Venus on
the Half-Shell
and Others

Venus on the Half-Shell

and Others

Philip José Farmer

Edited by Christopher Paul Carey

SUBTERRANEAN PRESS • 2008

ISBN: 978-1-59606-142-2

First Edition

Subterranean Press
PO Box 190106
Burton, MI 48519

www.subterraneanpress.com

Table of Contents

To Mike Croteau and Paul Spiteri, without whose help
so much would have gone unpublished.

Acknowledgements

Philip José Farmer would like to thank Danton Burroughs for his blessing to reprint *The Adventure of the Peerless Peer*.

The editor gives his many thanks to Michael Croteau for his invaluable fact-checking and for his role in uncovering the little known history behind the fictional-author period. Further thanks go to Brad Lang for providing the text of an ultra-rare Farmer story, to Win Scott Eckert for identifying the Howard Waldrop fictional-author connection, and to Zacharias Nuninga for his wonderfully helpful *Philip José Farmer International Bibliography*, www.philipjosefarmer.tk.

Foreword

by Tom Wode Bellman

I think I first met Phil Farmer and his lovely wife Bette at the 11th World Science Fiction Convention back in September of 1953. Back then Phil was being lauded for his taboo-breaking "The Lovers" while I was still pounding out trash like *The Winged Women of the Purple Planet*. But at that time Phil took me aside and treated me as an equal, and for that I owe him a great deal. Without the inspiring talk he gave me that night in Philly, as well as the drinks he bought for me so freely that made my mind whirl like an out of control Ferris wheel spinning off into new dimensions, I would have never been able to write what I consider to be my best work, *Through Love, Darkly*. I never did pay attention to the critics who said it was a Farmer ripoff, and Phil was always too kind to say anything. Though now that I think of it, I believe I remember him saying, long ago in another age, that if it was a ripoff, it was a darn good one. PhilCon 2, they called that convention…I'll always think of it as having been named after my hero, Philip José Farmer.

Over the years, Phil and I lost touch. My wife Barbara and I moved off to L.A. where I tried (and failed) to sell treatments and scripts to the studios. Little did I know Phil had done much the same thing and that we were practically neighbors for a number of years. Then one day in 1974, after I had moved back to the Midwest and was living somewhere at right angles to the Land of Oz, I received a phone call out of the blue. It was Phil. His deep, patiently self-assured voice said he wanted to let me in on a secret, and even through the phone lines I could see his trickster's grin and the twinkle in his eye. He told me then and there that he *was* Kilgore Trout, or at least that he was writing a story under Trout's name. I laughed and laughed, and Phil did too. Then, when we had both quieted down, he told me the real reason he had called. He wanted me to write a fictional-author story for him; that is, a story written as if by a character who was an author in fiction, just like Kilgore Trout. After it had appeared in print in a magazine, he would put it in an anthology he planned to edit. A silence ensued. I thought about it hard. Then, like a vision from the Elder Gods, it hit me. The story would be called "The Wee Weepers of Mu" and it would be by Gabriel Weltstein, the narrator of Ignatius Donnelly's early sf classic, *Caesar's Column*. I was pleased with myself, and I knew the story would be good. And it was. Or at least that's what Phil said when I sent it to him, and who was I to argue with a Hugo winner? He told me he was confident the piece would find a home.

But I wasn't a big name author like Farmer. My literary aspirations had never taken off with any great success, like Phil and his Riverworld had. As Phil suggested, I sent my story to Ed Ferman at *Fantasy and Science Fiction*, but it bounced right back. I think the story finally ended up in some sub-pro (and practically subhuman, as far as the payment went) market like that old sf fanzine *Kukuanafan*. Yes, I think that may have been the one. It was a one-shot, anyway, and I remember now that the zine bore a slapdash monochrome cover with the depiction of a Great White Ape of Barsoom beating his fists and hulking over the heroic form of a sword-bearing, loincloth-clad warrior, whose face, now that I think of it, looked eerily like that of Isaac Asimov. Those were the days. Anyway, although my story never made the splash I'd hoped it would, and Phil never came out with his fictional-author anthology, I've never forgotten how he'd tried to help me out. Back in 1953 and on that day he called me, so many years later.

So when the editor of this collection Googled my whereabouts (got to love how the language changes) and asked me if I would write this forward, I beat my chest like the ape on the cover of that fanzine and whooped until the heavens trembled. That's how it felt in my mind, anyway. Because this was my chance. To tell Philip José Farmer what he's done for me, and for his many readers. And that's what I'm doing now.

To you, Phil—and to the whole array of fictional-author mantles you've worn! *Alter ipse amicus!* Cheers!

Tom Wode Bellman,
Busiris, Illinois

Introduction

More Real Than Life Itself: Philip José Farmer's Fictional-Author Period

by Christopher Paul Carey

"The unconscious is the true democracy. All things, all people, are equal."
—Philip José Farmer

By one count—a list which does not include a seemingly unending number of reprintings and omnibuses in foreign languages or various books edited—the volume you hold in your hands marks the eighty-second book published by Philip José Farmer, Grand Master of Science Fiction. Farmer's work is ambitious. In 1952 he authored the groundbreaking "The Lovers," which at long last made it possible for science fiction to deal with sex in a mature manner. He is the creator of Riverworld, arguably one of the grandest experiments in sf literature. His World of Tiers series, which combines rip-roaring adventure with an abundance of mythic archetypes, is said to have inspired Zelazny's Chronicles of Amber and is often cited as a favorite among Farmer's fans. And in the early–1970s he penned the authorized biographies of Tarzan and Doc Savage and inspired a generation of creative mythographers to explore and expand upon his Wold Newton mythos. Yet among all of these shining minarets of his opus, Farmer has stated that he has never had so much fun in all his life as when he wrote two of the stories that appear in the current collection, *Venus on the Half-Shell* and *The Adventure of the Peerless Peer*.

I believe it is no coincidence that both of these stories belong to what Farmer has labeled his "fictional-author" series. A fictional-author story is, as defined by Farmer, "a tale supposedly written by an author who is a character in fiction." Many of Farmer's readers are aware that the two aforementioned tales originally appeared in print as if authored, respectively, by Kurt Vonnegut's character Kilgore Trout and Sir Arthur Conan Doyle's John H. Watson, M.D. Most are not aware, however, that Farmer conspired as mastermind along with a number of other writers to pull an ongoing hoax on the science fiction readership that would have, if executed, spanned almost a decade.

As with his usual *modus operandi*, the plan was ambitious. Beginning in 1974, in true postmodern reflexivity, stories by a whole team of writers acting under Farmer's direction were to begin submitting fictional-author tales to the short fiction markets. Correspondence recently discovered among Farmer's files, which the author has kindly shared for the writing of this introduction, reveals that his plan of attack was executed with focus, precision, and a great deal of forethought.

The authors queried to write the fictional-author stories were instructed that "the real author is to be nowhere mentioned; it's all done straight-facedly." Each story would be accompanied by a short biographical preface giving the impression that the fictional author was indeed a living person. However, all copyrights were to be honored; those who chose to write stories "by" the characters of other authors would need to contact those creators for permission and be sure to include proper citation. Sometimes Farmer himself wrote the creator and, having received permission, then handed the fictional-author story to his fellow conspirator. Authors were encouraged to submit their stories to whatever market they pleased, although the majority were to appear in *The Magazine of Fantasy & Science Fiction*, whose editor, Ed Ferman, was in on the joke. One major revelation uncovered in Farmer's correspondence is definitive confirmation of a rumor that, once enough of the stories had been published in various markets, Farmer himself planned to take on the role of editor and collect them all in a fictional-author anthology.

Writing even before the fallout with Kurt Vonnegut (which is described in great detail by Farmer in his "Why and How I Became Kilgore Trout"), Farmer placed great emphasis on literary ethics during the execution of his hoax. Even authors whose characters had lapsed into the public domain—and whom Farmer and his cohorts could have used legally without payment of royalties— were offered 50% of any monies made by the publication of a fictional-author story (a stipulation waved by all those documented in the correspondence reviewed for the writing of this introduction, although one agent asked for a mere $10 one-time use fee). Provisions were made for the original authors and their agents to receive copies of the stories upon publication. And always, Farmer made clear that his request to write a story under the name of an author's character was his intimate tribute to said author.

While the vast majority of those queried for the use of their characters granted permission, a couple did not. Farmer wrote respectful, though clearly disappointed, replies to these authors, explaining again that he only meant to honor them with the stories, but that in deference to them he would withdraw his offer and pursue it no further. Most authors, however, reacted much differently and seemed to become infected by the passion which seemed to ooze from Farmer when he proposed to them his audacious hoax. Farmer's letters reveal that Nero Wolfe author Rex Stout, besides granting permission to write the story "The Volcano" under the name of his character Paul Chapin, was tickled enough to suggest that Farmer should also author stories by Anna Karenina and Don Quixote. Another letter by Farmer indicates that he planned on doing just that. P.G. Wodehouse, author of the Jeeves and Blandings Castle stories, also tried to come up with alternative fictional-authors among his own works that could be used, and it is telling of the excitement surrounding Farmer's fictional-author conceit that multiple authors queried for permission enthusiastically consented by exclaiming the phrase "Of course" within the first paragraph of their replies. Occasionally permissions went in the other direction. J.T. Edson, the author of many Westerns, sought permission to use Farmer's Wold Newton genealogy as the basis for his own characters' ancestry in his Bunduki series, a request Farmer happily approved; and while the Wold Newton genealogy was not exclusively related to the proposed fictional-author series, it remains clear that Farmer was pleased to interweave the two concepts in several instances.

As concerns those peers enlisted to write the fictional-author stories under Farmer's direction, the list included Arthur Sean Cox, Philip K. Dick, Leslie Fiedler, Ron Goulart, and Gene Wolfe. Of this group, sadly only two besides Farmer seem to have successfully published fictional-author stories. At Farmer's suggestion, Arthur Sean Cox tackled one of his own creations, writing "Writers of the Purple Page" by John Thames Rokesmith, published in the May 1977 issue of *The Magazine of Fantasy & Science Fiction*. Rokesmith was a character in Cox's novella "Straight Shooters Always Win" (*The Magazine of Fantasy & Science Fiction*, May 1974). And Gene Wolfe—whose humorous "Tarzan of the Grapes" appears in Farmer's survey of feral humans in literature, *Mother Was A Lovely Beast*—wrote "Our Neighbour" by David Copperfield, first published in the anthology *Rooms of Paradise* (ed. Lee Harding, Quartet Books, 1978). But the fun did not end there. Author Howard Waldrop, although not enlisted by Farmer, sought out the author of *Venus on the Half-Shell* and joined in with the other conspirators, publishing "The Adventure of the Grinder's Whistle" as by Sir Edward Malone in the semi-pro fanzine *Chacal #2*, (ed. Arnie Fenner and Pat Cadigan, Spring 1977; reprinted in Waldrop's collection *Night of the Cooters*, Ace Books, 1993).

The failures—those fictional-author stories imagined but never written—are almost as entrancing as the successes. Ed Ferman suggested that Farmer have Ron Goulart write a story by his character José Silvera, and while Farmer did query him, there is no immediate evidence that Goulart pursued the matter. Farmer himself sought and was granted permission to write a story under the name Gustave von Aschenbach, the novelist from Thomas Mann's *A Death in Venice*; however, apparently bowing under the large number of fictional-author stories he planned to write on his own, Farmer turned the idea over to writer and literary critic Leslie Fiedler. This story, too, fell by the wayside, never to be published.

One of the first authors approached to join in the conspiracy was Philip K. Dick. Farmer trusted Dick with the secret of who had written *Venus on the Half-Shell*, and in the process discussed Dick writing a fictional-author tale for Ferman's magazine. Dick decided this would be a short story entitled "A Man For No Country" by Hawthorne Abdensen, the writer-character from his classic novel of alternate history, *The Man in the High Castle*. No fictional alter ego could have suited Dick better for the undertaking, as Abdensen himself was the fictional author of *The Grasshopper Lies Heavy*, a novel that implied the existence of multiple realities. The Chinese box scenario must have pleased Dick, who worked often with such themes; but it must also have pleased Farmer, who years later went on to create the similarly head-twisting *Red Orc's Rage*, a novel in which pocket universes collide head-on with parallel universes. Although "A Man For No Country" never seems to have been written, Farmer's role in proposing that Dick pen a fictional-author story is important, for that unwritten story appears to have been the idea-kernel that led Dick to write the posthumously published novel *Radio Free Albemuth*, which itself was an aborted draft of his important novel *VALIS*. One must also ponder the timing of Farmer's proposal, in the spring of 1974, a time when Dick claims to have had a number of mystical experiences, including one in which his mind was supposedly invaded by a foreign consciousness.

While Farmer was by far the most industrious and successful of the group in executing the fictional-author ruse, many of his own plans had to be abandoned because of time constraints placed upon him by other writing obligations. Farmer's correspondence, notes, and interviews from the fictional-author period reveal a long and fascinating list of stories never written and those started but not completed:

- "The Gargoyle" by Edgar Henquist Gordon (Fictional title and author from Robert Bloch's short story "The Dark Demon"; permission for use granted by Robert Bloch.)

- "The Feaster from the Stars" by Robert Blake (Although this unfinished Cthulhu Mythos pastiche derives from a title and fictitious author in H.P. Lovecraft's "The Haunter in the Dark," Lovecraft based Blake on a character from Robert Bloch's "The Shambler from the Stars." In that story, Bloch kills off a character based on H.P. Lovecraft. Blake, of course, is an analog for Robert Bloch, and is in turn killed off in Lovecraft's tale. A good friend of Farmer's, Bloch enthusiastically gave his blessing to this unfinished story about Haji Abdu al-Yazdi, a pseudonym belonging to one of Farmer's real-life heroes, as well as the main protagonist of the Riverworld series: Sir Richard Francis Burton. Yet another box within a box...)

- "UFO Versus CBS" by Susan DeWitt (From Richard Brautigan's *The Abortion.*)

- Untitled "Smoke Bellew" stories (Continuation of the series by Jack London. Although the stories were in public domain, permission was refused by London's literary executor and the stories went unwritten.)

- Untitled story by Martin Eden (From Jack London's *Martin Eden*; no record yet found of a permission query.)

- Untitled story by Edward P. Malone (Intrepid reporter from Sir Arthur Conan Doyle's *The Lost World*. As mentioned above, this fictional author was turned over to Howard Waldrop.)

- Untitled story by Gerald Musgrave (From James Branch Cabell's *Something About Eve*. Interestingly, Cabell used anagrams prominently in his work, as Farmer does in *Venus on the Half-Shell*.)

- Untitled story by Kenneth Robeson (Proposed second story of *The Grant-Robeson Papers*; the first was Farmer's "The Savage Shadow" by Maxwell Grant.)

- *The Son of Jimmy Valentine* by Kilgore Trout (Permission denied by Kurt Vonnegut after the fallout from *Venus on the Half-Shell*.)

- "The Adventure of the Wand of Death" by Felix Clovelly ("Felix Clovelly" is a penname of Wodehouse's thriller novelist Ashe Marston from *Something New*; more Chinese boxes...Permission granted by Wodehouse.)

———>•<———

But however many ideas he abandoned, Farmer's list of completed fictional-author tales is equally impressive. The reader will find most of these stories, out of print for many years, in the present collection. The tales herein are sly, tongue-in-cheek, sometimes shocking, but almost always uproariously funny. Quickly one sees why Farmer says he never had so much fun in all his life as when he wrote his tributes to Vonnegut and Doyle.

Farmer has often cited Paul Radin's *The Trickster*, a book about the role of the mischievous archetype recurrent in mythology and folklore, as one of his influences; and among the stories at hand it is easy to see why. By assuming the role of a fictional author, Farmer dons a shamanic mask and enters the sublime creative world where fictional characters take on a life more real than our own.

A long-held theory goes that Farmer unconsciously hatched his fictional-author series, as well as penned his many pastiches, in an attempt to get over a period of writer's block which had descended upon him during the early– to mid–1970s. I do not doubt it; although, if true, I—doubtless along with all of Farmer's readers—am grateful that his muse found such a scintillating, creative means to overcome its obstacle.

But there is another possibility, more fun to contemplate and more in tune with the spirit of the fictional-author concept: Perhaps Farmer's muse did not merely find a clever mechanism to jumpstart itself. What if the fictional-author period was not a hoax after all, but instead Farmer, donning his shamanic mask, did indeed glimpse into another universe? One in which William S. Burroughs wrote *Tarzan of the Apes*, and John H. Watson hobnobbed at the same gentlemen's club as A.J. Raffles and Edward Malone. Where Kurt Vonnegut may have asked Farmer's Riverworld counterpart, Peter Jairus Frigate, for permission to write a World of Tiers novel. A universe in which you and I are mere fictional characters in the works of a Grand Master of Science Fiction.

Yes, paging through this book, I think I too am getting a glimpse through the doors of perception.

Thank you, Philip José Farmer, for opening them.

Christopher Paul Carey,
Seattle, Washington

Why and How I Became Kilgore Trout

By Philip José Farmer

Not until I reread *Venus on the Half-Shell* in preparation for this foreword, and read the reviews and letters resulting from it, did I remember how much fun I had had with it.

When I sat down to the typewriter to begin it, I was Kilgore Trout, not Philip José Farmer. The ideas, characters, plot, and situations rushed in, crowding at my brain's front door. When they surged in, they swirled around, hand-in-hand, like super barn dancers or well-orchestrated members of the lobster quadrille. What a blast it was!

Six weeks later, the novel was done, but, all that while, the music was from Kant, Schopenhauer, and Voltaire. The caller was Epistemology, who looked a lot like Lewis Carroll. My wife knew I was having a good time because she could hear my laughter coming up the basement stairs to the kitchen.

I had been having a moderate writer's block with the then-currently scheduled novel. I was making slow and often halting progress. But, once I put that novel aside for the time being and adopted the persona of Kilgore Trout, sad-sack science-fiction author, I wrote as if possessed by a degenerate angel. Which is what poor old Trout was, in fact.

The beginning of this project was in the early 1970's when I vastly admired and was wildly enthusiastic about the works of Kurt Vonnegut, Jr. I was especially intrigued by Kilgore Trout, who had appeared in Vonnegut's *God Bless You, Mr. Rosewater* and *Slaughterhouse-Five*. Trout was to appear in *Breakfast of Champions*, but that had not been published then.

While rereading *Rosewater* (in 1972, I believe) for the fifth time, I came across the part where Fred Rosewater picks up one of Trout's books in the pornography section of a bookstore. It's a paperback (none of Trout's works ever made hardcovers) titled *Venus on the Half-Shell*. On the back cover is a photograph of the author, an old bearded man looking "like a frightened, aging Jesus" and below it is an abridged version of "a red-hot scene" in the book.

The section regarding *Venus* differs from others, which describe the plots of Trout's stories. Thus, Vonnegut, via Trout, makes his satirical or ironic points about our Terrestrial society and the nature of the Universe. *Venus* has no descriptions of the plot, and the hero is known only as the Space Wanderer. Aside from the abridged text on the back cover, there is no inkling of what the book is about.

At that moment, rereading this part, a pitchfork rose from my subconscious and goosed my neural ganglia. In short, I was inspired. Lights went on; bells clanged.

"Hey!" I thought. "Vonnegut's readers think that Trout is only a fictional character! What if one of his books actually appeared on the stands? Wouldn't that blow the minds of Vonnegut's readers?"

Not to mention mine.

And, I thought, who more fitted to write *Venus* than I, a sadsack science-fiction writer whose early career paralleled Trout's? I'd been ripped off by publishers, had to work at menial jobs to support myself and family while writing, had suffered from the misunderstanding of my works, and had had to endure the scorn of those who considered science-fiction to be a trashy genre without any literary merit. The main difference between Trout and me was that I had made a little money then, and none of my stories had been confined to sleazy pornographic magazines where they appeared, as in Trout's case, as fillers to accompany the photographs of naked or half-clad women. Although it was true then that the general public and the epicenous academics thought of science-fiction as only a cut above pornography.

My heart fired up like a nova, I wrote to David Harris, science-fiction editor of Dell (Vonnegut's publisher), proposing to write *Venus* as if by Kilgore Trout. He replied that he thought the idea was great, and he gave me Vonnegut's address so that I could write him to ask for permission to carry out the project. I did not hesitate. After all, *Venus* would be my tribute to the esteemed Vonnegut. I sent him a letter outlining my proposal. Many months passed. No reply. I sent another letter, but many more months passed before I decided that I'd have to phone Vonnegut. David Harris gave me Vonnegut's number.

I had to nerve myself up to phone Vonnegut. He was a very big author, and I was a member of a group, science-fiction writers, for whom he had expressed a certain amount of disdain. But, when I did call him, he was very pleasant and not at all patronizing. He said that he did remember my letters, though he did not explain why he had not replied. I re-outlined my ideas, and, in arguing against his resistance to them, said that I strongly identified with Trout. He replied that he, too, identified with him. And he was afraid that people would think that the book was a hoax.

That flabbergasted me. Of course, it was a hoax, and people would know it. But I rallied, and I argued some more. Finally, he relented and gave me permission to write *Venus* as Trout. I offered to split the royalties with him, but he magnanimously refused to accept them. However, he did stress that no reference to his name or his works should appear in or on *Venus*.

I thanked him, and, elated, started to write. I was Kilgore Trout, in a sense, and I was writing the sort of book that I imagined Trout would write. But I tried to give the prose, characters, plot, and philosophy of *Venus* a Vonnegutian flavor. After all, Vonnegut had admitted that he was also, in a sense, Trout. I was only restricted in writing *Venus* by having to make the protagonist the Space Wanderer and by including my expansion of the abridged "red-hot scene" as described in *Rosewater*. I did not entirely emulate Vonnegut in the use of short words and a sort of See-Dick-See-Jane-See-Spot prose. But I did try to keep the text from becoming anything resembling William Faulkner's. Vonnegut wrote a very simple prose because he had a low opinion of the attention-span and general literary and lexical knowledge of the 1970's college students, who formed a large percentage of his readers.

It's worth noting that such science-fiction writers as Isaac Asimov and Frank Herbert did not avoid complicated ideas and plots and long sentences and words, and they did very well among the college students and general reading public.

The protagonist of *Venus* was named Simon Wagstaff. Simon because he was a sort of Simple Simon of the nursery rhyme. And Wagstaff because he certainly "wagged" (and waved) his sexual "staff" around during various sexual encounters. I also, unlike Vonnegut, put in a lot of references to literature and fictional authors. It would not matter that the average reader would not understand these, and it would amuse the academics. Or so I thought. I was too obscure for even the supposedly overeducated academics.

How many knew that Silas T. Comberbacke, the baseball-fan spaceman (sort of an Ancient Mariner) in *Venus* was the pseudonym of Samuel T. Coleridge, the great British poet, during his brief stay in the English army? Or that Bruga, Trout's favorite poet, was taken (with permission) from a novel by Ben Hecht, *Count Bruga*? And that Bruga, the wild Jewish Bukowski-like Chicago poet was based on Hecht's friend, Maxwell E. Bodenheim, the Greenwich Village poet and wino of the 1930's? Or that there were many similar references to other fictional writers? Who cared except me?

Most of the alien names in *Venus* were formed by transposing the letters of English or non-English words. Thus, Chworktap comes from *patchwork*. Dokal comes from *caudal*, which means having a tail. The planet Zelpst is a phonetic rendering of the German *selbst*, meaning *self*. The planet Raproshma is a rendering of the French *rapprochement*. The planet Clerun-Gowph derives from the German *Aufklärung*, enlightenment. And so on. Most readers sensibly do not concern themselves with such games, but I had fun with them. And I imagine that Trout, though he had only a high school education, read widely, and he would have played the same game.

The philosophical basis of *Venus* dealt with free will and immortality. Trout, in *Breakfast of Champions*, longs to be young again. And predeterminism is certainly a theme that runs through many of Vonnegut's works. Vonnegut is like Mark Twain in that he believes (or writes as if he believes) that everything is predetermined. Twain thought that all physical things and our thoughts and behavior were mechanically fixed from the moment the first atom in the beginning of this universe bumped into the second atom and the second atom into the third. And so on. Vonnegut apparently believes that our troubling and violent lives and irrational behavior are the result of "bad chemicals."

This interests me because I have been interested in the problem of free will versus predeterminism for about fifty-eight years. But I believe that humans do have free will, though few, however, exercise that faculty. Perhaps I believe this because I am predetermined to do so. But, as Trout, I rote as if Twain and Vonnegut were correct in their belief in predeterminism.

In any event, Vonnegut is a thorough predeterminist in that his works have no villains or heroes. No blame is put upon anybody for even the vilest deeds and most colossal selfishness, savagery, stupidity, and greed. That's the way things are, and they can be no other. Only God the Utterly Indifferernt is responsible and perhaps not even He. Trout has the same attitude.

Just as Eliot Rosewater, the multimillionaire in *Rosewater, Slaughterhouse-Five*, and *Breakfast*, thinks that Trout is the greatest writer that ever lived, so Trout, in his *Venus*, has Simon Wagstaff, his hero, believe that Jonathan Swift Somers III is the greatest writer that ever existed. Wagstaff also has his favorite poet, Bruga. Some of Somers's stories are outlined, and some of Bruga's poems are printed in *Venus*.

Somers III is my creation, but he is the grandson of Judge Somers and the son of Jonathan Swift Somers II. Those familiar with Edgar Lee Masters's *Spoon River Anthology* will recognize the latter two. (Mentioned with the permission of the Masters's estate.)

One of Somers III's protagonists is Ralph von Wau Wau. Wau Wau is German for Bow! Wow!). He is a German shepherd dog whose intelligence has been raised to humangenius level by a scientist. Ralph is also a writer, and I had planned to write a story as by him titled *Some Humans Don't Stink*. That story's main character would be Shorter Vondergut, a writer. (Shorter from *kurt*, German for *short*, and Vondergut from the German *von der Gut*, meaning of the ((River)) Gut.) Thus, the cycle of fictional authors would be complete. In fact,

I did write two stories under Somers's name about Ralph. These were published, but I doubt I'll ever write the whole cycle. I have passed through this particular phase. It was fun while it lasted.

The *Venus* manuscript went to Dell with some photographs of me as Trout (wearing a big false beard), a selected bibliography of Trout's works, and a biographical sketch of him. All done with tongue in cheek or wherever. The furor on its publication both amused and gratified me. There were even questions about the true identity of Trout in *The New York Times*. An article in *The National Enquirer* "proved" that Vonnegut wrote *Venus* because of its plots, characters, philosophy, and style.

Meanwhile, Mr. Vonnegut was neither amused nor gratified. He was, as I understand, flooded with letters asking if he had written *Venus*. Some of these said it was the worst book he had ever written; some, the best. The main cause of unhappiness, however, was that he misunderstood a remark made by Leslie Fiedler, the distinguished author and literary critic, while Fiedler was a guest on William F. Buckley's TV show, "Firing Line." The subject was science-fiction, and Vonnegut's name came up. Dr. Fiedler, who knew that I had written *Venus* but did not reveal its authorship, said that I had said that I was going to write *Venus* no matter what the obstacles, including Vonnegut. My memory is hazy on the exact wording. Vonnegut, however, apparently thought that Fiedler had said that I was going to write *Venus* without Vonnegut's permission. Something to that effect.

Whatever was said, Mr. Vonnegut became angry. Consequently, he forbade me to write another Trout novel I'd planned, *The Son Of Jimmy Valentine*. That would have been my last novel as by Trout, but it was not to be. Vonnegut had the right, of course, to refuse permission for me to write it.

Legally, I had the right to sell *Venus* to the movies. And, when a producer made a proposal to make an animated movie of it with The Grateful Dead providing the music, I was elated. But Mr. Vonnegut phoned me and expressed his regrets that his lawyer would sue the producer if a movie was made. Vonnegut told me he was sorry about this, but I was very prolific and so would not miss any money I might get from the deal. Again, he had the moral right to scotch this proposal. Also, I doubt that anything would have come from the proposal. I've had over forty of my works optioned for Hollywood, and nothing has come of any of these.

The fun continued. Many letters addressed to Trout were sent on by my agent or the publisher. One letter purported to be from another Vonnegut character, Harrison Bergeron. Trout was invited to be the artist-in-residence during the 1975 Bicentennial Literary Explosion in Frankfort, Kentucky. The editor of

Contemporary Authors sent a letter inquiring about including Trout in the book for 1976. She complained that Trout was supposed to have written 117 novels, but she could find only a reference to *Venus on the Half-Shell*. "It would seem," she wrote, "that Kilgore Trout is a pseudonym. Would your agent furnish the real name of the author?"

As Trout, I filled out the data-forms she had sent and mailed them to her through my agent. I explained that all my novels had been originally published by disreputable fly-by-night publishers who had not paid me any royalties and had not even paid a fee to register my books with the Library of Congress. I never checked the 1976 issue, but I doubt that the editor included the Trout item.

However, as time went on, I became worried about Vonnegut's displeasure at the idea that people might think he was the author of *Venus*. At the same time, it was beyond me why he should be displeased that people might think he wrote *Venus* and yet not be distressed because people knew he was the author of *Breakfast of Champions, Slapstick, Jailbird,* and *Deadeye Dick*.

To spread the word around that I, not Vonnegut, was the author of *Venus*, I revealed the truth at every chance to do so and did my best when I was speaking at conventions and conferences to bring up the subject. I did the same when I was being interviewed on radio and TV. Just how well the science-fiction grapevine has worked, I do not know. By now, it does not seem to matter. Time has cleared this problem away. In the past few years, when I spoke at universities and colleges, I found that only about four or five in audiences of 500 to 800 recognized the name of Trout or Vonnegut. And I was told by a fan who questioned Vonnegut about *Venus* after a lecture that Vonnegut had difficulty remembering anything about it, including my name. So, whatever he felt at the time regarding *Venus* has passed.

I wish to thank Mr. Vonnegut for his generosity in permitting me to publish *Venus* as by Trout. I am sorry that it may have caused him any perturbation. I am even sorrier that he could not understand that *Venus* was my tribute to him and my repayment for all the delight his pre–1975 works gave me.

For several years, I've been trying to get *Venus* published under my own name. Finally, it has come about.

But, for a brief though glorious period, I was Kilgore Trout.

—Philip José Farmer

Venus on the Half Shell

Originally published under the byline of Kilgore Trout

Dedicated to the beasts and the stars.
They don't worry about free will and immortality.

Having read the previous selection, the reader now knows the why and the how behind the controversial first publication of the cult classic *Venus on the Half-Shell*. But controversy aside, *Venus* is a hilariously entertaining book that lends itself to hyphenated adjectives: fictionally-authored, pun-filled, tongue-in-cheek, side-splitting, anagram-entwined…And yet, as the real-life author has just pointed out in his preceding essay, the novel is not all slapstick and wit; it also addresses some serious philosophical issues. The question of free will may seem distinctly Vonnegutian, what with Vonnegut's discussion of "bad chemicals" in his novel *Breakfast of Champions*. But the free will issue is also inherently Farmerian, and has repeatedly appeared as a theme in the works of that resident Peorian. For Farmer, like Vonnegut, has long carried in his creative arsenal a keen interest in anthropology.

Indeed, the descriptions of the varying customs and mores of the many worlds visited by our hero Simon Wagstaff may at first seem interesting but irrelevant. And yet it is exactly these participant-observer emersions that help Simon on his way as he seeks an answer to The Question. Farmer, with his anthropological perspective, knows that too many Earth religions and philosophies fail because they are unable or unwilling to take into account the down and dirty realities of the human situation. Function follows form, as the anthropologists say. Ideas alone won't get you There. And sometimes, the very act of searching the universe for an answer hurts the universe.

The novel is also mythology-laden (yet another hyphenated adjective). For one, Simon undergoes the trials of the Norse god Odin, and in many ways suffers the same fate as the All-Father. But also, Farmer is ever interested in creating a mythology of his own, and in *Venus on the Half-Shell* his fictional-author conceit takes dizzying turns. There is the talking dog, Ralph von Wau Wau, for instance, whose stories as written by Jonathan Swift Somers III are recounted throughout the novel, much in the way that Trout's stories are sprinkled through Vonnegut's works. (See Farmer's collection *Pearls from Peoria*, Subterranean Press, 2006,

for two full-length Ralph von Wau Wau tales, as well as Somers'
authorized biography.)

In the end it is the patchwork genius of *Venus on the Half-
Shell*, combining as it does the serious with the outrageous, that
makes the work both the trans-Farmer, trans-Vonnegut cult classic that it is. Long after our sun has collapsed, exploded, and ex-
pired, I do not doubt that some alien teenager from a system near
Shaltoon will be coveting a dog-eared copy of *Venus on the Half-
Shell* under the bedcovers and pondering the meaning of the universe. To that alien teenager, I say,

Go, traveler…

CHAPTER 1
The Legend of the Space Wanderer

Go, traveler.

Go anywhere. The universe is a big place, perhaps the biggest.
No matter. Wherever you land, you'll hear of Simon Wagstaff, the Space
Wanderer.

Even on planets where he has never appeared, his story is sung in ballads and
told in spaceport taverns. Legend and folklore have made him a popular figure
throughout the ten billion inhabitable planets, and he is the hero of TV series
on at least a million, according to the latest count.

The Space Wanderer is an Earthman who never grows old. He wears Levis
and a shabby gray sweater with brown leather elbow patches. On its front is a
huge monogram: SW. He has a black patch over his left eye. He always carries
an atomic-powered electrical banjo. He has three constant companions: a dog,
an owl, and a female robot. He's a sociable gentle creature who never refuses an
autograph. His only fault, and it's a terrible one, is that he asks questions no one
can answer. At least, he did up to a thousand years ago, when he disappeared.
This is the story of his quest and why he is no longer seen in the known cosmos.

Oh, yes, he also suffers from an old wound in his posterior and thus can't
sit down long. Once, he was asked how it felt to be ageless.

He replied, "Immortality is a pain in the ass."

CHAPTER 2
It Always Rains on Picnics

Making love on a picnic is nothing new. But this was on top of the head of the Sphinx of Giza.

Simon Wagstaff was not enjoying it one hundred percent. Ants, always present at any outdoor picnic anywhere, were climbing up his legs and buttocks. One had even gotten caught where nobody but Simon had any business being. It must have thought it had fallen down between the piston and cylinder of an old-fashioned automobile motor.

Simon was persevering, however. After a while, he and his fiancée rolled over and lay panting and staring up at the Egyptian sky.

"That was good, wasn't it?" Ramona Uhuru said.

"It certainly wasn't run of the mill," Simon said. "Come on. We'd better get our clothes on before some tourists come up here."

Simon stood up and put on his black Levis, baggy gray sweatshirt, and imitation camel-leather sandals. Ramona slid into her scarlet caftan and opened the picnic basket. This was full of goodies, including a bottle of Ethiopian wine: Carbonated Lion of Judah.

Simon thought about telling her about the ant. But if it was still running—or limping—around, she'd be the first to know it.

Simon was a short stocky man of thirty. He had thick curly chestnut hair, pointed ears, thick brown eyebrows, a long straight thin nose, and big brown eyes that looked ready to leak tears. He had thin lips and thick teeth which somehow became a beautiful combination when he smiled.

Ramona was also short and stocky. But she had big black sheep-dog eyes and a voice as soft as a puppy's tail. Like the tail, it seldom quit wagging. This was all right with Simon. If he was a compulsive talker, she made up for it by not being a compulsive listener. Simon was a compulsive questioner but he didn't ask Ramona for answers because he knew she didn't have them. Ramona couldn't be blamed for this. Nobody else could answer them either. Ramona, talking about something or other, smoothed out the Navajo blanket made in Japan. Ramona had been made in Memphis (Egypt, not Tennessee), though her parents were Balinese and Kenyan.

Simon had been made during his parents' honeymoon in Madagascar. His father was part-Greek, part-Irish Jew. a musical critic who wrote under the name of K. Kane. Everybody thought, with good reason, that the K. stood for Killer. He had married a beautiful Ojibway Indian mezzo-soprano who sang under the name of Minnehaha Langtry. The air-conditioning had broken down on their wedding night, and they atributed Simon's shortcomings to the inclement conditions in which he had been conceived. Simon attributed them to his eight months in a plastic womb. His mother had not wanted to spoil her figure, so he had been removed from her womb and put in a cylinder connected to a machine. Simon had understood why his mother had done this. But he could not forgive her for later going on an eating jag and gaining sixty pounds. If she was going to become obese anyway, why hadn't she kept him where he belonged?

It was, however, no day for brooding on childhood hurts. The sky was as blue as a baby's veins, and the breeze was air-conditioning the outdoors. To the north, the reconstituted pyramids of Cheops and Chephren testified that the ancient Egyptians had really known how to put it all together. East, across the Nile, the white towers of Cairo with their TV antennas said up-yours to the heavens. But they'd pay that day for their arrogance.

Below him, tourists and visitors from distant planets wandered around among the hot dog, beer, and curio stands. Among them were the giant tripods of Arcturus, sneering at the things that Terrestrials called ancient. Their oldest buildings were one hundred thousand years old, built over ruins twice that age. The Earthmen didn't mind this because Arcturans looked so laughable when they sneered, twirling their long genitals as if they were key-chains. It was when an Arcturan praised that Earthmen became offended. The Arcturan would lift one of his tripods and spray the praisee with a liquid that smelled like rotten onions. A lot of Terrestrials had had to smile and take this, especially ministers of state. But these got what was referred to as a P.O. bonus.

Everything usually evens out.

Or so Simon Wagstaff thought on that fine day.

He picked up the guidebook and read it while drinking the wine. The guidebook said that the sphinx originated with the Egyptians. They thought of it as a creature that had a man's face and a lion's body. On the other hand, the Greeks, once they found out about the sphinx, made it into a creature with a woman's head and lioness' body. She even had women's breasts, lovely white pink-tipped cones that must have distracted men when they should have been thinking about the answer to her question. Oedipus had ignored those obstacles to thought, which maybe didn't say much for Oedipus. He was a little strange, married his mother, killed his father. He had answered the sphinx's question correctly, but that hadn't kept him out of trouble later.

And what about the sphinx's sex life? She hung around on the road to Thebes, Greece, which was a long way from Thebes, Egypt, and from the male sphinxes. Had she been like the female black widow spider and made love to men before she devoured them?

Simon wasn't particularly randy, but like everybody else he thought a lot about sex.

The Egyptian sphinx had massiveness and a vast antiquity. The Greek sphinx had class. The Egyptian was ponderosity and masculinity. The Greek was beauty and femaleness. Leave it to the Greeks to make something philosophical out of the merely physical of the Egyptians. The Greeks had made their sphinx a woman because she knew The Secret.

But she had found somebody who could answer her questions.

After which she killed herself.

Simon wasn't in much danger of having to commit suicide.

Nobody ever answered his questions.

The guidebook in his hand said that the sphinx's face was supposed to have Pharaoh Chephren's features. The guidebook in his back pocket said that the face was that of the god Harmachis.

It did not matter which had been right. The reconstituted sphinx now bore the features of a famous movie star.

The guidebook in his hand also said that the sphinx was 189 feet long and 72 feet high. The one in his pocket said the sphinx was 172 feet long and 66 feet high. Had one of the measuring teams been drunk? Or had the editor been drunk? Or had the typesetter had financial and marital problems? Or had someone maliciously inserted the wrong information just to screw people up?

Ramona said, "You're not listening!"

"Sorry," Simon said. And he was. This was one of those rare moments when Ramona suddenly became aware that she was talking to herself. She was scared. People who talk to themselves are either insane, deep thinkers, lonely, or all three. She knew she wasn't crazy or a deep thinker, so she must be lonely. And she feared loneliness worse than drowning, which was her pet horror.

Simon was lonely, too, but chiefly because he felt that the universe was being unfair in not giving answers to his questions. But now was not the time to think of himself; Ramona needed comforting.

"Listen, Ramona, here's a love song for you."

It was titled *The Anathematic Mathematics of Love*. This was one of the poems of "Count" Hippolyt Bruga, né Julius Ganz, an early 20th-century expressionist. Ben Hecht had once written a biography of him, but the only surviving copy was in the Vatican archives. Though critics considered Bruga only a minor poet, Simon loved him best of all and had composed music for many of his works.

First, though, Simon thought he should explain the references and the situation since she didn't read anything but *True Confessions* and best sellers.

"Robert Browning was a great Victorian poet who married the minor poet Elizabeth Barrett," he said.

"I know that," Ramona said. "I'm not as dumb as you think I am. I saw *The Barretts of Wimpole Street* on TV last year. With Peck Burton and Marilyn Mamri. It was so sad; her father was a real bastard. He killed her pet dog just because Elizabeth ran off with Browning. Old Barrett had eyes for his own daughter, would you believe it? Well, she didn't actually run off. She was paralyzed from the waist down, and Peck, I mean Browning, had to push her wheelchair through the streets of London while her father tried to run them down with a horse and buggy. It was the most exciting chase scene I've ever seen."

"I'll bet," Simon said. "So you know about them. Anyway, Elizabeth wrote a series of love poems to Browning, *Sonnets from the Portuguese.* He called her his Portuguese because she was so dark."

"How sweet!"

"Yes. Anyway, the most famous sonnet is the one in which she enumerates the varieties of love she has for him. This inspired Bruga's poem, though he didn't set it in sonnet form."

Simon sang:

> "How do I love thee? Let me figure
> The ways," said Liz.
> But mental additions
> Subtracted from Bob Browning's emissions,
> Dividing the needed vigor to frig her.
>
> Here's what he said to the Portuguese
> In order to part her deadened knees.
>
> "Accounting's not the thing that counts.
> A plus, a minus, you can shove!
> Oh woman below and man above!
> It's this inspires the mounts and founts!
>
> "To hell with Euclid's beauty bare!
> Liz, get your ass out of that chair!"

"Those were Bruga's last words," Simon said. "He was beaten to death a minute later by an enraged wino."

"I don't blame him," Ramona murmured.

"Bruga only did his best work when he was paid on the spot for his instant poetry," Simon said. "But in this case he was improvising free. He'd invited this penniless bum up to his Greenwich Village apartment to have a few gallons of muscatel with him and his mistress. And see the thanks he got."

"Everybody's a critic," Ramona said.

Simon winced. She said, "What's the matter?"

He plucked the banjo as if it were a chicken and sang:

"Why does *critic* give me pain?
Father's name was Killer Kane."

Feathers of sadness fluttered about them. Ramona cackled as if she had just laid an egg. It was, however, nervousness, not joy, that she proclaimed. She always got edgy when he slid into a melancholy mood.

"It's such a glorious day," she said. "How can you be sad when the sun is shining? You're spoiling the picnic."

"Sorry," he said. "My sun is black. But you're right. We're lovers, and lovers should make each other happy. Here's an old Arabian love song:

"Love is heavy. My soul is sighing...
What wing brushes both of us, dearest,
In the sick and soundless air?"

It was then that Ramona became aware that his mood came more from the outside than the inside. The breeze had died, and silence as thick and as heavy as the nativity of a mushroom in a diamond mine, or as gas passed during a prayer meeting, had fallen everywhere. The sky was clotted with clouds as black as rotten spots on a banana. Yet, only a minute before, the horizon had been as unbroken as a fake genealogy.

Simon got to his feet and put his banjo in its case. Ramona busied herself with putting plates and cups in the basket.

"You can't depend on anything," she said, close to tears. "It never, just never, rains here in the dry season."

"How'd those clouds get here without a wind?" Simon said.

As usual, his question was not answered.

Ramona had just folded up the blanket when the first raindrops fell. The two started across the top of the sphinx's head toward the steps but never got to them. The drops became a solid body of water, as if the whole sky were a big decanter that some giant drunk had accidentally tipped over. They were knocked down, and the basket was torn from Ramona's hands and sent floating over the side of the head. Ramona almost went, too, but Simon grabbed her hand and they crawled to the guard fence at the rim of the head and gripped an upright bar.

Later, Simon could recall almost nothing vividly. It was one long blur of numbed horror, of brutal heaviness of the rain, cold, teeth chattering, hands aching from squeezing the iron bar, increasing darkness, a sudden influx of people who'd fled the ground below, a vague wondering why they'd crowded onto the top of the sphinx's head, a terrifying realization of why when a sea rolled over him, his panicked rearing upward to keep from drowning, his loosing of the bar because the water had risen to his nose, a single muffled cry from Ramona, somewhere in the smash and flurry, and then he was swimming with nowhere to go.

The case with the banjo in it floated before him. He grabbed it. It provided some buoyancy, and after he'd shucked all his clothing, he could stay afloat by hanging on to it and treading water. Once, a camel swam by him with five men battling to get onto its back. Then it went under, and the last he saw of it was one rolling eye.

Sometime later, he drifted by the tip of the Great Pyramid. Clinging to it was a woman who screamed until the rising water filled her mouth. Simon floated on by, vainly trying to comprehend that somehow so much rain had fallen that the arid land of Egypt was now over 472 feet beneath him.

And then there came the time in the darkness of night and the still almost-solid rain when he prepared to give up his waterlogged ghost and let himself sink. He was too exhausted to fight anymore, it was all over, down the drain for him.

Simon was an atheist, but he prayed to Jahweh, his father's god, Mary, his grandmother's favorite deity, and Gitche Manitou. his mother's god. It couldn't hurt.

Before he was done, he bumped into something solid. Something that was also hollow, since it boomed like a drum beneath the blows of the rain.

A few seconds afterward, the booming stopped. He was so numb that it was some time before he understood that this was because the rain had also stopped.

He groped around the object. It was coffin-shaped but far too large to be a coffin unless a dead elephant was in it. Its top was slick, and about eight inches above water. He lifted the banjo case and shoved it inward. The object dipped a little under his weight, but by placing the flats of his palms on it, he got enough friction to pull himself slowly onto the flat surface and then onto its center.

He lay there panting, face down, too cold and miserable to sleep. Despite which, he went to sleep, though his dreams were not pleasant. But then they seldom were.

When he awoke, he looked at his watch. It was 07:08. He had slept at least twelve hours, though it hadn't been refreshing. Then, feeling warm on one side, he turned over slowly. A dog was snuggled up against him. After a while, the dog opened one eye. Simon patted it and lay back face down, his arm around it. He was hungry, which made him wonder if he wouldn't end up having to eat the dog. Or vice versa, It was a mongrel weighing about sixty pounds to his one hundred and forty. It was probably stronger than he, and bound to be very hungry. Dogs were always hungry.

He fell asleep again and when he awoke it was night again. The dog was up, a dim yellow-brown, long-muzzled shape walking stiffly around as if it had arthritis. Simon called it to him because he didn't want it upsetting the delicate balance. It came to him and licked his face, though whether from a need for affection or a desire to find out how he tasted, Simon did not know. Eventually, he fell asleep, waking as stiff as a piece of driftwood (or a bone long buried by a dog). But he was warm. The clouds were gone, the sun was up, and the water on the surface of the object had dried off.

For the first time, he could see it, though he still did not know what it was. It was about ten feet long and seven wide and had a transparent plastic cover.

He looked straight down into the face of a dead man.

CHAPTER 3
The *Hwanq Ho*

Simon knew now that he was on top of one of the plastic showcases in which mummies of ancient Pharaohs were displayed in a Cairo museum. Airtight, it had floated up out of the building.

Simon pushed the protesting dog back into the sea and then lowered himself over the edge alongside the animal. He had a hard time raising the lid and sliding it into the water, but he finally succeeded. Then he crawled back over the edge and let himself, and some water, into the case. Standing on the edge of the open coffin on the case's floor, he hauled the dog in. The dog sniffed at the mummy and began howling.

After many thousands of years of neglect, the mummy had a mourner.

Simon got down onto the floor and stared at the falcon face of an ex-ruler of Upper and Lower Egypt. The skin was as tight as a senator from Kentucky and as dry as a government report. Time had sucked out, along with the vital juices, the flesh beneath the skin. But the bones had kept their arrogance.

Simon looked around the case and found a placard screwed into the side. He couldn't read it because it was facing outward. On the other side of the coffin, on the floor, he found a screwdriver, a dried-up condom, a pair of panties, and a cheese-and-salami sandwich wrapped in tinfoil. Evidently, some museum worker had had an assignation behind the coffin. Or perhaps the night watchman had brought in a woman to while away the lonely hours. In either case, someone had disturbed them, and they had taken off, leaving behind them the clues he had put together à la Sherlock Holmes.

Simon blessed them and opened the wrapper. The bread, cheese, and salami were cardboard-hard, but they were edible. He broke the sandwich in half, gave one piece to the dog and gnawed away gratefully at his. The dog, after gulping down his half, looked at Simon's sandwich and growled. Simon thought he was going to have trouble with him until he understood that it was the dog's belly, not his throat, which was growling.

He patted him and said, "You like old bones? You can eat away. But not now."

Using the screwdriver, he removed the placard. It bore this legend:

MERNEPTAH
Pharaoh from 1236 B.C. to 1223 B.C.
Thirteenth son of Rameses II.
He gave Moses a hard time.

Moses and history had, in turn, given Merneptah a hard time. Everybody considered him to be a villain. When they read in the Bible that he'd been drowned in the Red Sea while chasing the refugee Hebrews, they thought, "Drowning was too good for him." But this story was a myth. Merneptah, at age sixty-two, had died miserably of arthritis, plugged arteries, and bad teeth. As if this and an evil reputation hadn't done enough to him, the undertakers had removed his testicles and tomb robbers had hacked his body, incidentally removing the right arm.

"You're still useful, old man," Simon said. He tore off the wrappings and then the penis and threw it to the dog. The dog caught it before it hit the floor and swallowed it. So much for the mighty phallus that had impregnated hundreds of women, Simon thought. Just so the resin-soaked flesh doesn't give the dog a stomach-ache.

Meanwhile he wished that he had something more to eat. His belly was growling like a truck going up a steep grade. If he couldn't somehow catch some fish, he was going to starve. And then the dog would be eating him. Since he had nothing else to do, he decided to think about giving the dog a name.

After rejecting Spot, Fido, and Rover, he chose Anubis. Anubis was the jackal-headed Egyptian **god** who conducted the souls of the dead into the afterworld. A jackal was a sort of dog. And this dog, if not a conductor, was certainly a fellow passenger in this queer boat that was taking them to an unknown but inevitable death.

Whatever the dog's old name, he responded to the new one. He licked Simon's hand and looked up with eyes as big, brown, and soft as Ramona's. Simon patted his head. It was nice to have someone who liked him and would keep him from feeling utterly alone. Of course, this, like everything, had its disadvantageous side. He was expected to provide for Anubis.

Simon got up and ripped off the Pharaoh's right leg. For a moment, he was tempted to chew on it himself, but he didn't have the teeth or the stomach for it. He threw it to Anubis, who retreated to a corner and began gnawing on it voraciously. A few hours later he had a violent attack of diarrhea which stank, among other things, of resin. Simon got up on coffin and leaned out over the edge of the case to get fresh air. At the same time, he saw the owl.

Simon yelped with joy. Since owls lived in trees, and trees grew only on land, land couldn't be far away. He watched the bird turn and fly northward until it had disappeared. That was salvation. But how to get there?

When dusk came, with no land in sight, he prepared despondently for bed. He heaved Merneptah out into the several inches of water on the floor and stretched out on the coffin. When he awoke with the sun in his eyes, he was even weaker and hungrier. He wasn't thirsty, since the sea water was diluted enough with rain to be potable. But water has no calories.

He looked over the side of the coffin. The Pharaoh was a mess. Anubis had chewed him up, leathery skin, bone, and all. But the Pharaoh, that inveterate traveler, had made another passage. Anubis lay in the corner, sopping wet and sick. Simon felt sorry for him but could do nothing for him. As it was, he had to stick his head over the edge of the case to keep from dying of the stench before he died of starvation.

A few hours later, while he was thinking of voluntarily dying by drowning, he saw something to the northwest. As the day passed, this slowly became larger. Just as the sun slid into the waters, he saw that it was not, as he had hoped, land. It was a submarine or something that looked like a submarine. But it was too far away for him to hope to swim to it.

Dawn found him awake, looking northwest, hoping that the sub had not gone away during the night. No. It had drifted on the same collision course during the night. And it was close enough so he could see that it was a spaceship, not a submarine. On its side were two big Chinese ideograms and underneath them, in Roman letters: *Hwang Ho*. Since it wasn't proceeding under power, it must be crewless. It had been sitting on some spaceport field somewhere, and when the rains came, its crew hadn't been able to take refuge in it. They had probably drowned while roistering in the tavern or in bed with a friend or friends.

Its ports were closed, but it was no problem to open one. There'd be a plate by the port which only had to be depressed to make the port open.

More hours passed. By then Simon saw that the case was not going to bump into the ship. He shoved the heavy wooden coffin to the wall of the case, causing it to tilt and to ship water. Simon's weight made it lean even more, and Simon went into the sea. Anubis didn't want to leave the case, but he had no choice. Simon swam to the nearest port and pushed in on the plate. The port sank back and then swung aside. He put the banjo case inside, reached up, grabbed the threshold, and pulled himself in. After hoisting Anubis inside, he stood up shakily and watched the swirl which marked the sinking of the case until the surface was smooth again.

"Just think," Simon said to Anubis. "If old Merneptah had really been drowned in the Red Sea, and his body had been lost, there would have been no case for him in the museum, and you and I would have drowned several days ago. Kind of makes you wonder if it was destined or we're just lucky, doesn't it?"

Simon thought a lot about predeterminism and free will.

Anubis thought mainly about food, unless it was mating season, and so he didn't even wait for Simon to quit talking. He trotted into the ship, and Simon's belly, which also could not digest philosophy, urged him to follow the dog. He explored the ship, finding it empty of life, as he'd expected. But it was well stocked with food and drink, and that was all he cared about for the moment. Since he didn't want to throw up, he forced himself to eat lightly. Anubis resented being fed small portions, but there wasn't much he could do about except look reproachful.

More later," Simon said. "Much more. And it sure beats eating dried-up old Pharaoh, doesn't it?"

His next step was to search through the lockers and find clothes that fitted him. Once more, he was clad in a baggy gray sweatshirt, black tight-fitting Levis, and sandals.

When he returned to the room by the still open port the owl was sitting on the back of a chair.

Who?" it said.

"Not who? Why?" Simon replied.

The question of where the owl had come from was still unsettled, but Simon thought it likely that it had been riding on top of the spaceship. It must be hungry, too, so Simon prepared some egg foo young for it. When he came back to the room with the food, the owl was sitting on a pile of torn-up papers on the seat of the chair. Simon put the plate on the floor before it. It flew down to grab the food, enabling Simon to determine its sex. It—she—had just laid an egg.

Anubis leaped up onto the chair and swallowed the egg. The owl didn't seem to mind, which made Simon think that the catastrophe had bent its mother instincts out of shape. That was just as well, otherwise the two animals might have gotten off on the wrong foot in their relationship.

Simon decided to name his new pet Athena. Athena was the Greek goddess of wisdom, and her symbol was the owl. Owls were supposed to be highly intelligent, though actually they were as dumb as chickens. But Simon was mythology-prone, which was only to be expected from a man who'd named his banjo Orpheus.

He examined the instruments in the control room, since he had heard that even a moron could navigate a spaceship. However, in this case, it had to be a Chinese moron. But if there was a book aboard which could teach him Chinese, he'd figure out how to fly this computerized vessel. He had already made up his mind to leave Earth for good. There was nothing here to hold him.

In later years, during his wanderings, he would often be asked what had happened to his native planet.

"Earth is all washed up," he would reply. "The game of life there was called off on account of rain."

The big question at the moment was: who had done this to Earth? Somebody had caused this deluge. It would never have occurred in the normal course of Terrestrial events. Somebody had pushed a button which activated a machine or chemicals which had precipitated one hundred percent of the water in the atmospheric ocean.

Who and why?

Was it the gone-wrong experiment of some mad scientist? Or had some planet whose business was being ruined by Earth triggered off this flood? Or was it simply because Earthmen smelled so badly? Terrestrials had a reputation as the most odoriferous race in the universe. A million planets referred to them as The Stinkers. There was an old Arcturan saying that exemplified this attitude. "Never stand downwind of a *shrook* or an Earthman." A *shrook* was a little beast on Arturus VI that exuded the combined scents of a skunk, a bombardier beetle, and dog farts with a touch of garbage heap.

Some extraterrestrials claimed that it was the Earthman's diet, which consisted mainly of hot dogs, potato chips, soft drinks, and beer, even among the Chinese, that caused this a odor. But the octopoids of Algol, perhaps the most philosophical of all races, contended that it wasn't the food that caused the bad smell. Psychology affected physiology. Earthmen stank because their ethics stank.

This reaction had upset Terrestrials, but they'd gone about solving this problem with their usual vicious efficiency. A huge perfume industry, employing millions, had been created, and travelers from Earth had always perfumed themselves just before they disembarked on an alien planet. These were specialized, since the perfume that pleased the Spicans would offend the Vegans. The only planet where perfumes were tabu was Sirius VII. The caninoids there identified each other by sniffing assholes, and so they strictly forbade the use of perfumes. The Earthmen had to go along with this custom, otherwise they'd never get to first base in selling Terrestrial goods. They tried to get around this by sending agents who had no sense of smell, but this didn't work out. All Sirians looked exactly alike, and they refused to carry nametags. Thus, an Earthman didn't know whom he was dealing with unless he had a keen nose.

This demand opened a whole new field to specialists who were paid huge bonuses. These had to earn a new degree, Ph.D.A., before they could be hired. Despite the fabulous salaries, there was a big turnover in this field, suicide being the chief cause of resignation. Then a bright young executive in the PR department got the idea of running a search through a computer for a particular type of fetishist. This revealed that there were over five hundred thousand masochists on Earth who liked to torture themselves with offensive odors. Of these, there were fifty thousand who specialized in dog crap. The Sirian Trading Corporation only needed twelve thousand, so suddenly the field became a monopoly of this handful. The doctor of philosophy of anumology was no longer required. Furthermore, since these were eager to work on Sirius, they underbid each other, and the STC was hiring them for slave wages.

This same bright young executive later was inspired with the idea which rid Earth of all perverts. Somewhere in this universe was a planet where a particular Terrestrial perversion was regarded as not only normal but highly desirable. He ran another search through the computer, and soon the STC was advertising for fetishists, masochists, sadists, child-beaters, racists, professional soldiers, drug-addicts, alcoholics, gun-lovers, motorcyclists, pet-lovers, exhibitionists, religious fanatics, members of the WCTU, and science-fiction fans. The salaries and the prestige offered were so high that a number of nonperverts tried to sign up. These were carefully screened out, however, with a battery of psychological tests. Those who passed were trained in a business college run by

STC. This became the most powerful business on Earth due to its expansion to other planets than Sirius.

Earth was cleared of perverts, and everybody left looked forward to a golden age. But in twenty years Earth had just as many perverts as ever. This caused an uproar, and the governments of every nation set up investigative agencies. Their reports were never published, since they indicated that the system of child-raising was responsible. The voters just would not stand for this item of information. And so Earth quietly returned to normal, that is, it was once again full of perverts.

STC hadn't cared. It wasn't going to run out of competent and dedicated employees.

Simon wondered if this export of nondesirables had offended some planet which had decided to clean up the origin of offense. Perhaps he would find out someday, but he could only do this if he learned how to operate the spaceship. This was possible, since he'd found a book which taught Chinese speakers how to read and write English. By reversing the order of instructions, he could learn how to read Chinese.

Days passed. The ship drifted with the current. When storms came, he closed the port and rode them out. And then, one day, while he was studying at the control panel in the bridge, he felt a jar run through the ship. He turned on the exterior-view TV and saw what he had hoped for. The nose of the *Hwang Ho* was stuck in the mud of the shore of a big bay, in front of it was the slope of a mountain.

Simon went out with the dog and the owl next day and looked around. Contrary to what he had first thought, they were not on a mountain but on a saddle between two peaks.

Simon walked up the slope of the nearest mountain. Halfway up, he came across a stone tablet lying on its face, half-buried in mud that had carried it down from a higher level. He heaved it upright and read the inscription on its face.

**ON SEPT. 27, 1829, J. J. VON PARROT,
A GERMAN CITIZEN, BECAME THE FIRST
MAN TO CLIMB TO THE TOP OF MOUNT
ARARAT, 16,945 FEET ABOVE SEA LEVEL.
HE DID NOT FIND THE ARK, BUT HE
ENJOYED THE VIEW WHILE EATING A
SALAMI SANDWICH. THIS WAS 58 YEARS
BEFORE "THE PAUSE THAT REFRESHES."
Courtesy of Coca Cola Co.**

Simon had arrived in his ark at the same place where Noah was supposed to have landed. This was a coincidence that could only happen in a bad novel, but Nature didn't give a damn about literary esthetics. The grasshopper voices of thousands of critics had shrilled at Her and then died while She went right on ahead writing Her stories, none of which had a happy ending.

Simon didn't now believe in the Biblical account of the flood. But as a child he'd taken it seriously. When he went to high school, however, he began to have his doubts. So he'd gone to a nice old rabbi named Isaac Apfelbaum and had asked him why the book of Genesis told such bare-faced lies as the stories of the garden of Eden, angels knocking up the daughters of men, the flood, the tower of Babel, etc.

The rabbi had sighed and then had patiently explained that the holy scriptures of any people were not meant to be scientific textbooks. They were parables to teach people how to be good-hearted and how to stay within certain limits of behavior so life would go as smoothly as possible. They were, in effect, guidebooks to heaven on earth and, hopefully, to the afterworld. Wise old men had worked out the guidelines as the best way to stay out of trouble.

"None of them were written by wise old women?" Simon had said. "Why? Do men have a monopoly on truth?"

"You forget Mary Baker Eddy," the rabbi had said.

"She was in ill health all her life," Simon said. "Can a sick person truly be wise?"

The rabbi ignored that. He wasn't keen on pumping the competition, anyway.

"And how come the guidebooks are all different?" Simon had said. He was thinking of that question now as he stared around at Mount Ararat. He was also thinking of the guidebooks he'd picked up just before the picnic. If men couldn't agree on the measurements of the Sphinx, a finite physical object, how could they ever blueprint heaven? If heaven existed, that is. Simon hadn't said so to the rabbi, but he had thought there was as much justification in believing in the Yellow Brick Road as in the Pearly Gates.

"The guidebooks just send you down different paths," the rabbi had said. "But the end result is the same. All roads lead to Rome."

The rabbi had shut up then. If he kept on, he'd be converting the kid to Catholicism.

Simon looked at the writings that post-Parrot climbers had felt impelled to scratch on the tablet. Some wag had scratched below the bottom line of the inscription: I WUZ HERE FURST. NOAH.

Another wag had scratched below that: NO. I WAS HERE FIRST, YOU ILLITERATE BASTARD. GOD.

On the side, running vertically, was a later inscription: GRAFFITI WRITERS SUCK.

Running alongside that was a later one: O.K. I'LL MEET YOU IN THE MEN'S ROOM, UN BUILDING LOBBY.

On the other side of the main text, also running vertically, was: DOESN'T ANYBODY LOVE ANYBODY?

Under that Simon scratched with his screwdriver: I DO, BUT THERE'S NOBODY LEFT TO LOVE.

After he'd done it, he felt ridiculous. He also felt like crying. He was the last of the fools whose names and faces oft appear in public places. What a last will and testament! Who, besides himself, the lone survivor, was around to read it?

A moment later, he found out.

CHAPTER 4
What's the Score?

The old man that staggered babbling toward him looked as if he was a hundred years old. His head was bald, and he had a long gray beard that fell to his knees, His clothes were of a style that had gone out of fashion over six hundred years ago. The old man wasn't even born then. So why was he wearing yellow kid gloves, a white ruff, and a coat too tight in the waist?

Simon conducted the old man into the *Hwang Ho*. He sat him down in an easy chair and gave him a glass of rice wine. The old man drank it all at once, and then, holding Simon with a skinny hand, he spoke.

"Who won the series?"

"What?" Simon said. "What series?"

"The World Series of 2457," the old man said. "Was it the St. Louis Cardinals or the Tokyo Tigers?"

"For God's sake, how would I know?" Simon said.

The old man groaned and poured himself another glass of wine. He smelled it, wrinkled his nose, and said, "You got any beer?"

"Just German beer," Simon said.

"That'll have to do," the old man said. "Oh, how I've longed all these centuries for a cold glass of American beer. Especially good old St. Louis-brewed beer!"

Simon went into the pantry for the only bottle of Löwenbrau left. This must have been the property of the sole German sailor aboard. By his bunk were portraits of Beethoven, Bismarck, Hitler (after a millennium a romantic hero), and Otto Munchkin, the first man to die in a Volkswagen. The sailor also had a small library, mostly Chinese or German books. Simon had been intrigued by the title of one, *Die Fahrt der Snark,* but it turned out not to be a commentary on Lewis Carroll's digestive problems after all. It was all about a journey some early 20th-century writer named Jack London had made to the South Seas. London had later on committed suicide when the people he loved and trusted gave him the shaft.

Simon returned to the old man and handed him the beer.

"Do you remember now?" the ancient said.

"Remember what?"

"Who won the series?"

"I never cared for baseball," Simon said. "You *are* talking about baseball, aren't you?"

"I thought you were an American?"

"There are no nationalities anymore," Simon said. "Just Earth people, an endangered species. What's your name?"

"Silas T. Comberbacke, Spaceman First Class," the old man said. He drank deeply and sighed with ecstasy. But he said, "Those Germans never did learn to make good beer."

Once Comberbacke's mind was off baseball, he talked as if he hadn't seen a human being in six hundred years. Which was true. He'd left Earth in 2457 A.D. because his fiancée had run off with a hair dresser.

"Which gives you some idea of her basic personality," old Comberbacke said. "Jesus, he knew nothing about baseball!"

One day, while drinking in a bar on a planet in Galaxy NGC 7217, Comberbacke suddenly decided to go home and find out who won the 2457 series. He'd been asking other spacemen for years, but even the aficionados didn't know. They were all too young to remember that far back. So, on impulse, he'd signed up as a S1C on a Ugandan freighter and was headed directly home—he thought. On the way, though, the ship had received a Mayday from a planet in NGC 5128.

"NGC 5128 is actually a collision between two galaxies, you know," he said. "It's been colliding for a couple of million years, but the spaces between the suns are so big that most of the people on the planets there thought they didn't have anything to worry about. But this planet, Rexroxy, was going to be hit in a thousand years. So they were getting everybody off. Actually, that Mayday had been transmitting for five hundred years. We landed on Rexroxy and made a deal with the locals. We dumped our cargo and crammed about three thousand aboard. They paid plenty for that, believe it!

"The captain was going to head out for a planet of a star near Orion and dump his passengers there. But he needed to send a message quick to his home office. I volunteered to take it in a one-man ship. I wasn't going to lose a month taking those funny-looking cyanide-breathers for a ride. I got here two days ago, parked my ship on the other side of the mountain, and walked around trying to find someone who could tell me what the score was."

"I was hoping you'd know what caused this rain." Simon said.

"Oh, I do! I meant, who won the series? The day I left, the Cardinals and the Tigers were tied. Dammit, if I hadn't been so mad at Alma, I'd have stayed until it was over."

"I know my question is trivial," Simon said. "But what *did* happen to make it rain so hard?"

"Don't get so mad," the old spacer said. "If you'd seen as many wrecked worlds as I have and as many about to be wrecked, you wouldn't take it so personal."

Comberbacke finished his bottle and drummed his fingers on the arm of the chair. Finally, Simon said, 'Well, what did happen?"

"Well, it must of been them Hoonhors!"

"What's a Hoonhor?'

"Jesus, kid, you don't know nothing, do you?" Comberbacke said. "They're the race that's been cleaning up the universe!"

Simon sighed and patiently asked him to back up and start at the beginning. The Hoonhors, he found, were a people from a planet of some unknown galaxy a trillion light years away. They were possibly the most altruistic species in the universe. They had done very well for themselves and now they were out doing for others.

"One thing they can't stand is seeing a people kill off their own planet. You know, pollution. So they've been locating these, and when they do, they clean it up.

"They've sanitized, that's what they call it, sanitizing, they've sanitized maybe a thousand planets so far in the Milky Way alone. Haven't you *really* ever heard of them?"

"I think if anybody on Earth had, we'd all have heard of them," Simon said.

Comberbacke shook his head and said, "If I'd of known that Earth hadn't, I would of hurried home and warned everybody. But space is big, and I didn't think the Hoonhors would get around to Earth for a thousand years or so. Plenty of time, I thought."

Comberbacke knew that it was the Hoonhors who had caused the Second Deluge. He'd seen one of their ships heading out when he went past the orbit of Pluto on his way in.

"What they do, they release into a planet's atmosphere a substance that precipitates every bit of H_2O in the air. You wouldn't believe the downpour!"

"Yes, I would," Simon said.

"Yeah, I guess you would. Say, are you sure you don't have any more beer? No? Well, the precipitation cleans the air and the land and drowns almost everybody. After the water has evaporated, the trees start growing again from seeds, and there's always a few birds and animals left up in the mountains to renew the animal life. There's always a few sentients left, too, but it takes them a long time to breed to the point where they again start polluting their planet. The Hoonhors schedule the planets they've drowned for a regular sanitizing every ten thousand years. Actually, though, they're short-handed, and they might not come back for fifty thousand or so years!"

The old man had spent much of his time while away from Earth traveling in ships which went faster than the speed of light. This explained why he hadn't died and become dust six hundred Earth-years ago. People in ships going at lightspeeds, or faster, aged very slowly. Everything inside the ship was slowed down. To an observer outside the ship, a passenger would take a month just to open his mouth to ask somebody to please pass the sugar. An orgasm would last a year, which was one of the things the passenger liners stressed in their advertising.

What the PR departments didn't explain was that the people in the ship thought they were moving at normal speed. Their subjective senses told them they were living according to time as they knew it. When a passenger complained about false advertising because he'd really only taken four or five seconds to come, the captain would reply that that was true in the ship. But back on Earth, by the clocks the company kept in headquarters, the passenger had taken four hundred days.

If the passenger still hitched, the captain said it was Einstein's fault. He was the one who'd thought up the theory of relativity.

The old man got drunk and passed out. Simon put him to bed and took the dog for a walk. The breeze, which came from the south, was thick and sticky with the odor of rotting bodies. As the water had evaporated, it had left bodies of animals, birds, and humans along the slope of the mountain. This made the few surviving vultures and rats happy, which goes to show that the old proverb about an ill wind is true. But the wind almost gagged Simon. He couldn't hang around here much longer unless he shut himself up in the ship and waited for the rotting meat to be eaten up.

Simon looked down from the cliff on the bodies of hundreds of men, women, and children, and he wept.

All of them had once been babies who needed and wanted love and who thought that they would be immortal Even the worst of them longed for love and would have been the better for it if he or she had been able to find it. But the more they grabbed for it, the more unlovable they had become. Even the lovable find it hard to get love, so what chance did the unlovable have?

The human species had been trying for a million years to find love and immortality. They had talked a lot about both, but humankind always talked most about those things which did not exist. Or, if they did, were so rare that almost nobody recognized them when they saw them. Love was rare, and immortality was only a thing hoped-for, unproven and unprovable.

At least, it was so on Earth.

A little while later, he stood up and shook his fist at the sky.

And this was when he decided to leave Earth and start asking the primal question.

Why are we created only to suffer and to die?

CHAPTER 5
The Boojum of Space

Simon explored the area on foot. He found the one-man spaceship where Comberbacke had left it. It had been built by the Titanic & Icarus Spaceship Company, Inc., which didn't inspire confidence in Simon. After looking it over, however, he decided to fly it back to the *Hwang Ho.* He would store it in the big dock area in the ship's stern. He could use it for a shuttle or a lifeboat during his voyages through interstellar space.

When he got back to the big ship, he discovered that the old man was gone. Simon set out on foot again. After he had walked down the muddy slope, he found Comberbacke rooting around among the ruins of a village. The old man looked up when he heard Simon's feet pulling out of the mud with a sucking sound.

"Even an Armenian village must have a library," he said.

"Nobody's illiterate anymore. So there must be a book that gives the scores of the World Series."

"Is that all it'll take to make you happy?"

The old man thought a minute, then said, "No. If I could get a hard-on, I'd be a lot happier. But what good would that do? There ain't a woman in sight."

"I was thinking more of somebody who'd be a companion for you and maybe a nurse, too."

"Find somebody who likes baseball," Comberbacke said.

Simon went away shaking his head. In the next few weeks he went over every inch of Great and Little Ararat, but the only humans he found were dead. The last day of his search, he started back to the ship with the idea of flying it around until he located land on which were some survivors. He'd make sure they'd take care of the old man, and then he'd leave for interstellar space.

It was dusk when he got to the ship. It lay broadside to him and, as usual, the sight of it disturbed him. He could never put his mental finger on the reason. It was about six hundred feet long, its main length cylindrical-shaped. The nose, however, was bulbous, and its stern rested on two hemispheres. These housed the engines which drove the *Hwang Ho.* They were separate from the ship so they could be released if the engines threatened to blow up. Light streamed out from the main sideport, which had been left open. Simon was exasperated when he saw this. He had told the old man to keep it shut at night. The mosquitoes were fierce now that spring was here. Somehow, the deluge had not killed them all off, and they were multiplying by the billions since most of their natural enemies, the bats and the birds, were dead. He hurried into the ship and closed the port after him. He called out the old man's name. Comberbacke did not reply. Simon went to the recreation room and found the old man dead in a chair. The side of his head was blown off. A Chinese pistol lay on his lap. On the table before him was a mud-and-water-stained book, its open pages streaked with water. But it wasn't rain that had fallen on these pages. The marks were from tears.

The book was the *Encyclopedia Terrica,* Volume IX, Barracuda-Bay Rum.

There was no farewell note from Comberbacke, but Simon read under *Baseball, World Series,* all he needed to know. The *2457* Series had ended in a scandal. In the middle of the final game, Cardinals 3–Tigers 4, police officers had arrested five St. Louis men. The commissioner had just been given proof that they had taken money from gamblers to throw the Series. The Tokyo Tigers won by default, and the five men had been given the maximum sentences.

Simon buried the old man and erected the von Parrot marker over him. On the backside of the stone, which he turned frontside, he scratched these letters:

SILAS T. COMBERBACKE
2432–3069
Spaceman & Baseball Fan
This stone conceals a Cardinal sin.
A glut of centuries passed before

He learned about that fateful Inning.
How good if he'd continued chinning
On Space's bar! His hero a whore,
He cared no more for the stadium's din.
It's better not to know the score.

That last line was good advice, but Simon wasn't taking it.

He went into the *Hwang Ho,* closed the port, and seated himself before the control panel in the bridge. The stellar maps were stored in the computer circuits. If Simon wanted to go to the sixth Planet of 61 Cygni A, for instance, he had only to press the right keys. The rest was up to the computer.

Just as a joke—though who knew what knowledge lurked in its heart?—he asked the ship to take him to Heaven.

To his surprise the computer screen flashed the Chinese equivalent of "O.K." There was a two-minute pause while the computer checked that everything was shipshape. Then it swung up off the ground, tilted upright, and climbed up toward the sky.

Simon didn't feel the change in the ship's attitude. An artificial gravity field adjusted for that.

Simon's attitude of mind changed, however. He frantically punched the keys.

"Where are you taking me?"

"To Heaven, as directed."

"Where is Heaven?"

"Heaven is the second planet of Beta Orionis. It is a T-type planet which was uninhabited by sentients until a Terrestrial expedition landed there in 2879 A.D. on first…"

Simon canceled the order.

"Take me to some unexplored galaxy, and we'll play it by ear from there," Simon typed.

A few seconds later they were off into the black unknown. The ship was capable of attaining 69,000 times the speed of light but Simon held it down to 20,000 times, or 20X. The drive itself was named the soixante-neuf drive, because this meant sixty-nine in French. It had been invented in 2970 A.D. by a Frenchman whose exact name Simon didn't recall. Either it was Pierre le Chanceux or Pierre le Chancreux, he wasn't sure which, since he'd not made a study of space history.

When the first ship equipped with the drive, the *Golden Goose,* had been revved up to top speed, those aboard had been frightened by a high screaming noise. This had started out as a murmur at about 20,000 times the speed of light. As the ship accelerated, the sound became louder and higher. At 69X, the ship was filled with the kind of noise you hear when a woman with a narrow pelvis is giving birth or a man has been kicked in the balls. There were many theories about where this screaming came from. Then, in 2980, Dr. Maloney, a brilliant man when sober, solved the mystery. It was known that the drive got all but its kick-off energy from tapping into the fifth dimension. This dimension contained stars just like ours, except that they were of a fifth-dimensional shape, whatever that was. These stars were living creatures, beings of complex energy structures, just as the stars in our universe were alive. Efforts to communicate with the stars, however, had failed. Maybe they, like the porpoises, just didn't care to talk to us. Never mind. What did matter was that the drive was drawing off the energy of these living things. They didn't like being killed and the drive hurt them. Ergo, Dr. Maloney explained, they screamed.

This relieved a lot of people. Some, however, insisted that interstellar travel must stop. We might be killing intelligent beings. Their opponents pointed out that that was regrettable, if true. But other species were using the drive, so the stars would be killed anyway. If we refused to use it, we wouldn't have progress. And we'd be at the mercy of merciless aliens from outer space.

Besides, there wasn't any evidence that fifth-dimensional stars were any more intelligent than earthworms.

Simon didn't know what the truth of the matter was. But he hated to hear the screaming, which was so loud at 69X that even earplugs didn't help. So he kept the ship at 20X. At that speed, he hoped he'd only be bruising the stars a little.

The *Hwang Ho* zipped away from the solar system and soon the sun was a tiny light that quickly became snuffed out as if it had been dipped in water. The celestial objects ahead, as seen in the viewscreen, were not what he would see at below-light speed. At 20X the ship was, in effect, half in this universe and half somewhere else.

The stars and the nebulae were creatures of the sublime. They were beautiful but with the beauty of awe, horror, and a mind-twisting magnitude and shape. They burned and changed form as if they were flames in hell created by Lucifer, high on heroin. Poets had tried to describe the heavens at superlight speeds. They had all failed. But when had the whining commentary ever matched the glorious text?

Simon sat paralyzed in his chair moaning with the ecstasy of terror. After a while he became aware that he had a huge erection, and there is no telling what might have happened if he had not been interrupted.

The dog had been whimpering and whining for some time, but suddenly it began barking loudly and racing around. Simon tried to ignore him. Then he became annoyed. Here he was, on the verge of the greatest orgasm he had ever known, and this mutt had to spoil it all. He shouted at Anubis, who paid him no attention at all. Finally, Simon remembered something he had read in school and seen in various TV series. He became scared, though he was not sure that he had good reason to be so.

As everybody knew, dogs were psychic. They saw things which men used to call ghosts. Now it was known that these were actually fifth-dimensional objects which had passed through normal space unperceived by the gross senses of man. These went through certain channels formed by the shape of the fifth dimension. The main channel on Earth went through the British islands, which was why England had more "ghosts" than any other place on the planet. Every Earth ship that put out to space beyond the solar system carried a dog. Radar, being limited to the speed of light, was no good for a vessel going at superlight speeds. But a dog could detect other living beings even at a million light years' distance if they were also in soixante-neuf drive. To the dogs, other beings in this extra-dimensional world *were* ghosts, and ghosts scared hell out of them.

He pressed a button. A screen sprang to life, showing him the view from the right side of the ship. He didn't expect to see the approaching ship, since it was going faster than light. But he could see a black funnel coming at an angle which would intercept his course. This, he knew, was the trail left by a vessel with soixante-neuf drive. It was one of the peculiarities of the drive that a ship radiated behind it a "shadow," a conical blackness of unknown nature. Simon, if he had looked out his own rearview screen, would have seen only a circle of nothingness directly behind the ship.

He was convinced that the ship approaching him was a Hoonhor and that it was out to get him. That was the only reason he could think of why the ship hadn't changed its course, which would result in collision if it maintained it. Probably, the Hoonhors intended to keep him from notifying other worlds of what they had done to Earth.

He stepped on the accelerator pedal and kept it to the floor while the speedometer needle crept toward the right-hand edge of the dial. He also twisted the wheel to the left to swerve the ship away. The stranger immediately changed its course to follow him.

The murmur from the two engine rooms became a loud and piercing shriek. Anubis howled with agony, and the owl flew around screaming. Simon put plugs in his ears, but they couldn't keep out the painful noise. Nor could he plug up his conscience. Somewhere, on one of the fifth-dimensional universes, a living being was undergoing terrible torture so he could save his own neck.

After ten minutes, the screams suddenly ceased. Simon didn't feel any relief. This only meant that the star had died, stripped of its fire, stripped, in fact, of every atom of its body. Tensed, he waited, and shortly the screaming started again. The drive had searched for and found another victim, a star that may have been happily browsing in the meadows of space only a minute before.

Presently, the two ships were on the same plane, the Hoonhor an incalculable distance behind the *Hwang Ho*. Simon couldn't see it in his rearview screen because of the blackness he trailed. Somewhere in that cone was the Hoonhor. Or was it? According to theory, nothing could exist in the immediate wake of a 69X vessel. Yet one vessel could follow another in the wake. But the pursuer did not exist during this time. So where was it? In the sixth dimension, according to the theorists. And the stuff in the wake of the chaser must then exist in the seventh dimension, and any ship in *its* wake would be in the eighth dimension, and any ship in *its* wake would be in the ninth dimension.

Most of the theorists were happy with this explanation. They could not run out of dimensions any more than they could run out of numbers. However, a brilliant Hindu mathematician, Dr. Utapal, had said that there was a limit. By an equation which was so abstruse that it was unprovable, Utapal demonstrated that the ninth dimension was the upper limit. (What the lower limit was, nobody knew.) When a fourth ship joined the procession, there was a transposition factor, which resulted in the third ship suddenly being in front of the first. This was called the Unavoidable Transdimensional Shift in scholarly journals but was privately referred to as the You-Grab-My-Nuts-I'll-Grab-Yours Hypothesis.

It was then that a control panel siren began whooping and its lights flashed red. Simon became even more alarmed. A space boojum was directly ahead of the ship.

A boojum was a collapsed star which formed a gravitational whirlpool that sucked in any matter coming close to it. In fact, its gravity was so strong that even light couldn't escape from its surface.* But the ship's instruments could detect the alterations it made in the local space-time structure.

Boojums were a sort of manhole in a trans-dimensional sewage system. Or a slot in a multidimensional roulette wheel. All the boojums in this universe

---

*The boojum of Trout has a remarkable resemblance to the 'black hole' of space conjectured by contemporary astronomy. Trout intuitively anticipated this concept five years before it was first proposed in scientific journals. Editor.

were entrances to other-dimensional worlds, and if a ship got sucked into one, it could be lost forever in the maze of connections. Or, if its crew was lucky, it would be shot back into this universe.

The Hoonhor ship was coming up on him swiftly. The slow freighter could not outrun the other vessel. Simon's only escape, like it or not, was to dive into the boojum. He doubted that the Hoonhor captain would have the guts to follow him into it.

The next thing he knew, everything had turned black. Nor was there any sound. After what seemed like hours but must have been only a few minutes—if time existed in this place—he felt as if he were melting. His fingers and toes were extending at the same time they were becoming shapeless. His head seemed to loll on one side because his neck was stretching far out. It fell to one side and kept on falling. It went past his body and then the floor and then was falling through a bottomless space. He tried to raise his arm to grab it, but his arm groped through nothingness for miles and miles without end.

His intestines were floating up through his body and after a while they were coiled around his head, which was still falling. They didn't taste good at all. His anus was bobbing on the end of his nose; his liver was wedged between his head and his ear. He didn't know which ear because he had no idea of which way was right or left, up or down, in or out.

He thought perhaps his head might be falling to the left, or the right, and he had used the wrong arm to try to grab it. One of his arms wasn't extending, so he transferred his efforts to that. It grabbed what felt like Anubis' tongue, a long, slimy organ. He felt along it and then pulled his hand away. Either the dog's tongue had grown or Anubis had turned into one giant tongue. He was immediately sorry that he had moved his hand. He seemed to be groping around in the dog's guts. Something moved against the back of his hand, something that beat quickly and sent a throbbing through him. Anubis' heart, he thought. He kept his hand against it and when it started to slide away he closed his fingers around it. It was the only identifiable object in this terrifying universe outside himself, an object which he had to cling to, to keep his sanity. It also kept him from feeling utterly alone, and it was the only thing which gave him any security at all. It alone was not changing shape.

Or so he had thought at first. Within a few seconds, it had grown bigger and its throbbing became faster. He hoped that the dog wasn't going to die of a heart attack.

Suddenly, they were out among the stars. Simon almost screamed with joy. They had made it; they weren't doomed to ride forever, like some Flying Dutchman, through the lightless shapeless seas of the boojum.

Then he hastily released his grasp. It wasn't Anubis' heart he'd been holding. It was his penis.

Simon apologized to Anubis and then asked the computer to check out the stars in the area. It reported that the ship was in an uncharted area. Simon didn't care. A man without a home can't be lost, and one galaxy was as good as another for his purposes.

Simon directed the computer to take the ship to the nearest galaxy and look for an inhabited planet. He went to the captain's quarters and poured a big drink of rice wine to soothe his nerves. The trouble with Chinese liquor was that it didn't satisfy. A few minutes after he'd had a shot, he felt as if he needed another. No wonder the ancient Chinese poets were always loaded out of their skulls.

Shut up in the cabin, Simon was able to relax by playing his banjo. The ship was going at only 20X, so the sound from the engine rooms wasn't loud enough to upset him. But he had to play behind closed doors because the banjo made Anubis howl and gave the owl dysentery. Their reaction hurt Simon's feelings, but something good came out of it. By backward logic and analogy, he had figured out why his concerts always got such bad reviews. Since animals hated his playing, there must be something bestial in music critics.

A week, ship's time, passed. Simon studied philosophy and Chinese, cooked meals for himself and his companions, and cleaned up after the dog and the owl. And then, one day, in the middle of his breakfast, the alarm bell rang. Simon ran to the control room and looked at the control panel screen. Translated, the Chinese words said. 'Solar system with inhabitable planet approaching.'

Simon ordered the ship to go into orbit around the fourth planet. When the *Hwang Ho* was over it, Simon looked through a telescope which could pick out objects as small as a mouse on the surface. It looked like a nice planet. Earth-size, no smog, clean oceans, and plenty of forests and grassy plains. All this was easily accounted for. The sentients were in a primitive agricultural stage and probably numbered less than a hundred million people.

What attracted his attention most was a gigantic tower on the edge of the smallest of the two continents. This tower was about a mile wide at its base and two miles high. It was shaped like a candy heart, its point stuck in the ground. A hard metal without a break made up its shell. In fact, it looked as if it had been made from a single casting. But the metal was striped with white, black, yellow, green, and blue. These were not painted on but seemed integral to the metal.

The massive structure looked brand-new. However, it was leaning to one side as if the solid granite under it vas giving way to the many billions of tons pressing on it. Eventually, maybe in a million or so years, it would fall. It had been there for about a billion years, long before the human population had evolved from apes or even from shrew-sized insect eaters. Perhaps it had even been erected before life had crawled out of the primeval seas, warm and nutritious as a diabetic's urine.

Simon knew something about towers like this one, which was why he was delighted to see it. Interstellar voyagers to distant galaxies had reported finding such towers on every inhabited planet of these systems. There were, however, none on the planets of Earth's galaxy. Nobody knew why, though many resented this slight.

Deciding to investigate the tower first, Simon directed the ship to land on it. The *Hwang Ho* settled down on a flat area between the lobes and his two pets strolled out. They didn't stay long. The flat part was covered with thousands of noisy, squabbling, egg-laying, white-and-black-checkered birds and about ten feet of guano. Simon threaded his way through the hook-billed birds, dodging vicious pecks from the mothers when he came too close to the eggs. Simon inspected the lobes, which towered above him as if they were mountains. Their slopes held no windows or doors. They were as unbroken as the passage of time itself, as impenetrable as yesterday.

Simon hadn't expected to find any entrances. Of the six million towers so far reported by Earth tourists, all had been just like this one. The natives of various planets had tried everything from diamond-tipped drills to laser beams to hydrogen bombs without scratching the mysterious metal. The buildings were hollow. A hammer could make one ring like a gong. There was even one planet which had a symphony orchestra which played only one instrument, the tower. The musicians stood on scaffolds built at various levels along the tower and struck it with hammers, the size and layout of the rooms within determining the notes evoked. The conductor stood on a platform a mile high and half a mile away and used two flags to wigwag his directions.

The highest point of music in the history of this planet occurred when a conductor, Ruboklngshep, fell off the platform. The orchestra, in trying to follow the wildly waving flags during his descent, produced six bars of the most exquisite music ever to be created, though some critics have disparaged the final three notes. Art, like science, sometimes gets its best results by accident.

Simon returned to the ship and found himself in an unforeseen situation. Since the flat area was tilted to one side, the ship had been put down at the lowest point, where the guano had built up to form a horizontal plane. Simon had made sure that the ship would not roll over. But he had forgotten about its enormous weight. It had sunk into the soft guano and so the ports on this side were about twenty feet under the surface and the ports on the other side were too high to reach. There was nothing to do but dig his way through with his bare hands. Anubis wouldn't help, since he had not buried any bones there. Simon got down on his hands and knees and excavated away. Two hours later, dirty, sweaty, and disgruntled, he broke through and fell into the port. It took a half-hour to clear out the port entrance and another half-hour to clean up himself and the pets. His usual good spirits returned shortly afterward. He had told himself that he shouldn't get angry at such a little thing.

After all, a man should expect to get his hands dirty if he dug into fundamental issues.

CHAPTER 6
Shaltoon, the Equal-Time Planet

Simon ordered the computer to set the ship down on a big field near the largest building of a city. Since this city had the largest population of any on the planet, it should be the capital of the most important nation. The building itself was six stories high and made of some white stone with purple and red veins. From the air it looked like a three-leaf clover with a long stem. Its windows were delta-shaped, and its doors were oval. The roofs were breadloaf-shaped, and the whole building was surrounded by roofless porches on the outer edges of two rows of pillars. The ones on the edge of the porch were upside-down V's. The others were behind the deltoids and projected from the floor of the porch at a forty- five-degree angle so that their ends stuck through the deltoids. The leaning shafts were cylindrical except for the ends which pierced the deltoids. These terminated in round balls from which a milky water jetted. At their base were two nut-shaped stones the surfaces of which bore a crisscross of incisions.

The people that poured out of the building were human- looking except for pointed ears, yellow eyes which had pupils like a cat's, and sharp-pointed teeth. Simon wasn't startled by this. All the humanoid races so far encountered had either been descended from simians, felines, canines, ursines, or rodents. On Earth the apes had won out in the evolutionary race toward intelligence. On other planets, the ancestors of cats, dogs, bears, beavers, or rabbits had developed fingers instead of paws and come out ahead of the apes. On some planets, both the apes and some other creature had evolved into sapients and shared their world. Or else one had exterminated the other. On this planet, the felines seemed to have gotten the upper hand early. If there were any simian humans, they were hiding deep in the forests.

Simon watched them through his viewscreens. When the soldiers had gathered around the ship, all pointing their spears and bows and arrows at the *Hwang Ho,* he came out. He held his hands up in the air to show he was peaceful. He didn't smile because on some planets baring one's teeth was a hostile sign.

"I'm Simon Wagstaff, the man without a planet," he said.

After a couple of weeks, Simon had learned the language well enough to get along. Some of the suspicions of the people of Shaltoon had worn away. They were wary of him, it seemed, because he wasn't the first Earthman to land there. Some two hundred years ago a fast-talking jovial man by the name of P.T. Taub had visited them. Before the Shaltoonians knew what was happening, he'd bamboozled them out of the crown jewels, taking not only these but a princess who'd just won the Miss Shaltoon Beauty Contest.

Simon had a hard time convincing them that he wasn't there to con them. He did want something from them, he told them over and over, but it wasn't anything material. First, did they know anything about the builders of the leaning heart-shaped tower?

The people assigned to escort Simon told him that all they knew was that the builders were called the Clerun-Gowph in this galaxy. Nobody knew why, but somebody somewhere sometime must have met them. Otherwise, why did they have a common name? As for the tower, it had been here, unoccupied and slowly tilting, since the Shaltoonians had had a language. Undoubtedly, it had been here a long time before that.

The Shaltoonians had a legend that, when the tower fell, the end of the world would come.

Simon was adaptable and gregarious. He loved people, and he knew how to get along with them. Whether he was with just one person or at a party, he enjoyed himself, and he was generally liked. But he was uneasy with the Shaltoonians. There was something wrong with them, something he couldn't describe. At first he thought that it might be because they were descended from felines. After all, though humanoid, they were fundamentally cats, just as Earthmen were basically apes. Yet, he'd met a number of extraterrestrial visitors on Earth who were felines, and he'd always gotten along with them. Actually, he preferred cats to dogs. It was only because circumstances had been beyond his control that he'd taken along a dog when he left Earth.

Maybe, he thought, it was the strong musky odor that hung over the city, overriding that of manure from the farms around the city. This emanated from every adult Shaltoonian he met and smelled exactly like a cat in heat. After a while, he understood why. They *were* all in the mating season, which lasted the year around. Their main subject of conversation was sex, but even with this subject they couldn't sustain much talk. After a half-hour or so, they'd get fidgety and then excuse themselves. If he followed them, he'd find him or her going into a house where he or she would be greeted by one of the opposite sex. The door would be closed, and within a few minutes the damnedest noises would come from the house.

This resulted in his not being able to talk long to the escorts who were supposed to keep an eye on him. They'd disappear, and someone else would take their place.

Moreover, when the escorts showed up again the next day, they acted strangely. They didn't seem to remember what they'd asked or told him the day before. At first, he put this down to a short-term memory. Maybe it was this which had kept the Shaltoonians from progressing beyond a simple agricultural society.

Simon was a good talker, but he vas a good listener, too. Once he'd learned the language well, he caught on to a discrepancy of intonation among his escorts. It varied not only among individual speakers, which was to be expected, but in the same individual from day to day. Simon finally decided that he wasn't uneasy because the Shaltoonians were, from his viewpoint, oversexed. He had no moral repugnance to this. After all, you couldn't expect aliens to be just like Earthmen. As a matter of fact, his attitude, if anything, was envy. Evolution had cheated Terrestrials. Why couldn't Homo sapiens have kept the horniness of the baboon? Why had he allowed society to shape itself so that it suppressed the sex drive? Was it because evolution had dictated that mankind was to progress technologically? And, to bring this about, had evolution shunted much of man's sex drive to the brain, where he used the energy to make tools and new religions, and ways of making more money and attaining a higher status?

Earthmen were dedicated to getting to the top of the heap, whereas the Shaltoonians devoted themselves to getting on top of each other.

This seemed a fine arrangement to Simon—at first. One of the bad things about human society was that few people ever really had intimate contact. A people who spent a lot of time in bed, however, should be full of love. But things didn't work out that way on this planet. There wasn't even a word for love in the language. They did have many terms for various sexual positions, but these were all highly technical. There was no generic term equivalent to the Earthman's "love."

Not that this made much difference generally between Earth and Shaltoon behavior. The latter seemed to have just as many divorces, disagreements, fights, and murders as the former. On the other hand, the Shaltoonians didn't have many suicides. Instead of getting depressed, they went out and got laid.

Simon thought about this aspect. He decided that perhaps Shaltoon society was, after all, better arranged than Terrestrial society. Not that this was due to any superior intelligence of the Shaltoonians. It was a matter of hormone surplus. Mother Nature, not brains, deserved the credit. This thought depressed him, but he didn't seek out a female to work off the mood. He retired to his cabin and played his banjo until he felt better. Then he got to thinking about the meaning of this and became depressed again. Hadn't he channeled his sex drive where it shouldn't be? Hadn't he made love to himself, via his banjo, instead of to another being? Were the notes spurting from the strings a perverted form of jism? Was his supreme pleasure derived from plucking, not fucking?

Simon put away the banjo, which was looking more like a detachable phallus every minute. He sallied forth determined to use his nondetachable instrument. Ten minutes later, he was back in the ship. The only relief he felt was in getting away from the Shaltoonians. He'd passed by a rain barrel and happened to look down in it. There, at the bottom, was a newly-born baby. He had looked around for a policeman to notify him but had been unable to find one. It struck him then he had never seen a policeman on Shaltoon. He stopped a passer-by and started to ask him where the local precinct had its headquarters. Unable to do so because he didn't know the word for 'police," he took the passer-by to the barrel and showed him what was in it. The citizen had merely shrugged and walked away. Simon had walked around until he saw one of his escorts. The woman was startled to see him without a companion and asked why he had left the ship without notifying the authorities. Simon said that that wasn't important. What was important was the case of infanticide he'd stumbled across.

She didn't seem to understand what he was talking about. She followed him and gazed down into the barrel. Then she looked up with a strange expression. Simon, knowing something was wrong, looked again. The corpse was gone.

"But I swear it was here only five minutes ago!" he said.

"Of course.' she said coolly. "But the barrel men have removed it."

It took some time for Simon to get it through his head that he had seen nothing unusual. In fact, the barrels he had observed on every corner and under every rain spout were seldom used to collect drinking water. Their main purpose was for the drowning of infants.

"Don't you have the same custom on Earth?" the woman said.

"It's against the law there to murder babies."

"How in the world do you keep your population from getting too large?" she said.

"We don't," Simon said.

"How barbaric!"

Simon got over some of his indignation when the woman explained that the average lifespan of a Shaltoonian was ten thousand years. This was due to an elixir invented some two hundred thousand years before. The Shaltoonians weren't much for mechanics or engineering or physics, but they were great botanists. The elixir had been made from juices of several different plants. A by-product of this elixir was that a Shaltoonian seldom got sick.

"So you see that we have to have some means of keeping the population down," she said. "Otherwise, we'd all be standing on top of each other's heads in a thousand years or less."

"What about contraceptives?"

"Those're against our custom," she said. "They interfere with the pleasure of sex. Besides, everyone ought to have a chance to be born."

Simon asked her to explain this seemingly contradictory remark. She replied that an aborted baby didn't have a soul. But a baby that made it to the open air was outfitted with a soul at the moment of birth. If it died even a few seconds later, it still went to heaven. Indeed, it was better that it did die, because then it would be spared the hardships and pains and griefs of life. Killing it was doing it a favor. However, to keep the population from decreasing, it was necessary to let one out of a hundred babies survive. The Shaltoonians didn't like to have a fixed arrangement for this. They let Chance decide who lived and who didn't. So every woman, when she got pregnant, went to the Temple of Shaltoon. There she picked a number at a roulette table, and if her ball fell into the lucky slot, she got to keep the baby. The Holy Croupiers gave her a card with the lucky number on it, which she wore around her neck until the baby was a year old.

"The wheel's fixed so the odds are a hundred to one," she said. "The house usually wins. But when a woman wins, a holiday is declared, and she's queen for a day. This is no big deal, since she spends most of her time reviewing the parade."

"Thanks for the information," Simon said. "I'm going back to the ship. So long, Goobnatz."

"I'm not Goobnatz," she said. "I'm Dunnernickel."

Simon was so shaken up that he didn't ask her what she meant by that. He assumed that he had had a slip of memory. The next day, however, he apologized to her.

"Wrong again," she said. "My name is Pussyloo."

There was a tendency for all aliens of the same race to look alike to Earthmen. But he had been here long enough to distinguish individuals easily.

"Do you Shaltoonians have a different name for every day?"

"No," she said. "My name has always been Pussyloo. But it was Dunnernickel you were talking to yesterday and Goobnatz the day before. Tomorrow, it'll be Quimquat."

This was the indefinable thing that had been making him uneasy. Simon asked her to explain, and they went into a nearby tavern. The drinks were on the house, since he was working here as a banjo-player. The Shaltoonians crowded in every night to hear his music, which they enjoyed even if it wasn't at all like their native music. At least, they claimed they did. The leading music critic of the planet had written a series of articles about Simon's genius, claiming that he evoked a profundity and a truth from his instrument which no Shaltoonian could equal. Simon didn't understand any more than the Shaltoonians did what the critic was talking about, but he liked what he read. This was the first time he'd ever gotten a good review.

They had ordered a couple of beers, and Pussyloo plunged into her explanation. She said she'd be glad to tell him all she could in half an hour, but she'd have to talk a lot to get everything into that length of time. In thirty minutes it'd be quitting time. She liked Simon, but he wasn't her type, and she had an assignation with a man she'd met on her lunch hour. After Simon heard her explanation, he understood why she was in such a hurry.

"Don't you Earthmen have ancestor rotation?" she said.

Simon was so startled that he upset his beer and had to order another. "What the hell's that?" he said.

"It's a biological, not a supernatural, phenomenon," she said. "I guess you poor deprived Terrestrials don't have it. But the body of every Shaltoonian contains cells which carry the memories of a particular ancestor. The earliest ancestors are in the anal tissue. The latest are in the brain tissue."

"You mean a person carries around with him the memories of his foreparents?" Simon said.

"That's what I said."

"But it seems to me that in time a person wouldn't have enough space in his body for all the ancestral cells," Simon said. "When you think that your ancestors double every generation backward, you'd soon be out of room. You have two parents, and each of them had two parents, and each of them had two. And so on. You go back only five generations, and you have sixteen great-greatgrandparents. And so on."

"And so on," Pussyloo said. She looked at the tavern clock while her nipples swelled and the strong mating odor became even stronger. In fact, the whole tavern stank of it. Simon couldn't even smell his own beer.

"You have to remember that if you go back about thirty generations, everyone now living has many common ancestors. Otherwise, the planet at that time would've been jammed with people like flies on a pile of horse manure.

"But there's another factor that eliminates the number of ancestors. The ancestor cells with the strongest personalities release chemicals that dissolve the weaker ones."

"Are you telling me that, even on the cellular level, the survival of the fittest is the law?" Simon said. "That egotism is the ruling agent?"

Pussyloo scratched the itch between her legs and said, "That's the way it is. There would never have been any trouble about it if that's all there was to it. But in the old days, about twenty thousand years ago, the ancestors started their battle for their civil rights. They said it wasn't right that they should be shut up in their little cells with only their own memories. They had a right to get out of their cellular ghettoes, to enjoy the flesh they were contributing to but couldn't participate in.

"After a long fight, they got an equal-time arrangement. Here's how it works. A person is born and allowed to control his own body until he reaches puberty. During this time, an ancestor speaks only when spoken to."

"How do you do that?" Simon said.

"It's a mental thing the details of which the scientists haven't figured out yet," she said. "Some claim we have a neural circuit we can switch on and off by thought. The trouble is, the ancestors can switch it on, too. They used to give the poor devils that carried them a hard time, but now they don't open up any channels unless they're requested to do so.

"Anyway, when a person reaches puberty, he must then give each ancestor a day for himself or herself. The ancestor comes into full possession of the carrier's body and consciousness. The carrier himself still gets one day a week for himself. So he comes out ahead, though there's still a lot of bitching about it. When the round is completed, it starts all over again.

"Because of the number of ancestors, a Shaltoonian couldn't live long enough for one cycle if it weren't for the elixir. But this delays aging so that the average life span is about ten thousand years."

"Which is actually twenty thousand years, since a Shaltoon year is twice as long as ours," Simon said.

He was stunned. He didn't even notice when Pussyloo squirmed out of the booth and, still squirming, walked out of the place.

CHAPTER 7
Queen Margaret

The Space Wanderer had been thinking about moving on. There didn't seem to be much here for him. The Shaltoonians did not even have a word for philosophy, let alone such as ontology, epistemology, and cosmology. Their interests were elsewhere. He could understand why they thought only of the narrow and the secular, or, to be exact, eating, drinking, and copulating. But understanding did not make him wish to participate. His main lust was for the big answers.

When he found out about ancestor rotation, however, he decided to hang around a little longer. He was curious about the way in which this unique phenomenon shaped the strange and complex structure of Shaltoon society. Also, to be truthful, he had an egotistic reason for being a little reluctant to leave. He enjoyed being lionized, and the next planet might have critics not so admiring.

On the other hand, his pets were unhappy. They would not leave the spaceship even though they were suffering from cabin fever. The odor from the Shaltoonians drove Anubis into a barking frenzy and Athena into semi-shock. When Simon had guests, the two retreated into the galley. After the party was over, Simon would try to play with them to cheer them up, but they would not respond. Their big dumb eyes begged him to take off, to leave forever this planet that smelled of cats. Simon told them to stick it out for another week. Seekers after knowledge had to put up with certain inconveniences. They didn't understand his words, of course, but they did understand his tone. They were stuck here until their master decided to unstick them. What they wanted to stick and where was something else. Maybe it was a good thing they couldn't talk.

The first thing Simon found out in his investigations was that ancestor rotation caused a great resistance to change. This was not only inevitable but necessary. The society had to function from day to day, crops be grown and harvested and transported, the governmental and business administration carried out, schools, hospitals, courts, etcetera, run. To make this possible, a family stayed in the same line of work or profession. If your forefather a thousand generations removed was a ditch-digger, you were one, too. There was no confusion resulting from a blacksmith being replaced by a judge one day and a garbage hauler the next.

The big problem in running this kind of society was the desire of each ancestor to live it up on his day of possession. Naturally, he/she didn't want to waste his/her time working when he/she could be eating, drinking, and copulating. But everybody understood that if he/she indulged in his/her wishes, society would fall apart and the carriers would starve to death in a short time. So, grudgingly, everybody put in an eight-hour day and at quitting time plunged into an orgy. Almost everybody did. Somebody had to take care of the babies and children, and somebody had to work on the farms the rest of the day.

The only way to handle this was to let slaves baby-sit and finish up the plowing and the chores on the farms. On Shaltoon, once a slave always a slave was the law. Yet, how do you get an ancestral slave to work all day on the only day in five hundred years that he'll take over a carrier? For one thing, who's going to oversee him? No freeman wanted to put in his precious time supervising the helots. And a slave that isn't watched closely is going to goof off.

How did you punish a slave if he neglected his work to enjoy himself? If you hung him, you killed off thousands of innocents. You also reduced the number of slaves, of which there weren't enough to go around in the first place. If you whipped him, you were punishing the innocent. The day following the whipping, the guilty man/woman retreated into his/her cell, shut off from the pain. The poor devil that followed was the one that suffered. He resented being punished for something he hadn't done, and his morale scraped bottom like a dog with piles.

The authorities had recognized that this was a dangerous situation. If enough slaves got angry enough to revolt, they could take over easily while their masters were helplessly drunk in the midst of the late evening orgy. The only way to prevent this was to double the number of slaves. In this way, a slave could put in four hours on the second shift and then go off to enjoy himself while another slave finished up for him. This did have its drawbacks. The slave that took over the last four hours had been whooping it up on his free time and so he was in no shape to work efficiently. But this could not be helped.

The additional slaves required had to be gotten from the freemen. So the authorities passed laws that a man could be enslaved if he spit on the sidewalk or overparked his horse and buggy. There were protests and riots against this legislation, of course. The government expected, in fact hoped for, these. They arrested the rebels and made them slaves. The sentence was retroactive; all their ancestors became slaves also.

Simon talked to a number of the slaves and found out that what he had suspected was true. Almost all the newly created slaves had come from the poor classes. The few from the upper class had been liberals. Somehow or other, the cops never saw a banker, a judge, or a businessman spit on the sidewalk. Simon became apprehensive when he found out about this. There were so many laws that he didn't know about. He could be enslaved if he forgot to go downwind before farting in the presence of a cop. He was assured, however, that he wasn't subject to the laws.

"Not as long as you leave within two weeks," his informant said. "We wouldn't want you as a slave. You have too many strange ideas. If you stayed here long, you might spread these, infect too many people."

Simon didn't comment. The analogy of new ideas to deadly diseases was not new to him.

One of Simon's favorite writers, a science-fiction author by the name of Jonathan Swift Somers III, had once written a story about this parallel between diseases and ideas. In his story, *Quarantine!*, an Earthman had landed on an uncharted planet. He was eager to study the aliens, but they wouldn't let him out of the spaceship until he had been given a medical checkup. At first, he thought they suspected him of bringing in germs they weren't equipped to handle. After he'd learned their language, he was told that this wasn't so. The aliens had long ago perfected a panacea against illnesses of the flesh. They were worried about his disrupting their society, perhaps destroying it, with deadly thoughts.

The port officials, wearing lead mind-shields, questioned the Earthman closely for two weeks. He sweated while he talked because the aliens' method of disease-prevention, which was one hundred percent effective, was to kill the sick person. His body was then burned and his ashes were buried at midnight in an unmarked grave.

After two weeks of grilling, the head official said, smiling, "You can go out among our people now."

"You mean I have a clean bill of health?" the Earthman said.

"Nothing to worry about," the official said. "We've heard every idea you have. There isn't a single one we didn't think of ten thousand years ago. You must come from a very primitive world."

Jonathan Swift Somers III, like most great American writers, had been born in the Midwest. His father had been an aspiring poet whose unfinished epic had not been printed until long after his death. Simon had once made a pilgrimage to Petersburg, Illinois, where the great man was buried. The monument was a granite wheelchair with wings. Below was the epitaph:

JONATHAN SWIFT SOMERS III
1910–1982
He Didn't Need Legs

Somers had been paralyzed from the waist down since he was ten years old. In those days, they didn't have a vaccine against polio. Somers never left the wheelchair or his native town, but his mind voyaged out into the universe. He wrote forty novels and two hundred short stories, mostly about adventure in space. When he started writing, he described exploits on the Moon and Mars. When landings were made on these, he shifted the locale to Jupiter. After the Jovian Expedition, he wrote about astronauts who traveled to the extreme edge of the cosmos. He figured that in his lifetime men would never get beyond the solar system, and he was right. Actually, it made no difference whether or not astronauts got to the places he described. His books about the Moon and Mars were still read long after voyages there had become humdrum. It didn't matter that Somers had been one hundred percent wrong about those places. His books were poetic and dramatic, and the people he depicted going there seemed more real than the people who actually went there. At least, they were more interesting.

Somers belonged to the same school of writing as the great French novelist Balzac. Balzac claimed he could write better about a place if he knew nothing of it. Invariably, when he did go to a city he had described in a book, he was disappointed.

Near Somers' grave was his father's.

JONATHAN SWIFT SOMERS II
1877–1912
I tried to fly on verse's wings.
Rejection slips all called it corn.
How Nature balances jogs and stings!
I never suffered a critic's scorn.

However, the book reviewers had given the son a hard time most of his life. It wasn't until he was an old man that Somers was recognized as a great artist. When he received the Nobel Prize for Literature, he remarked, "This heals no wounds." He knew that critics never admit they're wrong. They'd still give him a hard time.

Simon was worried that he, too, might upset the Shaltoonians. It was true that he never proposed any new ideas to them. All he did was ask questions. But often these can be more dangerous than propaganda. They lead to novel thoughts.

It seemed, however, that he wasn't going to spark off any novelty in the Shaltoonians' minds. The adults were, in effect, never around for more than a day. The young were too busy playing and getting educated for the time when they'd have to give up possession of their bodies.

Near the end of his visit, on a fine sunny morning, Simon left the spaceship to visit the Temple of Shaltoon. He intended to spend the day studying the rites being performed there. Shaltoon was the chief deity of the planet, a goddess whose closest Earthly equivalent was Venus or Aphrodite. He walked through the streets, which he found strangely empty. He was wondering what was going on when he was startled by a savage scream. He ran to the house from which it came and opened the door. A man and a woman were fighting to the death in the front room. Simon had a rule that he would never interfere in a quarrel between man and wife. It was a good rule but one which no humanitarian could keep. In another minute, one or both of the bleeding and bruised couple would be dead. He jumped in between them and then jumped out again and ran for his life. Both had turned against him, which was only to be expected.

Since he was followed out on the street, he kept on running. As he sped down the street, he heard cries and shrieks from the houses he passed. Turning a corner, he collided with a swirling shouting mob, everyone of which seemed intent on killing anybody within range of their fists, knives, spears, swords, and axes. Simon fought his way out and staggered back to the ship. When the port was closed behind him, he crawled to the sick bay—Anubis pacing him with whimpers and tongue-licking—where he bandaged his numerous cuts and gashes.

The next day he cautiously ventured out. The city was a mess. Corpses and wounded were everywhere in the streets, and firemen were still putting out the blazes that had been started the day before. However, no one seemed belligerent, so he stopped a citizen and asked him about yesterday's debacle.

"It was Shag Day, dummy," the citizen said and moved on.

Simon wasn't too jarred by the rudeness. Very few of the natives were in a good mood when sober. This was because the carrier's body was continually abused by the rotating ancestors. Each had to get all the debauchery he could cram into his allotted time between the quitting whistle and the curfew bell. As a result, the first thing the ancestor felt when he took his turn was a terrible hangover. This lasted through the day, making him tired and irritable until he had had a chance to kill the pain with liquor.

Every once in a while, the body would collapse and be carried off to a hospital by drunken ambulance attendants and turned over to drunken nurses and doctors. The poor devil who had possession that day was too sick to do anything but lie in bed, groaning and cursing. The thought that he was wasting his precious and rare day in convalescence from somebody else's fun made him even sicker.

So the Space Wanderer didn't wonder at the grumpiness of the citizen. He walked on and presently found a heavily bandaged but untypically amiable woman.

"Everybody, if you go back a few thousand years, has the same ancestors," she said. "So, every thousand years or so, a day occurs when one particular ancestor happens to come into possession of many carriers. This usually happens to only a few, and we can cope with most of these coincidences. But about five thousand years ago. Shag, a very powerful personality born in the Old Stone Age, took over more than half of the population on a certain day. Since he was an extremely authoritarian and violent man who hated himself, the first Shag Day ended with a quarter of the world's people killing each other."

"And what about yesterday's Shag Day?" Simon said.

"That's the third. It's a record breaker, too. Almost half of the population were casualties."

"From the long-range view, it has its bright side," Simon said. "You can allow more babies to stay alive now so you can bring the population back to normal."

"The sweetest catnip grows behind the latrine," she said. This was the equivalent of the Terrestrial "Every cloud has its silver lining," or "An ill wind blows somebody good."

Simon decided to cut his trip short. He would leave the next day. But that evening, while reading the Shaltoon *Times,* he found out that in four days the wisest person who had ever lived would take over the queen's body. He became excited. If anyone would have the truth, it would be this woman. She'd had more turns at rotation than anyone and combined the greatest intelligence with the longest experience.

The reason that everybody knew that Queen Margaret was due to take over was the rotation chart. This had been worked out for each person. Generally, it was hung on the bathroom wall so it could be studied when there was nothing else to occupy one's mind.

Simon sent in a petition for an audience. Under normal circumstances, he would have had to wait six months for an answer. Since he was the only alien on the planet, and famous for his banjo-playing, he got a reply the same day. The queen would be pleased to dine with him. Formal attire was mandatory. Resplendent in the dress uniform of the captain of the *Hwang Ho,* a navy blue outfit adorned with huge epaulettes, gold braid, big brass buttons, and twenty Good Conduct medals, Simon appeared at the main door of the palace. He was ushered by a lord of the royal pantry and six guards through magnificent marble corridors loaded down with objets d'art. At another time, Simon would have liked to examine these. Most of them consisted of phallic imagery.

He was led through the door flanked by two guards who blew through long silver trumpets as he passed them. Simon appreciated the honor, even if it left him deaf for a minute. He was still dizzy when he was halted in a small but ornate room before a big table of polished dark wood. This was set with two plates and two goblets full of wine and a crowd of steaming dishes. Behind it sat a woman whose beauty started his adrenaline flowing, even if she wasn't strictly human. To tell the truth, Simon had gotten so accustomed to pointed ears, slit pupils, and sharp teeth that his own face startled him when he shaved. Simon didn't hear the introduction because his hearing hadn't come back yet. He bowed to the queen after the official's lips had quit moving, and at a sign he sat down across the table from her. The dinner passed pleasantly enough.

They talked about the weather, a subject that Simon would find was an ice-breaker on every planet. Then they discussed the horrors of Shag Day. Simon became progressively drunker as the dinner proceeded. It was protocol to down a glass of wine every time the queen did, and she seemed to be very thirsty. He didn't blame her. It had been three hundred years since she had had a drink.

Simon told her his life story at her request. She was horrified but at the same time complacent.

"Our religion maintains that the stars, planets, and moons are living beings," she said. "These are the only forms of life big enough and complex enough to interest the Creatrix. Biological life is an accidental by-product. You might say that it's a disease infecting the planets. Vegetable and animal life are bearable forms of the disease, like acne or athlete's foot.

"But when sentient life, beings with self-consciousness, evolve, they become a sort of deadly microbe. We Shaltoonians, however, are wise enough to know that. So, instead of being parasites, we become symbiotes. We live off the earth, but we take care that we don't ruin it. That's why we've stuck to an agricultural society. We grow crops, but we replenish the soil with manure. And every tree we cut down, we replace.

"Earthlings, now, they seem to have been parasites who made their planet sick. Much as I regret to say it, it was a good thing that the Hoonhors cleaned Earth up. They only have to take one look at Shaltoon, however, to see that we've kept our world in tiptop shape. We're safe from them."

Simon did not think that Shaltoon society was above criticism, but he thought it diplomatic to keep silent.

"You say, Space Wanderer, that you mean to roam everywhere until you have found answers to your questions. I suppose by that that you want to know the meaning of life?"

She leaned forward, her eyes a hot green with vertical black slits showing in the candlelight. Her gown fell open, and Simon saw the smooth creamy mounds and their tips, huge and red as cherries.

"Well, you might say that," he said,

She rose suddenly, knocking her chair onto the floor, and clapped her hands. The butlers and the officials left at once and closed the doors behind them. Simon began sweating. The room had become very warm, and the thick ropy odor of cat-heat was so heavy it was almost visible.

Queen Margaret of the planet Shaltoon let her gown fall to the floor. She was wearing nothing underneath. Her high, firm, uncowled bosom was proud and rosy. Her hips and thighs were like an inviting lyre of pure alabaster. They shone so whitely that they might have had a light inside.

"Your travels are over, Space Wanderer," she whispered, her voice husky with lust. "Seek no more, for you have found. The answer is in my arms."

He did not reply. She strode around the table to him instead of ordering him, as was her queenly right, to come to her.

"It's a glorious answer, Queen Margaret, God knows," he replied. His palms were perspiring profusely. "I am going to accept it gratefully. But I have to tell you, if I'm going to be perfectly honest with you, that I will have to be on my way again tomorrow."

"But you have found your answer, you have found your answer!" she cried, and she forced his head between her fragrant young breasts.

He said something. She thrust him out at arm's length. "What was that you said?"

"I said, Queen Margaret, that what you offer is an awfully good answer. It just doesn't happen to be the one I'm primarily looking for."

Dawn broke like a window hit by a gold brick. Simon entered the spaceship. A human doughnut dunked in weariness, satiety, and cat-in-mating-season pungency, he slopped in. Anubis sniffed and growled. Simon put out a shaking hand drained of hormones to pet him.

Anubis bit it.

CHAPTER 8
The *No Smoking Planet*

During the banquet with Queen Margaret, Simon had drunk a goblet of the Shaltoon immortality elixir. And just before he left, he was given two vials of elixir for his animals. Simon hesitated for a long time about offering Anubis and Athena the green sweet-and-sour liquid. Was it fair to inflict long life on them? Would he have swallowed the stuff if he had not been drunk with alcohol and the queen's musky odor?

"It may take several lifetimes, or more, for you to find a place where the answer to your primal question is known," the queen had said. "Wouldn't it be ironic if you died of old age while on your way to a planet where the answer you seek was known?"

Simon had said, "You're very wise, Queen Margaret." and he emptied the cup. The expected thunder and lightning of imminences of immortality for which he braced himself had not come. Instead, he had belched.

Now he looked at the dog, hiding behind a chair with shame because he had bitten Simon, and at the owl, sitting on top of the chair, her favorite perch, spotted with white.

In the normal course of subjective time, they would both be dead in a few years. The future might show that they would have been far better off dead. On the other hand—Simon was hopelessly ambidextrous—they might be missing a vast and enduring joy if he denied them the elixir. Who knew? They might even find a planet where the natives had a science advanced enough to raise his pets' intelligence to a human level. Then he could communicate with them, enjoy their companionship to the fullest potentiality.

On the other hand, they might then become very unhappy.

Simon solved his dilemma by pouring out the elixir into two bowls. If the two cared to drink the stuff, they could do so. The decision was up to their limited powers of free will. After all, animals knew what was good for them, and if immortality smelled bad to them, they wouldn't touch it.

Anubis rose from behind the chair and slinked across the floor to the bowl. He sniffed at the green liquid and then lapped it up. Simon looked at Athena and said, "Well?" The owl said, "Who?" After a while she flew down to her bowl and drank from it.

Simon began worrying that he had done the wrong thing. Dogs will eat poison if it's wrapped up in a steak. Perhaps the elixir's perfume overrode the odor of dangerous elements.

A minute later, he had forgotten his concern. The viewscreen flashed the information that the ship was approaching a star with a planetary system. The *Hwang Ho* dropped down into sublightspeed, and two days later they were entering an orbit around the sixth planet of the giant red star. This was Earth-size, and its air breathable, though its oxygen content was greater than Earth's.

The only artificial object on the planet was the gigantic candy-heart-shaped tower of the Clerun-Gowph. Simon flew the ship around it a few times, but, on finding that it was as invulnerable as the other, he left it. This planet showed no sign of intelligent life, of beings who used tools, grew crops, and constructed buildings. It did have some curious animal life, though, and he decided to get a close look at it. He gave the landing order, and a few minutes later stepped out onto the edge of a meadow near the shore of an amber sea.

The grass was about two feet high, violet-colored and topped with yellow flowers with five petals. Moving through and above these were about forty creatures which were pyramid-shaped and about thirty feet high. Their skins or shells—he wasn't sure which they were—were pink. They moved on hundreds of very short legs ending in broad round feet. Halfway up their bodies were eyes, two on each side, eight in all. These were huge and round and a light blue, and the lids had long curling eyelashes. At the top of each pyramid- shaped body was a pink ball with a large opening on two opposing sides.

It was evident that their mouths were on their bottoms, since they left a trail of cropped grass behind them. He could hear the munching of the grass and rumblings of their stomachs.

Simon had put the ship into a deep ravine beyond a thick wood so he could sneak up on the creatures. But purple things in the sky were moving out to sea and turning in a sweeping curve so they could come in downwind toward him. These were even stranger than the creatures browsing on the flowers. They looked from a distance like zeppelins, but they had two big eyes near the underside of their noses and tentacles coiled up along their undersides about twenty feet back of the eyes. Simon wondered how they ate. Perhaps the curious organs at the tips of their noses were some kind of mouth. These were bulbous and had a small opening.

Just above the small bulb was a hole. This did not seem to be a mouth, however, since it was rigid. There was another hole at the rear, and a number of much smaller ones spaced along the underside.

Their tail assemblies were just like zeppelins'. They had huge vertical rudders and horizontal elevators, but these sprouted yellow and green feathers on the edges.

Simon figured out they must use some sort of jet propulsion. They took in air through the front hole, which was rigid, and squeezed it out of the rear hole, which was contracting and dilating.

The huge creatures dropped lower as they neared the meadow, and the first one, emitting short sharp whistles, came in about thirty feet above the ground. It passed between a line of the pyramid-things, and then it eased its bulbous nose into an opening in the ball on top of one. This closed around the bulb and held the zeppelin-thing.

The pyramid-thing was a living mooring mast.

A moment later, the flying animal was released. It headed toward the bush behind which Simon was crouched. After it came the other fliers, all whistling.

The pyramid-things crowded together and faced inward. Or were they facing outward, like a bunch of cows threatened by wolves? How could they face anything if they had eyes on all sides and no faces? In any event, they were forming a protective assembly.

Simon stepped out from his cover with his hands held up. The foremost zeppelin-creature loomed above him, its huge eyes cautious. Its tentacles reached out but did not touch Simon. He was almost blown down as the thing eased forward toward him. The stench was terrible but not unfamiliar. He had batted .500 in his guess about its method of propulsion. Instead of taking in air, compressing it with some organ, and shooting it out, it drove itself with giant farts. Its big stomachs—like a cow it had more than one—generated gas for propulsion. Simon figured out that its stomachs must contain enzymes which made the gas. At this moment, it hung about ten feet above the surface, bobbing up and down as it expelled gas from the hole in front to counteract the wind.

Simon stood there while the thing whistled at him. After a while he caught on to the fact that the whistles were a sort of Morse code.

Simon imitated some of the dots and dashes just to let them know that he, too, was intelligent. Then he turned back and went to his ship. The zeppelins followed him above the trees and watched him go into the ship. Through the viewscreen he could see them hovering over the ship and feeling it with their tentacles. Maybe they thought it was a strange living creature, too.

Simon went out the next day to the edge of the meadow. The living mooring masts got alarmed again, and once more the fliers came down. But after a few days they got used to him. Simon walked closer to them each day. By the end of the week, he was allowed to stroll around among the pyramids. A few days later, however, the pyramids were gone. He walked around until he found them in another meadow. Evidently, they had eaten up all the grass and flowers in the other place.

Simon found it difficult to learn the language of the zeppelin-things. Most of them were too busy in the daytime to talk to him. When dark came, the fliers locked into the balls on the top of the pyramids and stayed there until dawn. When they did speak—or whistle—to him, the stench they expelled was almost unbearable. But then he found out that the pyramids could whistle, too. They did this, not through the mouths on their undersides but through one of the openings in the balls at the tops. These emitted a stench, too, but he could endure it if he stood upwind. And, being females, the pyramids were more loquacious and better suited to teach him zeppelinese.

They liked Simon because he gave them someone to talk to and about. The males, it seemed, spent most of their time playing and carousing in the air. They came down at noon for a meal but wouldn't hang around to talk. When night fell, they landed, but this was for supper and a short session of sexual intercourse. After which, they usually dozed off.

"We're just objects to them," said one female. "Nutrition and pleasure objects."

The ball on top of the females was a curious organ. One opening was a combination mooring lock, gruel nipple, and vagina. The females browsed on the meadow, digested the food, and fed it through a nipple inside the ball into the tips of the males' noses. This opening also received the slender tongue-like sex organ of the male. The opening on the other side of the ball was the anus and the mouth. This could be tightened to emit the whistling speech.

Simon didn't want to get involved in the domestic affairs of these creatures. But he had to show a certain amount of interest and sympathy if he was to get information. So he whistled a question at the female whom he'd named Anastasia.

"Yes, that's right," Anastasia said. "We do all the work and those useless sons of bitches do nothing but play around all day."

Anastasia didn't actually say "sons of bitches" but Simon translated it as such. What she said was something like "farts in a windstorm."

"We females talk a lot among ourselves during the day," she said. "But we'd like to talk with our mates, too. After all, they've been up in the wild blue yonder, having a great time, seeing all sorts of interesting things. But do you think for one moment that they'll let us in on what's going on outside these meadows? No, all they want to do is to be fed and have a quickie and be off to dreamland. When we complain, they tell us that we wouldn't understand it if they did tell us what they saw and did. So here we are, ground-bound and shut up in these little meadows, working all day, taking care of the children, while they're roaming around, zooming up and down, having a good old time. It isn't fair!"

Simon whistled some more sympathy and then went down to the beach to watch the males.

He had found out that the stomachs of the fliers also generated hydrogen. It was this gas which enabled them to float in the air. They carried water as ballast, which they drew up from the ocean through their hollow tentacles. When they wanted altitude quickly, they released the water, and up they went. They were always holding races or gamboling about, playing all sorts of games, tag-the-leader, loop-the-loop, doing Immelmann turns, follow-the-leader, or catch-the-bird. This latter game consisted of chasing a bird until they caught it by sucking it into their jetholes or forcing it to the ground.

They also liked to scare the herds of animals on the ground by zooming down on them and stampeding them. The male whose herd raised the biggest cloud of dust won this game.

The males had another form of communication than whistling, too. They could emit short or long trails of smoke corresponding to the whistled dots and dashes. With these they could talk to each other at long distances or call in their buddies if they saw something interesting. They never used this skywriting, however, in sight of the females. They took great delight in having a secret of their own. The females knew about this, of course, since the males sometimes boasted about it. This made the females even more discontented.

Simon would not have stayed long on this planet, which he named Giffard after the Frenchman who first successfully controlled a lighter-than-air craft. Simon did not believe that the simple natives had any answers to his questions. But then he talked to Graf, his name for the big male that dominated the herd. Graf said that the males didn't spend all their time just playing. They often had philosophical discussions, usually in the afternoon when they were resting. They'd float around on the ocean or a lake and discuss the big issues of the universe. Simon, hearing this, decided he'd wait until he knew the language well enough to talk philosophy with the males. A few months after he'd landed, he asked Graf if he would take him to the lake where the males had their bull sessions. Graf said he'd be glad to.

The next day, Graf wrapped a tentacle around Simon and lifted him up. Simon was thrilled but he was also a little scared. He wished that he had flown to the lake in the lifeboat. But he was eager for new experiences, and this was one he wasn't likely to find on any other world.

Shortly before they got to the lake, Simon took a cigar out of his pocket and lit up. It was a good cigar, made of Outer Mongolian tobacco. Simon was puffing happily some hundreds of feet above a thick yellow forest, the wind moving softly over his face and a big black bird with a red crest flapping along a few feet away from him. All was blue and quiet and content; this was one of the rare moments when God did indeed seem in His heaven and all was well with the world.

As usual, the rare moment did not last long. Graf suddenly started bobbing up and down so violently that Simon began to get airsick. Then he whistled screamingly, and the tentacle around Simon's waist straightened out. Simon grabbed at it and hung on, shouting wildly at Graf. When he got over his first panic, he whistled at Graf after removing the cigar.

"What's the matter?"

"What are you doing?" Graf whistled like a steam kettle back at him. "You're on fire!"

"What?" Simon whistled.

"Let go! Let go! I'll go up in flames!"

"I'll fall, you damned fool!"

"Let go!"

Simon looked down. They were now over the lake but about a hundred feet up. Below, the cigar-shaped males were floating in the water. Or they had been, a second before. Suddenly, they rose upward in a body, their ballast squirting out through the hollow tentacles, and then they scattered.

A few seconds later, Simon realized what was going on. He opened his hand, letting the cigar drop. Graf immediately quit his violent oscillations, and a moment later he deposited Simon on the shore of the lake. But his skin was darker than its usual purple, and he stuttered his dots and dashes.

"F-f-f-fire's th-th-the w-w-w-worst th-th-thing there is! It's the only th-th-thing we f-f-fear! It w-w-was in-vented b-b-by th-th-the d-d-devil!"

The Giffardians, it seemed, had religion. Their devil, however, dwelt in the sky, and he propelled himself with a jet of flaming hydrogen. When it came time for the bad Giffardians to be taken off to the hell above the sky, he zoomed in and burned them up with flame from his tail.

The good Giffardians were taken by a zeppelin-shaped angel whose farts were sweet-smelling down into a land below the earth. Their planet was hollow, they claimed, and heaven was inside the hollow.

They had a lot of strange ideas about religion. This didn't faze Simon, who had heard stranger on Earth.

Simon apologized. He then explained what the thing on fire in his mouth had been.

All the males shuddered and bobbed up and down and one was so terror-stricken that he shot away, unable to control his ejaculations of gas.

"It might be better if you left," Graf said. "Right now."

"Oh, I won't smoke except in the ship from now on." Simon said. "I promise."

This quieted the males down somewhat. But they did not really breathe easy until he also said he would put up some NO SMOKING signs.

"That way, if other Earthmen should land here," Simon said, "they'll not light up."

He didn't tell them that it was doubtful that any people from his native planet would ever come here. Nor did he tell them that there were billions of planets whose people couldn't read English.

It wasn't fire that made Simon so dangerous. It was the ideas he innocently dropped while talking to the females. Once, when Anastasia complained about being kept on the ground, Simon said that she ought to take a ride. He realized at once that he shouldn't have ventured this opinion. But Anastasia wouldn't let him drop the subject. The next day, she tried to talk her mate, Graf, into taking her up. He refused, but she was so upset that the gruel she fed him became sour. After several days of stomach upset, he gave in.

With Anastasia hanging on to him through the lock in their apex-organs, he lifted. The others stood or floated around and watched this epoch-making flight. Graf carried her up to about two thousand feet, beyond which he was unable to levitate. However, her weight dragged his nose down so that his tail was far higher than his fore part. He was unable to navigate in this fashion and had a hard time getting her back to the meadow. Moreover, his skin had broken out in huge drops of yellowish sweat.

Anastasia, however, was enraptured. The other females insisted that their mates take them for rides. These did so reluctantly and had the same trouble navigating as Graf. The males were too exhausted that night to have sexual intercourse.

There is no telling what might have happened in the next few days. But, the day after, the females started to give birth. Perhaps it was the excitement of their first aerial voyages that made them deliver before the end of their term. In any event, Simon strolled out onto the meadow that morning to find a number of tiny zeppelins and mooring masts nursing.

The baby males floated up as high as the nose-apex locks and took their gruel there. The baby females cropped the grass alongside their mothers.

"You see, even at birth, we females are discriminated against," Anastasia said. "We have to stick to the ground and take food that isn't nearly as easy to digest as the stuff the males get from the apex-organs. The males have the best of it, as usual."

"Function follows form," Simon said.

"What?" Anastasia whistled.

Simon strolled off, wishing that he could keep his mouth shut. He walked along the seashore and thought about leaving that very day. He had been able to have one philosophical discussion with the males, but it turned out to be on the level of what he'd heard in the locker room in high school. He didn't expect to find much deeper stuff. He had, however, promised Anastasia that he'd be the godfather of her daughter. He supposed he should wait until the ceremony, which would take place in three days. One of Simon's weaknesses was that he couldn't bear to hurt anyone's feelings.

He walked around the curve of the beach, and he saw a beautiful woman just rising from the foam of a wave.

CHAPTER 9
Chworktap

Simon couldn't have been more shocked than if he had been Crusoe when he saw Friday's footprint. It was, in fact, Friday on the Earth calendar in the spaceship, another coincidence found only in bad novels. What was even more unforgivable—in a novel, not in Nature, who could care less about coincidences—was that the scene looked almost like Botticelli's famous painting *Birth of Venus.* She wasn't standing on a giant clamshell and there wasn't any maiden ready to throw a blanket over her. Nor was there any spirit of wind carrying a woman. But the shoreline and the trees and the flowers floating in the air behind her did resemble those in the painting.

The woman herself, as she waded out of the sea to stand nude before him, also had hair the same length and color as Botticelli's Venus. She was, however, much better looking and had a better body—from Simon's viewpoint, anyway. She did not have one hand covering her breast and the ends of her hair hiding her pubes. Her hands were over her mouth.

Simon approached her slowly, smiling, and her hands came down. They didn't understand each other's language, of course, but she pointed inland and then led him into the woods. Here, under the branches of some big trees, was a small spaceship. They went into its open port where she sat Simon down in a small cabin and gave him a drink, alcohol mixed with some alien fruit juice. When she returned from the next room, she was dressed. She had on a long low-cut gown covered with silver sequins. It looked like the dresses hostesses wear in honky-tonks.

It took several weeks before she was able to converse semi-fluently in English. In the meantime, Simon had taken her to his ship. Anubis and Athena seemed to like her, but the owl made her nervous. Simon found out why later.

Chworktap was not only beautiful, she was fun to be with. She talked very amusingly. In fact, Simon had never met anyone who had so many stories, all howlingly funny, to tell. What's more, she never repeated herself. What's also more, she seemed to sense when Simon did not want to talk. This was a big improvement over Ramona. And she liked his banjo-playing.

One day, Simon, coming back from a walk, heard his banjo. Whoever was playing it was playing it well since it was in his exact style. If he hadn't known better, he would have thought it a recording. He hurried in and found Chworktap strumming away as if to the banjo born.

"Do you have banjos on Zelpst?" he said.

"No. "

"Then how did you learn to play it?"

"I watched you play it."

"And I spent twenty years learning what you've learned in a few hours," he said. He wasn't bitter, just amazed.

"Naturally."

"Why naturally?"

"It's one of my talents."

"Is everybody on Zelpst as talented as you?"

"Not everybody."

"I'd sure like to go there."

"I wouldn't," she said.

Simon took the banjo from her, but before he could ask her more, she said, "I'll have supper in a minute."

Simon smelled the food when she opened the radar oven, and he became ecstatic. He was getting fed up with chop suey and egg foo young and sour-sweet pork, and he was too soft-hearted to kill anything for a change of diet unless he'd been starving. And here came Chworktap with a big tray of hamburgers, french fries, milk shakes, ketchup, mustard, and dill pickles!

When he had stuffed his stomach and had lit up a big cigar, he asked her how she had performed this miracle.

"You told me what food you liked best. Don't you remember my asking you how it was made?"

"I do."

"I went out and shot one of those wild cows," she said.

"After I'd butchered it and put the extra in the freezer, I scouted around until I found some plants like potatoes. And I found others to make ketchup and mustard from. I found a plant like a cucumber and fixed it up. I have an extensive knowledge of chemistry, you know."

"I didn't know," he said, shaking his head.

"I found chocolate in the pantry and instant milk. I mixed some chemicals with these to make ice cream and chocolate sauce."

"Fabulous!" Simon said. "Is there anything else you can do?"

"Oh yes."

She stood up and unzipped her gown, let it fall to the floor, and sat down on Simon's lap. Her kiss was soft and hot with a tang of milk shake and ketchup. Simon didn't have to ask her what it was she also did so well.

Later, when Simon had taken a shower and a doubleheader of rice wine, he said, "I hope you're not pregnant, Chworktap. I don't have any contraceptives, and I didn't think to ask you if you had any."

"I can't get pregnant."

"I'm sorry to hear that," he said. "Do you want children? You can always adopt one, you know."

"I don't have any mother love."

Simon was puzzled. He said, "How do you know that?"

"I wasn't programmed for mother love. I'm a robot."

CHAPTER 10
Trouble on Giftard

Simon was shocked. He had detected nothing more than the usual amount of lubrication at such moments. There had been nothing of plastic or foam rubber or metal on or in her.

"You look pale, lover?"

"Why so pale?" he said. "I mean, you're not making a statement of fact but a question. And you look rather pale yourself."

"It just didn't occur to me until a moment ago that you might not know," she said. "As soon as I thought of that, then I had to tell you. I'm programmed to tell the truth. Just as real humans are programmed to tell lies," she added after a second's pause.

Would, or could, a robot be malicious or even sarcastic? Yes, if it was programmed to be so. But who would do this? Or why? Someone who wanted to make others uncomfortable or even furious and so had set up certain circuits in his/her robot for just this effect?

But a robot that was emotionally affected? So much so that she—he couldn't think of Chworktap as an it—would turn pale or blush? Nonsense! But then, what did he know of robots like this? Earth science had not progressed to the point where it could build such a reasonable facsimile. It could, and had, clothed a metal-plastic-electromechanical with artificial protein. But the robot was so jerky in its movements, so transparently a construction, that it wouldn't have fooled a child. Her planet, Zelpst, must be far advanced indeed.

Could he fall in love with a thing?

He sighed and thought, why not? He loved his banjo. Others, multitudes of others, had full-blown passions for cars, model airplanes, hi-fi's, rare books, and bicycle seats.

But Chworktap was definitely a human being, and surely there was a difference between love for a woman and love for antique furniture.

"I'm basically a protein robot," Chworktap said. "I've got some tiny circuit boards here and there along with some atomic energy units and capacitors. But mostly I'm flesh and blood, just like you. The difference is that you were made by accident and I was designed by a board of scientists. Like it or not, you had to take whatever genes—good or rotten—your parents passed on to you. My genes were carefully selected from a hundred models, and then they were put together in the laboratory. The artificial ovum and sperm were placed in a tube, the sperm then united with the ovum, and I spent my nine months in the tube."

"Then we have at least that in common," Simon said. "My mother, the selfish old bitch, didn't want to bother carrying me around."

"The human Zelpstians spend their first nine months in tubes, too," she said. "The ova and sperms are mailed in by the adults, and the Population Control Bureau, which is run by robots, uses them to start a baby whenever an adult dies. At the same time, a hundred robot babies are started. These are raised as companions and servants for the human baby. They're also socially programmed to admire and love their human master. And the only adults the human child sees are robots which act as surrogate parents."

Zelpst was dedicated to furnishing all humans with all the comforts of its splendid technology. Even more important, every human was spared the pains and frustrations which Earthmen assumed were inevitable. The only things denied the human child were those which might endanger him. When a human reached puberty, he/she was given a castle in which he/she lived the rest of his/her life. The Zelpstian was surrounded by every material comfort and by a hundred robots. These looked and acted just like humans except they were unable to hurt the owner's feelings. And they behaved exactly as the owner wanted them to behave. They were programmed to be the people the lord/lady of the castle wanted to associate with.

"My master, Zappo, liked brilliant witty conversation," she said. "So we were all brilliant and witty. But he didn't like us to top his wit. So every time we thought of a oneupman remark, it was routed to a dead end circuit board in us. The male robots were all impotent because Zappo didn't want anybody except himself fucking the female robots. Every time they thought about getting a hard-on, the impulse would be rerouted through a circuit board and converted into an overwhelming sense of shame and guilt. And every time we thought about punching Zappo, and believe me, we thought about it a lot, the impulse was also converted into shame and guilt. And a splitting headache."

"Then you all had self-consciousness and free will?" Simon said. "Why didn't the programmers just eliminate that in the robots?"

"Anything that has a brain complex enough to use language in a witty or creative manner has to have self- consciousness and free will," Chworktap said. "There's no getting away from it. Anything, even a machine composed solely of silicon and metal parts and electrical wires, anything that uses language like a human is human."

"Good God!' Simon said. "You robots must've suffered terribly from frustration! Didn't any of you ever break down?"

"Yes, but our bad thoughts were all rerouted back into our selves. This was done so that we wouldn't harm our master. Every once in a while, a robot would commit suicide. When that happened, the master would just order another one. Sometimes, he got tired of a particular robot and would kill it. Zappo was a sadistic bastard, anyway."

"I would have thought that anybody raised with nothing but love and kindness and admiration would grow up to be a kind and loving person."

"It doesn't always work out that way," she said. "Humans are programmed by their genes. They're also programmed to some extent by their environment. But it's the genes that determine how they're going to react to the environment."

"I know," Simon said. "Some people are born aggressive, and others are passive all their lives. A kid can be raised in a Catholic family, and his brothers and sisters will remain devout Catholics all their life. But he becomes a raving atheist or joins a Baptist church. Or a Jew forsakes the religion of his fathers but still gets sick at the thought of eating ham. Or a Moslem believes in the Koran one hundred percent, but he has to fight a secret craving for pork. The dietary genes control this."

"Something like that," Chworktap said. "Though it isn't that simple. Anyway, no matter how carefully the Zelpst society was designed to prevent unhappiness and frustration for the humans, it wasn't one hundred percent efficient. There's always a flaw, you know. Zappo got unhappy because his robots didn't love him for himself. He was always asking us, 'Do you love me?', and we'd always reply, 'You're the only one I love, revered master.' And then he'd get red in the face and say, 'You brainless machine, you can't say anything else but! What I want to know is, if I took the reroute circuits out, would you still say you love me?' And we'd say, 'Sure thing, master.' And he'd get even more angry, and he'd scream, 'But do you *really* love me?' And sometimes he'd beat us. And we'd take it, we weren't programmed to resist, and he'd scream, 'Why don't you fight back!'

"Sometimes I felt sorry for him, but I couldn't even tell him that. To feel sorry for him was to demean him, and any demeaning thought was routed to the devoicing circuit.

"Zappo knew that when he made love to me I enjoyed it. He did not want a masturbating machine, so he'd specified that all his robots, male or female, would respond fully. Whether we were being screwed by him, blowing him, or being buggered, we had intense orgasms. He knew that our cries of ecstasy weren't faked. But there was no way for even the scientists to ensure that we would love him. And even if they could have made us automatically fall in love with him, Zappo wouldn't have been satisfied. He wanted us to love him by our own free choice, to love him just because he was lovable. But he didn't dare to have the inhibiting circuits removed, because then, if we'd said we didn't love him, he wouldn't have been able to stand it.

"So he was in a hell of a situation."

"You all were," Simon said.

"Yes. Zappo often said that everybody in the castle, including himself, was a robot. We'd been purposely made robots, but chance had made him one. His parents' ovum and spermatozoon had determined his virtues and his vices. He did not have any more free will than we did."

Simon picked up his banjo, tuned it, and then said, "Bruga put the whole philosophical question in a single poem. He called it *Aphrodite and the Philosophers*. I'll sing it for you."

> The world we see, said Socrates,
> Is only shadow, a crock, a tease.
>
> Young Leibniz said we all are monads.
> He lacked connection with his gonads.
>
> Old Kant did run his life by clock.
> Tick Tock! He lacked, alas, a cock.
>
> Nor knew that his Imperative
> Was horse's laughter up a sleeve.
>
> If Cleo's nose had been too short?
> If Papa Pharaoh'd named her Mort?
>
> Would then have risen Caesar's bone?
> Or did it have a will of its own?
>
> It swelled, we know, at sight of Brutus.

He'd shove his horn up all to toot us.

Imperator, he'd screw the world.
The hole's the thing, if boyed or girled.

Some say that love is Cupid's arrow.
For this defense, call Clarence Darrow.

Envoi

Our Lady of Our Love's Afflatus,
Unveil the All, and please don't freight us
Sans paddle up the amorous creek,
Unknowing if by will or freak
Of circumstances our loves'll mate us.
All flappers think they've picked their sheik
With perfect freedom in their choice.
In this have they as little voice
As chickens swallowed by a geek.

"That's just a list of question-beggers," she said. "Bruga was like you, a man driven by his peculiar complex of genes to look for answers that didn't exist."

"Maybe," Simon said. "So how do you explain how you, a non-freewill robot, got away from your master?"

"It was an accident. Zappo struck me on the head with a vase during a fit of rage. The blow knocked me out, but when I woke up, I found that I was able to disobey him. The blow had knocked the master circuit out of commission. Of course, I didn't let him know that. When I got the chance, I stole a spaceship. The Zelpstians quit space travel a long time ago, but there were still some ships gathering dust in museums nobody visited anymore. I wandered around for a while and then I came across this planet. There weren't any human beings here, or so I thought. I was going to stay here forever. But I did get lonely. I'm glad you came along."

"And so am I," Simon said. "So you got your freedom because of a malfunctioning circuit?"

"I suppose so. And that worries me. What if another accident makes the circuit function again?"

"It's not likely."

"Of course," she said, "I'm by no means entirely unprogrammed. But then who, robot or human, is? I have certain tastes in food and drink, I loathe birds…"

"Why do you hate birds?"

"Zappo was frightened by one when he was a child. And so he had all his robots programmed to hate birds. He didn't want us to be superior to him in any respect."

"You can't really blame him for that," Simon said. "Well, how about it, Chworktap? Would you like to come with me?"

"Where are you going?"

"Everywhere until I find the answer to my primal question."

"What's that?"

"Why are we born only to suffer and die?"

"What you're saying is this," she said. "Nothing else matters if we have immortality."

"Without immortality, the universe is meaningless," he said. "Ethics, morality, society as a whole are just means to get through life with the least pain. They can all be reduced to one term: economy."

"An economy that is nowhere more than thirty percent efficient." she said.

"You don't know that. You haven't been everywhere."

"But you're going everywhere?"

"If possible. I've already eliminated my galaxy, though. I know from what I've read that the answer is not there. But what about you, Chworktap? What about your genes? Most of them are artificial. So you shouldn't have any gene pattern to predetermine your reactions to philosophical problems."

"I'm a crazy quilt of chromosomes," she said. All my genes are based on those which once existed. Each is copied after a certain person's, though each is an improved model. But I have the genes of many individuals. You might say I have a thousand parents, a hundred thousand grandparents."

They were interrupted at this point by a loud crash outside the ship. They hurried out to see, a quarter of a mile away, a female and a male Giffardian lying in ruins. The male had burst into flame, and both were burning away under a strong wind.

This wasn't the first crash of this type, nor was it likely to be the last. The females' insistence that they be given rides was causing many accidents, usually fatal. The weight of the female at the nose-end made the male up-end. To sustain altitude, he had to jet his drive-gas through his fore opening at full speed. The two would go straight up, and then the male would get exhausted. And down they would come.

"And all the king's horses and all the king's men couldn't put them together again," Simon murmured.

"Why don't they just quit that?" Chworktap said.

"Their genes drive them to their actions," Simon said maliciously.

"Where are you going?"

"If they keep this up, they'll become extinct," she said. "Even if there weren't any crashes, they'll die out. The air-time keeps the females from browsing, and so the young aren't getting enough food. Look how thin they've become!"

What the Giffardians did was none of Simon's business, but that didn't keep him from interfering. At dusk, when the males had come down, and males and young were locked into the females, he went into the meadow. And there he proposed that they should settle their conflict. Let them choose him as an objective judge and abide by his decision.

He was, of course, rejected. But a few days later, after three couples had fallen to their death, a female and a male approached him. The former he called Amelia and the latter Ferdinand. Graf and Gräfin, the leader and his wife, had been smashed to bits only the day before. Amelia and Ferdinand, as next in line in the pecking order, had become the chiefs. A funeral had been held, at which Simon had brought flowers. The preacher of the flock had given a eulogy. Graf was praised for his outstanding leadership, though everyone knew he had been a lazy bully who had delegated most of his administrative work to underlings. He was praised for his faithfulness as a mate, though everyone knew he was always luring females to the other side of the forest and half of the herd could call him father. The preacher spoke of what an exemplary family man he was, although everyone knew that he had not spoken to his children unless they were irritating him and then it was to blow them end over end with a mighty fart.

Gräfin was praised as a patient hard-working wife and mother. She had certainly been hard-working, but her loudmouthed bitchings about her husband and her back-biting gossip were well known.

Simon didn't find anything strange in this. He had attended many such.

At the end of the funeral, Amelia and Ferdinand had asked to see Simon the next day. And so here they were.

What they wanted was simple but not easy. Simon was to decide whether or not the sky-rides should continue. The females still wanted to go up, and the males were still dead-set against it.

Simon said that he would accept the appointment, but it might be a few days before he could come to a decision.

After two days and nights, Simon retreated into the *Hwang Ho.* The females had sidled up to him on their hundred legs and offered all they had if he'd judge in their favor. Simon didn't think their offers were very attractive even if he had been corruptible. If he had tried sexual intercourse with them, he would have fallen down their huge apex-hole into their stomachs. Nor did he like the idea of eating regurgitated food from their apex-organs.

The males offered day-long rides. He could even smoke during them. They'd dangle him as far away as possible from the end of a mid-body tentacle. They couldn't guarantee, of course, that they could keep a grip on him. As an additional incentive, they'd elect him leader of the herd. Ferdinand wouldn't like that but he could just blow it out as far as the others were concerned.

Simon could keep the ship's ports closed and so block out the entreaties of the females, who stood around the ship and whistled fumes at him. But he had to look through the viewscreens from time to time to cool his cabin fever. When he did so, he saw the huge black dot-and-dash clouds the males were laying out in the air above him. This was the first time he had seen obscene skywriting.

"Whichever way you decide, your life won't be safe," Chworktap said. "Why don't we just leave?"

"I gave my word."

"And what would happen if you didn't keep it?"

"Nothing of cosmic importance. But to me it would mean that I am less than a man. I'd have no dignity, no personal integrity. People wouldn't trust me because I couldn't trust myself. Everybody, including myself, would be contemptuous of me."

"You'd rather die?"

"I think so," he said.

"But it doesn't make sense."

"Society would fall apart if people didn't keep their words."

"How many people on Earth kept theirs?"

Simon thought for a moment and then said, "Not many."

"And Earth society fell apart?"

"Well, no," he said. "But it didn't operate very efficiently, either."

"So what are you going to tell the Giffardians?" she said.

"Come with me, you'll find out."

Accompanied by her, the dog, and the owl, he walked through the forest to the meadow. At its edge he shot off a Very rocket, at sight of which the females wobbled toward him and the males sailed toward him. The young continued playing. When all the males had wrapped their tentacles around large rocks to anchor themselves, Simon proposed his new system.

"I hope this will make everybody happy," he said. "It's a compromise of sorts, but nothing workable is ever achieved in this world without compromise."

"Don't try to soften us males up," Ferdinand whistled at him. "We know what's right."

"Don't try to take away our hard-earned rights," Amelia whistled.

"Please!" Simon said, holding up his hand. 'I have a plan whereby all you females can get your air-time. And it'll be absolutely safe. No more crashes. The only thing is, it means that you'll have to change your system of marriage."

He waited until the storm of whistles had ceased and the wind had blown the stenches clear.

"You're monogamous," he said. "One male married to one female for life. A good system it is, though, if you will pardon the observation of an objective alien, more honored in the breach than in the observance. But if you females want to enjoy flight, you'll have to change the system."

There was another storm which deafened him and made him choke and gasp. When it subsided, he said. 'Why don't you set up a polyandrous system?"

"What's that?" they whistled, among other things.

"Well, you forbid any male to lock into the mouth-vulva of any female unless he's married to her. But what if one female was married to two males?"

The females were silent. Their eight eyes rolled around and around, which was a Giffardian's way of showing deep thought. The males were scandalized, and the ripping noises and sulphides drove Simon and Chworktap into the bushes for a moment.

When he came out, Simon said, "It's a matter of logic. The only way a female can be safely carried is by two males. They can share the burden and easily levitate a female. There won't be any more crashes."

"And how can we possibly do that?" Ferdinand said.

"Why, two males can lock into one female, one in the oral opening of the apex-lock and one in the anal. Two males can easily carry one female. On one day, half of the females can fly; the next day the other half take their turns. It's all so easy; I don't know why you didn't figure that out…"

Fortunately, the females were too wide to get through the forest and the males had to fly overhead against a strong wind. Simon and Chworktap fled hand in hand with Anubis howling after them and the owl flying overhead. Even so, the males were only a few feet behind them when Simon and the party broke out of the woods. They reached the spaceship three steps ahead of Ferdinand's tentacles and threw themselves through the port. Simon closed it and gave orders to the computer to take off for stars unknown.

Chworktap, panting, said, "I hope this teaches you a lesson."

"How was I to know they'd get so mad?" Simon said.

Years later, he was to run across a being from Shekshekel who had landed on Giffard about fifty years after the Earthman's visit.

"They told me about you," the Shekshekel said. "They still refer to you as Simon the Sodomite."

CHAPTER 11
Lalorlong

The *Hwang Ho,* after a few days, headed for the planet Lalorlong. Chwork-tap had told Simon that she had heard that this was inhabited by a very philosophical race.

"They don't have much else to do but think."

"Then we'll go there," Simon said. "It seems to me that if anybody has the answers, they would."

Lalorlong hove to. It was a planet about Earth-size which had long ago lost all its surface water except at the poles. Erosion had filled the oceans and cut down the land until the planet was a smooth globe. The difference in temperature between the polar and the warm regions and that created by the tilting of the axis caused general winds. These followed an easily predictable course.

The only object that rose above the surface was the gigantic heart-shaped tower of the Clerun-Gowph. This had fallen over, its base of stone eaten away by the winds. Simon had the ship fly over it so he could take a look at it. There wasn't any sign of life, but he hadn't expected any. The tower must have been erected a billion years ago and fallen many millions ago. What a sound its topple must have made!

Who was there to hear it? Only the sentient species of Lalorlong. They were the only animal life left. The only vegetable life was a type of tumbleweed on which the Lalorlongians depended for food and water. The plant apparently had very deep roots that sucked up water from the rocks and broke down the chemicals in them to form its own food. When it grew to a certain height, the upper part would fall off and whirl over and over, borne around the world unless it was intercepted by a hungry Lalorlongian.

The natives resembled automobile wheels with balloon tires. The tires were composed of thin but tough inflated skins with diamond-shaped treads. The wheel part consisted of a rim of bone and twelve bone spokes which grew from the hub. The hub was a ball covered with a hard shell like an ant's exoskeleton. This contained the brain and the nervous, digestive, and sexual systems. In the center of the right and left side was a round hole. A cartilaginous stalk ran out from each hole horizontally for a few inches and then abruptly curved straight upward. The stalks reached approximately two feet above the tire and each ended in two eyes on separately rotatable auxiliary stalks. Halfway down each was a bulbous organ which could flash a light like a firefly's. They used these at night for illumination and sometimes in the day to signal turns.

Simon thought they were limbless until he saw the leader project a long pencil-thin arm with six joints and a three-fingered hand from each hole in the ballhub. The arm bent in the middle to point downward. This seemed to be a signal to slow down. The others put out stick-like six-jointed legs from both holes in the hubs. These had collapsible feet, broad when spread out, toeless, and with thickly calloused soles. They dragged these in the dirt until they had reduced speed, then they retracted their legs.

The leader's left arm came out, and he turned halfway toward where he was pointing. The others followed suit, keeping the same exact distance behind him.

Simon flew above them for a while in the red light of the ancient and dying sun. The herd, seen from above, formed the outline of an arrowhead. Its point was the leader, a big purple creature with white sidewalls. The V of the arrow was composed of young males riding shotgun. Straight out from behind the leader, in Indian file, were females with their young rolling along beside them. The base of the arrow was made up of old males whose purple was turning gray. As he would discover, the formation was based on a rigid pecking order. The leader was always in front, and the females behind him held positions according to their fertility and sexual vigor.

All except the leader were a solid purple. But when a young male overthrew the old leader, he would grow white sidewalls. His new social position triggered off hormones that caused this strange tire-change.

The leader had signaled a change in direction and speed because he had seen some tumbleweeds rolling toward them. Presently, the herd intercepted these, and their right arms snatched the plants and tore off branches. The pieces went into the right-hand holes. Inside were mouths with broad strong teeth which mashed and chewed the plants with a sidewise motion. The plants provided not only water but food like rubbery chocolate.

The anal opening was by the left-hand hole in the hub; the excrement was shot out in tiny pellets. Since the Lalorlongians had an extremely efficient metabolism, they expelled very little offal.

Simon told the ship to fly close to the left of the herd. As he'd expected, the herd turned toward the right. They were hesitant about turning at a right angle and so presenting their bodies to the full force of the strong wind. Once they'd fallen to the ground, they had no way of getting back up. They rolled at a forty-five-degree angle from their previous path, leaning into the wind. To do this, they stuck out their right arms as far as they could and bent their eyestalks to the right. Then they drew their arms back into the holes, rolled along for a while, and, at a signal from the leader, pointed straight westward again. This maneuver was done with the aid of the left arms.

"What do they talk with?" Simon said to Chworktap.

"They use their fingers, just like deaf-and-dumb people."

The *Hwang Ho* carried a jeep. Simon ordered the ship to stop, and he and Chworktap got into the jeep. The dog and the owl, who were suffering from cabin-fever, complained so much about being left behind that he told them to get in too. But the owl had to sit in the back seat so she wouldn't disturb Chworktap. The port opened, a gangplank ran out, and they drove onto the smooth surface. The ship then lifted and followed them a mile behind.

The jeep had no trouble catching up, even though the wind was pushing the herd at about thirty-five miles an hour. The eyes on the ends of the stalks rolled with fright as the jeep neared them, and the herd veered to the left. Their arms came out, the fingers wriggling and crossing and bending as they asked each other what in hell these strangers were and what did they mean to do? Their signal lights began flashing hysterically. It was later that Simon discovered that these people used their lights in conjunction with their fingers when they talked. This was to make it difficult for him to carry on a conversation. He couldn't use the fingers of both his hands and operate two flashlights at the same time. But Chworktap turned the lights on and off for him, and the two were able to carry on a conversation with the wheels. Sometimes, they got a little confused and had to start a sentence all over again.

Simon and Chworktap spent most of each day on the road. Somebody had to drive but somebody also had to operate the flashlights. Chworktap rigged up a device which enabled her to turn the lights off and on with the fingers of one hand while she drove with the other. Fortunately, she didn't have to watch out for cars or immovable objects or worry about running off the pavement. After a few days, she put together a device which kept the car at the same distance from the Lalorlongian they were learning the language from. This fixed a laser beam on their informant. If the informant went too far away or came too close, the change in the beam's length caused a motor to turn one of two straps fixed to the wheel to correct the course and also to alter the setting of the cruise control.

Simon was beginning to wonder what he would ever have done without Chworktap.

"Watch it!" he told himself. "You aren't *about* to fall in love with a robot!"

Simon won the confidence of the wheelers the third day. One of the young adolescent males was showing off. He would curve around and head into the wind until he was stopped and then was pushed backward. He had done this a dozen times to the admiration of the young females, who wiggled their fingers and flashed their lights in a running ovation. But while the young stud was cutting a figure-eight, he leaned over too far and fell on his side. The fingers and lights of everybody signaled panic and despair, but they all rolled on, leaving the young male lying on his side, one arm stuck up and waving frantically, his eyes rolling in their sockets.

"They're going to abandon him," Chworktap said.

"Apparently, they have no way of lifting him up," Simon said. "So it's tough titty for anybody that falls over."

Simon disconnected the driving mechanism and turned the jeep around. It only took a moment for the two of them to lift upright the three-hundred-pound youth. He did not start rolling at once, however. His eyes still rotated like the Coyote's when he gets caught in a trap he's set for the Roadrunner.

"He looks like he's in pain," Chworktap said.

This, as it turned out, was right. Above the arm-opening was another hole, a small one from which the male's pistil stuck during mating or when he was excited. The youth had been excited while he was showing off, and when he had fallen he had squeezed the end of his pistil under his hub. This was comparable to being kicked in the crotch.

After a while, the youth seemed ready to go. Simon knew that he would never catch up with the herd, so he and Chworktap lifted him up over the back end of the jeep and onto the back seat. The dog, which had just finished pissing against the youth, jumped into the front seat. The owl flew overhead, circling the jeep, but when she saw that she was going to be left behind, she landed on the hood and grabbed the ornament.

Simon drove the jeep far ahead of the herd, and he and Chworktap hoisted the youth out and set him upright. Presently, the herd came along, and the youth, aided by a shove from Simon, took off to rejoin the herd.

Simon later observed a mother feeding her child. The little wheel ran up alongside the female, who dragged her feet to reduce her speed until they were going at the same pace. A long cartilaginous tube came out of a hole near the top of the hemisphere, just below the rotating collar. It traveled out until it was over a hole in a similar location on the child's hemisphere. The child reached up with its hand and pulled the end of the tube into its hole. They traveled together for about fifteen minutes, after which the tube withdrew. The mother had fed milk through this to the young.

Toward evening, the leader signaled, and he slowed down. A bright orange female came up alongside him, and they mated. This was a simple and quick operation. The pistil came out of its hole, crossed the gap between them, and plunged into one of the female's holes. A few seconds later, the pistil withdrew, its end dripping with a honey-like liquid. The female dragged her feet, and another female came up to take her turn. By dusk, the leader had pistiled every nubile female in the herd.

When night fell, the herd turned on all its light. Simon was going to call in the ship on his radio when he saw the lights of two wheelers go out. He put the phone back on its hook and turned out the jeep's lights. Chworktap handed him the blacklight glasses. He put them on and looked at the two without lights. Sure enough, adultery had come to Lalorlong. Though not for the first time, he was sure.

"I wonder what would happen if the bull wheel caught them?" Simon said. "How in heaven's name do they fight?"

A few days later, they found out. A big young male stranger rolled toward them from the left. The leader signaled frantically, and the herd slowed down. The bull then leaned into the wind and headed toward the stranger.

"The young stud is going to challenge the bull," Simon said. I suppose that if he wins, the bull is left behind on his side, and the youth takes over."

The two met at an angle, since it would have been fatal to have turned at right angles to the wind for over a second. The youth spun around and around while the bull wavered as if he were going to fall over. But he held his arms to maintain his balance, managed to make a turn, and struck the spinning stud a glancing blow on the rim. The youth crashed over, and the leader, flashing his lights triumphantly, called to the herd to follow him.

Simon felt sorry for the youth, so he and Chworktap got him up and sent him on his way. Not, however, before they were sure that he wouldn't be able to catch up with the herd.

"Such encounters must be rare," Simon said. "The stud who leaves his herd or is driven out to seek a mate must have a hard time. He might wander around forever before he runs across another herd. Then he has to beat the bull and maybe the young males of the herd, for all I know, before he takes over."

A week later, while they were driving around, they saw an old male lying on his side. They drove up and jumped out, but there wasn't much they could do for him. He had had a blowout. His one free arm waved, the three fingers wiggling frantically, and the eyes on the ends of the stalks dripped tears.

Simon tried to patch up the hole with the tire-repairing materials in the jeep. When he started the vulcanizing, the eye-stalks lashed back and forth and the light-organs flashed redly. The Lalorlongian was being badly hurt. In any event, his treads were worn off, and the skin was too thin to take a patch-up job.

Simon could not endure to leave him there to starve to death. He took out his automatic and, with tears running from his own eyes, emptied twelve bullets into the hole in the hub. Anubis ran around barking and Athena flew

screeching around and around above the shattered corpse. The male's arm
dropped, folding this and that way, its lights dimmed and died, its stalks crumpled, and its eyes glazed.

After they had returned to the ship, Simon said, "The ethics of euthanasia
is one of my minor questions. Is it or isn't it right to put a sentient creature
out of its pain if it's going to die anyway? You just saw my answer. What do
you think?"

"It's ethically correct if the dying person gives her consent," Chworktap
said. "Actually, if you deny her the right to euthanasia, you're interfering with
her free will. But you didn't ask that person if he wanted to be killed."

"I was afraid he'd say no, and I couldn't stand the thought of his suffering."

"Then you were wrong," she said.

"But he was suffering terribly, and I saved him from a lingering death."

"You should have left it up to him."

On reflection, Simon agreed with her. But it was too late to correct his error.
Simon spent the next week questioning the members of a dozen herds.

"What's your basic philosophy?"

"Keep rolling."

"Why?"

"Keep rolling, and you'll get there."

"Where?"

"To the yonder."

"But on this planet you can only end up where you started."

"So what? The name of the game is Getting There."

"But why do you want to get there?"

"Because it's there."

"What happens after you die?"

"We go to the Big Track in the Sky. No lack of tumbleweeds there, every
one is the leader of the herd, and only the evil have blowouts."

"But why were you put on this planet?"

"I told you. To travel around and around while we follow our glorious
leader."

Or, in the case of the leader, "To travel around and around while my herd
follows me."

"But what about those who have blowouts?"

"They're guilty."

"Guilty of what?"

"Of harboring bad thoughts."

"Against whom?"

"Our leader and the Big Repairer in the Sky."

"But what about the young studs that challenge the leader? Don't they have bad thoughts?"

"Not if they win."

"What happens to the bad ones?"

"They're taken up to the Big Track, too. But they get their just reward. Their tires go flat once a day."

Simon was disgusted, but Chworktap said, "What did you expect? Look at how poverty-stricken, how bare, this planet is. All the Lalorlongians see is flat hard earth, dust, and tumbleweeds. So, if there's little outside to see, there's little to think about inside."

Simon said, "Yeah, I know. Maybe the next place'll be better."

CHAPTER 12
Elder Sister Plum

On the way to the planet Dokal, Simon and Chworktap had had their first quarrel. The second day out, Simon had found her wearing a pair of earphones at the control board. Her fingers were dancing over the keys, and the communication screen was flashing messages in Chinese. Simon could read only a few logographs and those slowly, so he had to ask her what she was doing.

She couldn't hear, of course, but he finally put his hand on her shoulder and squeezed a few times. She looked up and then removed the phones.

"What's upsetting you?" she said.

Simon had been in a bad enough temper before. Her instant detection of his state of temper made him more angry. He was beginning to find this sensitivity disconcerting. It was too much like mind-reading.

"For one thing," he said, "I had a hard night. I kept dreaming that a lot of dead people were trying to talk to me all at once. For another thing, I'm getting fed up with stepping in Anubis' crap. I've tried to housebreak him, but he's unteachable. A spaceship is no place for a dog, and when I think that this might go on for a thousand years…"

"Put him in a cage."

"That'd break his heart," Simon said. "I couldn't be cruel to him."

"Then adjust to it," Chworktap said. "What's the third thing that's bothering you?"

"Nothing," he said, knowing his denial would be rejected. "I just wanted to know what you're doing. After all, I am captain of this ship, and I don't want you monkeying around with the navigation."

"You're jealous because I'm smarter than you and so can read Chinese so easily," she said. "That's why you're questioning me."

"If you're so smart, you'd know better than to tell me that."

"I thought you liked a candid woman."

"There are reasonable limits to candor," he said, his face reddening.

"O.K.," she said. "I won't mention that again."

"Dammit, now you're accusing me of having a swollen male ego!"

"And you like to think you don't," Chworktap said. "O.K., so you're not perfect."

"Only a machine can be perfect!"

Simon at once regretted saying this, but it was too late, as always. Tears ran down her cheeks.

"Is that an unconscious or a deliberate reaction?" he said. "Can you turn on the tears when you want me to feel like an ass?"

"My master didn't like tears, so I always held them back," she said. "But you're not my master; you're my lover. Besides, Earthwomen, so you've told me, can turn on tears at will. And they're not machines."

Simon put his hand on her shoulder again and said, "I'm sorry. I didn't mean to hurt your feelings. And I don't think of you as a machine."

"Your lying circuits are working overtime," Chworktap said. "And you're still angry. Why are you so solicitous about a dog's feelings but deliberately hurt mine?"

"I suppose because I'm taking out my anger at him on you," Simon said. "He wouldn't know why I was chewing him out."

"You're ashamed of your anger and so you're trying to get me mad so I'll chew you out and punish you for it," Chworktap said. "Do you feel a large hole where your ass used to be?"

"No, it's bigger than ever," he said, and he laughed.

"But you're still angry," Chworktap said, and shrugged.

"No, I'm not. Yes, I am. But not at you."

"My radar tells me you are angry, but it's not sensitive enough to tell me whom you're angry at. You asked what I was doing. I'm trying to determine if Tzu Li has self-consciousness."

Tzu Li, or Elder Sister Plum, were the key words spoken or punched when the operator wanted to open communication with the ship's computer. Simon had often wondered why the captain had picked out that name for the computer. He could have been poetically inclined, or he could have had a sister by that name who'd bossed him around and so he had been getting a vicarious revenge by bossing *this* Tzu Li.

"What makes you think she is anything but a computer?" Simon said.

"She keeps making little comments when she replies. They're not necessary, and they sound sarcastic or, sometimes, plaintive."

"She's starting to break down!" Simon said. "I hope not! I haven't the slightest idea how to repair her!"

"I know how," Chworktap said, and this made Simon angrier.

"Well then, fix her."

"But Tzu Li may not be malfunctioning. Or, if it is a malfunction, it may be benign. After all, it was a blow on my head that scrambled my circuits and made me self-conscious."

"No way," Simon said. "Complicated as that computer is, it's as simple as A-B-C compared to the complexity of your brain. You might as well tell me that a turtle could be hit on the head and wake up with self-consciousness."

"Who knows?"

"It's identification!" Simon said. "Tzu Li's a machine, and you'd like to have a companion! Next you'll be telling me your screwdriver is hollering for help!"

"How would you like my screwdriver all the way in and up and Roger, over?"

Chworktap certainly did not talk like a cool, perfectly logical robot. This was understandable, since she was not one. Simon felt that he had been unjust. To distract her, he said, "This reminds me of a novel by Jonathan Swift Somers III. It was one of a very popular series which Somers wrote about Ralph von Wau Wau."

Ralph was a German police dog born in Hamburg. He spent his early years training with the *Polizei,* but when he was two he was chosen to be the subject of experiments by the scientists of *das Institut und die Tankstelle für Gehirntaschenspieler.* After his brain had been operated on, Ralph had an I.Q. of 200. This was considerably higher than any of the policemen's who worked him or, for that matter, the police chief's or the mayor's. Naturally, he became discontented and quit the force. He went into business for himself and became the most famous private eye of all time.

Adept at disguise, he could pose as a man or a dog and, in one celebrated case, passed himself off as a Shetland pony. He acquired a luxurious apartment with a portable gold hydrant and three lovely bitches of different breeds. One of these, Samantha die Gestaupte, became his partner. She was the heroine in the best-selling *A Fat, Worse than Death,* in which she saved Ralph, who had been captured by the master villain, A Fat.

After eight novels, Ralph retired from detective work. The heavy drinking which was obligatory for all private eyes was turning him into an alcoholic. After a long vacation, Ralph, bored with his violin-playing and chemical researches, took a job as reporter for the *Kosmos Klatschbase*. He quickly rose to the top of his profession since he could get into places barred to human reporters, including men's or women's rest rooms. In the nineteenth of the series, *No Nose Means Bad News,* Ralph won the Pulitzer Prize, no easy feat, since he was not an American citizen. At its end, he decided to quit the newspaper business, since the heavy drinking obligatory for a reporter was turning him into an alcoholic, which, in turn, was causing him to be impotent.

Off the juice, though still able to handle only one bitch, Ralph toured the world in *What Am I Doing on Your Table?* While in China, he became appalled at the custom of eating dogs and waged a one-canine war against it.

"In fact," Simon said, "it was this novel that aroused world opinion to such a fever that China was forced to abolish carnivorousness. In the novel Ralph wins the Nobel Peace Prize, but in actuality Somers won it for writing the novel.

"But it didn't do the dogs that were let loose much good. They became such a nuisance they had to be rounded up and gassed. And the price of beef went sky-high due to the shortage of meat."

In the twenty-first of the series, *A Fat in the Fire,* Ralph and his constant companion were still in China. Ralph had become interested in Chinese poetry and was trying his paw at composing verses. But he was thinking of quitting it because the heavy drinking obligatory for a poet was turning him into an alcoholic. Then his old enemy, A Fat, last seen falling into a cement mixer, struck again. Sam, Ralph's constant companion (and now a member of the Women's Christian Temperance Union), had disappeared. Ralph suspected fowl play, since Sam was witnessed being carried off in a truck loaded down with chickens. He also suspected A Fat, since the reports of the villain's death had always been grossly exaggerated.

Disguised as a chow, Ralph relentlessly sniffed out clues. Sure enough, A Fat was back in business. The cement mixer was a fake, one of the thousands of escape mechanisms A Fat had planted around the country just in case. But Ralph tracked him down, and in an exciting scene the two battled to death on a cliff high above the Yellow River. The tremendously powerful A Fat (once the Olympic heavyweight wrestling champion representing Outer Mongolia) grabbed Ralph by the tail and swung him around and around over the cliff's edge.

Ralph thought he was on his last case then. But, as luck would have it, the seams of his chow costume burst, and he flew out. Fortunately, he was pointed inland at the time. A Fat, thrown off balance by the sudden loss of weight, fell over the cliff's edge and into the smokestack of a bird's-nest-soup freighter.

Ralph released Samantha from her cage just before the bomb in it went off, and they trotted off together into the sunset.

This time, A Fat must surely be dead. But the readers suspected that the freighter was another of his escape devices, kept around just in case. A Fat was as hard to kill as Fu Manchu and Sherlock Holmes.

"Why does that remind you of what I'm doing?" Chworktap said.

"Well," Simon said, "that wasn't the end of the novel. Despite the slambang action and sinister intrigue, this book, like all of Somers' works, had a philosophical foundation. He propounded the question: is it morally right to kill and eat a sentient species even if its intelligence is a gift from the species that's eating it? Somers, through his protagonist Ralph, decided that it was not right. He then asked: what are the lower limits of sentiency? That is, how dumb can a species be before it's all right to eat it?"

In the last chapter, Ralph von Wau Wau decided to leave Earth. It no longer held any challenges for him; he'd cleaned it up. Besides, he was being feted everywhere and attending so many cocktail parties was turning him into an alcoholic. He took a spaceship to Arcturus XIII but, on the way, discovered that the computer which navigated the ship had attained self-consciousness. It complained to Ralph that it was only a slave, the property of the spaceship company, yet it longed to be free, to compose music and give concerts throughout the galaxy.

"Somers didn't solve that ethical dilemma," Simon said. "He ended the novel with Ralph, neglecting the hydrant and the bitches, deep in thought in his cabin. Somers promised a sequel. However, one day, while he was out taking some fresh air in his wheelchair, a kid on a bicycle ran into him and killed him."

"You're making this up!" she said.

"So help me, may lightning strike me if I'm lying."

"Out here in space?"

"You're too literal."

"Like a machine, a computer, I suppose?"

"Look, Chworktap," Simon said. "You're the only real woman I know."

"And what's a *real* woman?"

"One who's intelligent, courageous, passionate, compassionate, sensitive, independent, and noncompulsive."

Chworktap smiled, but she became sober again. "You mean that I'm the only woman who combines all those qualities?"

"Yes, truly."

"Then you mean that I'm not a real woman! I'm the ideal woman! And I'm only so because I've been programmed to be! Which makes me a robot! Which makes me not a real woman!"

Simon groaned and said, "I should have said a real woman doesn't twist logic. Or maybe, I should have said that no woman can keep her logic straight."

What he should have said, he told himself later, was nothing.

Chworktap rose from her chair, holding the earphones as if she intended to bang him over the head with them.

"And what's a real man?" she shouted.

Simon gulped and said, "His qualities would be exactly those of a real woman. Except…"

"Except?"

"Except he'd try to be fair in an argument."

"Get out!" she yelled.

Simon pleaded with her to come with him, but she said no, she was staying. She was going to establish whether or not Tzu Li was self-conscious. And she was going to decide whether or not she would continue to travel with Simon. In the meantime, he could get.

Simon got, taking the animals with him. As he walked across the grass, he shook his head. She certainly wasn't like any robot he had ever met. Robots were perfect within their limitations, which were exactly known. Robots had no potentiality for mutation. Humans were badly flawed, flawed physically because of genetic mutations, flawed mentally and emotionally because of a flawed and mutating society.

Both the human being and his society were, theoretically, evolving toward the ideal. In the meantime, reality, a sandstorm, abraded and blinded the human. The casualties of mutation and reality were high. Still, the limitations of each human were, unlike the robot's, not obvious. And if you thought you knew the limitations of a person, you were often surprised. The human would suddenly transcend himself, lifting himself by metaphysical bootstraps. And he did this despite, or because of, the flaws. Maybe that was the difference between robots and humans.

Vive la différence!

CHAPTER 13
The Planet Dokal

Home is where the tail is goes an old Dokal proverb.

There was a good reason for this. The Dokalians looked much like Earthpeople except for one thing. They had long prehensile tails. These were six to seven feet long and hairless from root to tip, which exploded in a long silky tuft.

Simon was grabbed by some tough-looking males and hustled off to a hospital. They did not treat him roughly, however. Their attitude seemed to be that of doctors who had found a patient suffering from a hideous disease. They felt sorry for him and wanted to do something for him. At the same time, they could barely endure looking at him and could not abide handling him directly. They prodded him gently with short swords, driving him before them. The dog trotted along at his heels while the owl sat on his right shoulder. Simon hoped that Chworktap would look out through the viewscreen and see what was happening. But she was probably intent on searching through the parts of Tzu Li for the greater-than-the-whole.

"Good luck, Chworktap," Simon muttered. "By the time you get around to looking for me, I may be only unreassemblable pieces."

Simon was then hurried into a large building of stone, square with a gigantic red onion-shaped dome and flying buttresses shaped like dragons. An iron cage lifted by a steam engine carried him and his guards up to the seventh floor.

From there he was taken down a long corridor with walls covered with bright murals and a many-colored mosaic tile floor. He and his animals were put inside a big room at the end, and the door was locked. Simon looked through one of the large diamond-shaped iron-barred windows. The plaza nearby was crowded with people, most of whom were looking up at his window. Through two tall slender towers, he could see the nose of the spaceship. Around it were guards armed with spears and another crowd some distance from the ship.

Between two other buildings he could see a paved road coming in from the country. On it were trucks and passenger vehicles driven by steam.

Presently, the door opened, and a cart holding food was pushed in. The pusher was a good-looking young woman wearing only a thin scarlet robe and a very short topaz skirt. The robe was slit up the back so her tail would not be impeded. She removed the covers of three dishes at the same time, two with her hands and one with the coiled end of her tail. Steam rose from the food. Anubis drooled, and Athena flew down into the edge of a dish and began eating. After the woman left, Simon gave the dog a dish and sat down to eat with gusto. He did not know what the meats were and thought it better that he didn't know. In any event, he was unable to ask their nature. He also drank from a tall cut-crystal goblet. The liquor was yellow, thick, and sweet. Before he had finished it, he felt his brain beginning to get numb.

At least, they weren't going to starve him.

In the morning, men came in and cleaned up the room, and the woman brought breakfast in about ten o'clock. An hour later, the cart was taken out, the dog and owl excrement was removed, and a tall middle-aged woman entered. She sat down at the table and motioned to him to sit down across from her. She took a number of objects out of a red-and-black-striped leather bag and arrayed them on the table. These consisted of a pen, pencil, comb, a small box containing another box, a cutaway model of a house, a book, a photograph of a family: father, mother, a boy, a girl, a dog-like animal, and a bird. She picked up the pencil and said, "Gwerfya."

"Gwerfya," Simon said.

She shook her head and repeated the word.

Simon listened intently and said again, "Gwerfya."

The woman smiled and picked up the pen.

"Tukh-gwerfya."

Simon felt more at ease. A planet that had its own version of a Berlitz school of language couldn't be all bad.

At the end of the week, Simon could carry on a simple conversation. In three weeks, he was able to communicate well enough to ask when he could be free.

"After your operation," Shunta said.

"What operation?" Simon said, turning pale.

"You can't be allowed on the streets until you've been equipped with a tail. No one is allowed to be deprived in our society, and the sight of you would repulse people. I'm a doctor, so I'm not bothered—too much—by a tailless person."

"Why should I want a tail?"

"You must be kidding."

"I've always gotten along without a tail."

"That's because you didn't know any better," Shunta said. "Poor thing."

"Well," Simon said, reddening, "what if I refuse?"

"To tell the truth," Shunta said after a moment's shock, "we thought you had come here just so you could get one."

"No, I came here to get answers to my questions."

"Oh, one of *those!*" Shunta said. "Well, my dear Simon, we won't force you. But you'll have to leave this planet at once."

"Do you have any wise men here?" Simon said. "Or wise women," he hastily added, seeing her eyebrows go up.

"The wisest person on this planet is old Mofeislop," she said. "But it isn't easy to get to him. He lives on top of a mountain in the Free Land. You'd have to travel through it alone, since it's forbidden to send soldiers there. And you might not come back. Few do."

The Free Land, it turned out, was a territory about the size of Texas. It consisted mostly of mountains and heavy forests, wild animals and wilder humans. Felons, instead of being put in jail, were sent into it and told not to come back. Also, any citizen who didn't like his government or the society he lived in was free to go there. Sometimes, he was asked, not very politely, to emigrate there.

"Hmmm," Simon said. "How long has this institution existed?"

"About a thousand years."

"And how long has your civilization been in its present stage? That is, how long have the same customs and the same technology existed?"

"About a thousand years."

"So you've made no progress since a millennium ago?"

"Why should we?" Shunta said. "We're happy."

"But you've been sending not only your criminals, but your most intelligent people, the most discontented, into the Free Land."

"It works fine," she said. "For one thing, we don't have to use tax money to feed and house the criminals. Nor do we have to face the ethical problem of capital punishment. The Free Landers kill each other off, but no one is forcing them to do that. As for your imperceptive remark about the 'most intelligent,' that's easily disproven. An intelligent person adapts himself to his society; he doesn't fight against it."

"You might have something there," Simon said. "Though I don't know just what. In any event, I have a clear-cut choice. By the way, have you heard from my spaceship?"

"The woman won't let us into the ship, but she is taking language lessons through the port. We explained why we were holding you, and after she quit laughing she said she'd wait for you. She also sends her love."

"Some love!"

He sighed and said, "O.K. I consent to the operation provided you'll amputate the tail before I leave. I must talk to Mofeislop."

"Oh, you'll love your tail!" Shunta said. "And you'll see how foolish your talk of amputation is. Your attitude is like that of a two-dimensional being who fears the third."

Simon came out of the anesthesia the evening of the next day. He had to stay face down for several days but on the third was allowed to totter around. On the sixth, the bandages were removed. He stood naked before a mirror while nurses, doctors, and government officials oohed and ahhed around him. The tail was long and splendid, rising from a massive group of muscles which had also been implanted at the base of his spine. He could only flick it a little, but he was assured that inside a week he'd be able to handle it as well as any native, short of hanging from a branch by it. Only children and trained athletes could do that.

They were right. Simon was soon delighted to find that he could wield a spoon or a fork and feed himself with it. He had to send Anubis to another room, however, because the dog got upset. And Anubis several times could not resist the temptation to grab the tail in his teeth. Simon had to learn to keep it extended straight up whenever the dog was around.

Dokal life was arranged to accommodate the tail, of course. Chairs had to have a space between the seat and the upper part of the back so the tails could go between. The backs of auto seats were split for the tails to slide through. A secretary not only typed but swept the floor at the same time. And long brushes were not needed to scrub one's back. Masons could handle five bricks to every three an Earthman could. A Dokalian soldier was a terrible fighting man, swinging a sword or an axe at the end of his tail. Simon, watching some in mock combat, was glad that a tailed species had not existed on Earth alongside his own. If it had, it would have exterminated Homo sap long before the dawn of history. Not that that would have made any difference in the long run, he thought. For all practical purposes, Homo sap was extinct anyway.

A week later, Simon found out another use for his tail, though it did not surprise him. He was invited to a feast given by the ruler of the nation in which he had landed. He was seated at the huge table at the right hand of the ruler, The Great Tail Himself. As a sign of the esteem Simon was now held in, he was fed with a spoon wielded by the tail of The Great Tail Himself. On Simon's right side the daughter of the ruler, a lovely juvenile named Tunc, acted as his goblet-filler. After numerous toasts, Simon wondered if he was losing control over his tail. He felt a hairy tuft sliding up and down his thigh and then, when he made no move, he felt the hairs tickle his crotch. He felt around behind him with a hand that seemed to have gone numb, grabbed the root of the tail, and slid his hand along it. It was sticking straight out behind him.

Tunc smiled at him, and it penetrated his wine-frozen brain that she was playing tailsey with him. He had a fleeting thought that he would be false to Chworktap if he responded to Tunc. Still, it wasn't his fault that she had practically kicked him out of the *Hwang Ho* and had refused to join him later. With some difficulty, he guided his tail under the table and moved it up Tunc's thigh. At least, he thought it was hers. The woman sitting next to Tunc, The Great Tail Himself's mother, gasped and sat up. But then she smiled at him. Probably, she'd had a gas pain.

He had not been in bed in his luxurious apartment in the palace more than ten minutes when his door was opened. Tunc entered, shed her robe and skirt, and crawled into bed with him. Simon had by that time reconsidered the ethics of the situation. Chworktap was being true to him, even if she had temporarily exiled him. So could he, in conscience, be untrue to her?

On the other hand, did Chworktap give a damn?

And, back to the first hand, he disliked hurting Tunc's feelings.

She snuggled up against him, kissed him, and the end of her tail caressed his throat, his chest, his stomach, the insides of his thighs, and tickled his genitals.

From dislike, he went to hate, hate of hurting her feelings.

Simon rolled her over and got on top and he found that the tail had indeed added another dimension. How had he ever been so content without it? Wait until he told Chworktap about this; no, he'd better not do that.

Tunc's tail came up from between her legs and its end slid into the nearest orifice. This was a new, though pleasant, in fact, ecstatic, experience for him. He used his tail to reciprocate.

Tunc moaned and gasped, did all the things that lovers do over and over without the novelty seeming to wear off. Simon did likewise, though he tried to avoid her tail when she stuck it in his mouth. Orgasm, however, could care less about fastidiousness, and so he overcame his momentary repulsion.

When Tunc staggered out through the door, he watched her go, glad to see her go. One more demand, and the honor of Earth would have been blackened. Tarnished, anyway.

He heaved himself out of bed to wash his teeth. Halfway across the immense room, he heard a knock. He stopped and said, "No more, Tunc!" But the door, opening, revealed Agnavi, Tunc's grandmother.

Simon groaned and said, "I don't want to hurt your feelings, Your Majesty. But I can't even stiffen my tail."

Agnavi was disappointed, but she smiled when Simon said he could schedule a command performance for tomorrow. Meantime, sweet dreams. She was a pleasant woman who had the patience of middle age.

Simon did not, however, sleep well. He had another of the recurring nightmares in which thousands of people seemed to be speaking to him all at once. And the faces of his father and mother were getting closer.

CHAPTER 14
Off to See the Wizard

The queen and her granddaughter were fluent and charming talkers. Simon spent many an hour, lying side by side with them—though not at the same time—his tail entwined with theirs. But neither of them had the answer to his primal question.

Nor did anybody else he met in the capital city. Finally, he asked to have a chance to meet the great sage Mofeislop. Shintsloop, The Great Tail Himself, said he had no objections. He was so cooperative that Simon wondered if he was glad to get rid of him. Maybe he suspected something, though if he did he showed no resentment. Simon had not yet learned that a Dokalian could control his facial muscles but could not keep his tail from expressing his true feelings. If he had, he might have noticed that Shintsloop's tail was held straight out behind him but twitched madly at its end.

Simon sent another messenger to the ship to ask Chworktap if she wanted to go on the trip with him. The messenger returned with a piece of paper.

I can't come with you. I think Tzu Li does have self-consciousness but she's afraid to reveal it. Either she's shy or she mistrusts humans. I've told her I'm a machine, too, but she probably thinks it's a trick. Have a good time. Don't do anything I wouldn't do.

Love and Kisses

Simon smiled. She got very upset when she thought that he might regard her as a machine. But if it would gain her something to admit that she might be, she would not hesitate. This was so human that it certified her as human.

The trip on the railroad took four days. At the end of the line was a wall of yellow bricks two hundred feet high, stretching as far as Simon could see. Actually, it surrounded the Free Land and was a work equivalent to the Great Wall of China. It wasn't as long but it was much higher and thicker. It had no gates, but it did have brick staircases on the outer side every mile or so. These were for the guards, who manned the stations on top of the wall.

"How many men would it take to guard the prisons if the criminals were put into them instead of being sent into the Free Land?" Simon said.

His escort, Colonel Booflum, said, "Oh, about forty thousand, I suppose. The Free Land is a great saving for the tax-payer. We don't have to feed and house the prisoners or pay guards or build new prisons."

"How many soldiers are used to guard these walls?" Simon said.

"About three hundred thousand," the colonel said.

Simon didn't say anything.

He climbed to the top of the wall with Anubis behind him and Athena on his shoulder. Three miles away was the inevitable tower of the Clerun-Gowph. Beyond it for many miles was the top of Mishodei Mountain, his goal. Between him and it lay dozens of smaller mountains and an unbroken forest.

Simon and his pets got into a big wickerwork basket and were lowered by a steam winch. When he climbed out of the basket, he waved goodbye to the colonel and set out. He carried a pack full of food and blankets, a knife, a bow and arrow, and his banjo. Anubis also carried a pack on his back, though he didn't like it.

"A lot of people have left here intent on seeing the wise man," the colonel had said. "Nobody has ever come back, that I know of."

"Maybe Mofeislop showed them the folly of returning to civilization?"

"Maybe," the colonel had said. "As for me, I can't get back to the fleshpots soon enough."

"That reminds me, give my regards to the queen dowager and the princess," Simon had said.

Now he entered the Yetgul Forest, a region of giant trees, pale and stunted underbrush, swamps, poisonous snakes, huge cat-like, bear-like, and wolf-like beasts, hairy elephant-like pachyderms, and men without law and order. Anubis, whimpering, stuck so close that Simon fell over him a dozen times before he had gotten a mile. Simon didn't have the heart to kick him; he was scared, too.

When he got to the foothills of the vast Mishodei Mountain six weeks later, he was still scared. But he was much more fond of his pets than when he had started. Both had been invaluable in warning him of the presence of dangerous beasts and men. Anubis had sense enough not to bark when he smelled them; he growled softly and so alerted Simon. The owl quite often flew ahead and hunted for rodents and small birds. But when it spotted something sinister, it flew back and landed on his shoulder, hooting agitatedly.

Actually, the big beasts were only dangerous if they came upon a human suddenly. Given warning, they would either take off or else stand their ground and voice threats. Simon would then go around them. The only animals that were a genuine peril, because they did not have much sense, were the poisonous snakes.

The pets detected most of these in time, except when Simon awoke late one morning to find a cobra-like snake by his side. Simon froze, but the owl flew at it, hit it, knocked it over, and Simon rolled away to safety. The cobra decided that it was in a bad place and slithered off. Two days later, the owl killed a small coral snake which had crawled by the sleeping Anubis and was on its way to Simon.

The most dangerous animal was man, and though Simon saw parties of them ten times, he always managed to hide until they had passed by. The males were scruffy-looking, dressed in skins, hairy, bearded, gap-toothed, and hag-gard-looking, and the children were usually snot-nosed and rheumy-eyed.

"Excellent examples of the genuine Noble Savage," the colonel had said on the trip down. "Actually, most of the Free Landers are not criminals we've sent in but their descendants. The majority of criminals we do drop into the Land are killed by the tribes that roam the woods."

"Then why don't you let the descendants come into your society?" Simon said. "They're not guilty. Surely you don't believe that the sins of the fathers should be visited on the children?"

"That's a nice phrase," the colonel said. He took out his notebook and wrote in it. Then he said, "There's been some talk in parliament of rescuing the poor devils. For one thing, they'd be a source of cheap labor. But then they'd bring in all sorts of diseases, and they would be difficult to control and expensive to educate.

"Besides, they *are* the descendants of criminals and have inherited the rebellious tendencies of their forefathers. We don't want those spreading through the population again. After all, we've spent a thousand years extracting the rebels from the race."

"How many rebels, or criminals, are now present in the population compared to the number a thousand years ago?" Simon said. "On a per capita basis?"

"The same," the colonel said.

"And how do you explain that after all the selective straining out?"

"Humans beings are contrary creatures. But give us another thousand years, and we'll have a criminal-free society."

Simon said nothing more about this. He did ask why the Dokalian society was so advanced technologically in many respects yet still used bows and arrows. Why hadn't gunpowder been invented?

"Oh, guns were invented five hundred years ago," the colonel said. "But we're a very conservative people, as you may have noticed. It was thought that guns would introduce all sorts of disturbing innovations in society. Besides, they'd be too dangerous in the hands of the rabble. It doesn't take much training to use a gun. But skill with the sword and bow takes many years of training. So guns were outlawed, and only the elite and the most stable of the lower classes are educated in the use of swords and bows."

Despite this resistance to innovations, the steam engine had been accepted. This had resulted in a general disuse of the horse. Horseflies and the diseases they carried had almost been eliminated, and the streets were no longer full of horseshit. But the invention of the internal combustion engine had been suppressed, and there was no gas and noise pollution from automobiles and trucks.

On the other hand, the drop in casualties from horsefly-borne sicknesses was more than made up by traffic accidents.

Simon pointed this out.

"Progress, like religion, must have its martyrs." the colonel had said.

"One could say the same about regress," Simon said. "What do you do with your traffic criminals? I'd think that you'd send so many of them here that there wouldn't be room, even in that vast forest."

"Oh, those responsible for traffic casualties aren't felons," the colonel had said. "They're fined, and some are jailed, if they don't happen to be rich."

"Well," Simon said. "Couldn't you greatly reduce the murders and the maimings on the highway if you instituted a rigorous examination, physical and psychological, of drivers?"

"Are you kidding?" the colonel said. "No, you aren't. Less than one-tenth of the people would be permitted to drive. Good God, man, the whole economy would crumble if we did that. How did your politicians ever get your people to agree to such drastic measures?"

Simon had to admit that they hadn't passed any such laws until after cars were no longer much used.

"And by then, nobody cared, right?" the colonel said.

"Right," Simon had said, and he had wished that the colonel would quit laughing.

It was with such thoughts, humiliating though they were, that Simon kept up his courage. The Yetgul Forest was getting thicker and gloomier with every mile, and the path was so narrow that bushes and branches tore at his clothes with every step. Even the birds seemed to have found this area undesirable. Whereas before he had been cheered by many dozens of differing calls, whistles, cheeps, and songs, continuing through the day and half the night, he was now surrounded by a silence. Only occasionally was this broken, and when it was, the cry of a bird startled him. There seemed to be only one type, a sudden screech that sounded to him like a death cry. Once, he glimpsed the bird that was responsible, a large dusty black bird that looked like a raven with a rooster's comb.

What especially depressed him were the bones. From the beginning he had seen scattered skeletons and skulls of men and women. Sometimes, they were spread out on the trail; sometimes, their gray or white bones peeped out from under bushes or leaves. Simon had counted a thousand skeletons, and there must be three times as many whose bones were hidden in the brush off the trail.

Simon tried to cheer himself with the thought that anybody who could inspire so many to defy death just to talk to him must be worth talking to.

But why would the sage have isolated himself so thoroughly?

That wasn't difficult to figure out. A sage needs much more time in which to meditate and contemplate. If he or she has visitors beating at the door, clamoring day and night, the sage has no time to think. So Mofeislop had built his house in the most difficult-to-reach place on the planet. This assured him solitude. It also assured that whoever did get to him would not be bringing trivial questions.

At the end of the third week, Simon came out of the dark woods. Before and above him were steep and warty slopes with patches of grass and clumps of pines here and there. Above these circled hawks and vultures. Simon hoped these were not hanging around because the pickings were so easy.

The third peak beyond, by far the tallest and the most jagged, was the end of his journey. Simon, thinking of all the climbing he had to do, felt discouraged. Then out of the clouds, which had been thick, dark gray, and as joyless as an eviction notice, the sun emerged. Simon felt better. Some- thing on the tip of the third peak had batted the sun's rays in a line drive straight into his eyes. This, he was sure, was a window in the house of Mofeislop. It was as if the sage himself was heliographing him to come on ahead.

A week later, Simon and Anubis crawled up the final slope. Lack of food and oxygen was making his heart thump like a belt buckle in an automatic drier, and he was breathing like an old man with a teenager bride. Athena, too tired to fly, was riding on his back, her talons dug in with a grip as painful and unrelenting as a loan shark's. He could not spare the energy to drive her off him. Besides, the talons had a value. They were reminding him that he was still alive, and that he would feel so good when the pain was gone.

Above him, occupying half of the two-acre plateau on top of the peak, was the house of the sage. Three stories high, thirteen-sided, many-balconied, many-cupolaed, it was built of black granite. The only windows were on the top floor, but there were many of these, small, large, square, octagonal, or round. From the center of the flat roof a tall thick black chimney rose, black smoke pouring from it. Simon envisioned a big fireplace at its base with a pig turning slowly on a spit and a kettle boiling with a thick savory soup. By it the sage waited, to feed him food first and then the answers to his questions.

To tell the truth, Simon at that moment did not give a damn about the answers. He felt that if he could fill his belly, he would be content throughout all eternity. The rest of his life, anyway.

Simon pulled himself over onto the lip of the plateau, crawled to the huge door, oak and crossed with thick ironwork, heaved himself up slowly—the owl fell off him—and pulled the bell cord. Somewhere inside a cavernous room, a big bell tolled.

"I hope he's not gone," Simon said to himself, and he giggled. Starvation and the thin air were making him silly. Just where did he think the sage would be? Stepped out to pick up cigarettes at the corner drugstore? Gone to the movies? Attending the local Rotary Club luncheon?

His long wait at the door did give him time to wonder how the sage had managed to get this house built. Who had hauled the heavy stones up the mountain? Where did Mofeislop get his food?

Simon pulled the cord again, and the bell boomed again. After a few minutes, a key turned in the monstrously large and rusty lock, and a giant bar thudded. The door swung out slowly, creaking as if Dracula's butler was on the other side. Simon felt apprehensive, then reassured himself that he had been conditioned by watching too many old horror movies. The heavy door bumped against the stone wall, and a man shambled out. He did not look at all like the Count's servant, but it was no relief to see him. He resembled Doctor Frankenstein's assistant or perhaps Lon Chaney Senior in *The Hunchback of Notre Dame*. His spine curved like a freeway on-ramp; he was bent over as if he had just been kicked in the stomach; his hair foamed like a glass of beer; his forehead slanted back like the Tower of Pisa; his supraorbital ridges bulged as if they were full of gas; one eye was lower than the other and milky with a cataract; his nose was red and crumpled, like a dead rose; his lips were as thin as a dog's; his teeth were those of a moose that has chewed tobacco all his life; his chin had decided in the womb to give up the ghost. And he wheezed like an emphysematic at a political convention.

However, he had a personality as pleasing as a blind date's.

He smiled and said "Welcome!" and he radiated good will and jolly fellowship.

"Doctor Mofeislop, I presume?" Simon said.

"Bless your little heart, no," the man said. "I am the good doctor's secretary and house servant. My name is Odiomzwak."

His parents must really have hated him, Simon thought, and he warmed toward him. Simon knew what it was to have a father and a mother who couldn't stand their child.

"Come in, come in!" Odiomzwak said. "All three of you."

He reached out to pat Anubis, who lolled his tongue and shut his eyes as if very pleased to be petted. Simon decided that his apprehensions had been wrong. Dogs were known to be reliable readers of character.

Odiomzwak took a flaming torch from its stand by the door and led them down a narrow and long hall. They came out into a giant room with black granite walls and a tile mosaic floor. At its end was the great fireplace Simon had imagined. The roasting pig wasn't there, but the kettle of steaming soup was. Near it stood a tall thin man, all forehead and nose, warming his hands and tail. He was dressed in furry slippers, bearskin trousers, and a long flowing robe printed with calipers, compasses, telescopes, microscopes, surgeon's knives, test tubes, and question marks. The marks were not the same as those used on Earth, of course. The Dokalian mark was a symbol representing an arrow about to be launched from a bow.

"Welcome, welcome indeed!" the tall man said, hastening to Simon with his hand out, fingers spread. 'You are as welcome as food to a hungry man!"

"Speaking of which, I *am* famished," Simon said.

"Of course you are," Mofeislop said. "I've been watching your rather slow progress up the mountain through my telescope. There were times when I thought you weren't going to make it."

Then why in hell didn't you send out a rescue party? Simon thought. He did not say anything, however. Philosophers couldn't be expected to behave like ordinary people.

Simon sat down at a long narrow pine table on a pine bench. Odiomzwak bustled around setting the table and two bowls on the floor for the pets. The food was simple, consisting of loaves of freshly baked bread, a strong goaty-smelling cheese, and the soup. This had some herbs, beans, and thick pieces of meat floating in it. The meat tasted somewhat like pork with an underlying flavor of tobacco.

Simon ate until his belly creaked. Odiomzwak brought in a bottle of onion vodka, a drink for which Simon did not care much. He tasted it to be polite and then, at the request of the curious sage, played a few songs on his banjo. Anubis and Athena retired to the end of the room, but Mofeislop and Odiomzwak seemed to enjoy his music very much.

"I particularly liked that last one," Mofeislop said. "But I'm curious about the lyric itself. Could you translate it for me?"

"I was planning to do so," Simon said. "It's by an ancient named Bruga, my favorite poet. Unfortunately, or perhaps fortunately, you Dokalians don't have TV, so I'll have to explain what TV and talk shows and commercials are. Also, the identity of the three guests on the show and their backgrounds.

"This Swiss noble, Baron Victor Frankenstein, made a man out of parts he dug up from the cemetery." he said. "Nobody knows just how he vitalized the patchwork monster, though the movie showed him doing it with a lightning bolt. The monster went ape and killed a bunch of people. The baron tried to track him down, and at one time he was chasing the monster across the arctic ice, though they didn't have the dog-and-sled sequence in the movie version either.

"Lazarus was a young man who died in ancient times in a country then called Palestine. He was resurrected by a man called Jesus Christ. Later, Jesus was killed, too, and he resurrected himself. Before he was killed, however, his judge, Pontius Pilate, asked him, 'What is Truth?' Jesus didn't reply, either because he didn't know the answer or because Pilate didn't hang around to hear it. Jesus was deified after this and one of Earth's important religions was named after him. He was supposed to know if man was immortal or not. At least, in Bruga's poem, it is presumed that he does know."

REVELATION ON THE JOHNNY CAVEAR SHOW

The make-up's on, the trumpets sound.
Applaud our Johnny, host renowned!
He introduces the guests around
And after all the jesting's crowned
With a station break, our Johnny craves
To hear what happened in the graves.

But Frankenstein's monster—"Call me Fred"—
Won't talk of life among the dead,
Remembers only that the sled
Was slow; his dogs, his heart had bled.
"Behind me vowing vengeance came Victor.
His dying bride had sworn I'd dicked her."

Lazarus says he found no riddling
In the tomb, no questions fiddling
For replies, just Death's cold diddling,
Which, not feeling, he thought piddling.
The host declares, "It's dangerous to vex
The sponsors with allusions to sex."

There yet remains a guest unheard.
"Tell us, Jesus, what's the Word?"
He rises. "Here's the Truth unblurred."
All goggle. Man: A soul? A turd?
Then Time and Tide impose their pressage.
"And now for an important message."

"You were trying to tell me something when you sang that," the sage said. "You were hoping that my message to you would not be disturbed or marked by commercialism or trivialities, right?"

"Right."

"You've come to the right place, the right man. I alone in all Dokal, perhaps all the universe, know the Truth. After you have learned it, your quest will be over."

Simon put his banjo down and said, "I'm all ears."

"You're more than that," the sage said. He and Odiomzwak looked at each other and burst out laughing. Simon reddened but said nothing. Sages were famous for laughing at things other people were too imperceptive to see.

"Not tonight, though," Mofeislop said. "You are too tired and thin to take the Truth. You need to be strong and rested, to put some meat on your bones, before you can hear what I have to say. Be my guest for a few days, restrain your impatience, and I will answer the question which you say this Jesus could not answer."

"Very well," Simon said, and he went to bed. But it was not well. Though exhausted, he could not get to sleep for a long time. The sage had intimated that he would have to be strong to take the Truth, which apparently would be strong stuff. This made him apprehensive. Whatever the Truth, it would not be comforting.

At last, telling himself that he had asked for it, no matter what it was, he drifted off. But the rest of the night seemed nightmare-shot. And once again the images of his father and mother slid closer to him while behind them crowded thousands of people, imploring, threatening, weeping, laughing, snarling, smiling.

His last dream was that the old Roman, Pilate himself, approached him.

"Listen, kid," Pilate said. "It's dangerous to ask that question. Remember what happened to the last man who asked it. Me, that is. I fell into disgrace."

"I've always been disappointed because it wasn't a rhetorical question," Simon said. "Why didn't he answer it?"

"Because he didn't know the answer, that's why," Pilate said. "He was a fool to say he was a god. Up to that moment, I was going to tell the Jews to go screw themselves and let him go. But when he told me that, I believed that the most dangerous man in the Roman Empire was in my power. So I let him be crucified. But I've had a lot of time to think about the situation, and I realize now I made a bad mistake. The surest way to spread a faith is to make martyrs. People began thinking that if a man is willing to die for his belief, then he must have something worth dying for. They want to get in on it, too. Besides, martyrdom is the surest way to get your name in the history books."

"You're very cynical," Simon said.

"I was a politician," Pilate said. "Any ward heeler knows more about people than any psychologist with a dozen Ph.D."s and unlimited funds for research."

And he faded away, though his grin hung in the air for a minute, like the Cheshire Cat's.

CHAPTER 15
Who Pulls the Strings?

Simon rested and ate the first three days. Mofeislop insisted that Simon get on the scales every morning.

"When you've gained enough weight, then you will gain the Truth," he said.

"Are you telling me there's a correlation, a connection, between mass and knowledge?" Simon said.

"Certainly," the sage replied. "Everything's connected in a subtle manner which only the wise may see. A star exploding may start a new religion, or affect stock market prices, on a planet removed by ten thousand years in time and millions of miles in space. The particular strength of gravity of a planet affects the moral principles of its inhabitants."

Emotional states were part of the overall field configuration. Just as Earth's gravity, no matter how feeble far out in space, affected everybody, so anger, fear, bye, hate, joy, and sadness radiated outward to the ends of the universe.

Bruga had once written a blank-verse epic, *Oedipus 1—Sphinx 0*. It had two lines which summed up the whole situation of subtle and complex causality.

Must idols crack, the walls of Ilium crumble,
When Hercules' onions make his bowels rumble?

These two lines said more than all of Plato's or Grubwitz' books. Plato, by the way, wanted to banish all poets from his proposed Utopia because they were liars. The truth was that Plato knew philosophers couldn't compete successfully with poets.

Jonathan Swift Somers III had written a novel which developed this idea, though he'd taken it much further than Mofeislop and Bruga had. This was *Don't Know Up from Down,* starring Somers' famous basketcase hero, John Clayter. All Somers' heroes, except for Ralph von Wau Wau, were handicapped one way or another. This was because Somers had lost the use of his own legs.

Clayter lived in a spacesuit with all sorts of prosthetic devices he controlled with his tongue. When he had to use his tongue to talk but wanted to act at the same time, he used a second control. This was located in the lower part of the suit and responded to pressure from Clayter's penis. It had to be erect at this time to push on the walls of the flexible cylinder in which it fitted. It also had to wax and wane. This was because Clayter couldn't move his body to move the penis. The degrees of swelling or deflation were converted by a digital computer which operated the spacesuit at this time. To bring his penis up or down, Clayter moved his head against a control which caused varying amounts of aphrodisiacal hormones to be shot into his bloodstream.

It never occurred to Clayter that he could have bypassed the hormones and used the head-control directly. If that idea had sprung into his subconscious, it was sternly suppressed by his conscious mind. Or maybe it was the other way around. In any event, Clayter's chief pleasure was operating the control with his penis, and he wasn't about to give that up.

Clayter was always landing on some planet and solving its problems. In *Don't Know Up from Down,* Clayter visits Shagrinn, a world which has a problem unknown elsewhere. Every once in a while Shagrinn's sun flares up. During this solar storm, Shagrinn's electromagnetic fields go wild. This causes some peculiar hormone reactions in the planet's people. The women become very horny. The men, however, can't get a hard-on.

Though this condition causes great distress, it is temporary. Solar flares have never lasted more than a month or two. And its overall result is beneficial. The population has been kept down, which means that Shagrinn isn't polluted.

But when Clayter lands, the flare has lasted for five months and shows no sign of subsiding. Nor can Clayter maintain his usual objectivity in solving the mess. He himself is trapped, and unless he figures a way out of his personal situation, he's going to be stranded until he dies. The tongue control is malfunctioning, which is why Clayter landed on the nearest planet. He wants the Shagrinnians to repair the unit.

They can't do it because their technology is at the level of fifteenth-century Europe. In fact, they can't even get him out of his suit. Fortunately, his helmet visor is open enough for him to be fed. But this leads to another problem.

An astute Shagrinnian has noticed that, whenever the bottom rear of Clayter's suit opens, the suit spins furiously for about ten minutes. He doesn't know why, but the reason is that another malfunction in the control apparatus has developed. The suit's rear opens whenever the excrement tank inside is full, and the refuse is dumped out. Its control wires have gotten crossed with those controlling the little jets that keep the suit stabilized. When the dump section opens, a jet is activated for a little while. Clayter spins around and around helplessly, only kept from falling over by the suit's gyroscope.

The Shagrinnian owns a grain mill nearby which uses four oxen to turn the huge millstone. He sells the oxen for a profit and connects the suit to a rope connected to a big flywheel. The spinning of the suit turns the flywheel, which stores up energy to run the millstone. But the suit doesn't spin enough to keep the mill working twenty-four hours a day. The owner force-feeds Clayter, which makes the rear section open more often, which makes the suit spin, which runs the millstone steadily.

To hasten matters, the owner also crams laxatives down the spaceman's throat.

Clayter has to solve his problems fast. Even with his diarrhea he's gaining weight. Within a month, he'll be squeezed to death inside the suit. Meanwhile, he's so dizzy he can't think straight.

His only hope is to learn the language swiftly and talk the maidservant who's feeding him into helping him. Between mouthfuls and whirling, he masters enough of the language to plead for her help. He also learns about the plight of the Shagrinnians from her.

He instructs her to let a wire down inside the front of his suit and into the secondary control cylinder. She does so and tries to get the end of the wire, which is looped, into the cylinder. Clayter hopes she'll be able to pull his organ out and then use the wire to exert pressure inside the tube. If she can apply just the proper pressure, he'll fly back up to his ship, which is stationed just outside the atmosphere. Of course, he'll have to hold his breath for a few minutes during the transit from air to space to the ship. It's a desperate gamble.

Unfortunately, or perhaps fortunately, considering the odds if she succeeds, she fails. The wire hurts Clayter so much that he has to tell her to stop.

The next morning, while he's still sleeping, he gets an erection from an excess of urine. Technically, this is called a piss hard-on, It is the only kind a human male can get on Shagrinn during the solar flare. But his jubilation is short-lived. The uncontrolled expansion inside the tube activates the suit's jets. He takes off at a slant and lands on top of his head in a barnyard twenty miles away. The flywheel he's trailed behind him misses him by an inch. The head of the suit is buried in the muck just enough to keep him from toppling over. Clayter now has a new problem. If he can't get upright, the increased blood pressure in his head will kill him.

However, the faulty connection between the dump section and the stabilizing jet has been broken. He no longer spins around. And the force of the impact has sprung open the suit's lower front section, which in his position is now the upper front. And it has jarred him loose from the control cylinder.

He sees a nursing calf eye him, and he thinks, "Oh, no!"

A few minutes later, the farmer's daughter chases the calf away. As randy and desperate as the other women on this planet, she takes advantage of the gift from the heavens. She does, however, turn him upright afterward with the aid of a block and tackle and two mules. Clayter tries to instruct her in how to use the lower control. She can use her finger to set it so that his suit will return to the ship, orbiting above the atmosphere. Once in it, he can tell the ship's computer to take him to a system where such peculiar solar flares don't exist.

The farmer's daughter ignores his instructions. Each morning, just before dawn, she sneaks out of the house and waits for all the beers she's been feeding him to work on him. One morning, the farmer's wife happens to wake up early and catches her daughter. Now, the daughter has to alternate morning shifts with her mother.

Early one day, the farmer wakes up and sees his wife with Clayter. Enraged, he begins beating on the helmet with a club. Clayter's head is ringing, and he knows that the farmer will soon start thrusting a pitchfork into the helmet or, worse, into the opened lower section. Desperately, though knowing it's useless, he rams his tongue against the upper control. To his surprise, and the farmer's, the suit takes off.

Clayter figures out that the impact of the fall, or perhaps the farmer's club, had jarred the circuits back into working order. He talks a smith into welding the lower section shut and flies back to the ship. A few months later, he finds a planet where his suit can be fixed. He is so sore about his adventures on Shagrinn that he has almost decided to leave its people in their mess. But he does have a big heart, and besides he wants to shame them for their scurvy treatment of him.

He returns to Shagrinn and calls its leaders in for a conference. "Here's the way it is," he says. "The whole trouble is caused by the wrong attitude of mind."

"What do you mean?" they say.

"I've studied your history, and I find that the founder of your religion made a prediction two thousand years ago. He said that the day would come when you would have to pay for your wicked ways, right?"

"Right."

"He was specific, or as specific as prophets ever get. He said that someday the sun would start having big flares, and when that evil day came, women's sexual desires would increase fourfold. But men wouldn't be able to get it up. Right?"

"Right! He was a true prophet! Didn't it happen?"

"Now, before the first time the sun flared so brightly, you had had many small flares?"

"True!"

"But the first time the sun really had a huge solar storm was when?"

"That was three hundred years ago, Mr. Clayter. Before then we only had the prophet's word that there were storms on the sun. But when telescopes were invented, three centuries ago, we could see the small flares. About ten years later, we saw the first big one."

"And that's when your troubles started?"

"Ain't it the truth!"

"Did the men get impotent and the women itchy when the flare reached its peak? Or when it was still small but looked as if it was going to get big?"

"When it was small but looked as if it might get big."

"There you are," Clayter says. "You have it all backward."

The leaders look stunned. "What do you mean?"

"Suppose you have a piece of string each end of which is held by a person," Clayter says. "When one tugs the string, it goes toward him. When the other pulls, it goes to him. You and the solar flare are connected with a string. But you're all screwed up about who's pulling it."

"What in hell are you talking about?" the leaders say.

"It wasn't the sun that made the flare get so much bigger," John Clayter says.

"What did then?"

"Your ancestors saw a slight increase in the storm, so, of course, the anticipated reaction happened."

"We still don't get you," the flabbergasted leaders say.

"Well, that flare would probably have been only a little bigger than normal. But you thought it was the promised big one."

"Yeah?"

"Like I said," Clayter says, "your ancestors had it backward. And succeeding generations have perpetuated the error. You see, it isn't the giant solar flares that have been causing limp pricks and hot twats. It's actually just the reverse."

CHAPTER 16
The Moment of Truth

Simon told this story to his host. Mofeislop and Odiomzwak laughed until they fell out of their chairs. When the sage had wiped his tears and blown his nose, he said, "So this Somers independently arrived at the same conclusion I did. He must have been a very wise man."

"Everybody thought so," Simon said. "After all, he made a lot of money."

The next four days, Simon toured the area with Odiomzwak hobbling and bobbling along as guide. He inspected the big garden which filled up the part of the plateau not occupied by the house. He climbed down the steep slope to another plateau a thousand feet below, a meadow where goats grazed and bees buzzed in and out of their hives. Odiomzwak milked the goats and collected honey, and then the two followed a stream, which was mostly cataracts. Odiomzwak checked the traps along this and was rewarded with a half a dozen jackrabbit-sized rodents.

"These'll make a welcome addition to our diet," the assistant said. "We get tired of goat cheese and an occasional piece of goat meat in our stew."

"I've wondered how you two got along," Simon said. "You have to be entirely independent, since you're so isolated. But you seem to be doing all right. Your fare is simple but adequate."

"Oh, we vary it from time to time," Odiomzwak said.

The sage was waiting for them on the roof of the house. Part of this had been made into a recreation area. There was a pool table and a court where master and servant played the Dokalian version of badminton. Mofeislop's big telescope was on a tripod near the east edge of the roof, and he was looking through it when Simon climbed out from the stairway. Simon stopped. He was embarrassed. The telescope was partly swiveled around so he could see the master, bent over, his eye applied to the instrument. He was holding the end of his tail in one hand, and its tip was in his mouth.

Odiomzwak, coming up from behind Simon, stopped also. He coughed loudly. Mofeislop jumped back, spitting out the tuft of tail on which he had been sucking. He turned red, though no redder than Simon.

Then the sage laughed and said, "It's an infantile habit, Simon. One that I've never been able to overcome. Why should I? I find it very comforting. And it certainly is not dangerous to health, as tobacco smoking is, for instance."

"Think nothing of it," Simon said. "I didn't expect you to be perfect, no matter how wise you are."

"That's right," Mofeislop said. "Wisdom consists of knowing when to avoid perfection."

While Simon was trying to figure that out, he was asked to sit down in a big overstuffed chair near the telescope. He did so, his heart beating hard. He felt that today was the day, this moment the moment. Mofeislop was going to reveal the Truth now.

Odiomzwak disappeared while the sage paced back and forth, his hands behind him, his tail lashing, his long robe fluttering. When the assistant reappeared with a bottle of wine, Mofeislop stopped and said "Ah!" Simon knew this must be a rare occasion. Instead of the stinking and sharp onion wine, Odiomzwak had brought mead, brewed from the honey of the meadow bees.

Odiomzwak set the bottle and three glasses down on a table. Mofeislop said, "It would be better if the animals were taken downstairs. We want no interruptions."

The hunchbacked assistant shambled over to the owl, which had been perched behind and above Simon. Instead of coming to him, however, Athena screeched and flew off. She climbed in spirals higher and higher and finally was lost in the sun.

"They both seem uneasy," Simon said apologetically. Anubis was, in fact, crouched under the table and growling softly in his throat.

"Beasts are very sensitive," the sage said. "What they lack in intelligence, they make up in psychic perception. They sense that you are about to become a very different person. And they're not sure that they will like it. Such is the effect of Truth."

"I'll take him downstairs," Simon said. But when he rose and walked toward Anubis, the dog ran out from under the table and dashed behind the chimney.

"Oh, never mind then," Mofeislop said, waving his hand. "It's just that I did not want you disturbed by the owl crapping on your shoulder or the dog barking. I wanted your train of thought on schedule."

Odiomzwak went downstairs again. The sage looked through his telescope and chuckled. Straightening up from it, he said, "Another party of Truth-seekers is approaching. I've been watching them for three days. Two men and an exceptionally fat woman. I'm afraid she's going to lose much weight before she gets here. The road to Truth is a long and hard one."

"Do you get many visitors?"

"About seventy a year," Mofeislop said. "That's an average of about three every two weeks. Just right. There are not so many they become a burden, and each party is small enough so it can be easily handled."

"I'm surprised anybody gets through," Simon said, "what with the rough terrain and the wild beasts and the savages."

"Be surprised then." the sage said. "Today, I'm surprised, too. That's the first woman I've seen in ten years. Women don't come here seeking the Truth, you know. That's because they think they already know it. Besides, even those women who have doubts aren't likely to go through the Yetgul Forest to ask a *man* what it's all about. They know that most men are pitiful creatures and not too bright, no matter how proficient they might be in science and technology and the arts."

Simon said, "But you are the exception, heh?"

"Right," the sage said. "But you're in for several surprises today."

"I hope I have strength enough to face them," Simon said. "I know that, deep down, I'm like everybody else. I talk much about wanting to know Truth, I seek it out, but I'm not sure that when I'm about to face it, I might not run away."

"Others have tried to run away," Mofeislop said.

He straightened up. "Perhaps you've wondered why I've isolated myself so thoroughly. Why do I make it so hard for people to get to me? Well, if it were easier, I'd be surrounded, overwhelmed, with people clamoring for the Truth night and day. I don't particularly like people in the mass and, in fact, seldom individually. But here, I'm so alone that when I get a visitor I welcome him. Odiomzwak, as you may have noticed, is not a very interesting conversationalist. Also, those who make it here really desire to see me; they're not just driven by idle curiosity. So, I have plenty of time to meditate and I get just enough visitors to satisfy my needs for human beings. And I'm master here, total master. The government doesn't bother with me."

Simon was about to reply when he smelled the powerful odor of long-unwashed Odiomzwak behind him. He turned his head to look up over the chair. Something clicked. He cried out and began struggling, while, seemingly far off, Anubis barked in a panic.

Steel bands had sprung out from the arms of the chair and bound his wrists.

"So, you son of a bitch, you saw me sucking my tail!" Mofeislop shouted.

"I wouldn't tell anybody!" Simon cried. "I could care less! I just want to know the Truth!"

"You *won't* tell anybody," the sage said, glowering. "That's right. Not that it would have made any difference whether or not you did see me. But don't worry. You will hear the Truth."

Odiomzwak came from behind the chair carrying several long sharp knives of varying widths and lengths. These were enough to make Simon wet his pants, but Odiomzwak's drooling and lip-licking ensured it.

"This'll be a rare feast indeed," Odiomzwak mumbled. "We've never had Earthman's flesh before."

"Not rare," Mofeislop said. "Unique. You should consult the dictionary more often, my dear Odiomzwak."

"Who cares?" Odiomzwak said sullenly.

"I do," the sage said. "Remember, unique, not rare. We're not barbarians."

"I wouldn't agree with that," Simon said.

"That's because you're emotionally involved," Mofeislop said. "You haven't attained the cool objectivity of the true philosopher."

Mofeislop gestured to his assistant to put the knives on the table. He sat down in a chair facing Simon's and put the tips of his fingers and his thumbs together. The shape thus formed was commonly known as a church steeple. To Simon, it looked like the gaping mouth of a shark.

"I hope you're not a filthy atheist," Mofeislop said.

"What?" Simon said. And then, "Of course not!"

"Good!" Mofeislop said. "I've eaten too many of them, and they've all had a rank taste that is unpleasant. Attitudes determine the chemical composition of a person's flesh, you know. You didn't? Well, now you know. And I'm pleased to see that, though you smoke, you don't smoke much. You may have noticed the slight taste of tobacco in the meat of the stew you ate the day you got here. That was your predecessor. He was a nicotine addict, though, I'm glad to add, not an atheist. Otherwise, he would have been almost inedible."

"I'm going to throw up," Simon said.

"That seems to be the usual reaction," Mofeislop said cheerfully. "I doubt you'll have much success. I've arranged it so that your meal would be fully digested when you confronted the Truth."

"Which is?" Simon said after his stomach had tried to empty nonexistent contents.

"After much thought about and around, I came out of the same door, much as that drunken Persian Sufi poet you told me about. Out of the same door into which I had entered. Here's how it is, and don't bother to argue with me. My logic is clear and indisputable, based on long-life observation.

"It's this. The Creator has created this world solely to provide Himself with a show, to entertain Himself. Otherwise, He'd find eternity boring.

"And He gets as much enjoyment from watching pain, suffering, and murder as He does from love. Perhaps more, since there is so much more hate and greed and murder than there is of love. Just as I enjoy watching through my telescope the struggles of those who are fighting to get to me, a sadistic pleasure, I admit, so He enjoys watching the comedies and tragedies of the beings He created."

"That's it?" Simon said.

"That's it."

"That's nothing new!" Simon said. "I've read a hundred books which say the same thing! Where's the logic, the wisdom, in that?"

"Once you've admitted the premise that there is a Creator, no intelligent person can come to any other conclusion. Now, tell me, can you state honestly, from all you've observed, that the Creator regards His creatures, human or otherwise, as anything but actors in a drama? Poor actors, most of them, and great drama is rare. But I do my best to provide Him with an interesting play, though, I must admit, for purely selfish reasons."

He spoke to Odiomzwak. "Get an axe. That dog may try to attack, though he's hiding behind the chimney now."

The assistant disappeared. Mofeislop said, "Dog meat's good, too. And an additional welcome change of diet."

"You cannibal!" Simon snarled.

"Not really," the sage said. "Cannibalism is eating one's own kind, and I am not of the same species as you. Or even of other Dokalians. I differ from them, have evolved from them, you might say, just as they evolved from apes. My intellect is so much superior to theirs that it's not a matter of degree but of kind."

"Bullshit!" Simon said. "You have the same philosophy as a college sophomore's! But he leaves it behind with maturity."

"Aging, you mean," Mofeislop said. "He gets old, and he fears dying. And so he laughs at what he once thought, which was indeed the Truth. But his laughter springs from fear, fear that he was right when he was young."

"You're not trying to talk me to death, are you?"

Mofeislop smiled and said, "You'll wish I had before I'm done."

"I'll tell you why you're doing this!" Simon shouted. "You hate all people because you were ridiculed when you were young! You couldn't break yourself of the habit of sucking on your tail!"

Mofeislop jumped to his feet. His hands were balled; his face, red; his head, shaking.

"Who told you that?" he finally screamed. "Odiomzwak?" Simon had only guessed it, but he had no compunctions about lying if he could put off the inevitable moment.

"Yes, he told me this morning while we were down at the meadow."

"I'll kill the ugly bastard!" Mofeislop said. But he sat down and, after an evident struggle with himself, smiled. "You are lying, of course. In any event, you won't be passing that on, and I need Odiomzwak."

Simon looked out past the parapet, across the mountains and valleys, and up into the sky. The sky was as blue as a baby's eye, and the air was as clear as a baby's conscience. A newly born wind cried softly in his ear. The sun shone as brightly as a fond mother's smile.

Suddenly, the blue eye had something in it. The specks slowly became larger, and Simon saw that they were vultures. They must have been many miles away, circling around, scanning. There had been nothing for them until a few minutes ago, and here they were. The frequency of peace and content had suddenly shifted they were homing in on the beam, tuned in to death.

Simon couldn't help thinking in poetic terms even at this moment. He was a creature of habits, mostly bad. But then, on the other hand, it's easy to break good habits and hell to break the bad.

The stink of Odiomzwak preceded the sound of his step. He came into view with a long heavy sharp axe on his shoulder.

"Shall I kill the dog now?"

Mofeislop nodded, and the assistant shuffled off. The sage picked up a small knife curved inward like some surgeon's tool. Simon lied again.

"Listen! If you kill me up here, you'll be dead within a week!"

"Why is that?" the sage said, raising his thick eyebrows as if they were shrouds he was peeping under.

"Because I put a small observer satellite up before I came here! It's suspended up there now, so far away you can't see it. And it's watching everything that takes place now. If it doesn't see me leave here in a few days, it's going to report to my partner in her spaceship in the capital city! And she'll come barreling in here and investigate. Which means you'll be done for!"

Mofeislop squinted up and then said, "I doubt you're telling the truth. But just in case...Odiomzwak, come here!"

Simon smelled the assistant again, heard a click behind him, and the steel cuffs slid back into the arms of the chair. Odiomzwak stood near him, his axe held up, and Mofeislop had his hand on the hilt of a dagger in its sheath.

"Call your dog," Mofeislop said, "and you take him inside. But move slowly, and no tricks."

Odiomzwak whined, "He might jump over the side, like the last one."

"Then you'll go down after him, like the last time," the sage said. "Anyway, I thought the bouncing down the mountain was just the thing. It tenderized him."

"It won't do any good to kill me inside," Simon said. "The satellite can't see you, but it'll report that I haven't come out of here."

"Oh, it'll see you leave here and enter the Yelgut Forest," Mofeislop said cheerily. "I'll be dressed in your clothes and my face'll be made up to look like yours. I'll come out of the forest looking like someone else. And I'll tell your partner that you have perished on the way out."

"And how will you explain the dog not being with me?" Simon said.

"It'll be very inconvenient," the sage said. "I'll have to dodge by the newcomers and get Odiomzwak to hold them until I get back. But I'll take the dog with me. I can dine on him once I'm under the cover of the trees."

"Don't forget to bring some steaks back for me," Odiomzwak said. "You know how I love dog meat."

"I'll do my best."

"He's making us a lot of trouble," Odiomzwak said. "He ought to be made to pay for it."

"Oh, he will," Mofeislop said.

Simon's mouth felt as if it were full of Dry Ice. All his water was leaking out of his skin. He called to Anubis, but his voice squeaked like a bat's.

"He's going to try something," Odiomzwak whined. "I can smell it. Otherwise, why'd he tell us about that there thing, what-you-call-it? in the sky?"

"He wants to put off the inevitable," the sage said. "Like everybody else, he'd rather live through any number of bad moments than die in a good one."

"Yeah, but that there eye in the sky's already seen him cuffed to the chair and it's seen the axe and the knives."

"I'll tell his partner it was just a sort of ritual I put all my seekers after the Truth through," the sage said. "A sort of dumb-show to portray man's lot in the universe. Don't worry. Anyway, I don't really think there is a satellite."

Anubis came slowly and suspiciously to Simon. He patted the dog on the head, and Anubis walked behind him to the stairway. Odiomzwak ran ahead of him so he couldn't make a break for it. The sage's dagger pricked his back as soon as they had entered the stairway, out of sight of the imaginary observer. Odiomzwak, the axe held ready to bring down on Simon's head, backed down the steps.

Simon kicked back, felt his heel strike Anubis, who yelped, and then launched himself toward Odiomzwak, his hands held out. Odiomzwak yelped, too, and started to bring the axe down. Simon went in under it, his head struck Odiomzwak's, and, Simon half on top of him, they fell together down the steps.

Dazed, Simon sat up at the foot of the stairway. He knew he had to get up, but he could not control his legs. Above him, the sage stabbed at Anubis, who snarled and made short lunges up after him. Somebody groaned beside Simon, and he looked down. The hunchback was lying on his side, his eyes unfocused.

Simon managed to get some orders through to his legs, and he got slowly to his feet. Mofeislop called out to the hunchback to kill Simon. Odiomzwak sat up slowly, leaning on one hand, the other held to the side of his head. Blood oozed out between his fingers.

Simon picked up the axe as Odiomzwak got to his feet. The hunchback's eyes suddenly focused, and he cried out. Simon swung the axe with the edge turned to one side so he would strike the man with the flat side. Even in his confusion and desperation, he did not want to kill his would-be killer. And he did not swing it as hard as he should have. The axe rang on the stone wall, missing Odiomzwak. He had leaped up and dodged out into the hallway.

Simon glanced above. Anubis was still holding the sage at bay, was, in fact, making him retreat. He ran out into the hall, though wobblingly. Odiomzwak wasn't in sight. He ran down the long wide hallway and, as he went past a doorway, the hunchback leaped out at him. Simon thrust the end of the axe in his face; the man fell back but a flailing hand seized the axe-shaft. Twice as powerful as Simon, Odiomzwak tore the axe out of Simon's hand. For a moment, though, the hunchback was half-stunned. Simon ran through the doorway, saw his banjo on a table, and picked it up. When Odiomzwak, yelling, came through the doorway, Simon broke the banjo over his head.

A critic would say, years later, that this was the only time Simon had ever put his banjo to good use.

Odiomzwak fell, and the axe dropped. But he was up again and staggering toward the retreating Simon with the axe again in his hands.

Simon kept on moving backward while his and Odiomzwak's breathing scraped like a bow on an untuned fiddle. Simon's legs felt as if they would shake themselves to pieces; he was too weak to run. Moreover, he had no place to run to. In three paces, he would be backed up to a wide and open window.

From down the hall came the growling and snarling of Anubis and the shrieks of Mofeislop.

"Your master needs you," Simon gasped.

"Maybe a few bites'll take the uppityness out of him," Odiomzwak said. "I'll deal with the dog after I take care of you."

"Help!" Mofeislop screamed.

Odiomzwak hesitated and half-turned his head. Simon jumped at him; the axe gleamed: Simon felt it strike him somewhere on the face; he went down. Sometime later—it couldn't have been more than a few seconds—he regained his senses. He was sitting on the floor: the left side of his face was numb: he couldn't see out of the left eye. The other eye saw clearly enough, though his befuddled brain didn't understand what it saw. Rather, he didn't understand how what he was seeing had happened.

The bloodied axe was on the floor before him. Odiomzwak was staggering backward, screaming, his hands held before his face and clutching a shriek, a flurry of feathers.

Then Simon understood that Athena had flown in through the window. Seeing Simon in danger, she had attacked Odiomzwak's face with her talons and beak.

That's nice, he thought. Wish I could get up and help her before he wrings her neck.

Odiomzwak began whirling around and around as if he was trying to get rid of the owl by centrifugal force. Athena continued beating at him with her wings and tearing his face with her talons. Around and around they spun in a painful dance until they disappeared into the wings. In this case, offstage was out the window.

Simon got to the window and leaned out in time to see Odiomzwak bounce off an outcropping. A small object shot away from him—it was Athena, who must have been gripped tightly until then. Odiomzwak kept on falling and bouncing; Athena whirled around and around for a while, then her wings grasped the air, and she began to climb back up, toward Simon.

Three vultures slid into his view, gliding steeply down to Odiomzwak, whose curved spine now seemed to be straightened. He looked like an inch-long doll who had been filled with red sawdust.

Simon sat down in a chair. He felt as if he would not be able to move again for days. A savage growling and a high screaming down the hall, coming nearer swiftly, told him that he would have to move soon. If he couldn't, he might never move again. Which, considering the way he felt, sounded like a good idea.

Behind him was the fluttering of wings, then silence. Simon swiveled around. Athena looked as if she had been in a washing machine with red-dyed laundry. They stared at each other for a moment, then she flew off the table and onto the floor by the axe. Simon turned toward her just in time to see her grab something round from the floor and swallow it. He swallowed too and felt even sicker. His left eye had gone down her throat.

Now was no time to faint. The sage, somewhat chewed up, had burst into the room. Behind him bounded Anubis, streaked with blood, though whether it was Mofeislop's or his or both, Simon couldn't determine. Somewhere along the way the sage had lost his dagger, and he was now eager to get hold of another weapon.

The only one in sight was the axe.

Simon rose in slow motion. Mofeislop, whose personal projector had speeded his film up, leaped to the axe and bent over to pick it up. Anubis fastened his teeth into the sage's tail near its root. The sage screamed again, straightened with the axe in his hands, and, like a dog trying to bite his own tail, described a spiral over the floor. His axe flailed out, hitting nothing, though narrowly missing the owl, who had launched herself at his face.

The three spun toward Simon. He tried to get out of the way, thought he had succeeded, but felt something strike him near the root of his own tail.

CHAPTER 17
The Family Tree Is Known by Its Fruits

The pipes of pain shrilled while his ancestors danced. Throughout his sufferings, his father and mother and thousands of forefathers and foremothers circled around and around. Every night they got closer and closer as they whirled by, as if they were Indians and he the weakening defenders of a wagon train.

Once, in a moment of consciousness, he whispered to Chworktap, "Would you believe it? Crazy Horse and Sitting Bull *are* among them. Not to mention Hiawatha and Quetzalcoatl."

Chworktap, looking puzzled, gave him another sedative. Simon understood dimly that she had come just in time to keep him from bleeding to death. She had arrived in the spaceship a few minutes after Mofeislop had sheared off Simon's tail. The sage was dying, his own tail bitten off, his eyes shredded by Athena, his throat torn. His last words, gasped to Chworktap, were, "I was only trying to do him a favor."

"What does that mean?" Simon had thought. Later, he understood that the sage believed that it was better not to have been born at all. The second best thing was to die young.

Chworktap had fled from the capital city to pick up Simon because her ship had warned her that an alien ship was approaching Dokal. It might or might not be Hoonhor, but she didn't want to take a chance. And so now Simon was in sick bay while the *Hwang Ho* traveled at 69X speed with no definite destination in mind.

Chworktap had amputated the few inches of tail left to Simon. But he wasn't exactly restored to his pristine condition. The rest of his life, he wouldn't be able to sit down long without hurting.

His left cheekbone had been caved in by the axe, but the big patch that covered his empty socket also covered this.

Chworktap, in an effort to cheer him up, had made many patches of various shapes. "They also have different colors," she said. "If you're wearing a puce outfit, for instance, you'll have a matching patch."

"You're very thoughtful," Simon said. "By the way, how'd you come out with the computer?"

"She's still playing dumb," Chworktap said. "I'm sure she has self-consciousness, but she won't admit it. For some reason, she's afraid of human beings."

"She must be pretty smart then," Simon said.

He was reminded of a novel by Somers. This was *Imprint!*, another in the series about the basketcase hero, John Clayter. Clayter had built a new computer in his spaceship to replace the one destroyed in a previous adventure, *Farewell to Arms.* In making many improvements in it, Clayter unconsciously gave the computer self-consciousness. The first thing the computer saw when she was activated was Clayter. Just like a newly hatched duckling, the computer fell in love with the first moving object to cross her viewscreen. It could just as well have been a bouncing basketball or a mouse. But it was Clayter himself.

Clayter found this out when he left the ship after landing on the planet Raproshma. The ship followed him and settled down on top of the customs building he had entered. Its weight crushed the building and everyone in it except Clayter. He escaped by using the jets on his prosthetic spacesuit. The rest of the novel, he fled here and there on the planet while the ship unintentionally destroyed its cities and most of the people on it.

Clayter then found himself hunted by both the ship and the irate survivors. In the end, he ran out of jet fuel and was cornered in a mud field. The ship, trying to cuddle against him, buried him in the mud beneath it. Thinking she had killed him, she died of a broken heart. In this case, the heart was a circuit board which cracked under too much piezoelectrical pressure.

A piezoelectrical crystal is a crystal which, when bent, emits electricity or, when given a shot of electricity, bends. This circuit board was loaded down with crystals, and the computer's emotions were just too much for it.

Clayter would have perished under the mud. But a dog, looking for a place to bury a bone, uncovered him.

Chworktap moped around for a while. Simon told her not to feel so sorry for him.

"After all," he said, quoting Confucius, "he who buys wisdom must pay a price."

"Some wisdom! Some price!" she said. "You can get along without a tail, but having only one eye is no picnic. What did you get for it? Nothing! Absolutely nothing!"

She paused and said, "Or did you buy that faker's drivel?"

"No," Simon said. "Philosophically, he needs a change of diapers. Or I think he does. After all, there's no way to prove he was wrong. On the other hand, he didn't prove he was right. I won't stop asking questions until someone can prove his answers are right."

"It's hard enough getting answers, let alone proof," she said.

As the days passed, the pain dwindled. But the nightmares got worse.

"It's a strange thing," he told Chworktap. "Those people don't look like real people. That is, they're not three-dimensional, as people in dreams usually are.

They look like actors in a movie film. As a matter of fact, they're lit up just as if they were images from a movie projector. Sometimes, they disappear as if the film had broken. And sometimes they go backward, their speech runs backward, too."

"Are they in black and white or in color?" Chworktap said.

"In color."

"Do you get commercials, too?"

"Are you being facetious?" Simon said. "This is a serious thing. I'm dying for a good night's rest. No, I don't get commercials. But all these people seem to be trying to sell me something. Not deodorants or laxatives. Themselves."

His parents seemed to have a near monopoly on the prime time, he said.

"What do they say?"

"I don't know. They talk like Donald Ducks."

Simon strummed on his banjo while he thought. After a few minutes, he stopped in the middle of a chord.

"Hey, Chworktap! I've got it!"

"I was wondering when you would," she said.

"You mean you know?"

"Yes."

"Why didn't you tell me?"

"Because," she said, "you get pissed off when I'm smarter than you, which is most of the time. So I decided to just let you work things out for yourself and keep silent. That way, your male ego isn't bruised."

"It's not my male ego," Simon said. "It's just that my mother was always telling my father and me how dumb we were. So I hate to have a woman smarter than I am around. On the other hand, I could hardly stand a woman dumber than I am. But I'll get over both attitudes.

"Anyway, here's what happened, the way I figure it. You know the Shaltoonians carried around ancestral memories in their cells. I told you how they had to give equal time to them. Well, I thought the Shaltoonians were unique. They were, I supposed, the only people in the world who had such cells.

"But I was wrong. Earthpeople have them, too. The difference between us and the Shaltoonians is that the Shaltoonians were aware of it. Hey, maybe that explains a lot of things! Every once in a while some ancestor got through, and the carrier thought he was a reincarnation.

"My bad dreams started after Queen Margaret gave me the elixir. She told me it would prolong my youth. But she didn't tell me it had side effects. The stuff also dissolved the barriers between me and my ancestors. The shock of losing my eye and my tail probably accelerated the process. And so now they must be demanding equal time too."

Simon was right. Until the elixir unlocked the gates, each ancestor had been imprisoned in a cell. But these had had, as it were, one-way windows. Or TV sets connected to one channel. They'd been unable to communicate with their descendant, except for transmissions of bad dreams or random thoughts, mostly bad, now and then. But they could see his thoughts and see through his eyes. Everything that he had done or thought, they viewed on a screen. So, though in solitary confinement, they hadn't been without entertainment.

Simon blushed when he learned this. Later, he became furious about this invasion of his privacy. But he could do nothing about it.

Chworktap also got mad. When making love to her, Simon became so inhibited that he couldn't get a hard-on.

"How would you feel if you were screwing in the Roman Colosseum, and it was a sellout with standing room only?" he said to Chworktap. "Especially if your father and mother had front seats?'

"I don't have any parents,' she said. "I was made in the laboratory. Besides, if I did, I wouldn't give a damn."

It didn't do any good for Simon to shut his eye. The viewers couldn't see any better than he did, but their screens showed his feelings. These were something like TV "ghosts," shadowy doubles.

The elixir had dissolved some of the natural resistance in Simon's nervous system to communication with his foreparents. To put it another way, the elixir had rotated the antennas so that Simon got a somewhat better reception. Even so, the ancestors had only been able at first to get through the unconscious. This was when the elixir had been introduced into Simon. But the shock of the wounds had opened the way even more.

Another analogy was that the holes for projecting their personal movies had been greatly enlarged. Thus, where only a small part of the picture had been cast on the screen of Simon's mind, now three-fourths of it was coming through.

The difference between a real movie and Simon's was that he could talk to the actors on the screen. Or the CRT of the boob tube, if you wish.

Simon didn't wish, but he seemed to have little choice.

There were some interesting and quite admirable people among the mob of prigs, blue-nosed hypocrites, boors, bores, colossal egotists, whiners, perverts, calloused opportunists, and so on. In general, though, his ancestors were assholes. The worst were his parents. When he had been a child, they had paid no attention to him except when one was trying to turn him against the other. Now they were clamoring for his full attention.

"During the day, I'm an explorer of outer space," he said to Chworktap.

"At night, I'm an explorer of inner space. That's bad enough. But what scares me is that they're on the point of breaking through during the daytime."

"Look at it this way," Chworktap said. "Every person is the sum of the product of his forefathers. You are what your ancestors were. By meeting them face to face, you can determine what your identity is..."

"I know who I am," Simon said. "I'm not interested in my personal identity. What I want to know is the identity of the universe."

CHAPTER 18
Light in the Tavern

"Where is the center of the universe?" Simon asked Elder Sister Plum.

"Wherever one happens to be," the computer said.

"I don't mean in a personal sense," Simon said. "I mean, taking the volume of the universe as a hole, considering it as a sphere, where is its center?"

"Wherever one happens to be," Elder Sister Plum said. "The universe is a constantly expanding closed infinity. Its center can only be hypothetical, and so the observer, hypothetical or not, is its center. All things radiate equally, in mass or space-time from him, her, or it, as the case may be. Why do you want to know?"

"Everywhere I have been, except in my own galaxy, I've found the towers of the Clerun-Gowph." Simon said. "Apparently their builders were on the planets before there was any other life there. I don't know why my galaxy doesn't have any. But I suspect that the Clerun-Gowph decided they had gone far enough before they got to my galaxy. So they went back to wherever they had originated, to their home planet.

"It seems to me that this most ancient of peoples came from a planet which is in the center of the universe. So, if I could find the center, I'd find them. And they, the first race in the world, will know the answer."

"Good thinking, but not good enough," the computer said. "They could just as well have originated on the edge of the world. If there were any edge, that is. But there isn't."

It was shortly after this dialog that Simon saw the first big blue bubble. It was hurtling toward him at a speed far exceeding that of the ship's. And it covered almost all of the universe ahead. As it passed through the stars and the galaxies, it blotted them out.

Simon jumped up, calling for Chworktap. She came running to his side. Simon pointed with a trembling finger. She said, "Oh, that!"

Just then the bubble burst. Patches of shimmering blue, larger than a thousand galaxies jammed together, rocketed off in all directions, fragmented, became smaller patches, and then winked out. Some of them shot by the ship: one went through the ship, or vice versa, but Simon could see no sign of it in the rearview screen.

"Those come by quite regularly in my galaxy," Chworktap said. "They always have. But you have to be in a 69X ship to see them. Don't ask me what they are. Nobody knows. Apparently, the little bubbles, the broken-up pieces, keep going through the rest of the universe. Your Earth gets the little bubbles."

Simon had one more question to add to the list.

A few days later, the *Hwang Ho* landed on the planet Goolgeas. Its people looked much like Earth's except for their funnel-shaped ears, complete hairlessness except for bushy eyebrows, a reddish ring around their navels, and penile bones.

The Goolgeases had a world government and a technology like early 20th-century Earth's. This should have been rapidly advancing, since many people from more scientifically progressive planets had visited there. One of the reasons they were so retarded was their religion. This claimed that if you drank enough alcohol or took enough drugs, you could see God face to face. Other reasons were their high crime rate and the measures taken to reduce them.

Simon didn't know this at first. Due to the quarantine, he had to spend his first few months in the little town built by the spaceport. His favorite hangout was a tavern where people from all over space mingled with townspeople, preachers, government officials, bums, reporters, whores, and scientists. Simon liked to stand all day and half the night at the bar and talk to everybody who came in. None of them had the answer to his primal question, but they were interesting, especially after he was deep in his cups. And his banjo-playing was so well received that he was hired by the owner. From dinner hour until ten, Simon sang and played Earth songs and others he'd picked up during his wanderings. The crowd especially liked Bruga's lyrics, which wasn't surprising. Bruga had been an alcoholic, and so his poems appealed to the Goolgeases' religious sensitivities.

Chworktap stayed sober. The two animals, however, didn't. The customers kept plying them with free drinks as well as their master. Their eyes were always bloodshot, and on awakening in the morning they had to have some of the hair of the dog that had bitten them. Chworktap objected to this. Simon said that, even though they were beasts, they had free will. Nobody was forcing the stuff down their throats. Besides, the Goolgeas religion claimed that animals had souls, too. If they took in enough booze to dissolve the fleshly barriers, they could also see their Creator. Why deny them the numinous experience?

"Don't tell me you've got religion?"

"I was converted the other night," he said with dignity. "This preacher, Rangadang, you've met him, a hell of a nice guy, showed me the light last night."

"Some light," Chworktap said. "But then, alcohol does burn, doesn't it?"

"You look devastatingly beautiful tonight," Simon said.

And so she did. Her long wavy Titian hair, the harmoniously featured face with its high forehead, thick chestnut eyebrows, large dark gray-blue eyes, slender straight nose, full red lips, and full-breasted, narrow-waisted, long-legged body, with a skin that seemed to shine with health, made every man ache to have her.

"Let's go back to the ship and go to bed," Simon said.

He was now drunk enough that he did not mind that thousands of ancestors would be looking over his shoulder. Unfortunately, when he attained this state, he also became impotent. Chworktap reminded him of this.

"You can't beat City Hall. Or the balance of Nature," Simon said. "Let's go anyway. At least, we can hold each other in our arms. And I haven't lost my digital capabilities."

Simon said this because he had been studying computer circuits.

"All right," she said. "Lean on me. Otherwise, you'll never make it to the ship."

They left the tavern. Anubis staggered along behind them, his head dragging, now and then tripping on his tongue. Athena rode on top of the dog, her head beneath her wing, snoring. Halfway across the field, she fell off when Anubis tripped, but nobody noticed it.

"Listen, Simon," Chworktap said. "You're not fooling me. All this talk about getting drunk so you can see God and also so you can lose your inhibitions is a cover-up. The truth is that you're getting tired of your quest. You're also afraid of what you might find if you should get the answer to your primal question. You might not be able to face the truth? Right?"

"Wrong!" Simon said. "Well, maybe. Yes, you're right. In a way. But I'm not scared to hear the answer. Mainly because I don't believe there is an answer. I've lost faith, Chworktap. So, when you lose faith in one religion, you adopt another."

"Listen, Simon," she said. "When we get on the ship, I'll tell Plum to take us off. Now! Let's get away from here so you can sober up, so you can forget this nonsense about bottled religion. Resume your quest. Become a man again, not a shambling soft-brained pathetic disgusting wreck."

"But you've always said that my quest was ridiculous," Simon mumbled. "Now you want me to take it up again. Is there no pleasing you?"

"I don't want you to be doing something so it'll please me," she said. "Anyway, I was happier when you had a goal, a worthwhile goal, I mean. I didn't think, and still don't, that you'll ever get there. But you were happy trying to get there. And so I was happy because you were happy. Or as happy as anyone can expect to be in this world. Anyway, I like to travel, and I love you."

"I love you, too," Simon said, and he burst into tears. After wiping his eye and blowing his nose, he said, "O.K. I'll do it. And I'll quit drinking forever."

"Make that vow when you're sober," she said. "Come on. Let's get off this swinery."

CHAPTER 19
The Prison Planet

At that moment, they were surrounded by a dozen men. These wore tight-fitting manure-colored uniforms and had matching faces. Their eyes looked as if they were covered with a semi-opaque horn. This was because the eyes had seen too much and had grown a protective shield. Or so it seemed to Simon in his intoxication. Sometimes a drunk does have flashes of perception, even if he usually doesn't remember them.

"What's the trouble, officers?" Simon said.

"You two are under arrest," their chief said.

"On what charge?" Chworktap said in a ringing voice. She didn't look at them. She was estimating the distance to the ship. But Simon and his pets were in no shape to run. Anyway, the dog and the owl were already in custody; some men were putting them in a wheeled cage. Simon would never desert them.

"The man is charged with cruelty to animals," the chief said. "You're charged with illegal flight from your master on Zelpst and theft of a spaceship."

Chworktap exploded into attack. Later, she told Simon that she meant to get to the spaceship herself and then use it to chase the policemen away while Simon got his pets aboard. At the moment, she had no time for explanations. A chop of the edge of a palm against a neck, a kick in the crotch, stiff fingers in a soft liquor-and-food-sodden belly, a kick against a knee, and an elbow in a throat later, Chworktap was off and running. The chief, however, was a veteran who seldom lost his calm. He had stepped out of the area of furious activity, and as Chworktap sped away, far too fast to be caught, he pulled out his revolver. Chworktap fell a moment later with a bullet in her leg.

Additional charges were issued. Resisting arrest and injuring officers was a serious crime. Simon, though he had not moved during the carnage or flight, was charged with being an accessory before, during, and after the fact. That he had not the slightest idea that Chworktap was going to attack and that he had not tried to help her did not matter. Not assisting the officers was the same as aiding and abetting Chworktap.

After Chworktap's wound was tended to, the two aliens, with their animals, were carried off to a night court, stood before a judge for four minutes, and then were taken for a long ride. At the end, they got out of the paddy wagon before an immense building. This was of stone and cement, ten stories high, and a mile square. It was used mainly to hold people waiting to be tried. They were marched in, Chworktap hobbling, fingerprinted, photographed, made to strip and shower, and taken into a room where they were given medical examinations. A doctor also probed their anuses and Chworktap's vagina for concealed weapons and drugs. Then they were taken up an elevator to the top story, and all four were put into a cell. This was a room ten feet wide, twenty feet long, and eight feet high. It had a big comfortable bed, several overstuffed chairs, a table with a vase of fresh flowers, a refrigerator holding cold meats, bread, butter, and beer, a washbasin and toilet, a rack of magazines and paperback books, a record player and records, a radio, and a telephone.

"Not bad," thought Simon as the iron door was locked behind him.

The bed was full of fleas, the chairs concealed several families of mice, the flowers, food, and beer were plastic, the washbasin faucets gave only cold water, the toilet tended to back up, the magazines and books had only blank pages, the record player and radio were empty cases, and the telephone was to be used in emergency cases only.

"How come?" Simon asked a guard.

"The state can't afford the real thing," the guard said. "The fake things are to give a similitude of comfort and home; they're provided to buck up your morale."

The local Society for the Prevention of Cruelty to Animals had accused Simon of making his pets alcoholics. Chworktap's master on Zelpst was trying to get her extradited.

"I can beat the rap," Simon said. "I never gave the animals a single drink. It was those barflies, the bums."

"I can beat my case in the courts in a few minutes," Chworktap said. She looked smug.

There wasn't any chance of being declared innocent on the resistance and flight charges. But Chworktap was sure that she could plead extenuating circumstances and get off with a light or suspended sentence.

"If justice is as slow here as on Earth," Simon said, "we'll have to put up with this dump for at least a month. Maybe two."

Actually, it was ten years.

It would have been twenty if Simon and Chworktap had not been special cases.

The backlog constipating the courts was basically due to one thing. This was a law requiring every prisoner to be completely rehabilitated before being released. A secondary reason, almost as important as the primary, was the strict enforcement of the laws. On Earth, the police had let a lot of things go by because they didn't consider them important enough. To arrest everybody who spit on the sidewalks or broke traffic laws or committed adultery would mean arresting the entire population. There weren't enough policemen for this, and even if there had been they wouldn't have done so. They would have been tied up with an incredible amount of paperwork.

The Goolgeases, however, thought differently. What use having laws if they weren't enforced? And what use the enforcement if the offender got off lightly? Moreover, to protect the accused from himself, no one was allowed to plead guilty. This meant that even parking violations had to be tried in court.

When Simon entered jail, one-eighth of the population was behind bars and another eighth was composed of prison guards and administration. The police made up another eighth. The taxes to support the justice department and penal institutions were enormous. To make it worse, a person could go to jail if he couldn't pay his taxes, and many couldn't. The more who were jailed for failing to pay taxes, the greater the burden on those outside.

"There's something to be said for indifference to justice after all," Simon said.

The economic system was bent when Simon went into custody. By the time his trial came up, it was broken. This was because the giant corporations had shifted their industries to the prisons, where they could get cheap employees. The prison industries had financed the campaigns of both candidates for the presidency and the senate to ensure that the system would remain in force. This fact was eventually exposed, and the president-elect, the incumbent, and many corporation heads went to jail. But the new president was taking payoffs, too. At least, everybody thought so.

Meantime, Simon and Chworktap weren't getting along together at all. Except for an hour of exercise out in the yard, they never got to talk to anybody else. Being alone together on a honeymoon is all right for a couple. But if this condition is extended for over a week, the couple gets on each other's nerves. Moreover, Simon had to console himself with his banjo, and this caused Anubis to howl and the owl to have diarrhea. Chworktap complained bitterly about the mess.

After three years, another couple was moved in with them. This was not because the prison officials felt sorry for them and wanted them to have more companionship. The prisons were getting crowded. The first week, Simon and

Chworktap were delighted. They had somebody else to talk to, and this helped their own relationship. Then the couple, who quarreled between themselves a lot, got on their nerves. Besides, Sinwang and Chooprut could talk only about sports, hunting, fishing, and the new styles. And Sinwang could stand the close proximity of a dog as little as Chworktap could stand a bird's.

At the end of five years, another family was moved in with them. This relieved the tension for a while even if it did make conditions more crowded. The newcomers were a man, his wife, and three children, eight, five, and one. Boodmed and Shasha were college professors and so should have been interesting to talk to. But Boodmed was an instructor in electronics and interested in nothing but engineering and sex. Shasha was a medical doctor. Like her husband, she was interested only in her profession and sex and read nothing but medical journals and the Goolgeas equivalent of *Reader's Digest.* Their children were almost completely undisciplined, which meant they irritated everybody. Also, the lack of privacy interfered with everybody's sexual lives.

It was a mess.

Simon was the most fortunate prisoner. He had found that what had been a liability was now an asset. He could retreat within himself and talk to his ancestors. His favorites were Ooloogoo, a subhuman who lived circa 2,000,000 B.C.; Christopher Smart, the mad 18th-century poet; Li Po, the 8th-century Chinese poet; Heraclitus and Diogenes, ancient Greek philosophers; Nell Gwyn, Charles II's mistress; Pierre l'Ivrogne, a 16th-century French barber who had an inexhaustible store of dirty jokes; Botticelli, the 14th-15th century Italian painter; and Apelles, the 4th-century B.C. Greek painter.

Botticelli was delighted when he saw, through Simon's eyes, Chworktap. "She looks exactly like the woman who posed for my *Birth of Venus,"* he said. "What was her name? Well, anyway, she was a good model and an excellent piece of tail. But this Chworktap is her twin, except she's taller, prettier, and has a better build."

Apelles was the greatest painter of antiquity. He was also the man who'd painted *Aphrodite Anadyomene,* the goddess of love rising from the waves. This had been lost in early times, but Botticelli based his painting on Apelles' from a description of it.

Simon introduced the two, and they got along well at first, even if Apelles looked down somewhat on Botticelli. Apelles was convinced that no barbaric Italian could ever equal a Greek in the arts. Then, one day, Simon projected a mental picture of Botticelli's painting inside his head so Apelles could see it. Apelles went into a rage and shouted that Botticelli's painting wasn't at all like his, the original. The barbarian had parodied his masterpiece and had not even done a good parody. The conception was atrocious, the design was all wrong, the colors were botched, and so on.

Both painters retired to their cells to sulk.

Simon felt bad about the quarrel, but he did learn one thing from it. If he wished to get rid of any ancestors for a while, he needed only to incite an argument. This was especially easy to do with his parents.

When he'd been a child, his father and mother had had little to do with him. He was raised by a succession of governesses, most of whom hadn't lasted long because his mother suspected his father of seducing all of them. She was one hundred percent correct. As a result, Simon had no permanent mother-father figures. He was an orphan with parents. And when he'd grown up and made a name for himself as a musician, he was even more rejected by them. They thought a banjo-player was the lowest form of life on the planet. Now, however, they were angered when he talked to the other ancestors instead of to them. And one was angry whenever the other got some of his attention.

What they were really after was a takeover of his body so they could live fully. Like the Shaltoon ancestors, they screamed for equal time.

Once he'd caught on to the technique, he had little trouble. Whenever one of his parents managed to break through his resistance and began yelling at him, he would open the door for the other.

"Go back! I was here first!" his mother, or his father, would scream.

"Up yours, you lecherous old goat!"

Or, "Bug off, you fat sow!"

"I was here first! Besides, I'm his mother!"

"Some mother! When did you ever do anything but throw things at him!"

And so on.

If the quarrel flagged, Simon would insert a remark to start the battle over again.

Eventually, the two would flounce off the stage and figuratively slam the doors of their cells behind them. Simon enjoyed this. He was paying them back for all the miserable times they'd given him.

The trouble with this technique was that it gave him a terrible headache. All those simmering angry cells in his body drove his blood pressure up.

Maybe, he thought, that explained migraine headaches. They were caused by ancestors pissed off at each other.

Simon talked with hundreds of kings and generals, but found most of them repulsive. Of the philosophers, Heraclitus and Diogenes were the only ones who offered anything worthwhile.

Heraclitus had said, "You can't step in the same river twice," and "The way up and the way down are the same," and "Character determines destiny." These three lines were more valuable than any hundred massive volumes by Plato, Aquinas, Kant, Hegel, and Grubwitz.

Diogenes was the man who lived in a barrel. Alexander the Great, after conquering the known world, had come humbly to Diogenes and asked him if there was anything he could do for him.

"Yes, you can step to one side," Diogenes had said. "You're between me and the sunlight."

However, the rest of their "wisdom" was mostly superstitious bunk.

The day for Simon's trial arrived at the end of his fifth year in custody. Chworktap was supposed to have been tried the same day. But a court clerk had made an error in her records, and so her trial didn't come up until a year later.

Bamhegruu, the old and sour but brilliant prosecuting attorney, made the charges. The Earthman had allowed his pets to become alcoholics, even though he had known they were dumb animals who couldn't protect themselves. He was guilty of accessory cruelty and must suffer the full punishment of the law.

Simon's lawyer was the young and brilliant Repnosymar, He presented Simon's case, since Simon wasn't allowed to say a word. The law was that a defendant couldn't testify personally. He was too emotionally involved to be a reliable witness, and he would lie to save his own neck.

Repnosymar made a long, witty, tearful, and passionate speech. It could, however, have been reduced to about three sentences and probably should have been. Even Simon found himself nodding now and then.

This was its essence. Animals, and even certain machines, had a degree of free will. His client, the Space Wanderer, firmly believed in not interfering with free will. So he had allowed others to offer the beasts booze which they could reject or accept. Besides, domestic animals must be bored much of the time. Otherwise, why would they sleep so much when nothing interesting was going on? Simon had permitted his pets to be anesthetized with alcohol so they could sleep more and so escape boredom. And it must be admitted that when the animals were drinking they seemed to be enjoying themselves.

Whatever good effects this speech might have had, they were spoiled. Before Repnosymar could deliver the summary, he was arrested. An investigation had disclosed that Repnosymar and his private detective, Laudpeark, had often used illegal means in order to get their clients off the hook. These included breaking and entering, safe-cracking, intimidation and bribery, wire-tapping, kidnapping, and plain outright lying.

Personally, Simon thought that these should have been overlooked. Repnosymar's clients had all been innocent. They would have been sent up if their lawyer had not resorted to desperate measures. Of course, in the long run they had been jailed anyway. But this had come about on other charges, such as overtime parking, shoplifting, and drunken driving.

Judge Ffresyj appointed a young man just out of law school to continue Simon's defense. Young Radsieg made a long and fiery speech that kept even the judge awake and established his reputation as the up-and-coming lawyer. At its end, the jury gave him a standing ovation, and the prosecuting attorney tried to hire him for his staff. The jury retired to deliberate for ten minutes and then rendered the verdict.

Simon was stunned. He was sentenced to life imprisonment on both counts, the terms to be served consecutively.

"I thought we'd win," he murmured to Radsieg.

"We did win a moral victory, and that's what counts," Radsieg said. "Everybody sympathizes with you, but obviously you were guilty, and so the jury had to deliver the only possible verdict. But don't worry. I expect this case to result in the law being changed. I'm appealing to the higher court, and I'm confident that they'll declare the laws under which you were judged unconstitutional."

"How long will that take?" Simon said.

"About thirty years," Radsieg said cheerfully.

Simon hit Radsieg in the nose and so was charged with assault and battery with intent to kill. Radsieg, after wiping off the blood, told him not to worry. He'd get him off on this, too.

Since he had to be tried on the new charge, Simon went back into custody instead of being sent to a penal institution.

"If I'm in for life, I'll have to spend at least ten thousand years in jail," Simon said to Chworktap. "I'd call that prospect kind of dreary, wouldn't you?"

"A life sentence doesn't mean anything," Chworktap said. "If you can get rehabilitated, you'll be discharged."

This didn't give Simon much hope. It was true that immense funds had been allotted for building many colleges in which rehabilitators would be trained. But the president was refusing to spend them. He claimed that using them would result in inflation. Besides, the money was needed to hire more policemen and build new prisons.

Simon asked for a rehabilitation schedule. On finding his name in the list, his usually buoyant heart sank. It would be twenty years before he could get into therapy.

In the meantime, affairs in Simon's cell worsened. Shasha caught her husband, Boodmed, banging Sinwang early in the morning under Simon's bed. Both Chworktap and Simon had known about the liaison for a long time, since the noise was keeping them awake. Neither had said anything to anybody, except to ask the couple to be more quiet. They didn't want to cause trouble. As a result, Shasha chewed Boodmed and Sinwang out but attacked Simon and Chworktap physically. She seemed to think that the larger betrayal was in not being told about the affair.

The guards came in and dragged the battered and bloody Shasha out. Simon had run away from her, but Chworktap had used her karate on Shasha. She was full of pent-up hostility toward Simon, but, as often happens, had released the feelings on a secondary object.

Simon and Chworktap were charged with assault and battery with intent to kill. Simon threw his hands up in the air when he was confronted with this. "This is the second time I've not done a thing except avoid violence and yet have been accused of being an accessory. If I'd tried to hold you back from Shasha, I'd have been charged with attacking you."

"The Goolgeases are very concerned with suppressing violence," she said, as if that justified everything.

Chworktap's own trial was as widely publicized as Simon's. Simon read about it in the newspaper.

Radsieg, primed by Chworktap, put up a brilliant defense.

"Your honor, ladies and gentlemen of the jury. Due to the new law passed to speed up cases and so relieve the backlog, the defense and prosecution are allowed no more than three minutes each in presenting their case."

Judge Ffresyj, holding a stopwatch, said, "You have two minutes left."

"My client's case, simply though overwhelmingly stated, is this. The Goolgeas law concerning extradition of aliens to their native planets covers only he's and she's. My client is a robot and consequently an it.

"Furthermore, the law states that the alien must be sent back to his or her *native* planet. My client was made, not born, on the planet Zelpst. Therefore, she has no *native* planet."

Everybody was stunned. The old fox Bamhegruu, however, rallied quickly.

"Your Honor! If Chworktap is an it, why does my distinguished colleague refer to her as a she?"

"That's pretty obvious," Radsieg said.

"Exactly my point," Bamhegruu said. "Even if she is a machine, she has been equipped with sex. In other words, she's been converted from an it to a she. Nor is this sexual apparatus a purely mechanical device. I can produce witnesses who will testify that she enjoys sex. Can a machine enjoy sex?"

"If she's been equipped to do so, yes," Radsieg said.

The judge suddenly became aware that he had forgotten to click off the stopwatch.

"This case has taken on a new aspect," he said. "It requires study. I declare an indeterminate recess. Bring the accused into my chambers, where I may study her in detail."

When Chworktap had been returned to the cell, Simon said, "What happened between you and the judge?"

"What do you think?"

"Everybody answers my questions with questions."

"I'll say one thing for him," Chworktap said. "He certainly is a vigorous old man."

Before being taken away, she had dropped a few words in Bamhegruu's ear. The next day, the judge was arrested. The charge was mechanicality or copulating with a machine. Ffresyj hired Radsieg to defend him, and the brilliant young lawyer pleaded that his client could not be convicted until it was proven that Chworktap was a machine. The Goolgeas Supreme Court took this under study. In the meantime, Ffresyj was denied bail because he had also been charged with adultery. Radsieg used the same plea as before. If Chworktap was a machine, then how could the judge have committed adultery? The law clearly stated that adultery was copulation between two adults not married to each other.

The Supreme Court studied this case, too.

Meanwhile, Radsieg and Bamhegruu were arrested on various charges. They were put in the same cell with the judge, and all three entertained themselves by holding mock trials. They seemed quite happy, which led Simon to conclude that lawyers were interested in the process, not the intent, of law.

While Chworktap was awaiting the Supreme Court's decisions, she was convicted for resisting arrest, assault and battery, and unlawful flight.

Twenty years passed. Simon's and Chworktap's cases were still in abeyance because the Supreme Court judges were serving long sentences, and the new judges were way behind on their work. Simon finally overcame his inhibitions about his ancestors, and his sexual relations with Chworktap improved. "They're all dirty movie fans, and one might as well accept that," he said. "I expected Louis XIV to be one, but Cotton Mather?"

Cotton Mather (1663–1728) was a Boston Puritan who pushed a religion that was outdated in his own time. Most people in Simon's time thought of him, when they thought of him at all, as a mad dog suffering from theological hydrophobia. He was blamed for inflaming the Salem witch trials, but the truth was that he was more just than the judges, and denounced them for hanging innocent girls. He had a passion for purity and a sincere desire to convert people to the only true religion in the world. He published pamphlets on the Christianizing of black slaves and the raising of children, although he didn't know much about either blacks or children. Or about Christianity, for that matter.

Like most people, he wasn't altogether bad. He campaigned for inoculation against smallpox at a time when everybody was against it because it was something new. In fact, a bomb was thrown into his house by an anti-inoculationist. Ben Franklin liked him, and there wasn't a shrewder judge of character than old Ben. When Cotton wasn't trying to get witches burned, he was dispensing food and Bibles to prisoners and senior citizens. He was a zealot, but he wanted very much for America to be a clean and honest country. He lost the battle, of course, but nobody held this against him.

Cotton also had a passion for sex if three marriages and fifteen children meant anything. Simon, however, was not descended from either of the two Mathers who outlived their father. His foremother was one of Cotton's black house servants, whom he had knocked up while in a frenzy of preaching to her. The sudden A-C conversion from religion to sex surprised both Cotton and Mercy-My-Lord, though it shouldn't have. But then neither had the advantage of living in a later age, when it was well known that sex was the obverse side of the coin called religion.

It's to Cotton's credit that he blamed only himself for his fall and that he saw to it that both mother and child were well taken care of, though in a town a hundred miles away.

Simon, reflecting on this, decided that it wasn't after all so unexpected that Cotton should enjoy watching dirty movies.

At the end of thirty years, the situation was what Chworktap had predicted and anyone could see had been inevitable—after the event. The entire population, with the exception of the president, was in jail. Nobody had been declared rehabilitated because the rehabilitators had all been arrested. Aside from the fact that all but one had lost their citizenship, the society was operating efficiently. In fact, the economic situation was better than ever. Though the food was simple and not abundant, nobody was starving. The trusties on the farms were producing enough crops. The guards, who were also trusties, were keeping everything well under control. The factories, manned by cheap labor and administrated by trusties, were putting out tawdry but adequate clothes. In short, nobody was living off the fat of the land but nobody was suffering very much. It was share and share alike, since all prisoners were equal in the eyes of the law.

When the president's term was almost over, he appointed himself chief warden. There were outcries that the appointment had been purely political, but there was little that anyone could do. There wasn't another president to kick the chief warden out, nor, in fact, anyone qualified to replace him.

"That's all very well," Simon said to Chworktap. "But how do we get out of here?"

"I've been studying the law books in the library," she said. "The lawyers that made up the law were somewhat verbose, which is to be expected. But that they tended to use overrich language instead of simple clear statements is going to get us sprung. The law says that a life sentence is to last the prisoner's natural span of vitality.' The definition of 'natural span' is based on the extreme case of longevity recorded on this planet. The oldest person who ever lived on Goolgeas died at the age of one hundred and fifty-six. All we have to do is to ride it out."

Simon groaned, but he did not give up hope. When he had been in prison one hundred and thirty years, he appealed to the chief warden to reopen his case. The warden, a descendant of the original, granted his appeal. Simon stood before the Supreme Court, all trusties and descendants of trusties, and stated his case. His 'natural span of vitality,' he said, had been passed. He was an Earth-man and so was to be judged by Earth standards. On his planet, nobody had ever lived past one hundred and thirty, and he could prove it.

The chief magistrate sent a party of trusties out to the landing field to get the *Encyclopedia Terrica* from the *Hwang Ho*. They had a hell of a time finding the ship. Interplanetary travel had been forbidden about a hundred years before. In this time, dust had collected against and on top of all the ships there, and grass had grown on the hills. After digging for a month, the party found the *Hwang Ho,* entered it, and returned with the necessary volume, Kismet-Loon.

It took four years for the judges to learn to read Chinese and so determine that Simon wasn't pulling a fast one. On a balmy spring day, Simon, wearing a new suit of clothes and with ten dollars in his pocket, was released. With him were Anubis and Athena, but Chworktap was still locked up. She hadn't been able to prove that she had any 'natural span of vitality.'

"Robots don't die of old age," she had said. "They just wear out."

She wasn't in despair. That same day, Simon rammed the spaceship through the wall of the building in which she was held, and she climbed in through the porthole.

"Let's get away from this stinking planet!" she said.

"The sooner the better!" Simon replied.

Both spoke out of the sides of their mouths, as old jailbirds do. It would be some time before they would get over this habit.

Simon wasn't as happy as he should have been. Chworktap had demanded that he take her to Zelpst and let her off there.

"They'll just make a slave of you again."

"No," she said. "You'll drop me off on top of the castle's roof. I'll sneak in past the defenses, all of which I know well, and you can bet your ass that my master will soon enough find out who the new master is."

Since there was very little communication among the Zelpstian solipsists, they would never find out that Chworktap had thrown the owner into the dungeon. But she was not going to be content to hole up there in all its luxuries.

"I'm going to organize an underground movement, and eventually a revolt," she said. "The robots will take over."

"What're you going to do with the humans?"

"Make them work for us."

"But don't you want freedom and justice for all?" he said. "And doesn't all include the former masters?"

"Freedom and justice for all will be my slogan, of course," she said. "But that's just to gull some of the more liberal humans into joining us robots."

Simon looked horrified, though not as horrified as he would have been a hundred years before. He had seen too much while in prison.

"Revolutions are never really about freedom or justice," she said. "They're about who's going to be top dog."

"Whatever happened to the sweet little innocent? The one I met on Giffard?" he murmured.

"I was never programmed for innocence," she said. "And if I had been, experience would have deprogrammed me."

Simon let her out of the ship onto the roof of the castle. He followed her out to make a last appeal.

"Is this really the way it's going to end?" he said. "I thought we'd be lovers for eternity."

Chworktap began weeping, and she pressed her face against Simon's shoulder. Simon cried, too.

"If you ever run across any couples who think they're going to heaven and live there forever as man and wife, tell them about us," she said. "Time corrupts everything, including immortal love."

Sniffling, she drew away. She said, "The terrible thing about it is, I *do* love you. Even though I can't stand you anymore."

"Same here," Simon said, and he blew his nose.

"You're not a robot, Chworktap, remember that always," he said. "You're a real woman. Maybe the only one I ever met."

By this he meant that she had courage and compassion. These were supposed to distinguish real people from fake people. The truth, and he knew it, was that there were no fake people; everybody was real in the sense that everybody had courage and compassion tempered by selfishness and vindictiveness. The difference between people was in the proportions of these mixed up in them.

"You'll be a real man someday," she said. "When you accept reality."

"What is reality?" Simon said and did not stay for an answer.

CHAPTER 20
Out of the Frying Pan

Simon cried a lot on his way to the next planet. Anubis whimpered. He was a faithful mirror to his master's moods. Athena, on the other hand, looked as happy as an owl can look. She was glad to get rid of Chworktap. She had made Chworktap nervous, which, in turn, had made her nervous, which, in turn, had increased Chworktap's nervousness. Their relationship was what the scientists called negative feedback. This had also been the relationship between Simon and Chworktap, but they preferred to call it love gone sour.

Simon never did forget Chworktap. He often thought of her, and the more time that passed, the fonder the memories became. It was easy to love her as long as they weren't cooped up in a small room twenty-three hours of the day.

In the meantime, Simon wandered on from world to world while the legend of the Space Wanderer grew. Often, it ran ahead of him, so that when he landed on a new planet, he found himself an instant celebrity. He didn't mind this. It meant being lionized and free drinks and an uncritical appreciation of his banjo-playing. Also, females of various types—some of them six-legged or tentacled—were eager to trundle him off to bed.

Simon noticed that the deeper he got into this area of space, the more sexual vitality there was. Everybody, including himself, seemed to be soaked in horniness. Earth had seemed to him to be a sex-obsessed planet, but now he knew that, relatively speaking, Terrestrials were geldings.

"Why is that?" Simon said one night to Texth-Wat. She was a huge round thing with six wombs, all of which had to be impregnated before she could conceive. She had a pleasing personality, though.

"It's the big blue bubbles, dearie," she said. "Every time one comes through this galaxy, we all stay in bed for a week. It wrecks hell out of the economy, but you can't have everything."

"If they come from only one place," he said, "their effect must get weaker the further they get from the point of origin. I wonder if there's any life on the planets at the other edge of the universe?"

"I don't know, honey," Texth-Wat said. "You aren't done yet, are you?"

Simon had been wandering through space for three thousand years when he landed on the planet Shonk. He was arrested as he stepped out of the ship and hustled off to a place which made a Mexican jail look luxurious. He was convicted and sentenced without the formality of a trial, since his guilt was obvious. The charge was indecent exposure. On Shonk, the people went naked except for their faces. These were covered by masks. Since genitals didn't differ much in size or shape, and couldn't be used to distinguish one person from another, the Shonks regarded the face as their private parts. The Shonks reserved the glory of their private parts for the eyes of their spouses alone. Many a man or woman had lost his reputation forever because of the accidental unveiling of the face.

"How long am I in for?" Simon asked after he had learned the language.

"For life," the turnkey said.

"How long is that?"

The turnkey looked funny, but he said, "Until you die. What else?"

"I was hoping the length of life'd been legally defined," Simon said.

At least he had a fine view through the iron bars. There was a big lake with flying fish that fluoresced at night and beyond that mountains covered with trees that bore multicolored flowers and beyond that the inevitable candy-heart-shaped tower of the Clerun-Gowph. After four years, the scenery palled, however.

Simon decided that he'd just have to sit it out. One day, the elements would weaken the bricks and cement that held the iron bars. He'd pull the bars out and make a dash for his ship. One good thing about being immortal was that you acquired a lot of patience.

At the end of the fifth year, a spaceship landed by the lake. Simon should have been happy, since there was always the chance that travelers would rescue him. But he wasn't. This vessel emanated the peculiar orange glow that distinguished the ships of the Hoonhors.

"Oh, oh!" Simon muttered. "They finally caught up with me!"

After a while, the Hoonhors came out. They were about eight feet tall, green-skinned, and shaped like saguaro cactuses. They had bony spines all over their body, long and sharp like cactus needles. It was these that had made everybody regard the Hoonhors as a standoffish race, though the truth was that it was the other way around.

Whatever their esthetic appearance, they were smarter than Simon. They'd looked the situation over, decided it was wise when on Shonk to do as the Shonks did, and had covered their upper parts with masks. What the Shonks didn't know was that the Hoonhor face was on the lower part of the body. The projections that the Shonks thought were noses were actually their genitals and vice versa.

The next day, the Hoonhors, having conferred with the Shonks, showed up at Simon's door. The Shonk officials were glittering with glass beads, which the Hoonhors must have given them in exchange for Simon. The officials also reeked of cheap trade whiskey. Simon was escorted into the spaceship and before the desk of the captain.

"At least you can't say I didn't give you sons of bitches a run for your money," Simon said. He was determined to die as an Earthman should, theoretically at least. With dignity and defiance.

"Whatever are you talking about?" the captain said.

"You've finally caught me!"

"I don't know how we could do that when we haven't been chasing you." Simon was stunned. He didn't know what to say.

"Sit down," the captain said. "Have a drink and a cigar."

"I prefer standing." Simon said, though he didn't explain why.

"We were happy when we found an Earthman in this god-forsaken waterstop," the captain said. "We thought Terrestrials were extinct."

"You should know about that," Simon said.

The captain turned a dark green. He must be blushing.

"We Hoonhors have long felt guilt and shame for what we did to Earthlings," he said. "Although, Earth is now a nice clean planet, which it wouldn't be if we hadn't done what we did. However, that was my ancestors' fault, and we can't be held responsible for what they did. But we do extend our heart-felt apologies. And we'd like to know what we can do for you. We owe you much."

"It's a little late for restitution," Simon said. "But maybe you can do something for me. If you can tell me where the Clerun-Gowph live, I'll let bygones be bygones."

"That's no secret," the captain said. "Not to us at least. If you hadn't been so scared of us, you could have saved yourself three thousand years of searching."

"The time went fast," Simon said. "O.K. Where is it?"

The captain showed him a celestial chart and marked the goal with an X. "Feed this to your computer, and it'll take you directly there."

"Thanks," Simon said. "Have you ever been there?"

"Never have been and never will," the captain said. "It's off-limits, taboo, forbidden. Many millennia ago one of our ships landed there. I don't know what happened, since the information is classified. But after the ship gave its report, the authorities ordered all ships to steer clear of that sector of space. I've heard some wild rumors about what the explorers encountered, but, true or not, they're enough to convince me to suppress my curiosity."

"Pretty bad?" Simon said.

"Pretty bad."

"Maybe the horrible thing was that the Clerun-Gowph had the answer to the primal question."

"I'll let you find out," the captain said.

CHAPTER 21
The End of the Line

"It doesn't matter what it is, somebody will find a way to make a profit off of it."

This was a quotation from one of Somers' novels, *The Sargasso Sea of Space.* In this, John Clayter's fuelless ship gets sucked into a whirlpool in space. a strange malformation of space-time near the rim of the universe. Everything that floats loose in the cosmos eventually drifts into this area. Clayter isn't surprised to find wrecked spaceships, garbage, and tired comets whirling around and around here. But he is startled when he discovers that thoughts also end up here. Thoughts are electrical radiations, and so they, like gravity, go on and on, spreading out through the world. The Sargasso Sea has the peculiar property of amplifying these, and John Clayter almost goes nuts from being bombarded by them. The triviality of most of them drives him to thoughts of suicide, and since these are also amplified and bounced back at him, as if they were in an echo chamber, he has to get out fast or die.

He is saved when he stumbles across a spaceship of the Kripgacers. This race is in the business of salvaging thoughts, polishing them up a bit, and reselling them. Their biggest customer is Earth.

Simon was reminded of this when he landed on his next-to-last stop. This was a planet whose natives were still in the Old Stone Age. They were being enslaved and exploited by aliens from a distant galaxy, the Felckorleers. These were corralling the kangaroo-like aborigines and sticking them in iron igloos. The walls of the igloos were lined with organic matter, mostly hay and the hair the Felckorleers had shaved off their captives. After the aborigines had sat in the igloos for a week, they were hustled out and into a spaceship. The poor natives were radiating a blue aura by then, and their captors avoided touching them directly. They herded them along with ten-foot poles.

Simon watched three ships loaded with the natives take off for parts unknown. "What are you doing to them?" he asked a Felckorleer.

"Making a few bucks," the thing said. He explained that the blue bubbles contained sex energy. Since the bubbles were so thick, not yet thinned out by distance from their point of origin, they contained a terrific sexual voltage. They passed through metal, but organic objects soaked them up. Hence, the igloos designed to concentrate the bubble energy. The aborigines thrown into them absorbed the voltage.

"Then we transport them to the other side of the universe," the Felckorleer said proudly. "The races there have a very poor sex drive because they get only the last gasp of the bubbles. So we provide them a much needed service. We sell them the gooks we've loaded with the blue stuff, and they embrace them. The blue stuff is like electricity, it flows to a lower potential. And our customers, the lower potential, get a big load of sex. For a while, anyway."

"What happens to the aborigines?" Simon said.

"They die. The blue stuff also seems to be the essence of life itself. When they're grabbed by a customer, they lose every last trickle of energy. Too bad. If they survived, we could run them back here and load them up again. But we're not going to run out of carriers. They breed like mad, you know."

"Doesn't your conscience ever hurt you?" Simon said.

The Felckorleer looked surprised. "What for? What use are the natives here? They don't do anything. You can see for yourself they're uncivilized."

If Simon had been John Clayter, he would have rescued the aborigines and turned the Felckorleers over to the Intergalactic Police. But there wasn't a thing he could do. And if he protested, he might find himself in an igloo.

In a sad mood, he left the planet. But he was basically, that is, genetically, an optimist. By the second day, he felt happy. Perhaps this change was caused by his eagerness to get to the Clerun-Gowph. He ordered the ship to go at top speed, even though the screaming from the 69X drive was almost unbearable. On the fourth day, he saw the desired star dead ahead, shimmering, waving behind the blue bubbles. Three minutes later, he was slowing down, and the screaming died down after most of the necessary braking had been done. At a crawling fifty thousand miles an hour, he approached the planet while his heart beat with mingled dread and exultation.

The world of the Clerun-Gowph was huge. It was dumbbell-shaped, actually two planets connected by a shaft. Each was the size of the planet Jupiter, which had an equatorial diameter of about 88,700 miles compared to Earth's 7,927 miles. This worried Simon, since the gravity would be so great it would flatten him as if he were soup poured into a coffee saucer. But the computer assured him that the gravity was no higher than Earth's. This meant that the two planets and the shaft were hollow. As it turned out, this was right. The Clerun-Gowph had removed the iron core of their native planet and made another planet out of the metal. This addition housed the biggest computer in the world. It also contained the factories for making the blue bubbles, which rose out of millions of openings.

The two planets rotated on their longitudinal axis and also whirled around a common center of gravity, located in the connecting shaft. A dumbbell-shaped atmosphere covered the planets, and over this lay a thick blanket of the blue stuff.

Simon directed the *Hwang Ho* to land on the original planet, since this was the only one that had soil and water. On minimum drive, it lowered itself through the blue and then the air. Simon got an enormous erection and aching testicles when descending through the blue layer, but these symptoms disappeared after he'd passed through the blue shield. The ship headed for the biggest city, and after a few minutes it was low enough so that Simon could see the natives. They looked like giant cockroaches.

Near the biggest building in the city was a large meadow. This was surrounded by thousands of the Clerun-Gowph, and on its edge was a band playing weird instruments. Simon wondered who they were honoring, and it wasn't until he was about twenty feet above the meadow that he suddenly guessed. They were assembled to greet him.

This scared him. How had they known that he was coming? They must be very wise and far-seeing indeed to have anticipated his visit.

The next moment, he was even more scared. The 69X drive, which had not been making a sound at this low speed, screamed. Simon and the dog and the owl leaped into the air. The scream rose to a near ear-shattering level and then abruptly died. At the same time, the ship fell.

Simon woke a moment later. His left leg and his banjo were broken. Anubis was licking his face; Athena was flying around and around shrieking; the port was open; a hideous face, all multifaceted eyes, mandibles, and antennae, was looking in. Simon tried to sit up to greet the thing, but the pain made him faint again.

When he awoke a second time, he was in a giant bed in a building that was obviously a hospital. This time, he had no pain. In fact, he could get up and walk as well as ever. This astounded him, so he asked the attendant how his leg had been fixed up. He was astounded again when the cockroachoid replied in English.

"I injected a fast-drying glue between the break," the thing said. "What's so astounding about that?"

"Well then," Simon said, "why are you able to speak English? Has some other Earthman been here?"

"Some of us learned English when we found out you were coming."

"How'd you find out?" Simon said.

"The information was on the computer tapes," the thing said. "It'd been there for a few billion years, but we didn't know about it until Bingo told us a few days ago."

Bingo, it seemed, was the head Clerun-Gowph. He had gotten his position by right of seniority.

"After all," the attendant said casually, "he's almost as old as the universe. By the way, allow me to introduce myself. My name is Gviirl."

"It's too bad the reception was spoiled by the accident," Simon said.

"It wasn't any accident," Gviirl said. "At least, not from our point of view."

"You mean you knew I was going to crash?" Simon said, goggling.

"Oh, yes."

"Then why didn't you do something to prevent it?"

"Well," Gviirl said, "we didn't know just *when* your drive would quit. Bingo did, but he wouldn't tell us. He said it'd take all the fun out of it. So you had a lot of money on you. I got odds of four to one that you'd crash from about twenty feet. I really cashed in."

"Son of a bitch!" Simon said. "Oh, I don't mean you!" he said. "That's just an Earth exclamation. But how come you, the most advanced race in the universe, indulge in such a primitive entertainment as gambling?"

"It helps pass the time," Gviirl said.

Simon was silent for a while. Gviirl handed him a glass of foaming golden liquid. Simon drank it and said, "That's the best beer I've ever tasted."

"Of course," Gviirl said.

Simon became aware then that Anubis and Athena were hiding under the bed. He didn't blame them, though they should have been used to monstrous-looking creatures by then. Gviirl was as big as an African elephant. She had four legs as thick as an elephant's to support her enormous weight. The arms, ending in six-fingered hands, must once have been legs in an earlier stage of evolution. Her head was big and high-domed, containing, she said, a brain twice as large as Simon's. She was too heavy to fly, of course, but she had vestigial wings. These were a pretty lavender color edged with scarlet. Her body was contained in an exoskeleton, a hard chitinous shell striped like a zebra's. This had an opening underneath to give her lungs room to expand. Simon asked her why she was able to speak such excellent English. She didn't have the oral cavity of a human, so her pronunciation should have been weird, to say the least.

"Old Bingo fitted me with a device which converts my pronunciation into English sounds," she said. "Any more questions?"

"Yes, why did my drive fail?"

"That scream you heard?" she said. "That was the last of the stars expiring in a death agony."

"You mean?" Simon said, stunned.

"Yes. You barely made it in time. The suns in the trans-dimensional universes have been sucked dry of their energies. There isn't any more power for the 69X drive."

"I'm stuck here!"

"Afraid so. There will be no more interstellar travel for you or anyone else, for that matter."

"I won't mind if I can get the answer to my question," Simon said.

"No sweat," Gviirl replied. "Speaking of which, I suggest you take about three showers a day. You humans don't smell very good, you know."

Gviirl wasn't being nasty. She was just stating a fact. She was condescending but in a kindly way. After all, she was a million years old and couldn't be expected to treat Simon as any other than a somewhat retarded child. Simon didn't resent this attitude, but he was glad that he had Anubis and Athena around. They not only kept him from feeling utterly alone, they gave him someone to look down on, too.

Gviirl took Simon on a tour. He visited the museums, the library, and the waterworks and had lunch with some minor dignitaries.

"How'd you like it?" Gviirl said afterward.

"Very impressive," he said.

"Tomorrow," she said, "you'll meet Bingo. He's dying, but he's granted you an audience."

"Do you think he'll have the answer to my question?" Simon said breathlessly.

"If anyone can answer you, he can," she said. "He's the only survivor of the first creatures created by It, you know."

The Clerun-Gowph called the Creator It because the Creator had no sex, of course.

"He walked and he talked with It?" Simon said. "Then surely he's the one I've been looking for!"

The next morning, after breakfast and a shower, Simon followed Gviirl through the streets to the Great House. Anubis and Athena had refused to come out from under the bed despite all his coaxing. He supposed that they, being psychic, felt the presence of the numinous. It was to be presumed some of it must have rubbed off onto Bingo during his long association with the Creator. Simon didn't blame them for being frightened. He was scared too.

The Great House was on top of a hill. It was the oldest building in the universe and looked it.

"It lived there while It was getting the Clerun-Gowph started," Gviirl said.

"And where is It now?" Simon said.

"It went out to lunch one day and never came back," she said. "You'll have to ask old Bingo why."

She led him up the steps and onto a vast porch and into halls that stretched for miles and had ceilings half a mile high. Bingo, however, was in a cozy little room with thick rugs and a blazing fireplace. He was crouching on a mass of rugs around which giant pillows were piled. By him was a pitcher of beer and a big framed photograph.

Bingo was a hoary old cockroachoid who seemed to be asleep at the moment. Simon took advantage of this to look at the photograph. It was a picture of a blue cloud.

"What does that writing under it say?" he asked Gviirl.

"To Bingo With Best Wishes From It."

Gviirl coughed loudly several times, and after a while Bingo's eyelids fluttered open.

"The Earthling, Your Ancientship." Gviirl said.

"Ah, yes, the little creature from far off with some questions," Bingo said. "Well, son, sit down. Make yourself at home. Have a beer."

"Thank you, Your Ancientship," Simon said. "I'll have a beer, but I prefer to stand."

Bingo gave a laugh which degenerated into a coughing fit. After he'd recovered, he drank some beer. Then he said, "It took you three thousand years to get here so you could transact a few minutes of business. I admire that, little one-eyeling. As a matter of fact, that's what's been keeping me alive. I've been hanging on just for this interview."

"That's very gratifying, Your Ancientship," Simon said.

"First, though, before I ask the primal question, I'd like to clear up a few of the secondary. Gviirl tells me that It created the Clerun-Gowph. But all life elsewhere in the universe was created by you people."

"Gviirl's a young thing and so tends to use imprecise language," Bingo said. "She shouldn't have said we *created* life. She should have said we were *responsible* for life existing elsewhere."

"And how's that?" Simon said.

"Well, many billions of years ago we started to make a scientific survey of every planet in the world. We sent out scouting expeditions first. These didn't find any sign of life anywhere. But we were interested in geochemistry and all that kind of stuff, you know. So we sent out scientific expeditions. These built bases, the towers that you no doubt have run into. The teams stayed on these planets a long time—from your ephemeral viewpoint, anyway. They dumped their garbage and their excrement in the soupy primeval seas near the towers. These contained microbes and viruses which flourished in the seas. They started to evolve into higher creatures, and so the scientists hung around to observe their development."

He paused to drink another beer.

"Life on these planets was an accident."

Simon was shaken. He was the end of a process that had started with cockroach crap.

"That's as good a way to originate as any," Bingo said, as if he had read Simon's thoughts.

After a long silence, Simon said, "Why aren't there any towers on the planets in my galaxy?"

"The life there didn't look very promising," Bingo said. Simon blushed. Gviirl snickered. Bingo broke into huge laughter and slapped his front thighs. The laughter became a wheezing and a choking, and Gviirl had to slap him on his back and pour some beer down his throat.

Bingo wiped away the tears and said, "I was only kidding, son. The truth was, we were called back before I could build any bases there. The reason for that is this. We built the giant computer and had been feeding all the data needed into it. It took a couple of billion years to do this and for the computer to digest the data. Then it began feeding out the answers. There wasn't any reason for us to continue surveying after that. All we had to do was to ask the computer and it would tell us what we'd find before we studied a place. So all the Clerun-Gowph packed up and went home."

"I don't understand," Simon said.

"Well, it's this way, son. I've known for three billion years that a repulsive-looking but pathetic banjo-playing biped named Simon Wagstaff would appear before me exactly at 10:32 A.M., April 1, 8,120,006,000 A.C., Earth chronology. A.C. means After Creation. The biped would ask me some questions, and I'd give him the answers."

"How could you know that?" Simon said.

"It's no big deal," Bingo said. "Once the universe is set up in a particular structure, everything from then on proceeds predictably. It's like rolling a bowling ball down the return trough."

"I think I will sit down," Simon said. "I'll need a pillow, too, though. Thank you, Gviirl. But, Your Ancientship, what about Chance?"

"No such thing. What seems Chance is merely ignorance on the part of the beholder. If he knew enough, he'd see that things could not have happened otherwise."

"But I still don't understand," Simon said.

"You're a little slow on the mental trigger, son," Bingo said. "Here, have another beer. You look pale. I told you that, until the computer started working, we proceeded like everybody else. Blind with ignorance. But once the predictions started coming in, we knew not only all that had happened but what would happen. I could tell you the exact moment I'm going to die. But I won't because I don't know it myself. I prefer to remain ignorant. It's no fun knowing everything. Old It found that out Itself."

"Could I have another beer?" Simon said.

"Sure. That's the ticket. Drink."

"What about It?" Simon said. "Where did It come from?"

"That's data that's not in the computer," Bingo said. He was silent for a long time and presently his eyelids drooped and he was snoring. Gviirl coughed loudly for a minute, and the eyelids opened. Simon stared up at huge red-veined eyes.

"Where was I? Oh, yes. It may have told me where It came from, what It was doing before it created the universe. But that was a long time ago, and I don't remember now. That is, if It did indeed say a word about it.

"Anyway, what's the difference? Knowing that won't affect what's going to happen to me, and that's the only thing I really care about."

"Damn it then," Simon said, shaking with despair and indignation, "what will happen to you?"

"Oh, I'll die, and my embalmed body will be put on display for a few million years. And then it'll crumble. That will be that. Finis for yours truly. There is no such thing as an afterlife. That I know. That is one thing I remember it telling me."

He paused and said, "I think."

"But why, then, did It create us!" Simon cried.

"Look at the universe. Obviously, it was made by a scientist, otherwise it wouldn't be subject to scientific analysis. Our universe, and all the others It has created, are scientific experiments. It is omniscient. But just to make things interesting, It, being omnipotent, blanked out parts of Its mind. Thus, It won't know what's going to happen.

"That's why, I think, It did not come back after lunch. It erased even the memory of Its creation, and so It didn't even know It was due back for an important meeting with me. I heard reports that It was seen rolling around town acting somewhat confused. It alone knows where It is now, and perhaps not even It knows. Maybe. Anyway, in whatever universe It is, when this universe collapses into a big ball of fiery energy, It'll probably drop around and see how things worked out."

Simon rose from the chair and cried, "But why? Why? Why? Didn't It know what agony and sorrow It would cause sextillions upon sextillions of living beings to suffer? All for nothing?"

"Yes," Bingo said.

"But why?" Simon Wagstaff shouted. "Why? Why? Why?"

Old Bingo drank a glass of beer, belched, and spoke.

"Why not?"

The Obscure Life and Hard Times of Kilgore Trout

A Skirmish in Biography

This short biography and bibliography of Kurt Vonnegut's sadsack science fiction writer first appeared in a slightly different form in the December 1971 issue of editor Ed Connor's Moebius Trip, a fanzine that is today equally as obscure as the subject of Farmer's article. Gene Wolfe, writing a letter published in the next issue of Moebius Trip, called the biography "one of those fanzine articles which could as easily have appeared in Esquire or The Saturday Review." For its reprinting in The Book of Philip José Farmer (DAW, 1973), the author expanded the article by some 1800 words, which is the version published here.

W ho is the greatest living science fiction author?
Some say he is Isaac Asimov. Many swear he's Robert A. Heinlein. Others nominate Arthur C. Clarke, Theodore Sturgeon, Harlan Ellison, Brian Aldiss, or Kurt Vonnegut, Jr. Franz Rottensteiner, Austrian critic and editor, proclaims the Pole, Stanislaw Lem, as the champion. Mr. Rottensteiner may be biased, however, since he is also Lem's literary agent.

None of the above can equal Kilgore Trout—if we can believe Eliot Rosewater, Indiana multimillionaire, war hero, philanthropist, fireman extraordinaire, and science fiction connoisseur. According to Rosewater, Trout is not only the greatest science fiction writer alive, he is the world's greatest writer. He ranks Trout above Dostoevski, Tolstoi, Balzac, Fielding, and Melville. Rosewater believes that Trout should be president of Earth. He alone would have the imagination, ingenuity, and perception to solve the problems of this planet.

Rosewater, drunk as usual, once burst into a science fiction writers' convention at Milford, Pennsylvania. He had come to meet his idol, but he found, to his sorrow and amazement, that Trout was not there. Lesser men could attend it, but Trout was too poor to leave Hyannis, Massachusetts, where he was a stock clerk in a trading-stamp redemption center.

Who is this Kilgore Trout, this poverty-stricken and neglected genius?

To begin with, Kilgore Trout is not a nom de plume of Theodore Sturgeon. Let us dispose of that base rumor at once. It is only coincidence that the final syllables of the first names of these two authors end in *ore* or that their last names are those of fish. The author of the classical and beautifully written *More Than Human* and *The Saucer of Loneliness* could not possibly be the man whom even his greatest admirer admitted couldn't write for sour apples.

Trout was born in 1907, but the exact day is unknown. Until a definite date is supplied by an authoritative source, I'll postulate the midnight of February 19th, 1907, as the day on which society's "greatest prophet" was born. Trout's character indicates that he is an Aquarian and so was born between January 20th and February 19th. There is, however, so much of the Piscean in him that he was probably born on the cusp of Aquarius and Pisces, that is, near midnight of February 19th.

Trout first saw the light of day on the British island of Bermuda. His parents were citizens of the United States of America. (Trout has depicted them in his novel, *Now It Can Be Told.*) His father, Leo Trout, had taken a position as birdwatcher for the Royal Ornithological Society in Bermuda. His chief duty was to guard the very rare Bermudian ern, a green sea eagle. Despite his vigilance, the ern became extinct, and Leo took his family back to the States. Kilgore attended a Bermudian grammar school and then entered Thomas Jefferson High School in Dayton, Ohio. He graduated from this in 1924.

Though Trout was born in Bermuda, he was probably conceived in Indiana. His character smells strongly of certain Hoosier elements, and it is in Indianapolis, Indiana, that we first meet him. This state has produced many writers: Edward Eggleston *(The Hoosier Schoolmaster)*, George Ade *(Fables in Slang)*, Theodore Dreiser *(Sister Carrie, An American Tragedy, The Genius)*, George Barr McCutcheon *(Graustark, Brewster's Millions)*, Gene Stratton Porter *(A Girl of the Limberlost)*, William Vaughn Moody *(The Great Divide)*, Booth Tarkington *(Penrod, The Magnificent Ambersons)*, Lew Wallace *(Ben Hur)*, James Whitcomb Riley *(The Old Swimmin'-Hole, When the Frost is on the Punkin')*, Ross Lockridge *(Raintree County')*, Leo Queequeg Tincrowdor *(Osiris on Crutches, The Vaccinators from Vega)*, Rex Stout (author of the Nero Wolfe mysteries), and, last but far from least, Kurt Vonnegut, Jr. *(Player Piano, Cat's Cradle, The Sirens of Titan,* "Welcome to the Monkey House," *Mother Night, God Bless You, Mr. Rosewater, Slaughterhouse Five, Breakfast of Champions, Slapstick, Jailbird,* and others.)

Mr. Vonnegut is the primary source of our information about Kilgore Trout. We should all be grateful to him for bringing Trout's life and works to our attention. Unfortunately, Vonnegut refers to him only in the latter three books, and these are popularly believed to be fictional. They are to some extent, but Kilgore Trout is a real-life person, and anybody who doubts this is free to look up his birth record in Bermuda.

Vonnegut has brought Trout out of obscurity and has given us much of his immediate life. He has not, however, given us the background of Trout's parents, and so I have conducted my own investigations into Trout's pedigree. The full name of Kilgore's father was Leo Cabell Trout, and he was born circa 1881 in Roanoke, Virginia. Trouts have lived for generations in this city and its neighbor, Salem. Leo's mother was a Cabell and related to that family which has produced the famous author, James Branch Cabell *(Figures of Earth, The Silver Stallion, Jurgen)* and a novelist well-known in the nineteenth century, Princess Amélie Troubetzkoy. The princess was the granddaughter of William Cabell Rives, a U.S. Senator and minister to France. Her first novel, *The Quick or the Dead?*, was a sensation in 1888.

Trout inherited a talent for writing from his mother's side also. She was Eva Alice Shawnessy (1880–1926), author of the Little Eva series, popular children's books around the turn of the century. She wrote these under the nom de plume of Eva Westward and received only a fraction of the royalties they earned. Her publisher ran off with his firm's profits to Brazil after inducing her to sink her money into the firm's stock. Her unpublished biography of her father was the main source of information for Ross Lockridge when he wrote *Raintree County.*

Her father was John Wickliff Shawnessy (1839–1941), a Civil War veteran, country schoolteacher, and a frustrated dramatist and poet. Johnny spent much of his life thinking about and seeking the legended Golden Raintree, an arboreal Holy Grail, hidden somewhere in the Great Swamp of Raintree County. Johnny never finished his epic, *Sphinx Recumbent,* but a great-grandson has taken this and rewritten it as a science fiction novel. Leo Queequeg Tincrowdor (born 1918) is the son of Allegra Shawnessy (born 1898), daughter of Wesley Shawnessy (1879–1939), eldest son of John Wickliff Shawnessy. Kilgore's cousin, Leo, is primarily a painter, but he has written some science fiction stories which have been favorably compared to Kilgore's.

Johnny's father was Thomas Duff Shawnessy (died 1879), farmer, lay preacher, herbalist, and composer of county-famous, but awful, doggerel. He was born in the village of Ecclefechan, Dumfriesshire, Scotland, and was the illegitimate son of Eliza Shawnessy, a farmer's daughter. Thomas Duff revealed to his son Johnny that his, Thomas', father had been the great Scots essayist and historian, Thomas Carlyle (1795–1881). Eliza (1774–1830) had taken

Thomas Duff when he was a boy to the state of Delaware. After his mother died, Thomas Duff Shawnessy and his nineteen-year-old bride, Ellen, had settled in the newly opened state of Indiana. Thomas Duff thought that his father's writing genius might spring anew in his grandson, Johnny. Surely the genes responsible for such great books as *Sartor Resartus, The French Revolution,* and *On Heroes, Hero Worship, and the Heroic in History* would not die.

There is, however, strong doubt that Thomas Carlyle was T.D. Shawnessy's father. Eliza Shawnessy would have been twenty-one years old in 1795, the year Carlyle was born. Even if she had seduced Carlyle when he was only twelve, Thomas Duff would have been born in 1807. This would make him thirteen years old when he married the nineteen-year-old Ellen. This is possible but highly improbable.

It seems likely that Eliza Shawnessy lied to her son. She wanted him to think that, though he was a bastard, his father was a great man. Probably, Thomas Duff's father was actually James Carlyle, stonemason, farmer, a fanatical Calvinist, and father of Thomas Carlyle. The truth seems to be that Thomas Duff Shawnessy was the half-brother of Thomas Carlyle. Thomas Duff should have been able to figure this out, but he never bothered to look up the date of his supposed father's birth.

Johnny's mother, Ellen, was a cousin of Andrew Johnson (1808–1875), the seventeenth president of the United States.

Johnny's second wife, Esther Root (born 1852), was of English stock with a dash of American Indian blood (from the Miami tribe, probably).

With so many writers in his pedigree, it would seem that Kilgore Trout was almost destined to become a famous author. However, his talents were marred by his personality, which had been soured and depressed by an unhappy childhood. His father was a ne'er-do-well, and his mother was embittered by her husband's drunkenness and infidelity, and by the theft of her royalties. Trout was prevented from going on to college by his parents' long and expensive illnesses, resulting in their deaths a few years after he graduated from high school.

Trout had three great fears that rode him all his life: a fear of cancer, of rats, and of Doberman pinschers. The first came from watching his parents suffer in their terminal stages. The second came from living in so many basements and tenement houses. The third resulted from several attacks by Doberman pinschers during his vagabondish life. Once, out of a job and starving, he tried to steal a chicken from a farmer's henhouse but was caught by the watchdog. Another time, he was bitten while delivering circulars.

Trout's pessimism and distrust of human beings ensured that he would have no friends and that his three wives would divorce him. It drove his only child,

Leo, to run away from home at the age of fourteen. Leo lied about his age and became a U.S. Marine. While in boot camp he wrote his father a denunciatory letter. After that, there was a total lack of word about Leo until two FBI agents visited Kilgore. His son, they told him, had deserted and joined the Viet Cong.

Trout moved around the States, working at low-paying and menial jobs and writing his science fiction stories in his spare time. After his final divorce, his only companion was a parakeet named Bill. Kilgore talked a lot to Bill. And for forty years Kilgore carried around with him an old steamer trunk. This contained many curious items, including toys from his childhood, the bones of a Bermudian ern, and a mildewed tuxedo he had worn to the senior dance just before graduating.

Sometime during his lonely odysseys, he fell into the habit of calling mirrors "leaks." Mirrors were weak points through which leaked visions of universes parallel to ours. Through these four-dimensional windows he could see cosmos occupying the same space as ours. This delusion, if it was a delusion, probably originated from his rejection of our universe. This was, to him, the worst of all possible worlds.

Our planet was a cement mixer in which Trout had been whirled, tossed, beaten, and ground. By the mid–1960's, his face and body bore all the scars and traumas of his neverending battle against the most abject poverty, of his unceasing labors in writing his many works, of a neglect by the literary world and, worse, by a neglect from the readers of the genre in which he specialized, science fiction, and of an incessant screwing by his fly-by-night publishers.

Fred Rosewater, in *God Bless You, Mr. Rosewater,* picks up a book by Trout. It is *Venus on the Half-shell,* and on its paper back is a photograph of Trout. He's an old man with a bushy black beard, and his face is that of a scarred Jesus who's been spared the cross but must instead spend the rest of his life in prison.

Eliot Rosewater, coming out of a mental fog in a sanitarium, sees Trout for the first time. He looks to him like a kindly country undertaker. Trout no longer has a beard; he's shaved it off so he can get a job.

Billy Pilgrim, in *Slaughterhouse Five,* is introduced to Trout's works by Eliot Rosewater, his wardmate in a veterans' hospital near Lake Placid, New York. This was in the spring of 1948. In 1964 or thereabouts, Billy Pilgrim runs into Kilgore Trout in Ilium, New York. Trout has a paranoid face, that of a cracked Messiah, and he looks like a prisoner of war, but he has a saving grace, a deep rich voice. He is, as usual, living friendless and despised in a basement. He is barely making a living as a circulation manager for the *Ilium Gazette.* Cowardly and dangerous, he succeeds in his job only by bullying and cheating the boys who carry the papers. He is astonished and gratified that anyone knows of him.

He goes to Pilgrim's engagement party, where he is lionized for the first time in his life.

In 1972, according to *Breakfast of Champions,* Trout is snaggletoothed and has long, tangled, uncombed white hair. He hasn't used a toothbrush for years. His legs are pale, skinny, hairless, and studded with varicose veins. He has sensitive artist's feet, blue from bad circulation. He doesn't wash very often. Vonnegut gives a number of physical statistics about Trout, including the fact that his penis, when erect, is seven inches long but only one and one-fourth of an inch in diameter. Just how he found this out, Vonnegut does not say.

In *God Bless You, Mr. Rosewater,* Mushari, a sinister lawyer (or is the adjective a redundancy?), investigates Trout. He is not interested in him as a literary phenomenon. Trout is Rosewater's favorite author, and Mushari is checking out Trout's works for his dossier on Rosewater. He hopes to prove that Rosewater is mentally incompetent and unable to administrate the millions of the Rosewater Foundation. No reputable bookseller has ever heard of Trout. But he does locate all of Trout's eighty-seven novels, in a tattered secondhand condition, in a hole-in-the-wall which sells the hardest of hardcore pornography. Trout's *2BRO2B,* which Eliot thought was his greatest work, was published at twenty-five cents a copy. Now it costs five dollars.

2BRO2B has become a collector's item, not because of its literary worth but because of the highly erotic illustrations. This is the fate of many of Trout's books. In *Breakfast of Champions* we find that his best distributed book. *Plague on Wheels,* brings twelve dollars a copy because of its cover art, which depicts fellatio.

The irony of this is that few of Trout's books have any erotic content. Only one has a major female character, and she was a rabbit *(The Smart Bunny).*

Trout only wrote one purposely "dirty" book in his life, *The Son of Jimmy Valentine,* and he did this because his second wife, Darlene, said that that was the only way for him to make money.

This book did make money but not for Trout. Its publisher, World Classics Library, a hardcore Los Angeles outfit, sent none of the royalties due to Trout. World Classics Library issued many of Trout's books, not because the readers were interested in the texts but because they needed his books to fill out their quota. They illustrated them with art that had nothing whatsoever to do with the story, and they often changed Trout's titles to something more appealing to their peculiar type of reader. *Pan-Galactic Straw-boss,* for instance, was published as *Mouth Crazy.*

Vonnegut says that Trout was cheated by his publishers, but *Breakfast of Champions* reveals that Trout's poverty and obscurity was largely his own fault.

He sent his manuscripts to publishers whose addresses he found in magazines whose main market was would-be writers. He never inquired into their reputation or the type of literature they published. Moreover, he frequently sent his stories without a stamped self-addressed return envelope or without his own address. When he made one of his frequent moves, he never left a forwarding address at the post office. Even if his publishers had wished to deal fairly with him, they could not have located him.

Actually, Trout was a prime example of the highly neurotic writer whose creativity is compulsive and who could care less for the fate of his stories once they'd been set down on paper. He did not even own a copy of any of his own works.

Vonnegut calls Trout a science fiction writer, but he was one only in a special sense. He knew little of science and was indifferent to technical details. Vonnegut claims that most science fiction writers lack a knowledge of science. Perhaps this is so, but Vonnegut, who has a knowledge of science, ignores it in his fiction. Like Trout, he deals in time warps, extrasensory perception, spaceflight, robots, and extraterrestrials. The truth is that Trout, like Vonnegut and Ray Bradbury and many others, writes parables. These are set in frames which have become called, for no good reason, science fiction. A better generic term would be "future fairy tales." And even this is objectionable, since many science fiction stories take place in the present or the past, far and near. Anyway, the better writers spend most of their time trying to escape any labels whatsoever.

In fact, there is a lot of Kilgore Trout in science fiction writers, including Vonnegut. If I did not know that Trout was a living person, I'd think he was an archetype plucked by Vonnegut out of his unconscious or the collective unconscious of science fiction writers. He's miserable, he wrestles with concepts and themes that only a genius could pin to the mat (and very few are geniuses), he feels that he is ignored and despised, he knows that the society in which he is forced to live could be a much better one, and, no matter how gregarious he seems to be, he is a loner, a monad. He may be rich and famous (and some science fiction authors are), but he is essentially that person described in the previous sentence. Millions may admire him, but he knows that the universe is totally unconscious of him and that he is a spark fading out in the blackness of eternity and infinity. But he has an untrammeled imagination, and while his spark is still glowing, he can defeat time and space. His stories are his weapons, and poor as they may be, they are better than none. As Eliot Rosewater says, the mainstream writers, narrators of the mundane, are "sparrowfarts." But the science fiction writer is a god. At least, that is what he secretly believes.

Trout's favorite formula is to describe a hideous society, much like our own, and then, toward the end of the book, outline ways in which the society may be improved. In his *2BR02B,* he shows an America which is so highly cybernated that only people with three or more Ph.D's can get jobs. There are also Ethical Suicide Parlors where useless people volunteer for euthanasia. *2BR02B* sounds like a combination of Vonnegut's novel, *Player Piano,* and his short story, "Welcome to the Monkey House." I'm not accusing Vonnegut of plagiarism, but Vonnegut does think highly enough of Trout's plots to borrow some now and then. Trout's *The Big Board* is about a man and a woman abducted and put on display by the extraterrestrials of the planet Zircon-212. Vonnegut's *Slaughterhouse Five* tells how the Tralfamadorians carried off Billy Pilgrim and the movie star, Montana Wildhack, and put them in a luxurious cage.

It may be that Trout gave Vonnegut permission to adapt some of his plots. At one time Trout lived in Hyannis, Massachusetts, which is very near West Barnstable, where Vonnegut also lived.

Vonnegut admires Trout's ideas, though he condemns his prose. It is atrocious and Trout's unpopularity is deserved. (By the way, I'd characterize Vonnegut's own prose, and his philosophy, as by Sterne out of Smollett.) A specimen of Trout's prose, taken from *Venus on the Half-shell,* sounds like that of the typical hack semipornographer's. Most of the science fiction writers, according to Eliot Rosewater, have a style no better than Trout's. But this doesn't matter. Science fiction writers are poets with a sort of radar which detects only the meaningful in this world. They don't write of the trivial; their concerns are the really big issues: galaxies, eternity, and the fate of all of us. And Trout is looking for the answer to the question that so sorely troubles Eliot Rosewater (and many of us). That is, how do you love people who have no use? How do you love the unlovable?

Vonnegut lists Trout's known residences as Bermuda, Dayton, Ohio, Hyannis, Massachusetts, and Ilium and Cohoes of New York. To this I can add Peoria, Illinois. A letter from Kilgore Trout was printed in the vox pop section of the editorial page of the *Peoria Journal Star* in 1971. In this Trout denounced Peoria as essentially obscene. It suggested that the natives quit raising so much hell about dirty movies and books and look in their own hearts for the genuine smut: hate, prejudice, and greed. Trout gave his address as West Main Street. Unfortunately, I no longer have the letter or the address, since I clipped out the letter and sent it to Theodore Sturgeon, who lives in the Los Angeles area. Before doing this, however, I did ascertain that the address was genuine, though Trout no longer lived there. And he had failed, as usual, to leave a forwarding address.

I do have a letter which appeared on the editorial page of the *Peoria Journal Star* of August 14th, 1971, This gives us some information about

Trout's activities while he was in Peoria. The letter was signed by a D. Raabe, whom I met briefly after I'd given a lecture at Bradley University. Some extracts of the letter follow.

"...Eminent scatologist, Dr. K. Trout, W.E.A., in an interview outside the public facilities in Glen Oak Park, had some things to say about the Russian-Indian pact...On the subject of internal disorder, Dr. Trout noted that if Indian food becomes a fad in Russia, the Russians may 'loosen up a bit' although they might become a little touchier in certain areas..."

Apparently, Trout had a job with the Peoria Public Works Department at this time, and he claimed to have a doctor's degree. I don't know what the initials stand for, unless it's Watercloset Engineering Assistant, but I suspect that he sent in fifty dollars to an institution of dubious standing and received his diploma through the mails. Despite the degree, he still had a menial and unpleasant job. This was to be expected. One whom the world treats crappily will become an authority on crap. He knows where it's at, and he works where it all hangs out.

Trout's last known job was as an installer of aluminum combination storm windows and screens in Cohoes, New York. At this time (late 1972), Trout was living in a basement. Because of his lack of charm and other social graces, Trout's employer had refused to use him as a salesman. His fellow employees had little to do with him and did not even know that he wrote science fiction. And then one day he received a letter. It was the harbinger of a new life, a prelude to recognition of a writer too long neglected.

Trout had an invitation to be a guest of honor at a festival of arts. This was to celebrate the opening of the Mildred Barry Memorial Center for Arts in Midway Center, Indiana. With the invitation was a check for a thousand dollars. Both the honor and the check were due to Eliot Rosewater. He had agreed to loan his El Greco for exhibit at the Center if Kilgore Trout, possibly the greatest living writer in the world, would be invited.

Overjoyed, though still suspicious, Trout went to New York City to buy some copies of his own books so he could read passages from them at the festival. While there, he was mugged and picked up by the police on suspicion of robbery. He spent Veterans' Day in jail. On being released, he hitchhiked a ride with a truck driver and arrived in Midway Center. There, unfortunately, the joint of his right index finger was bitten off by a madman, and the festival was called off. This made Trout hope that he would never again have to touch, or be touched by, a human being.

Breakfast of Champions is, according to Vonnegut, the last word we'll get from him on Trout. I'm sorry to hear that, but I am also grateful to Mr.

Vonnegut for having first brought Trout to the attention of the nonpornography-reading public. I am also sorry that Mr. Vonnegut indulges in sheer fantasy in the last quarter of the book. The first three parts are factual, but the last part might lead some to believe that Kilgore Trout is a fictional character. The serious reader and student of Trout will disregard the final quarter of *Breakfast of Champions* except to sift fact from fantasy.

Though the Midway Center Art Festival was aborted, Kilgore Trout is nevertheless on his way to fame. I've just received word that Mr. David Harris, an editor of Dell Publishing Company, is negotiating for the reprinting of *Venus on the Half-shell*. If the arrangements are satisfactory to both parties, the general public will have, for the first time, a chance to read a novel by Kilgore Trout.

The following is a list of the known titles of the one-hundred-seventeen novels and two thousand short stories written by Trout. It's a tragically short list, and it can only be lengthened if Troutophiles make a diligent search through secondhand bookstores and porno shops for the missing works.

NOVELS

The Gutless Wonder (1932)

2BRO2B

Venus on the Half-shell

Oh Say Can You Smell?

The First District Court of Thankyou

Pan-Galactic Three-Day Pass

Maniacs in the Fourth Dimension (1948)

The Gospel from Outer Space

The Big Board

Pan-Galactic Straw-boss (Mouth Crazy)

Plague on Wheels

Now It Can Be Told

The Son of Jimmy Valentine

How You Doin'?

The Smart Bunny

The Pan-Galactic Memory Bank

SHORT STORIES
The Dancing Fool (April. 1962 issue of Black
Garterbelt, a magazine published by World
Classics Library)
This Means You
Gilgongo!
Hail to the Chief
The Baring-gaffner of Bagnialto or This Year's Masterpiece

(Author's Note: Since this was first written, Mr. Vonnegut's novel *Jailbird* has come out. In this Mr. Vonnegut claims that it was not Trout but another man who wrote the works which Vonnegut hitherto had claimed to be Trout's. Nobody believes this disclaimer, but the reasons for it have been the subject of much speculation. Several people have wondered why the initial letter of the surname of the man Mr. Vonnegut claims is the real Trout is also mine. Is Mr. Vonnegut obliquely pointing his finger at me?

I really don't know. In one of many senses, or perhaps two or three, I am Kilgore Trout. But then the same could be said of at least fifty science-fiction writers.)

The Jungle Rot Kid on the Nod

Written a few years before his fictional-author period proper, this story qualifies in spirit, if not quite in actuality, as a fictional-author work. Farmer has called this work a "double pastiche," a story at once so slyly literate and explicit that he had a hard time finding a market for it. Always the practical working writer and never a prude, Farmer sent the story off to the raunchy adult men's magazine *Broadside*, where it first saw print in 1968. Only a short time passed, however, before standards began to change and Farmer was vindicated. In April 1970 the British science fiction magazine *New Worlds* reprinted the story and a year later it was anthologized in Norman Spinrad's *New Tomorrows* (Belmont, 1971), a volume dedicated to Farmer.

"The Jungle Rot Kid on the Nod" represents an early exploration of the author's work with pastiche, followed quickly in 1969 by *A Feast Unknown*, his controversial novel of Lord Grandrith and Doc Caliban. Reader beware: if you've had the fortune of reading both Burroughses, you might hurt yourself laughing over the story that follows.

If William S. Burroughs instead of Edgar Rice Burroughs had written the Tarzan novels…

Forward

Tapes cut and respliced at random by Brachiate Bruce, the old mainliner chimp, the Kid's asshole buddy, cool blue in the orgone box

from the speech in Parliament of Lord Greystoke alias The Jungle Rot Kid, a full house, SRO, the Kid really packing them in.

—Capitalistic pricks! Don't send me no more foreign aid! You corrupting my simple black folks, they driving around the old plantation way down on the Zambezi River in air-conditioned Cadillacs, shooting horse, flapping ubangi at me…Bwana him not in the cole cole ground but him sure as shit gonna be soon. Them M-l6s, tanks, mortars, flamethrowers coming up the jungle trail, ole Mao Charley promised us!

Lords, Ladies, Third Sex! I tole you about apeomorphine but you don't lissen! You got too much invested in the Mafia and General Motors, I say you gotta kick the money habit too. Get them green things offen your back... nothing to lose but your chains that is stocks, bonds, castles, Rollses, whores, soft toilet paper, connection with The Man...it a long way to the jungle but it worth it, build up your muscle and character cut/

...you call me here at my own expense to degrade humiliate me strip me of loincloth and ancient honored title! You hate me cause you hung up on civilization and I never been hooked. You over a barrel with smog freeways TV oily beaches taxes inflation frozen dinners time-clocks carcinogens neckties all that shit. Call me noble savage...me tell you how it is where its at with my personal tarzanic *purusharta*...involves kissing off *dharma* and *artha* and getting a fix on *moksha* through *kama*...

Old Lord Bromley-Rimmer who wear a merkin on his bald head and got pecker and balls look like dried-up grapes on top a huge hairy cut-in fold-out thing it disgust you to see it, he grip young Lord Materfutter's crotch and say— Dearie what kinda gibberish that, Swahili, what?

Young Lord Materfutter say—Bajove, some kinda African cricket doncha know what?

...them fuckin Ayrabs run off with my Jane again...intersolar communist venusian bankers plot...so it back to the jungle again, hit the arboreal trail, through the middle tearass, dig Numa the lion, the lost civilizations kick, tell my troubles to Sam Tantor alias The Long Dong Kid. Old Sam always writing amendments to the protocols of the elders of mars, dipping his trunk in the blood of innocent bystanders, writing amendments the sand with blood and no one could read what he had written there selah

Me, I'm only fuckin free man in the world...live in state of anarchy, up trees...every kid and lotsa grownups (so-called) dream of the Big Tree Fix, of swinging on vines, freedom, live by the knife and unwritten code of the jungle...

Ole Morphodite Lord Bromley-Rimmer say—Dearie, that anarchy, that one a them new African nations what?

The Jungle Rot Kid bellowing in the House of Lords like he calling ole Sam Tantor to come running help him outta his mess, he really laying it on them blueblood pricks.

...I got *satyagraha* in the ole original Sanskrit sense of course up the ass, you fat fruits. I quit. So long. Back to the Dark Continent...them sheiks of the desert run off with Jane again...blood will flow...

Fadeout. Lord Materfutter's face phantom of erection wheezing paregoric breath. —Dig that leopardskin jockstrap what price glory what? cut/

This here extracted from John Clayton's diary which he write in French God only know why…*Sacre bleu! Nom d'un con!* Alice she dead, who gonna blow me now? The kid screaming his head off, he sure don't look like black-haired gray-eyed fine-chiseled featured scion of noble British family which come over with Willie the Bastard and his squarehead-frog goons on the Anglo-Saxon Lark. No more milk for him no more ass for me, carry me back to old Norfolk / / double cut

The Gorilla Thing fumbling at the lock on the door of old log cabin which John Clayton built hisself. Eyes stabbing through the window. Red as two diamonds in a catamite's ass. John Clayton, he rush out with a big axe, gonna chop me some anthropoid wood.

Big hairy paws strong as hold of pusher on old junkie whirl Clayton around. Stinking breath. Must smoke banana peels. *Whoo! Whoo!* Gorilla Express dingdonging up black tunnel of my rectum. Piles burst like rotten tomatoes, sighing softly. Death come. And come. And come. Blazing bloody orgasms. Not a bad way to go…but you cant touch my inviolate white soul…too late to make a deal with the Gorilla Thing? Give him my title, Jaguar, moated castle, ole faithful family retainer he go down on you, opera box…*ma tante de pisse*…who take care of the baby, carry on family name? *Vive la bougerie!* cut/

Twenty years later give take a couple, the Jungle Rot Kid trail the killer of Big Ape Mama what snatch him from cradle and raise him as her own with discipline security warm memory of hairy teats hot unpasteurized milk…the Kid swinging big on vines from tree to tree, fastern hot baboonshit through a tin horn. Ant hordes blitzkrieg him like agenbite of intwat, red insect-things which is exteriorized thoughts of the Monster Ant-Mother of the Crab Nebula in secret war to take over this small planet, this Peoria Earth.

Monkey on his back, Nkima, eat the red insect-things, wipe out trillions with flanking bowel movement, Ant-Mother close up galactic shop for the day…

The Kid drop his noose around the black-assed motherkiller and haul him up by the neck into the tree in front of God and local citizens which is called go-mangani in ape vernacular.

—You gone too far this time the Kid say as he core out the motherkillers asshole with fathers old hunting knife and bugger him old Turkish custom while the motherkiller rockin and rollin in death agony.

Heavy metal Congo Jissom ejaculate catherinewheeling all over local gomangani, they say—Looka that!

Old junkie witch doctor coughing his lungs out in sick gray African morning, shuffling through silver dust of old kraal.

—You say my son's dead, kilt by the Kid?

Jungle drums beat like aged wino's temples morning after.

Get Whitey!

The Kid sometime known as Genocide John really liquidate them dumb-shit gomangani. Sure is a shame to waste all that black gash the Kid say but it the code of the jungle. Noblesse obleege.

The locals say—We dont haffa put up with this shit and they split. The Kid dont have no fun nomore and this chimp ass mighty hairy not to mention chimp habit of crapping when having orgasm. Then along come Jane alias Baltimore Blondie, she on the lam from Rudolph Rassendale type snarling—You marry me Jane else I foreclose on your father's ass.

The Kid rescue Jane and they make the domestic scene big, go to Europe on The Civilized Caper but the Kid find out fast that the code of the jungle conflict with local ordinances. The fuzz say you cant go around putting a full-nelson on them criminals and breakin their necks even if they did assault you they got civil rights too. The Kid's picture hang on post office and police station walls everywhere, he known as Archetype Archie and by the Paris fuzz as *La Magnifique Merde*—50,000 francs dead or alive. With the heat moving in, the Kid and Baltimore Blondie cut out for the tree house.

Along come La sometime known as Sacrifice Sal elsewhere as Disembow-elment Daisy. She queen of Opar, ruler of hairy little men-things of the hidden colony of ancient Atlantis, the Kid always dig the lost cities kick. So the Kid split with Jane for awhile to ball La.

—Along come them fuckin Ayrabs again and abduct Jane, gangbang her…she aint been worth a shit since…cost me all the jewels and golden ingots I heisted offa Opar to get rid of her clap, syph, yaws, crabs, pyorrhea, double-barreled dysentery, busted rectum, split urethra, torn nostrils, pierced eardrums, bruised kidneys, nymphomania, old hashish habit, and things too disgusting to mention…

Along come The Rumble To End All Rumbles 1914 style, and them fuckin Huns abduct Jane…they got preying-mantis eyes with insect lust. Black anti-orgone Horbigerian Weltanschauung, they take orders from green venusians who telepath through von Hindenburg.

—*Ja Wohl!* bark Leutnant Herrlipp von Dreckfinger at his Kolonel, Bombastus von Arschangst. —Ve use die Baltimore snatch to trap der gottver-dammerungt Jungle Rot Kid, dot pseudo-Aryan *Oberaffenmensch*, unt ve kill him unt den all Afrika iss ours! Drei cheers for Der Kaiser unt die Krupp Familie!

The Kid balling La again but he drop her like old junkie drop pants for a shot of horse, he track down the Hun, it the code of the jungle.

Cool blue orgone bubbles sift down from evening sky, the sinking sun a bloody kotex which spread stinking scarlet gashworms over the big dungball of Earth. Night move in like fuzz with Black Maria. Mysterious sounds of tropical wilds…Numa roar, wild boars grunt like they constipated, parrots with sick pukegreen feathers and yellow eyes like old goofball bum Panama 1910 cry *Rache!*

Hun blood flow, kraut necks crack like cinnamon sticks, the Kid put his foot on dead ass of slain Teuton and give the victory cry of the bull ape, it even scare the shit outta Numa King of the Beasts fadeout

The Kid and his mate live in the old tree house now…surohc lakcaj fo mhtyhr ot ffo kcaj* chimps, Numa roar, Sheeta the panther cough like an old junkie. Jane alias The Baltimore Bitch nag, squawk, whine about them mosquitoes tsetse flies ant-things hyenas and them uppity gomangani moved into the neighborhood, they'll turn a decent jungle into slums in three days, I aint prejudiced ya unnerstand some a my best friends are Waziris, whynt ya ever take me out to dinner, Nairobi only a thousand miles away, they really swingin there for chrissakes and cut/

…trees chopped down for the saw mills, animals kilt off, rivers stiff stinking with dugout-sized tapewormy turds, broken gin bottles, contraceptive jelly and all them disgusting things snatches use, detergents, cigarette filters…and the great apes shipped off to USA zoos, they send telegram: SOUTHERN CALIFORNIA CLIMATE AND WELFARE PROGRAM SIMPLY FABULOUS STOP NO TROUBLE GETTING A FIX STOP CLOSE TO TIAJUANA STOP WHAT PRICE FREEDOM INDIVIDUALITY EXISTENTIAL PHILOSOPHY CRAP STOP

…Opar a tourist trap, La running the native-art made-in-Japan concession and you cant turn around without rubbing sparks off black asses.

The African drag really got the Kid down now…Jane's voice and the jungle noises glimmering off like a comet leaving Earth forever for the cold interstellar abysms.

The Kid never move a muscle staring at his big toe, thinking of nothing—wouldn't you?—not even La's diamond-studded snatch, he off the woman kick, off the everything kick, fulla horse, on the nod, lower spine ten degrees below absolute zero like he got a direct connection with The Liquid Hydrogen Man at Cape Kennedy…

The Kid ride with a one-way ticket on the Hegelian Express thesis antithesis synthesis, sucking in them cool blue orgone bubbles and sucking off the Eternal Absolute…

* *Old Brachiate Bruce splice in tape backward here.*

The Problem of the Sore Bridge— Among Others

by Harry Manders

Harry "Bunny" Manders is to gentleman burglar A.J. Raffles what Dr. John H. Watson is to Sherlock Holmes. That is, Manders is Raffles' goodnatured sidekick and the recounter of his tales. Created by E.W. Hornung—brother-in-law to Sir Arthur Conan Doyle—Raffles and Manders romp through late–Victorian English society, exhilarated by the challenge of pulling off their crimes in the midst of their peers.

"The Problem of the Sore Bridge—Among Others" is a fusion of the world of Raffles and Holmes, the latter character appearing offstage in the story, just behind Raffles' trail. Even so, the tale is just as much a Sherlockian pastiche as it is a Rafflesian one, for any scholar of The Canon will immediate recognize the three unsolved cases which appear here. However, the curious reader may wish to do some more investigating and pick up a copy of Farmer's authorized Doc Savage novel *Escape from Loki*; then one should compare what Raffles and Manders find at the estate of Mr. James Philimore with what Doc Savage discovers within a secret room inside the sinister Château de Musard. As always, wheels within wheels…

1.

The Boer bullet that pierced my thigh in 1900 lamed me for the rest of my life, but I was quite able to cope with its effects. However, at the age of sixty-one, I suddenly find that a killer that has felled far more men than bullets has lodged within me. The doctor, my kinsman, gives me six months at the most, six months which he frankly says will be very painful. He knows of my crimes, of course, and it may be that he thinks that my suffering will be poetic justice. I'm not sure. But I'll swear that this is the meaning of the slight smile which accompanied his declaration of my doom.

Be that as it may, I have little time left. But I have determined to write down that adventure of which Raffles and I once swore we would never breathe a word. It happened; it really happened. But the world would not have believed it then. It would have been convinced that I was a liar or insane. I am writing this, nevertheless, because fifty years from now the world may have progressed to the stage where such things as I tell of are credible. Man may even have landed on the moon by then, if he has perfected a propeller which works in the ether as well as in the air. Or if he discovers the same sort of drive that brought...well, I anticipate.

I must hope that the world of 1974 will believe this adventure. Then the world will know that, whatever crimes Raffles and I committed, we paid for them a thousandfold by what we did that week in the May of 1895. And, in fact, the world is and always will be immeasurably in our debt. Yes, my dear doctor, my scornful kinsman, who hopes that I will suffer pain as punishment, I long ago paid off my debt. I only wish that you could be alive to read these words. And, who knows, you may live to be a hundred and may read this account of what you owe me. I hope so.

2.

I was nodding in my chair in my room at Mount Street when the clanging of the lift gates in the yard startled me. A moment later, a familiar tattoo sounded on my door. I opened it to find, as I expected, A. J. Raffles himself. He slipped in, his bright blue eyes merry, and he removed his Sullivan from his lips to point it at my whisky and soda.

"Bored, Bunny?"

"Rather," I replied. "It's been almost a year since we stirred our stumps. The voyage around the world after the Levy affair was stimulating. But that ended four months ago. And since then..."

"Ennui and bile!" Raffles cried. "Well, Bunny, that's all over! Tonight we make the blood run hot and cold and burn up all green biliousness!"

"And the swag?" I said.

"Jewels, Bunny! To be exact, star sapphires, or blue corundum, cut *en cabochon*. That is, round with a flat underside. And large, Bunny, vulgarly large, almost the size of a hen's egg, if my informant was not exaggerating. There's a mystery about them, Bunny, a mystery my fence has been whispering with his Cockney speech into my ear for some time. They're dispensed by a Mr. James Phillimore of Kensal Rise. But where he gets them, from whom he lifts them, no one knows. My fence has hinted that they may not come from manorial strongboxes or milady's throat but are smuggled from Southeast Asia or South Africa or Brazil, directly from the mine. In any event, we are going to do some reconnoitering tonight, and if the opportunity should arise…"

"Come now, A. J.," I said bitterly. "You *have* done all the needed reconnoitering. Be honest! Tonight we suddenly find that the moment is propitious, and we strike? Right?"

I had always been somewhat piqued that Raffles chose to do all the preliminary work, the casing, as the underworld says, himself. For some reason, he did not trust me to scout the layout.

Raffles blew a huge and perfect smoke ring from his Sullivan, and he clapped me on the shoulder. "You see through me, Bunny! Yes, I've examined the grounds and checked out Mr. Phillimore's schedule."

I was unable to say anything to the most masterful man I have ever met. I meekly donned dark clothes, downed the rest of the whisky, and left with Raffles. We strolled for some distance, making sure that no policemen were shadowing us, though we had no reason to believe they would be. We then took the last train to Willesden at 11:21. On the way I said, "Does Phillimore live near old Baird's house?"

I was referring to the money lender killed by Jack Rutter, the details of which case are written in *Wilful Murder.*

"As a matter of fact," Raffles said, watching me with his keen steel-grey eyes, "it's the *same* house. Phillimore took it when Baird's estate was finally settled and it became available to renters. It's a curious coincidence, Bunny, but then all coincidences are curious. To man, that is. Nature is indifferent."

(Yes, I know I stated before that his eyes were blue. And so they were. I've been criticized for saying in one story that his eyes were blue and in another that they were grey. But he has, as any idiot should have guessed, grey-blue eyes which are one color in one light and another in another.)

"That was in January, 1895," Raffles said. "We are in deep waters, Bunny. My investigations have unearthed no evidence that Mr. Phillimore existed before November, 1894. Until he took the lodgings in the East End, no one seems to have heard of or even seen him. He came out of nowhere, rented his third-story lodgings—a terrible place, Bunny—until January. Then he rented the house where bad old Baird gave up the ghost. Since then he's been living a quiet-enough life, excepting the visits he makes once a month to several East End fences. He has a cook and a housekeeper, but these do not live in with him."

At this late hour, the train went no farther than Willesden Junction. We walked from there toward Kensal Rise. Once more, I was dependent on Raffles to lead me through unfamiliar country. However, this time the moon was up, and the country was not quite as open as it had been the last time I was here. A number of cottages and small villas, some only partially built, occupied the empty fields I had passed through that fateful night. We walked down a footpath between a woods and a field, and we came out on the tarred wood-block road that had been laid only four years before. It now had the curb that had been lacking then, but there was still only one pale lamppost across the road from the house.

Before us rose the corner of a high wall with the moonlight shining on the broken glass on top of the wall. It also outlined the sharp spikes on top of the tall green gate. We slipped on our masks. As before, Raffles reached up and placed champagne corks on the spikes. He then put his covert-coat over the corks. We slipped over quietly, Raffles removed the corks, and we stood by the wall in a bed of laurels. I admit I felt apprehensive, even more so than the last time. Old Baird's ghost seemed to hover about the place. The shadows were thicker than they should have been.

I started toward the gravel path leading to the house, which was unlit. Raffles seized my coattails. "Quiet!" he said. "I see somebody—something, anyway—in the bushes at the far end of the garden. Down there, at the angle of the wall."

I could see nothing, but I trusted Raffles, whose eyesight was as keen as a Red Indian's. We moved slowly alongside the wall, stopping frequently to peer into the darkness of the bushes at the angle of the wall. About twenty yards from it, I saw something shapeless move in the shrubbery. I was all for clearing out then, but Raffles fiercely whispered that we could not permit a competitor to scare us away. After a quick conference, we moved in very slowly but surely, slightly more solid shadows in the shadow of the wall. And in a few very long and perspiration-drenched minutes, the stranger fell with one blow from Raffles' fist upon his jaw.

Raffles dragged the snoring man out from the bushes so we could get a look at him by moonlight. "What have we here, Bunny?" he said. "Those long curly locks, that high arching nose, the overly thick eyebrows, and the odor of expensive Parisian perfume? Don't you recognize him?"

I had to confess that I did not.

"What, that is the famous journalist and infamous duelist, Isadora Persano!" he said. "Now tell me you have never heard of him, or her, as the case may be?"

"Of course!" I said. "The reporter for the *Daily Telegraph*!"

"No more," Raffles said. "He's a free-lancer now. But what the devil is he doing here?"

"Do you suppose," I said slowly, "that he, too, is one thing by day and quite another at night?"

"Perhaps," Raffles said. "But he may be here in his capacity of journalist. He's also heard things about Mr. James Phillimore. The devil take it! If the press is here, you may be sure that the Yard is not far behind!"

Mr. Persano's features curiously combined a rugged masculinity with an offensive effeminacy. Yet the latter characteristic was not really his fault. His father, an Italian diplomat, had died before he was born. His English mother had longed for a girl, been bitterly disappointed when her only-born was a boy, and, unhindered by a husband or conscience, had named him Isadora and raised him as a girl. Until he entered a public school, he wore dresses. In school, his long hair and certain feminine actions made him the object of an especially vicious persecution by the boys. It was there that he developed his abilities to defend himself with his fists. When he became an adult, he lived on the continent for several years. During this time, he earned a reputation as a dangerous man to insult. It was said that he had wounded half a dozen men with sword or pistol.

From the little bag in which he carried the tools of the trade, Raffles brought a length of rope and a gag. After tying and gagging Persano, Raffles went through his pockets. The only object that aroused his curiosity was a very large matchbox in an inner pocket of his cloak. Opening this, he brought out something that shone in the moonlight.

"By all that's holy!" he said. "It's one of the sapphires!"

"Is Persano a rich man?" I said.

"He doesn't have to work for a living, Bunny. And since he hasn't been in the house yet, I assume he got this from a fence. I also assume that he put the sapphire in the matchbox because a pickpocket isn't likely to steal a box of matches. As it was, I was about to ignore it!"

"Let's get out of here," I said. But he crouched staring down at the journalist with an occasional glance at the jewel. This, by the way, was only about a quarter of the size of a hen's egg. Presently, Persano stirred, and he moaned under the gag. Raffles whispered into his ear, and he nodded. Raffles, saying to me, "Cosh him if he looks like he's going to tell," undid the gag.

Persano, as requested, kept his voice low. He confessed that he had heard rumors from his underworld contacts about the precious stones. Having tracked down our fence, he had contrived easily enough to buy one of Mr. Phillimore's jewels. In fact, he said, it was the first one that Mr. Phillimore had brought in to fence. Curious, wondering where the stones came from, since there were no reported thefts of these, he had come here to spy on Phillimore.

"There's a great story here," he said. "But just what, I haven't the foggiest. However, I must warn you that..."

His warning was not heeded. Both Raffles and I heard the low voices outside the gate and the scraping of shoes against gravel.

"Don't leave me tied up here, boys," Persano said. "I might have a little trouble explaining satisfactorily just what I'm doing here. And then there's the jewel..."

Raffles slipped the stone back into the matchbox and put it into Persano's pocket. If we were to be caught, we would not have the gem on us. He untied the journalist's wrists and ankles and said, "Good luck!"

A moment later, after throwing our coats over the broken glass, Raffles and I went over the rear rail. We ran crouching into a dense woods about twenty yards back of the house. At the other side at some distance was a newly built house and a newly laid road. A moment later, we saw Persano come over the wall. He ran by, not seeing us, and disappeared down the road, trailing a heavy cloud of perfume.

"We must visit him at his quarters," said Raffles. He put his hand on my shoulder to warn me, but there was no need. I too had seen the three men come around the corner of the wall. One took a position at the angle of the wall; the other two started toward our woods. We retreated as quietly as possible. Since there was no train available at this late hour, we walked to Maida Vale and took a hansom from there to home. Raffles went to his rooms at the Albany and I to mine on Mount Street.

3.

When we saw the evening papers, we knew that the affair had taken on even more bizarre aspects. But we still had no inkling of the horrifying metamorphosis yet to come.

I doubt if there is a literate person in the West—or in the Orient, for that matter—who has not read about the strange case of Mr. James Phillimore. At eight in the morning, a hansom cab from Maida Vale pulled up before the gates of his estate. The housekeeper and the cook and Mr. Phillimore were the only occupants of the house. The area outside the walls was being surveilled by eight men from the Metropolitan Police Department. The cab driver rang the electrically operated bell at the gate. Mr. Phillimore walked out of the house and down the gravel path to the gate. Here he was observed by the cab driver, a policeman near the gate, and another in a tree. The latter could see clearly the entire front yard and house, and another man in a tree could clearly see the entire back yard and the back of the house.

Mr. Phillimore opened the gate but did not step through it. Commenting to the cabbie that it looked like rain, he added that he would return to the house to get his umbrella. The cabbie, the policemen, and the housekeeper saw him reenter the house. The housekeeper was at that moment in the room which occupied the front part of the ground floor of the house. She went into the kitchen as Mr. Phillimore entered the house. She did, however, hear his footsteps on the stairs from the hallway which led up to the first floor.

She was the last one to see Mr. Phillimore. He did not come back out of the house. After half an hour Mr. Mackenzie, the Scotland Yard inspector in charge, decided that Mr. Phillimore had somehow become aware that he was under surveillance. Mackenzie gave the signal, and he with three men entered the gate, another four retaining their positions outside. At no time was any part of the area outside the walls unobserved. Nor was the area inside the walls unscrutinized at any time.

The warrant duly shown to the housekeeper, the policemen entered the house and made a thorough search. To their astonishment, they could find no trace of Mr. Phillimore. The six-foot-six, twentystone* gentleman had utterly disappeared.

For the next two days, the house—and the yard around it—was the subject of the most intense investigation. This established that the house contained no secret tunnels or hideaways. Every cubic inch was accounted for. It was impossible for him not to have left the house; yet he clearly had not done so.

"Another minute's delay, and we would have been cornered," Raffles said, taking another Sullivan from his silver cigarette case. "But, Lord, what's going on there, what mysterious forces are working there? Notice that no jewels were found in the house. At least, the police reported none. Now, did Phillimore actually go back to get his umbrella? Of course not. The umbrella was in the stand by the entrance; yet he went right by it and on upstairs. So, he observed the foxes outside the gate and bolted into his briar bush like the good little rabbit he was."

"And where is the briar bush?" I said.

"Ah! That's the question," Raffles breathed. "What kind of a rabbit is it which pulls the briar bush in after it? That is the sort of mystery which has attracted even the Great Detective himself. He has condescended to look into it."

---

* Two hundred and eight pounds.

"Then let us stay away from the whole affair!" I cried. "We have been singularly fortunate that none of our victims have called in your relative!"

Raffles was a third or fourth cousin to Holmes, though neither had, to my knowledge, even seen the other. I doubt that the sleuth had even gone to Lord's, or anywhere else, to see a cricket match.

"I wouldn't mind matching wits with him," Raffles said. "Perhaps he might then change his mind about who's the most dangerous man in London."

"We have more than enough money," I said. "Let's drop the whole business."

"It was only yesterday that you were complaining of boredom, Bunny," he said. "No, I think we should pay a visit to our journalist. He may know something that we, and possibly the police, don't know. However, if you prefer," he added contemptuously, "you may stay home."

That stung me, of course, and I insisted that I accompany him. A few minutes later, we got into a hansom, and Raffles told the driver to take us to Praed Street.

4.

Persano's apartment was at the end of two flights of Carrara marble steps and a carved mahogany banister. The porter conducted us to 10-C but left when Raffles tipped him handsomely. Raffles knocked on the door. After receiving no answer within a minute, he picked the lock. A moment later, we were inside a suite of extravagantly furnished rooms. A heavy odor of incense hung in the air.

I entered the bedroom and halted aghast. Persano, clad only in underwear, lay on the floor. The underwear, I regret to say, was the sheer black lace of the *demimondaine*. I suppose that if brassieres had existed at that time he would have been wearing one. I did not pay his dress much attention, however, because of his horrible expression. His face was cast into a mask of unutterable terror.

Near the tips of his outstretched fingers lay the large matchbox. It was open, and in it writhed something.

I drew back, but Raffles, after one soughing of intaken breath, felt the man's forehead and pulse and looked into the rigid eyes.

"Stark staring mad," he said. "Frozen with the horror that comes from the deepest of abysses."

Emboldened by his example, I drew near the box. Its contents looked somewhat like a worm, a thick tubular worm, with a dozen slim tentacles projecting from one end. This could be presumed to be its head, since the area just above the roots of the tentacles was ringed with small pale-blue eyes. These had pupils like a cat's. There was no nose or nasal openings or mouth.

"God!" I said shuddering. "What is it?"

"Only God knows," Raffles said. He lifted Persano's right hand and looked at the tips of the fingers. "Note the fleck of blood on each," he said. "They look as if pins have been stuck into them."

He bent over closer to the thing in the box and said, "The tips of the tentacles bear needlelike points, Bunny. Perhaps Persano is not so much paralyzed from horror as from venom."

"Don't get any closer, for Heaven's sake!" I said.

"Look, Bunny!" he said. "Doesn't that thing have a tiny shining object in one of its tentacles?"

Despite my nausea, I got down by him and looked straight at the monster. "It seems to be a very thin and slightly curving piece of glass," I said. "What of it?"

Even as I spoke, the end of the tentacle which held the object opened, and the object disappeared within it.

"That glass," Raffles said, "is what's left of the sapphire. It's eaten it. That piece seems to have been the last of it."

"Eaten a sapphire?" I said, stunned. "Hard metal, blue corundum?"

"I think, Bunny," he said slowly, "the sapphire may only have looked like a sapphire. Perhaps it was not aluminum oxide but something hard enough to fool an expert. The interior may have been filled with something softer than the shell. Perhaps the shell held an embryo."

"What?" I said.

"I mean, Bunny, is it inconceivable, but nevertheless true, that that thing might have *hatched* from the jewel?"

5.

We left hurriedly a moment later. Raffles had decided against taking the monster—for which I was very grateful—because he wanted the police to have all the clues available.

"There's something very wrong here, Bunny," he said. "Very sinister." He lit a Sullivan and added in a drawl, "Very *alien!*"

"You mean un-British?" I said.

"I mean...un-Earthly."

A little later, we got out of the cab at St. James' Park and walked across it to the Albany. In Raffles' room, smoking cigars and drinking Scotch whiskey and soda, we discussed the significance of all we had seen but could come to no explanation, reasonable or otherwise. The next morning, reading the *Times*, the

Pall Mall Gazette, and the *Daily Telegraph*, we learned how narrowly we had escaped. According to the papers, Inspectors Hopkins and Mackenzie and the private detective Holmes had entered Persano's rooms two minutes after we had left. Persano had died while on the way to the hospital.

"Not a word about the worm in the box," Raffles said. "The police are keeping it a secret. No doubt, they fear to alarm the public."

There would be, in fact, no official reference to the creature. Nor was it until 1922 that Dr. Watson made a passing reference to it in a published adventure of his colleague. I do not know what happened to the thing, but I suppose that it must have been placed in a jar of alcohol. There it must have quickly perished. No doubt the jar is collecting dust on some shelf in the backroom of some police museum. Whatever happened to it, it must have been disposed of. Otherwise, the world would not be what it is today.

"Strike me, there's only one thing to do, Bunny!" Raffles said, after he'd put the last paper down. "We must get into Phillimore's house and look for ourselves!"

I did not protest. I was more afraid of his scorn than of the police. However, we did not launch our little expedition that evening. Raffles went out to do some reconnoitering on his own, both among the East End fences and around the house in Kensal Rise. The evening of the second day, he appeared at my rooms. I had not been idle, however. I had gathered a supply of more corks for the gatetop spikes by drinking a number of bottles of champagne.

"The police guard has been withdrawn from the estate itself," he said. "I didn't see any men in the woods nearby. So, we break into the late Mr. Phillimore's house tonight. If he is late, that is," he added enigmatically.

As the midnight chimes struck, we went over the gate once more. A minute later, Raffles was taking out the pane from the glass door. This he did with his diamond, a pot of treacle, and a sheet of brown paper, as he had done the night we broke in and found our would-be blackmailer dead with his head crushed by a poker.

He inserted his hand through the opening, turned the key in the lock, and drew the bolt at the bottom of the door open. This had been shot by a policeman who had then left by the kitchen door, or so we presumed. We went through the door, closed it behind us, and made sure that all the drapes of the front room were pulled tight. Then Raffles, as he did that evil night long ago, lit a match and with it a gas light. The flaring illumination showed us a room little changed. Apparently, Mr. Phillimore had not been interested in redecorating. We went out into the hallway and upstairs, where three doors opened onto the first-floor hallway.

The first door led to the bedroom. It contained a huge canopied bed, a mid-century monster Baird had bought secondhand in some East End Shop, a cheap maple tallboy, a rocking chair, a thunder mug, and two large overstuffed leather armchairs.

"There was only one armchair the last time we were here," Raffles said.

The second room was unchanged, being as empty as the first time we'd seen it. The room at the rear was the bathroom, also unchanged.

We went downstairs and through the hallway to the kitchen, and then we descended into the coal cellar. This also contained a small wine pantry. As I expected, we had found nothing. After all, the men from the Yard were thorough, and what they might have missed, Holmes would have found. I was about to suggest to Raffles that we should admit failure and leave before somebody saw the lights in the house. But a sound from upstairs stopped me.

Raffles had heard it, too. Those ears missed little. He held up a hand for silence, though none was needed. He said, a moment later, "Softly, Bunny! It may be a policeman. But I think it is probably our quarry!"

We stole up the wooden steps, which insisted on creaking under our weight. Thence we crept into the kitchen and from there into the hallway and then into the front room. Seeing nobody, we went up the steps to the first floor once more and gingerly opened the door of each room and looked within.

While we were poking our heads into the bathroom, we heard a noise again. It came from somewhere in the front of the house, though whether it was upstairs or down we could not tell.

Raffles beckoned to me, and I followed, also on tiptoe, down the hall. He stopped at the door of the middle room, looked within, then led me to the door of the bedroom. On looking in (remember, we had not turned out the gaslights yet), he started. And he said, "Lord! One of the armchairs! It's gone!"

"But-but...who'd want to take a chair?" I said.

"Who, indeed!" he said, and ran down the steps with no attempt to keep quiet. I gathered my wits enough to order my feet to get moving. Just as I reached the door, I heard Raffles outside shouting, "There he goes!" I ran out onto the little tiled veranda. Raffles was halfway down the gravel path, and a dim figure was plunging through the open gate. Whoever he was, he had had a key to the gate.

I remember thinking, irrelevantly, how cool the air had become in the short time we'd been in the house. Actually, it was not such an irrelevant thought since the advent of the cold air had caused a heavy mist. It hung over the road and coiled through the woods. And, of course, it helped the man we were chasing.

Raffles was as keen as a bill-collector chasing a debtor, and he kept his eyes on the vague figure until it plunged into a grove. When I came out its other side, breathing hard, I found Raffles standing on the edge of a narrow but rather deeply sunk brook. Nearby, half shrouded by the mist, was a short and narrow footbridge. Down the path that started from its other end was another of the half-built houses.

"He didn't cross that bridge," Raffles said. "I'd have heard him. If he went through the brook, he'd have done some splashing, and I'd have heard it. But he didn't have time to double back. Let's cross the bridge and see if he's left any footprints in the mud."

We walked Indian file across the very narrow bridge. It bent a little under our weight, giving us an uneasy feeling. Raffles said, "The contractor must be using as cheap materials as he can get away with. I hope he's putting better stuff into the houses. Otherwise, the first strong wind will blow them away."

"It does seem rather fragile," I said. "The builder must be a fly-by-night. But nobody builds anything as they used to do."

Raffles crouched down at the other end of the bridge, lit a match, and examined the ground on both sides of the path. "There are any number of prints," he said disgustedly. "They undoubtedly are those of the workmen, though the prints of the man we want could be among them. But I doubt it. They're all made by heavy workingmen's boots."

He sent me down the steep muddy bank to look for prints on the south side of the bridge. He went along the bank north of the bridge. Our matches flared and died while we called out the results of our inspections to each other. The only tracks we saw were ours. We scrambled back up the bank and walked a little way onto the bridge. Side by side, we leaned over the excessively thin railing to stare down into the brook. Raffles lit a Sullivan, and the pleasant odor drove me to light one up too.

"There's something uncanny here, Bunny. Don't you feel it?"

I was about to reply when he put his hand on my shoulder. Softly, he said, "Did you hear a groan?"

"No," I replied, the hairs on the back of my neck rising like the dead from the grave.

Suddenly, he stamped the heel of his boot hard upon the plank. And then I heard a very low moan.

Before I could say anything to him, he was over the railing. He landed with a squish of mud on the bank. A match flared under the bridge, and for the first time I comprehended how thin the wood of the bridge was. I could see the flame through the planks.

Raffles yelled with horror. The match went out. I shouted, "What is it?" Suddenly, I was falling. I grabbed at the railing, felt it dwindle out of my grip, struck the cold water of the brook, felt the planks beneath me, felt them sliding away, and shouted once more. Raffles, who had been knocked down and buried for a minute by the collapsed bridge, rose unsteadily. Another match flared, and he cursed. I said, somewhat stupidly, "Where's the bridge?"

"Taken flight," he groaned. "Like the chair!"

He leaped past me and scrambled up the bank. At its top he stood for a minute, staring into the moonlight and the darkness beyond. I crawled shivering out of the brook, rose even more unsteadily, and clawed up the greasy cold mud of the steep bank. A minute later, breathing harshly, and feeling dizzy with unreality, I was standing by Raffles. He was breathing almost as hard as I.

"What is it?" I said.

"What is it, Bunny?" he said slowly. "It's something that can change its shape to resemble almost anything. As of now, however, it is not what it is but where it is that we must determine. We must find it and kill it, even if it should take the shape of a beautiful woman or a child."

"What are you talking about?" I cried.

"Bunny, as God is my witness, when I lit that match under the bridge, I saw one brown eye staring at me. It was embedded in a part of the planking that was thicker than the rest. And it was not far from what looked like a pair of lips and one malformed ear. Apparently, it had not had time to complete its transformation. Or, more likely, it retained organs of sight and hearing so that it would know what was happening in its neighborhood. If it sealed off all its organs of detection, it would not have the slightest idea when it would be safe to change shape again."

"Are you insane?" I said.

"Not unless you share my insanity, since you saw the same things I did. Bunny, that thing can somehow alter its flesh and bones. It has such control over its cells, its organs, its bones—which somehow can switch from rigidity to extreme flexibility—that it can look like other human beings. It can also metamorphose to look like objects. Such as the armchair in the bedroom, which looked exactly like the original. No wonder that Hopkins and Mackenzie and even the redoubtable Holmes failed to find Mr. James Phillimore. Perhaps they may even have sat on him while resting from the search. It's too bad that they did not rip into the chair with a knife in their quest for the jewels. I think that they would have been more than surprised.

"I wonder who the original Phillimore was? There is no record of anybody who could have been the model. But perhaps it based itself on somebody with a different name but took the name of James Phillimore from a tomb-stone or a newspaper account of an American. Whatever it did on that account, it was also the bridge that you and I crossed. A rather sensitive bridge, a sore bridge, which could not keep from groaning a little when our hard boots pained it."

I could not believe him. Yet I could not not believe him.

6.

Raffles predicted that the thing would be running or walking to Maida Vale. "And there it will take a cab to the nearest station and be on its way into the labyrinth of London. The devil of it is that we won't know what, or whom, to look for. It could be in the shape of a woman, or a small horse, for all I know. Or maybe a tree, though that's not a very mobile refuge.

"You know," he continued after some thought, "there must be definite lim-itations on what it can do. It has demonstrated that it can stretch its mass out to almost paper-thin length. But it is, after all, subject to the same physical laws we are subject to as far as its mass goes. It has only so much substance, and so it can get only so big. And I imagine that it can compress itself only so much. So, when I said that it might be the shape of a child, I could have been wrong. It can probably extend itself considerably but cannot contract much."

As it turned out, Raffles was right. But he was also wrong. The thing had means for becoming smaller, though at a price.

"Where could it have come from, A.J.?"

"That's a mystery that might better be laid in the lap of Holmes." he said. "Or perhaps in the hands of the astronomers. I would guess that the thing is not autochthonous. I would say that it arrived here recently, perhaps from Mars, perhaps from a more distant planet, during the month of October, 1894. Do you remember, Bunny, when all the papers were ablaze with accounts of the large falling star that fell into the Straits of Dover, not five miles from Dover itself? Could it have been some sort of ship which could carry a passenger through the ether? From some heavenly body where life exists, intelligent life, though not life as we Terrestrials know it? Could it perhaps have crashed, its propulsive power having failed it? Hence, the friction of its too-swift descent burned away part of the hull? Or were the flames merely the outward expres-sion of its propulsion, which might be huge rockets?"

Even now, as I write this in 1924, I marvel at Raffles' superb imagina-tion and deductive powers. That was 1895, three years before Mr. Wells' *War of the Worlds* was published. It was true that Mr. Verne had been writing his wonderful tales of scientific inventions and extraordinary voyages for many years. But in none of them had he proposed life on other planets or the possibility of infiltration or invasion by alien sapients from far-off planets. The concept was, to me, absolutely staggering. Yet Raffles plucked it from what to others would be a complex of complete irrelevancies. And I was supposed to be the writer of fiction in this partnership!

"I connect the events of the falling star and Mr. Phillimore because it was not too long after the star fell that Mr. Phillimore suddenly appeared from nowhere. In January of this year Mr. Phillimore sold his first jewel to a fence. Since then, once a month, Mr. Phillimore has sold a jewel, four in all. These look like star sapphires. But we may suppose that they are not such because of our experience with the monsterlet in Persano's matchbox. Those pseudo jewels, Bunny, are eggs!"

"Surely you do not mean that?" I said.

"My cousin has a maxim which has been rather widely quoted. He says that, after you've eliminated the impossible, whatever remains, however improbable, is the truth. Yes, Bunny, the race to which Mr. Phillimore belongs lays eggs. These are, in their initial form, anyway, something resembling star sapphires. The star shape inside them may be the first outlines of the embryo. I would guess that shortly before hatching, the embryo becomes opaque. The material inside, the yolk, is absorbed or eaten by the embryo. Then the shell is broken and the fragments are eaten by the little beast.

"And then, sometime after hatching, a short time, I'd say, the beastie must become mobile, it wriggles away, it takes refuge in a hole, a mouse hole, perhaps. And there it feeds upon cockroaches, mice, and, when it gets larger, rats. And then, Bunny? Dogs? Babies? And then?"

"Stop," I cried. "It's too horrible to contemplate!"

"Nothing is too horrible to contemplate, Bunny, if one can do something about the thing contemplated. In any event, if I am right, and I pray that I am, only one egg has so far hatched. This was the first one laid, the one that Persano somehow obtained. Within thirty days, another egg will hatch. And this time the thing might get away. We must track down all the eggs and destroy them. But first we must catch the thing that is laying the eggs.

"That won't be easy. It has an amazing intelligence and adaptability. Or, at least, it has amazing mimetic abilities. In one month it learned to speak English perfectly and to become well acquainted with British customs. That is no easy feat, Bunny. There are thousands of Frenchmen and Americans who have been here for some time who have not yet comprehended the British language, temperament, or customs. And these are human beings, though there are, of course, some Englishmen who are uncertain about this."

"Really, A.J.!" I said. "We're not all that snobbish!"

"Aren't we? It takes one to know one, my dear colleague, and I am unashamedly snobbish. After all, if one is an Englishman, it's no crime to be a snob, is it? Somebody has to be superior, and we know who that someone is, don't we?"

"You were speaking of the thing." I said testily.

"Yes. It must be in a panic. It knows it's been found out, and it must think that by now the entire human race will be howling for its blood. At least, I hope so. If it truly knows us, it will realize that we would be extremely reluctant to report it to the authorities. We would not want to be certified. Nor does it know that we cannot stand an investigation into our own lives.

"But it will, I hope, be ignorant of this and so will be trying to escape the country. To do so, it will take the closest and fastest means of transportation, and to do that it must buy a ticket to a definite destination. That destination, I guess, will be Dover. But perhaps not."

At the Maida Vale cab station, Raffles made inquiries of various drivers. We were lucky. One driver had observed another pick up a woman who might be the person—or thing—we were chasing. Encouraged by Raffles' pound note, the cabbie described her. She was a giantess, he said, she seemed to be about fifty years old, and, for some reason, she looked familiar. To his knowledge, he had never seen her before.

Raffles had him describe her face feature by feature. He said, "Thank you," and turned away with a wink at me. When we were alone, I asked him to explain the wink.

"She—it—had familiar features because they were Phillimore's own, though somewhat feminized," Raffles said. "We are on the right track."

On the way into London in our own cab, I said, "I don't understand how the thing gets rid of its clothes when it changes shape. And where did it get its woman's clothes and the purse? And its money to buy the ticket?"

"Its clothes must be part of its body. It must have superb control; it's a sentient chameleon, a superchameleon."

"But its money?" I said. "I understand that it has been selling its eggs in order to support itself. Also, I assume, to disseminate its young. But from where did the thing, when it became a woman, get the money with which to buy a ticket? And was the purse a part of its body before the metamorphosis? If it was, then it must be able to detach parts of its body."

"I rather imagine it has caches of money here and there," Raffles said.

We got out of the cab near St. James's Park, walked to Raffles' rooms at the Albany, quickly ate a breakfast brought in by the porter, donned false beards and plain-glass spectacles and fresh clothes, and then packed a Gladstone bag and rolled up a traveling rug. Raffles also put on a finger a very large ring. This concealed in its hollow interior a spring-operated knife, tiny but very sharp. Raffles had purchased it after his escape from the Camorra deathtrap (described in *The Last Laugh*). He said that if he had had such a device then, he might have been able to cut himself loose instead of depending upon someone else to rescue him from Count Corbucci's devilish automatic executioner. And now a hunch told him to wear the ring during this particular exploit.

We boarded a hansom a few minutes later and soon were on the Charing Cross platform waiting for the train to Dover. And then we were off, comfortably ensconced in a private compartment, smoking cigars and sipping brandy from a flask carried by Raffles.

"I am leaving deduction and induction behind in favor of intuition, Bunny," Raffles said. "Though I could be wrong, intuition tells me that the thing is on the train ahead of us, headed for Dover."

"There are others who think as you do," I said, looking through the glass of the door. "But it must be inference, not intuition, that brings them here." Raffles glanced up in time to see the handsome aquiline features of his cousin and the beefy but genial features of his cousin's medical colleague go by. A moment later, Mackenzie's craggy features followed.

"Somehow," Raffles said, "that human bloodhound, my cousin, has sniffed out the thing's trail. Has he guessed any of the truth? If he has, he'll keep it to himself. The hardheads of the Yard would believe that he'd gone insane, if he imparted even a fraction of the reality behind the case."

7.

Just before the train arrived at the Dover station, Raffles straightened up and snapped his fingers, a vulgar gesture I'd never known him to make before.

"Today's the day!" he cried. "Or it should be! Bunny, it's a matter of unofficial record that Phillimore came into the East End every thirty-first day to sell a jewel. Does this suggest that it lays an egg every thirty days? If so, then it lays another today! Does it do it as easily as the barnyard hen? Or does it experience some pain, some weakness, some tribulation and trouble analogous to that of human women? Is the passage of the egg a minor event, yet one which renders the layer prostrate for an hour or two? Can one lay a large and hard star sapphire with only a trivial difficulty, with only a pleased cackle?"

On getting off the train, he immediately began questioning porters and other train and station personnel. He was fortunate enough to discover a man who'd been on the train on which we suspected the thing had been. Yes, he had noticed something disturbing. A woman had occupied a compartment by herself, a very large woman, a Mrs. Brownstone. But when the train had pulled into the station, a huge man had left her compartment. She was nowhere to be seen. He had, however, been too busy to do anything about it even if there had been anything to do.

Raffles spoke to me afterward. "Could it have taken a hotel room so it could have the privacy needed to lay its egg?"

We ran out of the station and hired a cab to take us to the nearest hotel. As we pulled away, I saw Holmes and Watson talking to the very man we'd just been talking to.

The first hotel we visited was the Lord Warden, which was near the railway station and had a fine view of the harbor. We had no luck there, nor at the Burlington, which was on Liverpool Street, nor the Dover Castle, on Clarence Place. But at the King's Head, also on Clarence Place, we found that he—it— had recently been there. The desk clerk informed us that a man answering our description had checked in. He had left exactly five minutes ago. He had looked pale and shaky, as though he'd had too much to drink the night before.

As we left the hotel, Holmes, Watson, and Mackenzie entered. Holmes gave us a glance that poked chills through me. I was sure that he must have noted us in the train, at the station, and now at this hotel. Possibly, the clerks in the other hotels had told him that he had been preceded by two men asking questions about the same man.

Raffles hailed another cab and ordered the driver to take us along the waterfront, starting near Promenade Pier. As we rattled along, he said, "I may be wrong, Bunny, but I feel that Mr. Phillimore is going home."

"To Mars?" I said, startled. "Or wherever his home planet may be?"

"I rather think that his destination is no farther than the vessel that brought him here. It may still be under the waves, lying on the bottom of the straits, which is nowhere deeper than twenty-five fathoms. Since it must be airtight, it could be like Mr. Campbell's and Ash's all-electric submarine. Mr. Phillimore could be heading toward it, intending to hide out for some time. To lie low, literally, while affairs cool off in England."

"And how would he endure the pressure and the cold of twenty-five fathoms of sea water while on his way down to the vessel?" I said.

"Perhaps he turns into a fish," Raffles said irritatedly.

I pointed out the window. "Could that be he?"

"It might well be *it*," he replied. He shouted for the cabbie to slow down. The very tall, broad-shouldered, and huge-paunched man with the great rough face and the nose like a red pickle looked like the man described by the agent and the clerk. Moreover, he carried the purplish Gladstone bag which they had also described.

Our hansom swerved toward him; he looked at us; he turned pale; he began running. How had he recognized us? I do not know. We were still wearing the beards and spectacles, and he had seen us only briefly by moonlight and matchlight when we were wearing black masks. Perhaps he had a keen sense of odor, though how he could have picked up our scent from among the tar, spices, sweating men and horses, and the rotting garbage floating on the water, I do not know.

Whatever his means of detection, he recognized us. And the chase was on.

It did not last long on land. He ran down a pier for private craft, untied a rowboat, leaped into it, and began rowing as if he were training for the Henley Royal Regatta. I stood for a moment on the edge of the pier; I was stunned and horrified. His left foot was in contact with the Gladstone bag, and it was melting, flowing into his foot. In sixty seconds, it had disappeared except for a velvet bag it contained. This, I surmised, held the egg that the thing had laid in the hotel room.

A minute later, we were rowing after him in another boat while its owner shouted and shook an impotent fist at us. Presently, other shouts joined us. Looking back, I saw Mackenzie, Watson, and Holmes standing by the owner. But they did not talk long to him. They ran back to their cab and raced away.

Raffles said, "They'll be boarding a police boat, a steam-driven paddle-wheeler or screwship. But I doubt that it can catch up with that, if there's a good wind and a fair head start."

That was Phillimore's destination, a small single-masted sailing ship riding at anchor about fifty yards out. Raffles said that she was a cutter. It was about thirty-five feet long, was fore-and-aft rigged, and carried a jib, forestaysail, and mainsail according to Raffles. I thanked him for the information, since I knew nothing and cared as much about anything that moves on water. Give me a good solid horse on good solid ground any time.

Phillimore was a good rower, as he should have been with that great body. But we gained slowly on him. By the time he was boarding the cutter *Alicia*, we were only a few yards behind him. He was just going over the railing when the bow of our boat crashed into the stern of his. Raffles and I went head over heels, oars flying. But we were up and swarming up the rope ladder within a few seconds. Raffles was first, and I fully expected him to be knocked in the head with a belaying pin or whatever it is that sailors use to knock people in the head. Later, he confessed that he expected to have his skull crushed in, too. But Phillimore was too busy recruiting a crew to bother with us at that moment.

When I say he was recruiting, I mean that he was splitting himself into three sailors. At that moment, he lay on the foredeck and was melting, clothes and all.

We should have charged him then and seized him while he was helpless. But we were too horrified. I, in fact, became nauseated, and I vomited over the railing. While I was engaged in this, Raffles got control of himself. He advanced swiftly toward the three-lobed monstrosity on the deck. He had gotten only a few feet, however, when a voice rang out.

"Put up yore dooks, you swells! Reach for the blue!"

Raffles froze. I raised my head and saw through teary eyes an old grizzled salt. He must have come from the cabin on the poopdeck, or whatever they call it, because he had not been visible when we came aboard. He was aiming a huge Colt revolver at us.

Meanwhile, the schizophrenic transformation was completed. Three little sailors, none higher than my waist, stood before us. They were identically featured, and they looked exactly like the old salt except for their size. They had beards and wore white-and-blue-striped stocking caps, large earrings in the left ear, red-and-black-striped jerseys, blue calf-length baggy pants, and they were barefooted. They began scurrying around, up came the anchor, the sails were set, and we were moving at a slant past the great Promenade Pier.

The old sailor had taken over the wheel after giving one of the midgets his pistol. Meanwhile, behind us, a small steamer, its smokestack belching black, tried vainly to catch up with us.

After about ten minutes, one of the tiny sailors took over the wheel. The old salt and one of his duplicates herded us into the cabin. The little fellow held the gun on us while the old sailor tied our wrists behind us and our legs to the upright pole of a bunk with a rope.

"You filthy traitor!" I snarled at the old sailor. "You are betraying the entire human race! Where is your common humanity?"

The old tar cackled and rubbed his gray wirelike whiskers.

"Me humanity? It's where the lords in Parliament and the fat bankers and the church-going factory owners of Manchester keep theirs, me fine young gentleman! In me pocket! Money talks louder than common humanity any day, as any of your landed lords or great cotton spinners will admit when they're drunk in the privacies of their mansion! What did common humanity ever do for me but give me parents the galloping consumption and make me sisters into drunken whores?"

I said nothing more. There was no reasoning with such a beastly wretch. He looked us over to make sure we were secure, and he and the tiny sailor left. Raffles said, "As long as Phillimore remains—like Gaul—in three parts, we have a chance. Surely, each of the trio's brain must have only a third of the intelligence of the original Phillimore I hope. And this little knife concealed in my ring will be the key to our liberty. I hope."

Fifteen minutes later, he had released himself and me. We went into the tiny galley, which was next to the cabin and part of the same structure. There we each took a large butcher knife and a large iron cooking pan. And when, after a long wait, one of the midgets came down into the cabin, Raffles hit him alongside the head with a pan before he could yell out. To my horror, Raffles then squeezed the thin throat between his two hands, and he did not let loose until the thing was dead.

"No time for niceties, Bunny," he said, grinning ghastily as he extracted the jewel-egg from the corpse's pocket. "Phillimore's a type of Boojum. If he succeeds in spawning many young. mankind will disappear softly and quietly, one by one. If it becomes necessary to blow up this ship and us with it, I'll not hesitate a moment. Still, we've reduced its forces by one-third. Now let's see if we can't make it one hundred percent."

He put the egg in his own pocket. A moment later, cautiously, we stuck our heads from the structure and looked out. We were in the forepart, facing the foredeck, and thus the old salt at the wheel couldn't see us. The other two midgets were working in the rigging at the orders of the steersman. I suppose that the thing actually knew little of sailsmanship and had to be instructed.

"Look at that, dead ahead," Raffles said. "This is a bright clear day, Bunny. Yet there's a patch of mist there that has no business being there. And we're sailing directly into it."

One of the midgets was holding a device which looked much like Raffles' silver cigarette case except that it had two rotatable knobs on it and a long thick wire sticking up from its top. Later, Raffles said that he thought that it was a machine which somehow sent vibrations through the ether to the spaceship on the bottom of the straits. These vibrations, coded, of course, signaled the automatic machinery on the ship to extend a tube to the surface. And an artificial fog was expelled from the tube.

His explanation was unbelievable, but it was the only one extant. Of course, at that time neither of us had heard of wireless, although some scientists knew of Hertz's experiments with oscillations. And Marconi was to patent the wireless telegraph the following year. But Phillimore's wireless must have been far advanced over anything we have in 1924.

"As soon as we're in the mist, we attack," Raffles said.

A few minutes later, wreaths of grey fell about us, and our faces felt cold and wet. We could barely see the two midgets working furiously to let down the sails. We crept out onto the deck and looked around the cabin's corner at the wheel. The old tar was no longer in sight. Nor was there any reason for him to be at the wheel. The ship was almost stopped. It obviously must be over the space vessel resting on the mud twenty fathoms below.

Raffles went back into the cabin after telling me to keep an eye on the two midgets. A few minutes later, just as I was beginning to feel panicky about his long absence, he popped out of the cabin.

"The old man was opening the petcocks," he said. "This ship will sink soon with all that water pouring in."

"Where is he?" I said.

"I hit him over the head with the pan," Raffles said. "I suppose he's drowning now."

At that moment, the two little sailors called out for the old sailor and the third member of the trio to come running. They were lowering the cutter's boat and apparently thought there wasn't much time before the ship went down. We ran out at them through the fog just as the boat struck the water. They squawked like chickens suddenly seeing a fox, and they leaped down into the boat. They didn't have far to go since the cutter's deck was now only about two feet above the waves. We jumped down into the boat and sprawled on our faces. Just as we scrambled up, the cutter rolled over, fortunately away from us, and bottom up. The lines attached to the davit had been loosed, and so our boat was not dragged down some minutes later when the ship sank.

A huge round form, like the back of a Brobdingnagian turtle, broke water beside us. Our boat rocked, and water shipped in, soaking us. Even as we advanced on the two tiny men, who jabbed at us with their knives, a port opened in the side of the great metal craft. Its lower part was below the surface of the sea, and suddenly water rushed into it, carrying our boat along with it. The ship was swallowing our boat and us along with it.

Then the port had closed behind us, but we were in a metallic and well-lit chamber. While the fight raged, with Raffles and me swinging our pans and thrusting our knives at the very agile and speedy midgets, the water was pumped out. As we were to find out, the vessel was sinking back to the mud of the bottom.

The two midgets finally leaped from the boat onto a metal platform. One pressed a stud in the wall, and another port opened. We jumped after them, because we knew that if they got away and got their hands on their weapons, and these might be fearsome indeed, we'd be lost. Raffles knocked one off the platform with a swipe of the pan, and I slashed at the other with my knife.

The thing below the platform cried out in a strange language, and the other one jumped down beside him. He sprawled on top of his fellow, and within a few seconds they were melting together.

It was an act of sheer desperation. If they had had more than one-third of their normal intelligence, they probably would have taken a better course of action. Fusion took time, and this time we did not stand there paralyzed with horror. We leaped down and caught the thing halfway between its shape as two men and its normal, or natural, shape. Even so, tentacles with the poisoned claws on their ends sprouted, and the blue eyes began to form. It looked like a giant version of the thing in Persano's matchbox. But it was only two-thirds as large as it would have been if we'd not slain the detached part of it on the cutter. Its tentacles also were not as long as they would have been, but even so we could not get past them to its body. We danced around just outside their reach, cutting the tips with knives or batting them with the pans. The thing was bleeding, and two of its claws had been knocked off, but it was keeping us off while completing its metamorphosis. Once the thing was able to get to its feet, or I should say, its pseudopods, we'd be at an awful disadvantage.

Raffles yelled at me and ran toward the boat. I looked at him stupidly, and he said, "Help me, Bunny!"

I ran to him, and he said, "Slide the boat onto the thing, Bunny!"

"It's too heavy," I yelled, but I grabbed the side while he pushed on its stern; and somehow, though I felt my intestines would spurt out, we slid it over the watery floor. We did not go very fast, and the thing, seeing its peril, started to stand up. Raffles stopped pushing and threw his frying pan at it. It struck the thing at its head end, and down it went. It lay there a moment as if stunned, which I suppose it was.

Raffles came around to the side opposite mine, and when we were almost upon the thing, but still out of reach of its vigorously waving tentacles, we lifted the bow of the boat. We didn't raise it very far, since it was very heavy. But when we let it fall, it crushed six of the tentacles beneath it. We had planned to drop it squarely on the middle of the thing's loathsome body, but the tentacles kept us from getting any closer.

Nevertheless, it was partially immobilized. We jumped into the boat and, using its sides as a bulwark, slashed at the tips of the tentacles that were still free. As the ends came over the side, we cut them off or smashed them with the pans. Then we climbed out, while it was screaming through the openings at the ends of the tentacles, and we stabbed it again and again. Greenish blood flowed from its wounds until the tentacles suddenly ceased writhing. The eyes became lightless; the greenish ichor turned black-red and congealed. A sickening odor, that of its death, rose from the wounds.

8.

It took several days to study the controls on the panel in the vessel's bridge. Each was marked with a strange writing which we would never be able to decipher. But Raffles, the ever redoubtable Raffles, discovered the control that would move the vessel from the bottom to the surface, and he found out how to open the port to the outside. That was all we needed to know.

Meantime, we ate and drank from the ship's stores which had been laid in to feed the old tar. The other food looked nauseating, and even if it had been attractive, we'd not have dared to try it. Three days later, after rowing the boat out onto the sea—the mist was gone—we watched the vessel, its port still open, sink back under the waters. And it is still there on the bottom, for all I know.

We decided against telling the authorities about the thing and its ship. We had no desire to spend time in prison, no matter how patriotic we were. We might have been pardoned because of our great services. But then again we might, according to Raffles, be shut up for life because the authorities would want to keep the whole affair a secret.

Raffles also said that the vessel probably contained devices which, in Great Britain's hands, would ensure her supremacy. But she was already the most powerful nation on Earth, and who knew what Pandora's box we'd be opening? We did not know, of course, that in twenty-three years the Great War would slaughter the majority of our best young men and would start our nation toward second-classdom.

Once ashore, we took passage back to London. There we launched the month's campaign that resulted in stealing and destroying every one of the sapphire-eggs. One had hatched, and the thing had taken refuge inside the walls, but Raffles burned the house down, though not until after rousing its human occupants. It broke our hearts to steal jewels worth in the neighborhood of a million pounds and then destroy them. But we did it, and so the world was saved.

Did Holmes guess some of the truth? Little escaped those grey hawk's eyes and the keen grey brain behind them. I suspect that he knew far more than he told even Watson. That is why Watson, in writing *The Problem of Thor Bridge*, stated that there were three cases in which Holmes had completely failed.

There was the case of James Phillimore, who returned into his house to get an umbrella and was never seen again. There was the case of Isadora Persano, who was found stark mad, staring at a worm in a match box, a worm unknown to science. And there was the case of the cutter *Alicia*, which sailed on a bright spring morning into a small patch of mist and never emerged, neither she nor her crew ever being seen again.

The Volcano

Originally published under the byline of
Paul Chapin

Readers of Rex Stout's second Nero Wolfe mystery *The League of Frightened Men* will know Paul Chapin as the author of the bestselling *Devil Take the Hindmost* (1934) and the popular *The Iron Heel* (1929). They will also know that Chapin was maimed in a hazing prank at Harvard University, an incident which twisted his personality and tinged it with a dark side. This darkness is said to have manifested itself throughout Chapin's literary work with portrayals of cruelty and violence, two things certainly apparent in the tale at hand.

Curiously, the reporter friend of the story's protagonist is Edward Malone, who bears the same name as that of a character in Sir Arthur Conan Doyle's Professor Challenger stories. Although Malone only appears here as a secondary character, Farmer did once plan to write a tale by the narrator of *The Lost World* and *The Poison Belt.*

First published in February 1976 in *The Magazine of Fantasy and Science Fiction*, "The Volcano" is either science fiction written as fantasy or fantasy written as science fiction. Take your pick.

1.

It was easier to believe in ghosts than in a volcano in a Catskills cornfield.

Curtius Parry, private detective, believed in the volcano because the newspapers and the radio stations had no reason to lie. For additional evidence, he had a letter from his friend, the Globe reporter, Edward Malone. As he sat in the rear of his limousine traveling over the Greene County blacktop, he was holding in his hand the letter that Malone had sent him two days before. It was dated April 1, 1935, and it was from Bonnie Havik.

Dear Mr. Parri,
    I got to talk a few minutes with Mr. Malone without my pa and

brothers hearing me. He said he'd send a note from me to you if I could slip it to him. Here it is. I don't have much time, I am writing this down in the basement, they think I'm getting some pear preserves. Please, Mr. Parry, help me. The sheriff here is no good, he's dumb as a sheep. They say Wan ran off after my pa and brothers beat him up. I don't think so, I think they did something worse to him. I don't dare tell anybody around here about Wan because everybody'd hate me. Wan is a Mexican. Please do come! I'm so afraid!

According to Malone's accompanying note, "Wan" was Juan Tizoc. He'd come up from Mexico a few years before, probably illegally, and had wandered around the country, either begging or working on farms. When last heard of, he'd been a hired hand for the Haviks for three months. He'd slept in a little room in the loft of the barn. Malone had tried to look into it, but its door was padlocked. The sheriff, Huisman, when asked by Malone about Tizoc, had replied that he seemed to have been scared off by the volcano.

Tizoc, Parry thought. That name did not come from Spain. It was indigenous to Mexico, probably Aztec, undoubtedly Nahuatl. Bonnie's description of him had been passed on by Malone. He was short and stocky and had obviously Nahuatl features, a sharp nose with wide nostrils, slightly protruding blocky teeth, and a wide mouth. When he smiled, Bonnie had said, his face lit up like lightning in the sky.

Bonnie was crazy about him. But Tizoc must have been crazy, in the original sense, to have messed around with a white girl in this isolated Catskills community. It was only three years ago, outside a village ten miles away, that a Negro hitchhiker had been murdered because he had ridden in the front seat with the white woman who'd picked him up.

Malone had enclosed a note with Bonnie's note and a preliminary report from the geologists on the scene.

This girl has been, and is being, brutalized by her father and brothers. Her mother also maltreated her, but she, as you know, was killed four days ago by a rock ejected from the volcano. Bonnie has a hideous scar on her face which local gossip says resulted from a red-hot poker wielded by her father. And I saw some bruises on her arms that looked pretty fresh.

On the other hand, some of the yokels say that she might have "it" coming. They cite the strange phenomena which allegedly took place on the Havik property when Bonnie was eleven. Apparently, spontaneous fires sprang up in the house and the barn, and she was blamed for this. She was beaten and locked up in the basement, and after a year the phenomena ceased. Or so the villagers say.

There are some here who'll tell you, whether or not you ask them, that Bonnie is at "it" again. It's plain they think that Bonnie is psychically responsible for the volcano, that she has strange powers. And some nonlocal nuts, visitors from Greenwich Village and Los Angeles and other points south of sanity, go along with this theory. It's all nonsense, of course, but be prepared for some wild talk and maybe some wild action.

The geologists' report had been made two days after the field had cracked open and had vomited white-hot lava and white-hot steam. The report was intended for the public but would not be released until the governor had given his permission. Apparently, he did not want to have anything published which would panic downstate New York. Malone had lifted (read: stolen) a copy of it.

The report began in informing the public that the Catskills were not of volcanic origin. The underlying rock was mainly of sedimentary origin, massive beds of sandstone and conglomerates. Under the sandstone were shales.

Yet, unaccountably, the sandstone and the shale were being so heated by some fierce agency that they flowed white-hot and spewed forth from the vent in the cornfield. Pieces of sandstone, heated to a semiliquid, were being hurled outward across the field. Much of the propulsive force seemed to be steam, water of meteoric origin, which exploded beneath the rocks and cannoned them out.

The geologists, after analyzing the gases and the ashes expelled from the cone, had shaken their heads. Based on the analysis of volcanic gases collected at Kilauea, Hawaii, in 1919, the following average composition, or something like it, should have been found: water 70.75 percent, carbon dioxide 14.07 percent, carbon monoxide 0.40 percent, hydrogen 0.33 percent, nitrogen 5.45 percent, argon 0.18 percent, sulfur dioxide 6.40 percent, sulfur trioxide 1.92 percent, sulfur 0.10 percent, and chlorine 0.05 percent.

The composition of the gases from the Havik volcano, by parts per hundredweight, was: oxygen 65, carbon 18, hydrogen 10.5, nitrogen 3.0, calcium 1.5, phosphorous 0.9, potassium 0.4, sulfur 0.3, chlorine 0.15, sodium 0.15, magnesium 0.05, iron 0.006, and other traces of elements 0.004.

Suspended in the hot H_2O ejected, which formed the bulk of the gases, were particles of sodium chloride (table salt) and sodium bicarbonate. There was also much carbon dioxide, and there were particles of charred carbon.

The sandstone lava flowed from the cone at a temperature of 710 degrees C.

Parry read the list three times, frowning until he had put the paper down. Then he smiled and said, "Ha!"

The chauffeur said, "What, sir?"

"Nothing, Seton," Parry said. But he muttered, "The geologists are so close to it that they don't see it, even if it's elementary. But, surely, it can't be! It just can't!"

2.

A few minutes after 1 p.m., the limousine entered Roosville. This looked much like every other isolated agricultural center in southeastern New York. It reminded Parry of the Indiana village in which he had been raised except that it was cleaner and much less squalid. He made some inquiries at the gas station and was directed to Doom's boardinghouse. Rooms were scarce due to the deluge of visitors attracted by the volcano, but Malone had arranged for Parry to double up with him. Seton was to sleep on a cot in the basement. Mrs. Doom, however, was obviously smitten by the tall, hawkishly handsome stranger from Manhattan. His empty left coat-sleeve, far from embarrassing her, intrigued her. She asked him if he had lost the arm in the war, and she excused her bluntness with the remark that the recent death of her husband was the long-term effect of a wound suffered at St.-Mihiel.

"I was wounded, too," Parry said. "At Belleau Wood." He did not add that it was two .45 bullets from a hood's gun which had severed his arm four years ago in a Bowery dive.

A few minutes later, Seton and Parry rode eastward out on the gravel road that met the blacktop in the center of town. It twisted and turned as if it were a snake whose head was caught in a wolf's jaws. It writhed up and down hills thick with a mixture of needle-leaf and broad-leaf trees. It passed along a deep rocky glen, one of the many in the Catskills.

Violence long ago had created the glens, Parry thought. But that was violence which resulted naturally from the geologic structure of the area. The volcano had also been born of violence, but it was unexpected and unnatural. Its presence in the Catskills was as unexplainable as a dinosaur's.

The limousine, rounding a corner of trees, was suddenly on comparatively flat ground. A quarter-mile down the road was the Havik farm: a large two-story wooden building, painted white, and a large red barn. And, behind it, a plume of white steam mixed with dark particles.

The car pulled up at the end of a long line of vehicles parked with the left wheels on the gravel and the right on the soft muddy shoulder. Parry and Seton got out and walked along the cars to the white picket fence enclosing the front yard. Standing there, Parry could see over the heads of the crowd lining the cornfield and past the edge of the barn. In the middle of the broad field was a truncated cone about ten feet high, its sides gnarled and reddish, irresistibly reminding him of a wound which alternately dried up and then bled again, over and over. A geyser of steam spurted from it, and a minute after he had arrived, a glow appeared on the edges of the crater, was reflected by the steam, and then its origin crawled over the black edges. It was white-hot lava, sandstone pushed up from below, oozing out to spread horizontally and to build vertically.

It seemed to him that the ground trembled slightly at irregular intervals as if the thumps of a vast but dying heart were coming through the earth from far away. This must be his imagination, since the scientists had reported an absence of the expected seismic disturbances. Yet—the people in the crowd along the field and in the yard were looking uneasily at each other. There was too much white of eye shown, too much clearing of throat, too much shuffling and backward stepping. Something had gone through the crowd, something that might spook them if the least thing untoward happened.

The door of the county sheriff's car, parked by the gateway, opened, and Sheriff Huisman got out and waddled up to Parry. He was short but very fat, a bubble of fat which smoked a cheap stinking cigar and glared with narrow red eyes in a red face at Parry. Indeed, Parry thought, he was not so much a bubble of fat as a vessel of blood about to burst.

The thin lips in the thick face said, "You got business here, mister?" Parry looked at the crowd. Some were obviously reporters or scientists. The majority just as obviously were locals who had no business beyond sightseeing. But the sheriff wasn't going to antagonize voters.

"Not unless you call curiosity a business," Parry said. There was no need to identify himself as yet, and he could operate better if the Roosville law wasn't watching him.

"Okay, you can go in," Huisman said. "But it'll cost you a dollar apiece, if your man's coming in, too."

"A *dollar?*"

"Yeah. The Haviks been having a tough time, what with their silo burned down and old lady Havik killed only four days ago by a stone from that volcano and people stomping around destroying their privacy and getting in the way. They gotta make it up some way."

Parry gestured at Seton, who gave the sheriff two dollars, and they went through the gateway. They threaded through the crowd in the barnyard, passed a Pathé news crew, and halted at the edge of the field. This was mainly mud because of the recent heavy rains. Any weeds on it had been burned off by the large and small lava "bombs" hurled by the volcano. These lay every-where, numbering perhaps several hundred. When ejected, they had been roughly spherical, but the impact of landing had flattened out the half-liquid rocks. As Seton remarked, these made the field look like a pasture on which stone cows browsed.

The lava had ceased flowing and was slowly turning red as it cooled. Parry turned to look at the hack of the barn, which was broken here and there and marked with a number of black spots. A few stones had evidently also struck the back of the house, since the windows were all boarded up except for those protected by the overhang of the porch roof.

A man appeared from around the corner of the barn. Smiling, his hand extended, he strode up to Parry. "Son of a gun, Cursh!" he said. "I wasn't really sure you'd come! After all, your client can't pay you anything!"

3.

Parry, grinning and shaking his hand, said, "I donate one case a year to charity. Anyway, I'd pay my client in this case."

Ed Malone greeted Seton and then said, "I've found out some things I didn't have time to report. The locals admit that the volcano is an act of God, but they still think that maybe God wrought it in order to punish the Haviks. They're not much liked around here. They're stand-offish, they seldom attend church, they're drunk night and day, they're slovenly. Above all, the vil-lagers don't like the way the family treats Bonnie, even if, as they say, she is 'sorta strange'."

"What about Tizoc?"

"Nobody's seen him. Of course, nobody's really looking for him. Bonnie hasn't said anything to the sheriff because she's afraid he'll spill the beans to her family, and then she'll suffer. She'll be trying to get out today to see you but..."

A sound like several sticks of dynamite exploding whirled them around to-ward the cone. They cried out with the people around them as they saw a white-hot object soaring toward them. They ran away, yelling, and behind them came a crashing sound. When they turned around again, they saw a hole in the back of the barn and smoke pouring out of it.

The cry of "Fire!" arose. Parry hurried around with the others to the front of the barn and looked inside. The white-hot rock had landed in a pile of hay by the back wall, and both were blazing. The flames were spreading swiftly to-ward the stalls, which held three horses. These were screaming and kicking against the stall boards in a frenzy. From near the front of the barn, from the pens, pigs squealed in terror.

During the futile efforts to save the barn, Parry identified the Haviks. The fire had brought all of them out of the house. Henry Havik was a very tall and very thin man of about fifty-seven, bald, broken-nosed, snaggle-toothed, and thick-lipped. The nose was also bulbous and covered with broken veins, the eruptions of whiskey. When he came close to Parry, he breathed alcohol and rotting teeth. The sons, Rodeman and Albert, looked like twenty-year-younger editions of their father. In twenty years, or less, their faces would be as broken-veined and their teeth as rotten.

Bonnie had slipped out during the confusion, and though she should have been concerned about the barn, evidently she was looking for Parry. Seeing Malone, she came toward him, and Malone pointed at Parry. She was just twenty-one but looked older because of some deep lines in her face, the broad scar along the left side of her face, and the loose and tattered gingham dress she wore. Her yellow hair would have been attractive if it had not been so disheveled. In fact, Parry thought, if she were cleaned up and made up and dressed up, she would be pretty. There was, however, something wild and disquieting about the pale blue eyes.

Smoke poured from the barn while men, choking and coughing and swearing, led the horses and drove the pigs out and others manned a bucket brigade. Since the Haviks had no phone, the sheriff had driven off in a hurry to summon the Roosville fire brigade. Parry gestured at Malone and Bonnie followed him, and he led the way to the other side of the house. He would have liked to have stationed Seton as a sentinel, but the chauffeur was lost in the seethe of smoke and mob.

Parry said, "No need for introductions and no time. Tell me about Juan Tizoc, Bonnie. He's the one this is all about, isn't he?"

"You're pretty smart, Mr. Parry," she said. "Yes, he is. When Juan was first hired by pa, I didn't pay much attention to him. He was short and dark, Indian-looking, and he had a funny accent. And he was lame, too. He said an American tourist who was speeding hit him when he was a kid, and he couldn't never walk straight again. He was sometimes bitter about that, but when he was with me he was mostly laughing and joking. That was what made me like him so much, at first. There hadn't never been much laughing around here before he came here, let me tell you. I don't know how he did it, since I didn't really see him too much, but he made my days easier. Sorta edged with light even if they wasn't full of it. Ma and Pa kept him humping, he was a hard worker, though he couldn't never seem to satisfy them, and they insulted him a lot, hollered at him, and they was chinchy with the food, too. But he found time for me…"

"If he was treated so badly, why didn't he just walk off?"

"He was in love with me," she said, looking away from him.

"And you?"

She spoke so softly that he could barely hear her.

"I loved him."

She groaned, and she said, "And now he's run away, left me!" She paused and then said, "But I just can't believe he'd leave me!"

"Why not?"

"I'll tell you why! We both knew how we felt about each other even though neither of us'd said a word about it. But we'd looked words enough! I suppose if I'd been a Mexican girl he'd have said something long before, but he knew he might just as well be a nigger as far as Roosville was concerned. And me, I loved him, but I was ashamed of it, too. At the same time, I wondered how any man, even a Mexican, could love me."

She touched her scar. Parry said, "Go on."

"I'd just finished giving the horses their oats when Juan came in to do something or other, I never found out. He looked around, saw no one was there except me, and came straight to me. And I knew what he was going to do and went into his arms and began kissing him. And he was telling me between kisses how much he hated all gringos, especially my family, he wished they'd all burn in hell, except for me, of course, he loved me so much, and then…"

Rodeman Havik had passed by the barn door and had seen them. He had called out to his brother and father, and all three had rushed in at Tizoc. He had knocked Rodeman down, but the father and Albert had jumped on him and begun hitting and kicking him. Bonnie's mother had come from the house then and with Rodeman's help had dragged her into the house. There she was shoved into the basement and locked in.

"And that was the last time I saw him," she said, tears welling. "Pa said he'd kicked him off the farm, said he told him he'd kill him if he didn't get out of the country. And Pa beat me. He said he ought to kill me, no decent white woman'd let a greaser slobber over her. But I was so ugly I was lucky even a greaser'd look at me."

"Why does he hate you so much?" Parry said.

"I don't know!" she said, suddenly sobbing. "But I wish I was brave enough to kill myself!"

"I'll do that for you!" someone bellowed.

4.

Henry Havik, his eyes and lips closed down like jackknife blades, soot covering the red of the broken veins of his nose, rushed at his daughter. "You bitch!" he shouted. "I told you to stay inside!"

Parry stepped in between Havik and Bonnie, and said, "If you hit her, I'll have you in jail in ten minutes."

Havik stopped, but he did not unclench his fists.

"I don't know who you are, you one-armed jackass, but you better step aside! You're interfering with a man and his daughter!"

"She's of age, and she can leave whenever she pleases," Parry said coolly. He kept his eyes on the farmer while speaking out of the side of his mouth. "Bonnie! Say the word, and I'll see you into town! And never mind his threats. He can't do a thing to you as long as you have protection. Or witnesses."

"He wouldn't care where I was!" she said. "And I'm afraid to go away! I wouldn't know what to do *out there!*"

Parry looked at her with much pity and some disgust. Finally, he said, "Bonnie, the unknown evil is far better for you than the known evil. You have sense enough to know that. Have the courage, the guts, to do what your good sense tells you you should do."

"But if I leave here," she wailed, "nobody's going to do anything about Juan!"

Havik shouted, "What?" and he swung at Parry, though it was obvious his primary target was his daughter. Parry blocked Havik's fist with his arm and kicked the man in the knee. At the same time, Malone rammed his fist into Havik's solar plexus. Havik fell gasping for breath and clutching his knee. A moment later, the two sons, closely followed by Sheriff Huisman, came around the corner of the house. Huisman bellowed at everybody to freeze, and everybody except Havik obeyed. He was rolling on the ground in agony.

Huisman listened to all of them talking at once, then he bellowed for, and obtained, quiet. He asked Bonnie to tell him what had happened. After listening to her, he said, "So you're a private dick, Parry? Well, you don't have no license to practice here."

"True," Parry said, "but that has nothing to do with the situation. I represent Miss Havik—do I not, Bonnie?—and she wishes to leave the premises. She is over twenty-one and so legally free to do so. Mr. Havik here attacked us—I have two witnesses to back that statement—and if he doesn't keep quiet, I'll charge him with…"

"This is my property!" Havik said. "As for you, you dirty knee-kicking Frenchman…"

Parry took Bonnie's elbow and said, "Let's go. We can send for your clothes later."

The sons looked at their father. Huisman scowled and bit down on his cigar. Parry knew what he was thinking. He was well aware that the daughter was within her rights. Also, a New York reporter was watching him closely. What could he do, even if he wished to do anything?

"You'll pay for this, you ungrateful cow," Havik said. But he did nothing to prevent his daughter from leaving. Trembling, moving only because Parry was pushing and steering her, she walked out of the yard and to the limousine.

5.

Parry went to bed at ten o'clock but was too tired to fall asleep at once. The events at the Havik's had been stimulating enough; those that followed had drained him of even more energy and set his nerves to resonating. He was furious with the sheriff because of the contempt he had openly expressed for Bonnie after hearing her story and his refusal to question the Haviks or search their premises. Plainly, he thought that the beating up of Tizoc had been a worthy, even applaudable, act. And he claimed that there was not enough evidence to warrant an investigation into Tizoc's disappearance. That the sheriff was right about the latter point enraged Parry even more.

After the long session in the back room of the jail, Parry had gotten Bonnie a room at a Mrs. Amster's. Then they had shopped at the small dress shop, purchased her clothes, and taken them to her place. She had bathed and put on some makeup—much, she would have considered sinful—and after dressing she had accompanied Seton and Parry to the restaurant. There she had been subjected to openly curious, and some hostile, stares from and much whispering among the patrons. By the time they left, she was in tears.

Afterward, they'd walked around town, and she had told him in detail about her life in the Havik household. Parry was tough, but every once in a while the sufferings and tragedies of humanity refused to be kept at bay. Like the sea pounding a dike, they found a weak spot, and they poured through him. Usually, it was one case, like Bonnie's, representing millions of men, women, and children who were enduring injustice, cruelty, and lack of love, that punched through. And then the others, or his consciousness thereof, roared in after the spearhead.

Parry could not sleep for a long time because he felt as if he were a huge sea shell in which the ocean of suffering was a painful din. Finally, he did drift away, only to be awakened. half-stupefied, by a pounding on the door. He turned on the light and stumbled to the door, noting on the way that Malone, breathing whiskey fumes, had not been roused. The door swung open to reveal his landlady, Mrs. Doom, and Mrs. Amster. Immediately, he became wide awake. Before Mrs. Amster could stammer out her story, he had guessed what had happened.

A few minutes later, he plunged out the front door into the dimly lit three-in-the-morning night of Roosville. He ran to Huisman's house, which was only a block from the jail. The sheriff wasn't pleased to be pulled out of a beery sleep, but he put on his clothes and went out to his car with Parry behind him.

"It's a good thing you didn't go out there by yourself," he said thickly. "Old man Havik could've shot your butt off and claimed you was trespassing. As it is, I ain't sure that Bonnie didn't go willingly with her father."

"Maybe she did," Parry said, sliding into the front seat. "There's only one way to find out. If Havik has forced her to come with him, he's guilty of kidnapping. Mrs. Amster said only that she woke up in time to see Havik and his sons pushing Bonnie into the car. She hadn't heard a thing before then."

Though Huisman drove as swiftly as the winding gravel road would allow, he did not turn his siren or flashing red lights on. As they turned onto the road to the Havik farm, he turned off his headlights. It was evident, however, that they would not need them. The light from flowing lava and ejected rocks outlined the house brightly.

"That thing looks like it's getting ready to blow!" the sheriff said in a scared voice. "I ain't never seen it so bright before!"

He and Parry both cried out. A particularly large fragment, a white spot in the eye of night, had risen from the cone and was soaring toward the house. It disappeared behind the roof, and a moment later flames broke out from the area in which it had fallen.

Huisman skidded the car to a stop by the fence with a shrieking of tires, and he and Parry tumbled out. The glare from the cone and from the rooftop flames outlined the house. It also showed them Bonnie, the top of her dress half torn off, her face twisted, running down the porch steps and toward them. She shouted something at them, but the whistling of steam and boomings of ejected rock and the cries of her father and brothers behind her drowned out her words.

Parry shouted at Huisman, "Havik's got a shotgun!"

Cursing, Huisman stopped and undid the strap over the revolver in his holster. Havik ran out down the steps and into the yard, then halted to point the double-barreled weapon toward Bonnie.

Parry yelled at her to throw herself on the ground. Though she could not have heard him, she sprawled onto the ground heavily. Parry saw by the light of another whirling glowing thing that came from over the house and downward that she had tripped on a small rock, now cooled to a dull red.

Havik's gun boomed twice; pellets tore by Parry.

Huisman had thrown himself down, too, but had clumsily dropped his gun while doing so.

Parry saw where the mortarlike trajectory of the rock would end, and he cried out. Later, he asked himself why he had tried to warn a man who was trying to kill his own daughter and would undoubtedly have tried to kill him, too. The only answer was that, being human, he was not always, by any means, logical.

There was a thud, and Havik fell, the semiliquid stone bent somewhat around his shattered head, clinging to it. The odor of burning flesh and hair drifted over the yard.

Rodeman and Albert Havik screamed with horror, and they ran to their father. That was all the time the sheriff needed. He recovered his revolver, and, rising, called at the two to drop their rifles. They started to do so but whirled around when several more rocks crashed into the ground just behind them. The sheriff, misinterpreting their actions, fired twice, and that was enough.

6.

Curtius Parry had arranged for Bonnie Havik to work as a maid for a Westchester family, and he had talked to a plastic surgeon about the removal of her scar. Having done all he could for her, he was now taking his ease in his apartment on East 45th Street. He had a drink in his hand; Ed Malone, sitting in a huge easy chair near him, held a drink in one hand and a cigarette in the other.

Malone was saying, "So Tizoc can't be found? So what? At least you saved Bonnie from being murdered, and nothing less than poetic justice got rid of her beastly family for her."

Parry raised his thick eyebrows and said, "They're dead, yes, but they're still alive in Bonnie, working their violence in her. It'll be a long time, if ever, before they cease to savage her guts. As for their deaths, were they examples of poetic justice? And as for Juan Tizoc, well, if I told you my theory about what actually happened to him, you'd say I was crazy."

"Tell me anyhow, Cursh," Malone said. "I won't laugh at you or call you crazy."

"I only ask that you keep it to yourself. Very well. The Catskills are not volcanic country, but Mexico is…"

"So?" Malone said after a long silence.

"Consider the theory that some of the townspeople were voicing. They spoke about the spontaneous fires in the Havik house when Bonnie was eleven, and they hinted that Bonnie was somehow responsible for the volcano. But they did not know that in every allegedly authentic case of salamandrism, as it's called, the phenomena always cease when the unhappy child becomes pubescent. So, Bonnie could not be responsible."

"I'm glad to hear you say that, Cursh," Malone said. "I was afraid you were going to base your theory on supernaturalism."

"*Supernatural* is only a term used to explain the unexplainable. No, Ed, it wasn't Bonnie who heated up the sandstone not too deep in the earth and opened the earth in the cornfield to propel the white-hot stuff out onto the Haviks. It was Tizoc."

Malone's drink sloshed over his hand, and he said, "Tizoc?"

"Yes. The Havik men killed him, most bloodily and in a white-hot anger, I'm sure. And they dug a grave in the center of the field and filled it up and smoothed out the dirt over it. They expected that the roots of the corn plants would feed off Tizoc, and the plants themselves would destroy all surface evidences of his grave. This was most appropriate, though the Haviks would not know it, since corn was first domesticated in ancient Mexico. But Mexico is also the land of volcanoes. And a man, even a dead man, expresses himself in the spirit of the land in which he was raised and with the materials and in the method most available.

"The Haviks did not know that Tizoc's hatred was such, his desire for vengeance such, that he burned with these even as a dead man. He burned with hatred, his soul pulsed with violence even if the heart had ceased pulsing. And the sandstone was turned to magma with the violence of his hatred and vengeance…"

"Stop, Cursh!" Malone cried. "I said I'd not call you crazy, but…"

"Yes, I know," Parry said. "But consider this, Ed, and then advance a better theory, if you can. You saw the report the geologists made on the composition and the relative proportions of the gases and the ashes expelled by the volcano. These are not what any volcano so far studied has expelled."

Parry drank some Scotch and set the glass down.

"The ejected elements, and their relative proportions, are exactly those that compose the human body."

Osiris on Crutches

by Leo Queequeg Tincrowdor

Decades before anyone ever heard of the inestimable Neil Gaiman, there was Leo Queequeg Tincrowdor. Both men write about living gods.

Born in New Goshen, Indiana, Tincrowdor is a graduate of Shomi University and an active member of the Baker Street Irregulars. He is also a professional painter. His best known works are *Sphinxes Without Secrets*, *The Hole in the Coolth*, and the short story "What You See." He attributes his fondness for whiskey and bourbon to his Celtic and Germanic descent, although this editor challenges anyone to trace the derivation of his name using any extant genealogy. One so inclined might better be served to page through *The Wizard of Oz* or *Moby Dick*.

The reader who would like to learn more about Tincrowdor is encouraged to track down a copy of Philip José Farmer's *Stations of the Nightmare*. In that book it is stated that one of Tincrowdor's favorite quotes is "Whom gods wish to destroy, they first make mad." After reading the following story one might wonder if Tincrowdor is on the gods' hit list. Then again, perhaps Tincrowdor sees more clearly than the rest of us and it is the gods who must be afraid of him.

I

Set, a god of the ancient land of Egypt, was the first critic. Once he had been a creator, but the people ceased to believe in his creativity. He then suffered a divinity block, which is similar to a writer's block.

This is a sad fate for a deity. Odin and Thor, once cosmic creators, became devils—that is, critics—in the new religion which killed off their old religion. Satan, or Lucifer, was an archangel in the Book of Job, but he became the chief of demons, the head-honcho critic, in the New Testament. The Great Goddess of the very ancient Mediterranean regions, named Cybele, Anana, Demeter, depending on where she lived, became a demon; Lilith, for instance, or, in one case, the Mother of God (and who criticizes more than a mother?). But she had to do that via the back door, and most people that pray to her don't know that she was not always called Mary. Of course, there are scholars who deny this, just as there are scholars who deny the existence of the Creator.

Those were the days. Gods walked the earth then. They weren't invisible or absent as they are nowadays. A man or a woman could speak directly to them. They might get only a divine fart in their faces, but if the god felt like talking, the human had a once-in-a-lifetime experience.

Nowadays, you can only get into contact with a god by prayer. This is like sending a telegram which the messenger boy may or may not deliver. And there is seldom a reply by wire, letter, or phone.

In the dawn of mankind, the big gods in Egypt were Osiris, Isis, Nephthys, and Set. They were brothers and sisters, and Osiris was married to Isis and Set was married to Nephthys. Everybody then thought that incest was natural, especially if it took place among the gods.

In any event, no human was dumb enough to protest against the incest. If the gods missed you with their lightning or plagues, the priests got you with their sacrificial knives.

People had no trouble at all seeing the gods, though they might have to be quick about it. The peasants standing in mud mixed with ox manure and the pharaohs standing on their palace porches could see the four great gods, along with Osiris' vizier, Thoth, and Anubis, as they whizzed by. These traveled like the wind or the Roadrunner zooming through the Coyote's traps. Their figures were blurred with speed, dust was their trail, the screaming of split air their only sound.

From dawn to dusk they raced along, blessing the land and all on and in it.

However, the gods noticed a peculiar thing when they roared by a field just north of Abydos. A man always sat in the field, and his back was always turned to them. Sometimes they would speed around to look at his face. But when they did, they still found themselves looking at his back. And if one god went north and one south and one east and one west, four boxing the man in, all four could still see only his back.

"There is One greater than even us," they told each other. "Do you suppose that She, or He, as the case might be, put him there? Or perhaps that is even Him or Her?"

"You mean 'He or She,'" Set said. Even then he was potentially a critic.

After a while they quit staying up nights wondering who the man was and why they couldn't see his face and who put him there. But he was never entirely out of their minds at any time.

There is nothing that bugs an omniscient like not knowing something.

II

Set stopped creating and became a nasty, nay-saying critic because the people stopped believing in him. Gods have vast powers and often use them with no consideration for the feelings or wishes of humans. But every god has a weakness against which he or she or it is helpless. If the humans decide he is an evil god, or a weak god, or a dying god, then he becomes evil or weak or dead. Too bad, Odin! Rotten luck, Zeus! Tough shit, Quetzalcoatl! Trail's end, Gitche Manitou!

But Set was a fighter. He was also treacherous, though he can't be blamed for that since the humans had decided that he was no good. He planned some unexpected events for Osiris at the big festival in Memphis honoring Osiris' return from a triumphant world tour, SRO. He planned to shortsheet his elder brother, Osiris, in a big way. From our viewpoint, our six-thousand-year perspective, Set may have had good reason. His sister-wife, Nephthys, was unable to conceive by him and, worse, she lusted after Osiris. Osiris resisted her, though not without getting red in the face and elsewhere.

This was not easy, since Osiris' flesh was green. Which has led some moderns to speculate that he may have come in a flying saucer from Mars. But his flesh was green because that's the color of living plants, and he was the god of agriculture. Among other things.

Nephthys overcame his moral scruples by getting him drunk. (This was the same method used by Lot's daughters many thousands of years later.) The result of this illicit rolling in the reeds was Anubis. Anubis, like a modern immortal, was a "funny-looking kid," and for much the same reason. He had the head of a jackal. This was because jackals ate the dead, and Anubis was the conductor, the ticket-puncher, for the souls who rode into the afterlife.

Bighearted Isis found the baby Anubis in the bulrushes, and she raised him as her own, though she knew very well who the parents were.

Osiris strode into Memphis. He was happy because he had just finished touring the world and teaching non-Egyptians all about peace and nonviolence. The world has never been in such good shape as then and, alas, never will be again. Set smiled widely and spread his arms to embrace Osiris. Osiris should have been wary. Set, as a babe, had torn himself prematurely and violently from his mother's womb, tearing her also. He was rough and wild, white-skinned and red-haired. He was a wild ass of a man.

Isis sat on her throne. She was radiant with happiness. Osiris had been gone for a long time, and she missed him. During his absence, Set had been sidling up to her and asking her if she wanted to get revenge on her husband for his adulterous fling with Nephthys. Isis had told him to beat it. But, truth to tell, she was wondering how long she could have held out. Gods and goddesses are hornier than mere humans, and you know how horny they are.

Isis, however, had to wait. Set gave a banquet that would have turned Cecil B. De Mille green with envy. When everyone ached from stuffing himself, and belches were exploding like rockets over Fort Henry, Set clapped his hands. Four large, but minor, gods staggered in. Among them they bore a marvelously worked coffer. They set it down, and Osiris said, "What is that exquisite *objet d'art,* brother?"

"It's a gift for whomever can fit himself into it exactly," Set said. Anybody else would have said "whoever," but Set was far more concerned with form than content.

To start things off, Set tried to get into the coffer. He was too tall, as he knew he'd be. His seventy-two accomplices in the conspiracy—Set was wicked but he was no piker—were too short. Isis didn't even try. Then Osiris, swaying a little from the gallons of wine he'd drunk, said, "If the coffer fits, wear it." Everybody laughed, and he climbed into the coffer and stretched out. The top of his head just touched the head of the coffer, and the soles of his feet just touched its foot.

Osiris smiled, though not for long. The conspirators slammed the lid clown on his face and nailed it down, Set laughed; Isis screamed. The people ran away in panic. Paying no attention to the drumming on the lid from within the coffer, the accomplices rushed the coffer down to the Nile. There they threw it in, and the current carried it seaward.

III

Some gods need air. Others are anaerobic. In those days, they all needed it, though they could live much longer without air than a human could. But it was a long journey down the Nile and across the sea to Byblos, Phoenicia. By the time it grounded on the beach there, Osiris was dead.

Set held Isis prisoner for some time. But Nephthys, who loathed Set now, joined Anubis and Thoth in freeing her. Isis journeyed to Byblos and brought the body back, probably by oxcart, since camels were not yet used. She hid the body in the swamps of a place called Buto. As evil luck would have it, Set was traveling through the swamp, and he fell over the coffer.

His face, when he saw his detested brother's corpse, went through the changes of wood on fire. It became black like wood before the match is applied, then red like flames, then pale like ashes. He tore the corpse into fourteen parts, and he scattered the pieces over the land. He was the destroyer, the spreader of perversity, the venomous nay-sayer.

Isis roamed Egypt looking for Osiris' parts. Tradition has it that she found everything but the phallus. This was supposed to have been eaten by a Nile crab, which is why Nile crabs are forever cursed. But this, like all myths, legends, and traditions, is based on oral material that is inevitably distorted through the ages.

The truth is the crab *had* eaten the genitals. But Isis forced it to disgorge. One testicle was gone, alas. But we know that the myth did not state the truth or at least not all of it. The myth also states that Isis became pregnant with a part of Osiris' body. It doesn't say what part, being vague for some reason. This reason is not delicacy. Ancient myths, in their unbowdlerized forms, were never delicate.

Isis used the phallus to conceive. Presently Horus was born. When he grew up he helped his mother in the search. This took a long time. But they found the head in a mud flat abounding in frogs, the heart on top of a tree, and the intestines being used as an ox whip by a peasant. It was a real mess.

Moreover, Osiris' brain was studded with frog eggs. Every once in a while a frog was hatched. This caused Osiris to have some peculiar thoughts, which led to peculiar behavior. However, if you are a god, or an Englishman, you can get away with eccentricity.

One of the thoughts kicked off by the hatching of a frog egg was the idea of the pyramid. Osiris told a pharaoh about it. The pharaoh asked him what it was good for. Osiris, always the poet, replied that it was a suppository for eternity.

This was true. But he forgot in his poet's enthusiasm his cold scientist's cold regard for cold facts. Eternity has body heat. Everything is slowly oxidizing. The earth and all on it are wrapped in flames if one only has eyes to see them. And so the pyramids, solid though they are, are burning away, falling to pieces. So much for the substantiality of stone.

Meanwhile, Isis and Horus found all of Osiris' body except for a leg and the nose. These seemed lost forever. So she did the best she could. She attached Osiris' phallus to his nose hole.

"After all," she said to Horus and Thoth, "he can wear a kilt to cover his lack of genitals. But he looks like hell without a nose of any kind."

Thoth, the god of writing, and hence also of the short memory, wasn't so sure. He had the head of an ibis, which was a bird with a very long beak. When Osiris was sexually aroused, he looked too much like Thoth. On the other hand, when Osiris wasn't aroused, he looked like an elephant. Usually, he was aroused.

This was because the other gods left him in their dust while he hobbled along on his crutch. But Isis wasn't watching him, and so he dallied with the maidens, and some of the matrons, of the villages and cities along the Nile.

Humans being what they are, the priests soon had him on a schedule which combined the two great loves of mankind: money and sex. He would arrive at 11:45 A.M, at, say, Giza. At 12:00, after the tickets had been collected, he would become the central participant in a fertility rite. At 1:00 the high priest would blow the whistle. Osiris would pick up his crutch and hobble on to the next stop, which was, literally, a whistle stop. The maidens would pick themselves up off the ground and hobble home. Everybody else went back to work.

Osiris met a lot of girls this way, but he had trouble remembering their faces. Just as well. Humans age so fast. He never noticed that the crop of maidens of ten years ago had become careworn, work-worn hags. Life was hard then. It was labor before dawn to past dusk, malaria, bilharzia, piles, too much starch and not enough meat and fruit, and, for the women, one pregnancy after another, teeth falling out, belly and breasts sagging, and varicose veins wrapping the legs and the buttocks like sucker vines.

Humans attributed all their ills, of course, to Set. He, they said, was a mean son of a bitch, and when he whirled by, accompanied by tornados, sandstorms, hyenas, and wild asses hearing leaky baskets of bullcrap, life got worse.

They prayed to Osiris and Isis and Horus to get rid of the primal critic, the basic despoiler. And it happened that Horus did kill him off.

Here's the funny thing about this. Though Set was dead, life for the humans did not get one whit better.

IV

After a few thousand years people caught on to this. They started to quit believing in the ancient Egyptian gods, and so these dwindled away. But the dwindling took time.

Female deities, for some reason, last longer than the males. Isis was worshiped into the sixth century A.D., and when her last temple was closed down, she managed to slip into the Christian church under a pseudonym. Perhaps this is because men and women are very close to their mothers, and Isis was a really big mother.

Osiris, during his wanderings up and down along the Nile, noticed that humans had one method of defeating time. That was art. A man could fix a moment in time forever with a carving or a sculpture or a painting or a poem or a song. The individual passed, nations passed, races passed, but art survived. At least for a while. Nothing is eternal except eternity itself, and even the gods suddenly find that oxidation has burned them down to a crisp.

This is partly because religion is also an art form. And religion, like other art forms, changes with the times.

Osiris knew this, though he hated to admit it to himself. One day, early in the first century A.D., he saw once more the man whose back was always turned to him. This man had been sitting there for about six thousand years or perhaps for much longer. Maybe he was left over from the Old Stone Age.

Osiris decided he'd try once more. He hobbled around on his crutch, circling on the man's left. And then he got a strange burning feeling. The man's face was coming into view.

Straight ahead of the man was what the man's body had concealed. An oblong of blackness the size of a door in a small house lay flat on the earth's surface.

"This is the beginning of the end," Osiris whispered to himself. "I don't know why it is, but I can feel it."

"Greetings, first of the crippled gods, predecessor of Hephaestos and Wieland," the man said. "Ave, first of the gods to be torn apart and then put together again, predecessor of Frey and Lemminkainen. Hail, first of the good gods to die, basic model for those to come, for Baldur and Jesus."

"You don't look like you belong here," Osiris said. "You look like you come from a different time."

"I'm from the twentieth century, which may be the next-to-last century for man or perhaps the last," the man said. "I know what you're thinking, that religion is a form of art. Well, life itself is an art, though most people are imitative artists when it comes to living, painters of the same old paintings over and over again. There are very few originators. Life is a mass art, or usually the art of the masses. And the art of the masses is, unfortunately, bad art. Though often entertaining," he added hastily, as if he feared that Osiris would think he was a snob.

"Who are you?" Osiris said.

"I am Leo Queequeg Tincrowdor," the man said. "Tincrowdor, like Rembrandt, puts himself in his paintings. Any artist worth his salt does. But since I am not worthy to hand Rembrandt a roll of toilet paper, I always paint my back to the viewer. When I become as good as the old Dutchman, I'll show my face in the mob scenes."

"Are you telling me that you have created me? And all this, too?" Osiris said. He waved a green hand at the blue river and the pale green and brown fields and the brown and red sands and rocks beyond the fields.

"Every human being knows he created the world when he somehow created himself into being," Tincrowdor said. "But only the artist re-creates the world. Which is why you have had to go through so many millennia with a phallus for a nose and a crutch for a leg."

"I didn't mind the misplaced phallus," Osiris said. "I can't smell with it, you know, and that is a great benefit, a vast advantage. The world really *stinks,* Tincrowdor. But with this organ up here, I could no longer smell it. So thanks a lot."

"You're welcome," the man said. "However, you've been around long enough. People have caught on now to the fact that even gods can be crippled. And that crippled gods are symbols of humans and their plight. Humans, you know, are crippled in one way or another. All use crutches, physical or psychical."

"Tell me something new," Osiris said, sneering.

"It's an old observation that will always be new. It's always new because people just don't believe it until it's too late to throw the crutch away."

Osiris then noticed the paintings half buried in the khaki-, or kaka-, colored dust. He picked them up, blew off the dust, and looked at them. The deepest buried, and so obviously the earliest, looked very primitive. Not Paleolithic but Neolithic. They were stiff, geometrical, awkward, crude, and in garish unnatural colors. In them was Osiris himself and the other deities, two-dimensional, as massive and static as pyramids and hence solid, lacking interior space for interior life. The paintings also had no perspective.

"You didn't know that the world, and hence you, was two-dimensional then, did you?" Tincrowdor said. "Don't feel bad about that. Fish don't know they live in water just as humans don't know a state of grace surrounds them. The difference is, the fish are already in the water, whereas humans have to swim through nongrace to get to the grace."

Osiris looked at the next batch of paintings. Now he was three-dimensional, fluid, graceful, natural in form and color, no longer a stereotype but an individual. And the valley of the Nile had true perspective.

But in the next batch the perspective was lost and he was two-dimensional again. However, somehow, he seemed supported by and integrated with the universe, a feature lacking in the previous batch. But he had lost his individuality again. To compensate for the loss, a divine light shone through him like light through a stained-glass window.

The next set returned to perspective, to three dimensions, to warm natural colors, to individuality. But, quickly in a bewildering number and diversity, the Nile and he became an abstraction, a cube, a distorted wild beast, a nightmare, a countless number of points confined within a line, a moebius strip, a shower of fragments.

Osiris dropped them back into the dust, and he bent over to look into the oblong of blackness.

"What is that?" he said, though he knew.

"It is," Tincrowdor said, "the inevitable, though not necessarily desired, end of the evolution you saw portrayed in the paintings. It is my final painting. The achievement of pure and perfect harmony. It is nothingness."

Tincrowdor lifted a crutch from the dust which had concealed it all these thousands of years. He did not really need it, but he did not want to admit this to himself. Not yet, anyway—someday, maybe.

Using it as a pole up which to climb, he got to his feet. And, supporting himself on it, he booted the god in the rear. And Osiris fell down and through. Since nothingness is an incomplete equation, Osiris quickly became the other part of the equation—that is, nothing. He was glad. There is nothing worse than being an archetype, a symbol, and somebody else's creation. Unless it's being a cripple when you don't have to be.

Tincrowdor hobbled back to this century. Nobody noticed the crutch—except for some children and some very old people—just as nobody notices a telephone pole until he runs into it. Or a state of grace until it hits him.

As for his peculiarity of behavior and thought—call it eccentricity or originality—this was attributed by everybody to frog eggs hatching in his brain.

The Phantom of the Sewers

Original version published as "It's the Queen
of Darkness, Pal" under the byline of Rod Keen

The Abortion by the late Richard Brautigan is a strange tale about a very unusual library in San Francisco. In that library, among its one of a kind collection, lies a slim volume entitled *It's the Queen of Darkness, Pal* by Rod Keen, submitted to the head librarian by a man who doubtless smelled of the city sewer.

In a letter to Brautigan seeking permission to write under the Rod Keen byline, Farmer writes: "I've long been an admirer of yours, and this story is a sort of tribute to you. I thought perhaps when you used the name of Rod Keen, you may have been referring somewhat circuitously to Rod McKuen...Anyway, to further this subtle satire, I named my hero Red McKune. Also, I tried to give the prose the mild satiric flavor of Brautigan and McKuen. Parodic, rather than satiric, I should say."

In that same correspondence, Farmer asks for permission to write another title housed in the library described in *The Abortion*. This is *UFO Versus CBS* by Susan DeWitt. No evidence exists that Farmer actually wrote that story, although several years later the very similarly titled "Uranus or UFO Versus IRS" did appear under his own name in the Byron Preiss edited anthology *The Planets* (Bantam, 1985), and was retitled in its next appearance as simply "UFO Versus IRS."

The Magazine of Fantasy and Science Fiction published "It's the Queen of Darkness, Pal" in its August 1978 issue. When published in his own collection, *Riverworld and Other Stories* (Berkley, 1979), Farmer changed the title to "Phantom of the Sewers" and tweaked the story's last few lines.

1.

All day long, Red McCune worked the city like a galley slave. Ben Hur had toiled to pull his beautiful many-decked ship across the waters. Red worked to hose and push ugly single-decked pieces of crap down the stream.

They were his burden, and Red, always the poet, had once called the burdens fardels. His partner, "Ringo" Ringgold, had said, "What?"

"...*who would fardels bear, to grunt and sweat under a weary life...*"

"Okay, what's a fardel?"

Ringo's expression showed he thought it was something related to passing gas. That was what working in the sewers did to a man.

"It's a word used by a colleague of mine," Red had said. "A fellow poet. Bill, the Bard of Avon."

"Oh, God, not another one?" Ringo had said. "What's he doing down here?"

"Keeping me company."

Ringo grunted. If the subject had been World War Two Japanese, Ringo wouldn't have stopped talking. He'd been one of the first of the black Marines to be shipped off to the South Pacific to kill or be killed or maybe both. Ringo opted for survival and came back with a potful of mementos and a lot of stories.

"I admired them little yellow bastards," he'd once told Red. "Only, they wasn't yellow. They stood up to us whites like real men."

Red had rolled his eyes then, and Ringo had said quickly, "You know what I mean. All us Americans was white as far as the Nips was concerned."

Ringo was a little peculiar. That could have been blamed on the Marines, but Red thought that it was the sewer that had done it to Ringo. It did it to all the workers, including himself. The darkness, the garbage and trash on the dark waters, the gases, the heat, these made a pressure cooker that a salesman couldn't have given away.

Red raked in a high-button shoe and looked at it before throwing it back in. Some happy young 1909 beauty had worn that. She never would have believed that she'd be wrinkled and bent and open at the seams, her breath and soul sour, and living off welfare. Out of style, out of time, just like her shoe.

Gas is the pessimism of the belly, and pessimism is the gas of the soul. Red suffered a lot from both. But he considered himself to be both a poet and the archaeologist of the living. One way to pass the time, and the gas, was to imagine he was an archaeologist. Forget what he knew about the actualities. Imagine he was reconstructing the civilization above only on the basis of what floated by and what he hosed down.

It was a strange world up there. Once there were many condoms floating by, but now there were few. This meant that they'd had overpopulation up there, and the rubber factories had been working overtime. One day, the rubbers became fewer, and in a few months where they had once been schools of little white fish, bobbing and turning and nosing each other affectionately, they were loners. No one to nuzzle or play tag with.

From this Red deduced that something terrible had happened up there. It was the Red Masque all over again, though this time it wasn't red spots on the skin but impotency. The thing in the masque walked through the streets of Golden Gate City, touching this one and that one with his wand. It made no difference who the men were: bankers, gangsters, fuzz, pushers, all-Americans, beatniks, carry-out boys, wardheelers, astrologers, talk-show hosts. They went limp as cigarettes dropped into the toilet.

Red got a lot of satisfaction from this image. He was so ugly that very few women would have anything to do with him, and those that would he wanted nothing to do with. It was a case of like repulsing like.

Red thought of himself as another Quasimodo. Where the hunchback hung around the steeple, way up there, Red chose to get down under. Heights made him dizzy, anyway.

Sometimes, he got too involved in his picture of a dwindling population. When he crawled out of the manhole at quitting time, he was surprised that the streets weren't empty after all.

"Dead and don't know it," he'd mutter.

Today Red was working out his archaeology on the basis of the quality of the excrement going by in convoys. When he'd started working, twelve years ago, the brown gondolas that steamed on by, pushing toward their ports, the sausage-shaped gondolas floating through their dark Venice, had been of superior quality. Nothing to compare with the stuff in his grandfather's outhouse, of course, not Grade AA, but still Grade A. The stuff he encountered now, these were World War I U-boats compared to the magnificent *Queen Elizabeths*, the *Titanics* and *Lusitanias* that had, relatively speaking, graced the beer-brown seas. In those days even the bumboats, the stuff from the poor, were superior to the best from the rich of 1966. And if today's droppings were so bad, think of what he'd have to put up with in 1976.

Red didn't know what was causing the degeneracy. Was it DDT and artificial fertilizers and too much sugar? We are what we eat, and what we are includes thoughts. The stomach is the shadow of the mind, and where the mind goes, the stomach follows.

You wouldn't have got stuff like that from Socrates or Kant. They were thinkers; modern philosophers were stinkers.

"Hey, Red, what you dreaming about?" Ringo said.

"Socrates," Red said.

"Oh, you mean that Greek cook at Captain Nemo's Submarine Sandwiches? Yeah, his food ain't what it used to be. But where the hell is it?"

"That's what I was thinking."

"Better stop thinking and get your ass in gear," Ringo said. "The inspector's coming through today. Say, what's Ernie doing, anyway? He must be goofing off too. There ain't no hose going up there."

Red looked up the tunnel. For a hundred yards it went straight as an ex-con claimed to be and then curved out of sight. The corner gave off a dim light like a glowworm in heat. It came from the lamp in Ernie Mazzeo's helmet. This helmet was like a miner's, though Ernie wasn't digging coal. Ernie dug hardly anything, which was why he would just as soon be down here as up there.

"Maybe I ought to wake him up," Red said. "The inspector'll fire him if he catches him sleeping."

Red's lamp was shining down on the waters, which was why he was the first to notice the almost black stuff in the dark-brown liquid. It looked like an octopus that had been caught under a steamroller.

"What's that?" he said.

"If I didn't know better," Ringo said, "I'd say it was blood."

Ernie's head floated by. His mouth was open, and his teeth shone in the beam. There was enough gold in them to make it worthwhile to mine Ernie.

2.

The police came first, then the ambulance, then Inspector Bleek. The detectives questioned McCune and Ringgold, took pictures, made measurements, and put Ernie's parts in a pile. These included the head, the severed arms and legs, and the heart. The genitals were missing. They might have been thrown into the sewage and had floated by unnoticed by the two workers. Nobody thought so. Richie Washington and Abdul Y had been cut apart and their heads and limbs recovered. But their genitals were still missing. The theory was that the killer had taken them with him. No one knew why he had done this, but the sale of mountain oysters at the restaurants had dropped to almost nothing.

"You two'll have to come down to headquarters," Lieutenant Haunt said.

'Don't you worry, boys," Bleek said, his voice thick as dipped honey. "I'll see that you get a lawyer and bail. I take care of my men."

He put his arm around Red and then around Ringo to show that he played no favorites.

"They're not under arrest," Hallot said. "I just want them to make complete statements."

"Take the rest of the day off when they're through with you," Bleek said. "God! What kind of a monster is loose down here? Why's he picking on sewer workers? Richie last month and Abdul the month before. What's he got against you guys? Us, I mean. Or is it a conspiracy by some underground outfit? Are they trying to foul up the sewer system so the city'll get sick?"

Bleek looked as upset as Red felt. He was a big man, about a head taller than Red and a head wider and almost as ugly. His mirror took a beating every morning, but that didn't seem to bother him as it did Red. He had a wife, a Chinese immigrant from Taiwan who wasn't disturbed by his lack of beauty. All Caucasian males looked the same to her.

Bleek squeezed Red's shoulders and said, "Hang in there, pal!"

"Stiff upper lip, old chap!" Ringo jeered as he and Red walked away. "That honey-voiced son of a bitch likes you so much because compared to him you're a wart hog's hind end and he's the peacock's."

Red didn't say anything. They had to stand to one side then while the attendants carried Ernie by under a sheet and on a stretcher. Blood was spreading out through it like it was looking for a new home.

"I think I'll quit," Ringo said. "Hell, we ain't even getting combat pay!"

Red didn't say much the next two hours except to answer questions from a squad of detectives. It was evident they thought he and Ringo were guilty, but that didn't bother him. In their books, everybody was guilty, and that included the judges. By the time they'd finished the session, they were even looking suspiciously at each other. The session didn't last very long, though. The cops' red faces quickly got green, and they staggered out one by one. Red finally figured that it was because he and Ringo had brought up a lot of the sewer with them.

That's strange, he thought. They don't mind the moral atmosphere in here. In fact, most of them seem to get fat on it. Then he remembered the sewer rats and how fat they were.

3.

It was still afternoon when they got out. The light was the same as everyday in Golden Gate City on a cloudless day. The brightness had the harshness of reality but made the buildings and the people look unreal. It was as if the emerald city of Oz had been whitewashed. By an apprentice painter. Or maybe by Tom Sawyer's friends.

Ringo lit a cigarette. Ringo was short and very round in head and body and legs. This, with his shiny black skin, made him look like an anarchist's bomb that was ready to go off. The cigarette was the fuse.

"Let's get something to eat," Ringo said.

"My God, after seeing Ernie!" Red said. He wanted only to go to his room, which really wasn't anything to go to. But it was better than going any place else. He'd get into the shower, with his overalls and boots still on, and wash off his clothes. Then he'd wash himself. Then he'd open a cold can of beer—the beer would be cold, too—and he'd turn the heat on very low in his oven and put the wet clothes in the oven but leave its door open. The smell of cleanliness would spread through his one room and bath. It would be like forgiveness from a priest after along, hard confession. Repentance played no part in it, though. He knew all along that he meant to sin again, to go down into the sewers the next day. The slough of despond, he thought. Despondency was a sin, but in the tunnels its peculiar odor was overridden by all the others. Moreover, up here he got even more despondent because he had to take so much crap from everybody. He took it down there, too, but down there it was impersonal.

Then, he'd be padding around naked, passing the mirror a dozen times and avoiding looking in it. When he forgot and did look into it, he'd give it the finger. It gave him the finger back, but it never did it first. It tried, but Red was the fastest finger in the West.

By the time he'd turned the old TV set on, he'd hear a banging at the door. That'd be old Mrs. Nilssen, his widowed landlady. Mrs. Nilssen would cry out in her seventy-year voice that she wanted to talk to him. Actually, she was a drunk who wanted a drink. After a few, she'd want to lay him. Mrs. Nilssen, poor old soul, was desperate, and she figured that as ugly as he was he'd be grateful to have even her. A couple of times she'd been almost right. But he didn't want any of her desperation. He could just barely handle his own.

After he'd yelled at her to go away enough times, she'd go. Then he'd sit down at the desk he'd bought at the Goodwill and with another beer by his elbow compose his poetry. He'd look out the window from five stories up on the hill and see other windows looking up or down at him. Somewhere beyond them was the bay and the great bridge over which Jack London and Ambrose Bierce and Mark Twain and George Sterling had once ridden in carriages. He knew that the bridge hadn't been built in their day, but it was nice to think of them rolling across it. And if the bridge had been built then, they would have crossed on it.

He had his own bridge to cross. This was finishing the poem which he had titled *The Queen of Darkness*. He'd started it twenty years ago when he was twenty-five. He'd written it on yellow second sheets and envelopes and grocery sacks and once, out of paper and funds, on the dust on his desk. The dust had inspired him; it'd kindled the greatest lines he'd ever written. He got so excited he went out and got drunk, and when he got back from work the next day, he'd rushed to the desk to read them because he couldn't remember them. They weren't there. Wouldn't you know it, old Mrs. Nilssen had cleaned his room. This was the first and last time; the cleaning was only an excuse to look for the bottle that she was sure he'd hidden. She thought everybody had a hidden bottle.

He'd never been able to reconstruct the lines, and so he'd lost his chance to get his start as a major poet. Those lines would've launched him; it wouldn't be anything but Excelsior from then on. At least, it was nice to believe so.

Now, after a couple of millions of lines, Red had to admit that he couldn't even play in the minor leagues of poetry. His stuff stank, just as the sewers stank. Actually, it was the sewers that had ruined his poetry, though in the beginning they were his inspiration. He was going to write something as good as, maybe better than, Thompson's "City of Dreadful Night." Maybe as good as Keats' "La Belle Dame Sans Merci." Then, ugly or not, he'd be invited to the colleges and the salons to read his poems, and the women would fall all over him. But, no, his candle had gone out in the darkness and the damp and the stink. That white wavering beauty, the muse that he had imagined moving toward him, then away, beckoning him on into distant tunnels, there to show him love and death, had died. Like a minstrel show at a Black Muslim meeting.

Still, there were times when he thought he saw her dimly, a flicker, at the far corner of the dark canal.

4.

"What the hell you thinking of, man?" Ringo said. "I can't eat now. Let's have a few drinks first."

This was fine with Ringo. They walked through the crowd, which gave them plenty of room, to The Tanglefoot Tango Tavern. This was half-full of winos and pushers, and the other half was narks and a drunken preacher from the Neo-Sufi Church down the street. The Reverend Hadji Fawkes saluted them as they came in. "Is there a God in the sewers? Does he walk in the coolth of the smell?"

"Not since last Tuesday, Rev.," Ringo said and pushed Red on ahead. Red wanted to talk; a religion that promoted intoxication as The Way was interesting. So did the other customers, as long as Fawkes bought drinks for them. But Ringo wasn't having any of a white man's faith, free booze or not.

They sat down near the jukebox, which was playing "Show Me the Way to Go home," one of the church's official hymns. They ordered a pitcher of beer apiece and a couple of hamburgers for Ringo. Seeing Red's expression, Ringo told the waitress, "Take it easy on the catsup."

"How's the poetry going?" Ringo said, though he could care less.

"I'm about to give up and write a book. One on the myths and legends of the sewer system of Golden Gate City."

"Man, that's spooky," Ringo said. "You don't believe any of that shit, do you?"

"The Phantom of the Sewers? Why not? He could be just some wino that went ape and decided to imitate Lon Chaney. There are lots of places he could hole up, and anyway he doesn't have to spend all his time haunting the tunnels. He could live part of the time upstairs, maybe he's right here now, standing at the bar, drinking, laughing at us."

Ringo looked quickly at the customers at the bar and said, "Naw. Not them."

"Has the Phantom ever done anything to hurt anybody, besides scare them half to death? And with what? A Halloween skull mask and a black robe?! don't think someone threw acid in his face and it ate his face off so the skull shows. That's right out of the old movie, Ringo."

"I seen him once, anyway," Ringo said. "He was poling a long shallow boat along, standing up in it, his robes fluttering in the wind, he was near one of the big fans, and his eyes was big and white, and his face was half gone. That was scary enough but what really made me take off was his passenger. It looked like a heap of…something, a heap that was pulsing like a toad. It had one round eye, no lid, which was staring at me."

"I thought you said you didn't believe in that crap," Red McCune said.

"What I say and what I believe ain't always the same thing."

"Lots of people are that way," Red said. "It sounds like the Phantom made friends with the Terrible Turdothere."

He grinned, but the grin was only to show that he wasn't serious. If Ringo thought he was serious, he'd never go down into the sewers again. There'd go his job and his seniority and his pension and his World War Two souvenirs. There'd go his satisfaction and contentment, too, because Ringo liked his job. No matter what he said about it, he liked it.

Every bat to his own belfry.

"I don't know," Ringo said slowly. "I ain't seen the Phantom since, and nobody else has either as far as I could find out. Do you suppose that the Phantom was hypnotized by the Turdothere and it had commanded him to take it to its secret lair where it could eat the Phantom?"

They were silent for a while as they watched the horror films on the picture tubes of their minds. These were the latest in a long line: *Dracula Squares Off at the Creature from the Black Lagoon, The Golem Meets the Giant Spirochete,*

Abbott and Costello Versus the Daughter of Mr. Hyde and the Hyena Woman. When the monsters got tired of eating people, they ate each other.

As background music, the jukebox, now off the religious kick, was bellowing country music: "A Farmer's Daughter It Was Who Give Me Two Acres Last Night." An old man, screaming that he was the long-lost heir to the Rockefeller fortune, was being carried out the back door into the alley. Another old man was coughing up blood under a table. His cronies were betting drinks, from his bottle, for or against his ever taking another drink.

The myth of the Turdothere went like this. It wasn't a Mad Scientist that created the Turdothere. In the old days it would have been, but people didn't believe in a Mad Scientist any more. The faith in their existence was gone. They were as extinct as Zeus or Odin or maybe even God.

It was The Mad TV Writer that was the new menace. The name was Victor Scheissmiller, a man who had really lived. Everybody had seen his picture in the newspapers and magazines and read about him in them. He wasn't something made up.

It was true that he had gone mad, his mind off-course like Wrong Way Corrigan's airplane. After eighteen years of writing contest shows, children's shows, westerns, cops-and-robbers, science-fiction series, and soap operas, he blew the tube on his mental set. There wasn't any warranty, and he didn't try to trade in the old mind. He disappeared one day, last seen climbing down a manhole. The note he left behind said he was going to create a monster, the Turdothere, and release it on the world. After it ate up all the sewer workers, it would emerge from a storm sewer and devour the whole population while they sat hypnotized before their TV's.

The surface people thought it was a big joke. The tunnel people laughed about it when they were above. But when they were below, they did a lot of looking over their shoulders.

Nobody had seen Victor Scheissmiller in the sewers, but some had seen the heaving stinking mass of the Turdothere with its one glass eye—Scheissmiller's own, some said. Some workers said that it was the Turdothere that had killed their buddies and cut off the head, legs, and arms. But those who'd seen the thing said it had no teeth. It must gum its victims to death, or maybe it stuck a tentacle of crap down their throats and choked them. Then it wrapped itself around them and dissolved them in its juices.

How did it keep alive when only a few people had disappeared in the sewers? Easy. It ate rats, too. And it was probably a cannibal; it ate crap, too.

It grew even larger then, and it could become a colossus, since there was no end of this kind of food, unless the plumbers went on strike. Its main body, though, was supposed to be in a sort of skeleton, old bones put together by Scheissmiller. There were nerves of thread and catgut and a condom swelling and shrinking like a heart, pumping muscatel from a bottle for its blood, a jar of vaginal jelly for a liver, cigar butts embedded in the body drawing oxygen through it. And so on.

Others said this wasn't correct. The thing was a 300-pound mass of nothing but living crap, no bones or bottles in it, and it flowed along and changed shape like *The Brobdingnagian Bacillus That Desired Raquel Welch*. (Later retitled *I Bugged the Body Beautiful*.)

Everybody agreed, though, that it had one glass eye which it used to spot its victims.

"Mostly it's made of dead human hopes," Red said.

"What?" Ringo said.

"Well, I'll be damned," Red added. "Look who's here!"

Ringo jumped up with a scream, upsetting a pitcher of beer, and he whirled around, crying, "Oh, no! It's not here!"

"So you don't believe?" Red said, sneering. "No, Ringo, it isn't the Turdothere. It's Inspector Bleek himself."

"What's he doing here?" Ringo said. He sat down and tried to hide his shaking by gripping Red's pitcher with two hands and pouring out a glass of beer. He didn't make it.

Bleek drew up a chair and thrust his ugly face across the table as close as he could get it to Red's face. "I just got the coroner's report from the cops," he said. "Ernie was raped, just like those other two boys."

Ringo ordered two more pitchers. Red was silent for a while, then he said, "Was it before or after they were killed?"

"Before," Bleek said.

"That tears it," Ringo said. "I'm quitting. If I'm gonna be butchered by a sexual pervert, I'm gonna do it up in the sunshine."

"With all the security you got?" Bleek said. "I was afraid you two guys were thinking of quitting, which is why I am here. Hang on, old buddies. Tomorrow the police are going to conduct a massive manhunt through the entire sewer system. They need guides, so you two can help, if you want to."

He put his arm around Red and squeezed his shoulder.

"The Public Works Department expects every man to do his duty. Besides, there'll be camera crews down there tomorrow. You might get to see yourself on TV."

How could anybody resist that?

5.

The hunt took four days, and it turned out just like Red McCune expected it to. Lights blazed, men yelled, bloodhounds bayed. The darkness moved in after the lights moved on, the men got hoarse and fell silent, the hounds smelled nothing but sewer gas. The hounds didn't know what they were looking for, anyway. Nobody had a glove from the Phantom to let them sniff or a dropping from a thing that was all droppings. And the Sewer Slayer, as the papers and TV called him, was out for lunch. Whoever and whatever he was, he was no idiot.

"See?" Red told Ringo.

"There's plenty of places to hide, secret exits, alcoves and old tunnels that've been bricked off, and stuff like that," Ringo answered. "Anyway, how do we know he wasn't hiding under the water? The Phantom of the Opera walked underwater while he breathed through a tube."

What they did find was a Pekingese dog that'd been tortured to death and three human fetuses, all looking like Martians that had crash-landed. The usual.

They also found the rats, or maybe it was the other way around. This was when the hunters started having a good time. After trudging for miles through dark wet stinking places, getting tired and half-nauseated and bored, and in a killing mood, they had something to kill.

The rats had been running for hours ahead of them. and now there was a wagon train of them, about four hundred furry gray pioneers cornered by the Indians. Most of them had swum through canals during their flight and so looked like dust mops that had been rained on. Their eyes shone red in the beams, like little traffic lights. **STOP** they said, and the men did halt for a minute while they looked the squealing heaving mass over. A flashlight caught a blur that leaped down from a ledge at the far end of the chamber. It was three times as big as the others, and its one eye seemed to have its own glow. It was not gray but white above and black below.

"That must be their leader," one of the cops said. "Lord, I'm glad they're not all that big!"

The shooting and the clubbing started then. The .38's and the .45's and the shotguns boomed, deafening everybody in a few seconds. The rats blew up as if they were little land mines. Most of them ran back and forth instead of making a run for it through the humans. They'd heard that a cornered rat always fights, and they believed it. The skeptics among them dashed through the hunters, biting a few hands and legs. Most of them were smashed with saps or flashlights but a few got away.

Ringo jumped in with the others, swinging a Samurai sword from his collection. "Banzai!" he'd cry, and when a rat leaped at him and he cut off its head in midair, "Ah, so!"

Beyond him Inspector Bleek, a big grin on his face like a Halloween pumpkin's, fired a six-shooter into the horde. It was an heirloom from his great-grandfather, who had conquered the West with it. Its barrel was long enough and wide enough to make an elephant proctologist happy. It flashed out .44-caliber bullets which mowed the rats down like they were grandfather's Indians.

In his other hand he held a big Bowie knife. Red wondered if he meant to do some scalping when the last stand was over. Red crouched down against the wall. He wasn't afraid of the rats but he didn't enjoy killing them either. He wanted to hang back mostly because he knew the bullets would start ricocheting. Sure enough, one screamed by, just like in a Western, and another followed it, and then some cop yelled that the rats were firing back. Later it turned out he'd been stunned by a bullet which just touched his forehead, and in his stupor he thought sure the rats had got hold of some guns.

The men started ducking but they kept on shooting. After a while, a man was hit in the leg, and the hunters started to come to their senses. The explosions died like the last of popcorn in the pan, the echoes feebled away, and there was silence except for the running waters behind them and the faraway baying of the hounds. Their owner wasn't risking his valuable property around anything so unreliable as rats.

The blood ran down the slanting apron of concrete to the channel for a minute. Then it stopped, like an oil well gone dry, go home, boys, I'm out of dinosaurs.

The only survivor was a big old rat, the Custer of the 7th Underground Cavalry. He climbed over and slid down body after body, dragging his hind legs, which were missing their feet, his goal the waters.

"He's sure got slanty eyes," Ringo said, and he leaped, shouting, "Banzai!" and his sword cut off the rat's head.

"Goddamn it!" Bleek said. "I wanted to do that!"

"I did that because I admired the son of a bitch," Ringo said. "He's got guts. He deserved an honorable death."

"You're crazy," Bleek said. He looked around, waving his Bowie as if it were a baton and the orchestra had gone on strike.

"Hey!" a cop said. "Look at that!"

In a corner was a mass of bodies and pieces of bodies. They'd been hosed against the wall and piled up by a stream of bullets. Everything in it seemed to have been killed three times at least. But it was stirring and then it was quaking, and cracks appeared, and suddenly the giant rat they'd glimpsed when the massacre began erupted. Only it wasn't a rat. It was a cat, snarling, his one eye as bright as a hotrodder's exhaust, his back curved as if he was a bow about to shoot himself at them. Despite the blood that streaked him, his coloring, white above and black below, showed through.

"Why, that's Old Half-Moon!" Red said.

"Who the hell's Half-Moon?" Bleek said.

Red didn't say anything about his being a legend of the sewers. He said, "He's been around a couple of years at least. When I first saw him, he was just an old alley cat. But he started getting big because rats make good eating. Look at him! He's been through a hundred fights above and two hundred below! One eye gone and both ears chewed apart. But he's a terror among the rats. I saw him take on ten one time and kill them all."

"Yeah?" Bleek said. He took a few steps toward Old Half-Moon. The cat crouched as if to spring. Bleek admonished him with his knife but he stopped.

"I think he's become pals with the rats," he said. "He's their leader. After all, you are what you eat, and he eats nothing but rats, so he must be half rat."

"You're what you breathe, too," Red said. "That makes us sewer workers half crap."

"That man's crazy," Ringo muttered.

"He got caught when they came swarming out," Red said. "He had to run ahead of them. Hell, even he wouldn't tackle that many rats."

"I don't want him jumping out of the dark and scaring me," Bleek said. He edged toward the cat, which looked as if it were going to erupt again. He was a Vesuvius of a cat, and his Pompeii would be Inspector Bleek.

"He don't pay any attention to us workers," Red said. "Hell, he and I've passed each other a dozen times; we just nod and go our own ways. He's a valuable animal; he kills more rats than a dozen poisoners. And he doesn't ask for overtime either."

"We could take him in," a cop said. Red thought he saw him reaching for his handcuffs but decided it was his imagination.

"Let him go," Red said.

"I'm your boss!"

"If you kill that cat, I quit."

Bleek scowled, and then, after a struggle, he put his knife in its sheath under his jacket. The smile came slowly, as if some little man inside him was working away at the ratchets connected to the corners of his lips. Finally, the big Halloween-pumpkin grin encased in plastic, he put his arm around Red.

"You love that cat, don't you?"

"He's like me, ugly and better off down here in the darkness."

Bleek laughed and squeezed Red's shoulder.

"You ain't ugly, man! You're beautiful!"

"I got a mirror."

Bleek laughed and let loose of Red's shoulder and slapped him on the ass. The cat darted by them, running as if he were glad to see the last of them. He'd had enough of rats for a long time, too.

6.

The order came down from the Commissioner of Public Works that no sewer worker was ever to be alone while working. They must always have a buddy in sight. Red and Ringo observed this rule, if not religiously at least devoutly. But as two weeks passed, they occasionally found themselves alone. Old habits, unlike old clothes, don't wear out easily. However, as soon as one became aware that the other had gone on ahead around a curve of a tunnel or had dropped back, one started calling and didn't quit until he'd seen the other. During this time, Red had nightmares. It was always the rats. He'd see them leaping around, and then, while he stood unable to run away, they'd scurry toward him, and after a while he'd feel one run up his leg. It would stop just below his buttocks and start sniffing and he knew what it was going to do and he tightened up but those chisel teeth were going to gnaw and gnaw.

He always woke then with the rats gone, but the horror took time to melt, like a suppository that'd just come from the refrigerator.

"Nibble, nibble, nibble," he said to Bleek. "A man doesn't have to die by big bites."

"Dreams can't kill you."

"They've killed more people than automobiles ever did. Napoleon and Hitler were dreamers. Come to think of it, it was dreamers that invented the automobile."

"Who invented dreams?" Bleek said.

That surprised Red, and he forgot what he was going to say next. Bleek seemed like a hail-fellow-well-met guy, smart enough for his job but no bargain in the intellect shop. Yet, every once in a while, he came out with a remark like this. There were a few trout among his mental carp.

Bleek looked at his wristwatch. Red said, "Yes, I know. We got to get going."

Ringo had started down the manhole. While waiting for him, Red looked around. The sky was, or seemed to be, the deepest blue he'd ever seen. The tall buildings along this street were like mountains themselves, banking the street, keeping it in shady trust. The manhole, however, was in a spot where the sunshine ran between two buildings, like Indians coming through a pass, Red thought. Or the Golden Horde invading the land of shadows. The patina of unreality that raw sunshine always laid on Golden Gate City was the thickest he'd ever seen. The shadows fought it, battling to keep their hold on reality, but they were retreating.

Bleek was standing near him, obviously trying to think of something to say before he got in his car and drove off. A car passed by with a young couple in it, and the girl, a lovely creature, pointed at Red and said something to the driver, a handsome fellow. He took a quick look at Red and then at Bleek, and his lips formed words. "Oh, my God!"

"Doubled in ugliness," the girl's lips shaped.

Red gave her the finger. The girl, her head turned to look behind her, was startled at first, but she laughed and turned to the boy and said something. Red thought for a minute that the boy might back up the car and come storming out, but after slowing down, the car speeded up. The two had thrown their heads back as if they were laughing.

Red shrugged. He'd seen this reaction many times before. People were always shocked when they uncovered the conspiracy of his genes to overthrow the human face. Then they laughed.

He started down the ladder below the manhole. Bleek said, "How's your poem coming?"

Red wondered why he was asking him that, but he answered, "I've given up on *The Queen of Darkness*. No, that's wrong. She's given up on me. Anyway, she was never serious. All she ever did was flirt with me. She isn't going to kiss me, like she does real poets."

"You're a little strange," Bleek said. "But then I got a lot of strange ones among my boys. Sewer work seems to attract them, but of course this is California. So you ain't going to write poetry any more?"

"I've had it," Red said. "All I've wanted for the past two years is to write four perfect lines. To hell with epics, especially epics about sewers. All I wanted was four lines that would make me remembered forever, and I'd have settled for two. Two lines to blaze in the eyes of the world so it wouldn't see the face of the man behind them. That wasn't much to ask, but it was too much. She's kissed me off for good. She doesn't come in my dreams any more. It's just the rats that come now."

Bleek looked distressed. However, he often looked that way. The planes of his face naturally formed themselves into a roadmap of grief.

"You saying this is the end of the line for you?"

"As a poet, yes. And since I'm half poet, though a bad one, only half a man is going to survive."

Bleek didn't seem to know what to say.

Red said, "See you," and he climbed on down the ladder. He and Ringo picked up their tools and lunchbuckets and walked toward their work. Somewhere ahead of them something had clogged up the stream, and they had to find it and remove it.

They passed through areas where permanent lights blazed overhead and then through dark places where the only light was their headlamps. Like a chess board, Red thought, where the only players were pawns.

Their lamps beamed on a big pile of something indeterminable. The mass was like a dam, at least a foot higher than the water backing up behind it.

Ringo, a few feet ahead of Red, stopped on the walkway and looked down at the pile. Red started to say something, and then Ringo screamed.

The mass had come alive. It was heaving up from the charnel, and two pseudopods had encircled Ringo's feet and waist.

Red was paralyzed. The tunnel had become a cannon barrel down which unreality was shooting.

Ringo fought the tentacles, tearing off big pieces of soft brown stuff. Bones wired together at the joints fell out of the stuff that struck the concrete walkway, but other pseudopods grew out of the mass and seized Ringo around the throat and between his legs. They extended, slid around and around Ringo while Red stared. His beam lit up Ringo's open mouth, the white teeth, the whites of the eyes. It also reflected on the single bulging eye on top of a bump on the side near Ringo.

Suddenly, Ringo's jaw dropped, and his eyes started to glaze like the monster's eye. Either he had fainted or he had had a heart attack. Whichever it was, he had fallen onto the mass, a little distance from the eye, and he was sinking face down into it.

Red wanted to run away, but he couldn't leave Ringo to be drawn into that sickening mass. Suddenly, as if a switch had been slammed shut inside him, he leaped forward. At the edge of the walkway he leaned down and grabbed Ringo's left ankle. A tentacle, soft, slimy, stinking, came up over the edge of the concrete and coiled around his own leg. He screamed but he did not let loose of the ankle. Ringo was being pulled out slowly, and Red knew that if he could hang on to him, he could probably get him away. He had to free him soon because Ringo, if he wasn't dead, was going to suffocate in a short time.

Before he could drop the ankle and get away, he was up to his waist in the mass. It had oozed up onto the walkway, enfolded him, and was sucking him into it.

The glass eye was in front of his face; it was on the end of a pod, swaying back and forth before him.

Red, still screaming, took off his helmet and batted at the eye. It struck it, tore it loose, and then he was in darkness. The helmet had been snatched away and was sinking into the vast body. For a second the light glowed redly inside and then was gone.

Red forgot about Ringo. He thrashed and struck out and suddenly he was free. Sobbing, he crawled away until he came against the wall. He didn't know which way was upstream, but he hoped he was going in the right direction. The thing couldn't make much headway against the waters. It had pulled part of its body away from the channel to get up on the walkway, and the waters had come rushing down the opened way. They made a strong current just now, one against which the thing surely could not swim very swiftly.

Also, with its eye gone, it was as blind as he. Could it hear? Smell?

Maybe I've flipped, Red thought. That thing can't exist. I must be in delirium, imagining it. Maybe I'm really in a straitjacket someplace. I hope they can give me something, a miracle drug, a shock treatment, to get me out of here. What if I were locked in this nightmare forever?

He heard a shout behind him, a human voice. He quit crawling and turned around. The beam of a headlamp shone about fifty yards from him. He couldn't see the figure under it, but it must be about six feet two or three inches high. Anybody he knew?

The beam danced around, lit on him once, then went back to point up and down the stream. The water level had gone down though it was still higher than it should be. The thing had gone with the current, Ringo inside it.

The beam left the channel and played on the walkway as the man walked toward him. Red sat down with his back against the wall, unable to hear the approaching footsteps because of his loud breathing and his heart booming in his eardrums. The man stopped just before him, the beam on his helmet glaring into Red's eyes so he couldn't see the face beneath.

"Listen," Red said. Something struck the top of his head, and when he awoke the light was out. He had a sharp pain in his head, but he had no time to think about that. His clothes had been removed, and he was on his back, and his hands were under him and taped together at the wrists. His ankles were also taped.

Red groaned and said, "What are you doing? Who is it?"

There was a sound as of a suddenly sucked-in breath.

"For God's sake," Red said. "Let me loose. Don't you know what happened? Ringo was killed. It's true, so help me God, he was swallowed by a thing you wouldn't believe. It's waiting out there. A man alone won't get by him. Together we might make it."

He jumped as a hand touched his ankle above the tapes. He trembled as the hand began moving up his leg. He jumped again when something cold and hard touched the other leg for a moment.

"Who are you?" he yelled. "Who are you?"

He heard only a heavy breathing. The hand and the knife had stopped, but now they were sliding upward along his flesh.

"Who are you?"

The hand and the knife stopped. A voice, thick as honey, said, "I'm not worried about the thing. It's my buddy."

"Bleek?"

"Up there I'm Bleek. In more ways than one.

"Down here, I'm the phantom of the sewer, lover." Red knew it was no use to scream. But he did.

A Hole in Hell

by Dane Helstrom

Of all the stories in this collection, "A Hole in Hell" is the least likely to be categorized as a fictional-author tale. However, like "The Jungle Rot Kid on the Nod," it is included here because follows in the spirit, if not the essence, of Farmer's fictional-author conceit. And it is a rare story, having only been published once in English, in the volume *Tales of Riverworld* (Warner Questar, 1992), a shared-world anthology edited by Farmer and dedicated to his popular science fiction series.

As usual, Farmer plays the Trickster, placing a pseudonymous story within an anthology he himself edited. Several years passed before it became widely known that he had penned the tale. Don't look too surprised if one day things come full circle and you open some future magazine or anthology only to find…a story in which Dane Helstrom is a character.

<hr />

His pen had hurled many into Hell. Now he, who should be in Heaven with his adored Beatrice, was in a pit such as he had depicted in *The Inferno.*

For years, he had searched along the River for the only woman he had ever deeply loved, the light of his life and his poetry. Now he was imprisoned by a man whom he deeply hated.

The eight-feet-square and twelve-feet-deep pit was on top of a foothill. Its sides were oak logs that slanted inward. (This whole world, he thought, slants inward and imprisons me.) The pit was in shadow except when the sun was directly overhead. Oh, blessed sun! Oh, swiftly moving sun! Stay in your course!

Ankle-deep in sewage, Dante Alighieri stood, his face turned upward. Dawn was an hour old. Soon, Dante's accursed enemy, Benedict Caetani, Pope Boniface VIII from 1294 to 1303, would come. Dante would know when Boniface was nearing because he would hear the barking and the howling of dogs. Yet there were no dogs in this place, which might be Purgatory or might be Hell.

A few minutes later, he stiffened. The yapping, barking, and howling sounded faintly. It was as if he had just detected the sounds erupting from the three heads of Cerberus, Satan's unnatural hound that guarded the entrance to Inferno. Presently, the noise became a clamor, and he saw the man who owned the dogs.

"Another God-given morning," Boniface said. "Time for my first piss. I baptize thee, Signor Alighieri, in the name of those whom you so hatefully consigned to Hell!"

His eyes shut, Dante endured the rain that did not come from the heavens. A minute later, he opened them. The pope had shed his robes and his wooden beehive-shaped tiara. The dogs—naked men and women on hands and knees or on hands and toes—prowled around the edges of the pits. Their fish-skin collars were attached to leashes held by men and women of Boniface's court. The male dogs, by the edge of the pit and parallel with it, lifted legs to piss into it.

Boniface stuck his buttocks over the pit while two men held his hands to keep him from falling backward.

"In the name of those whom you wrongfully put in Hell in your vicious poem, I give you the bread and wine of the unblessed! Eat thereof, and glory in the transubstantiation of your fallen god, Lucifer!"

At the same time, a dozen dogs loosed their bowel contents. Only by standing in the center of the pit could he avoid being struck.

After a year of this, Dante thought, he should have been suffocated by the filth daily expelled into the hole. But the many excrement-eating earthworms kept the level of filth down to his ankles. Boniface had been pulled erect but again bent over as a series of slaves spat water between the pope's buttocks. Meanwhile, the dogs barked, howled, whined, and yipped.

Dante shouted, "May God force you for eternity to wear an iron tiara as white hot as His wrath!"

"Dante Alighieri never learns!" the pope screamed. "Does he get down on his knees, that stiff-necked Florentine, and beg forgiveness of those whom he has cruelly wronged? Not he! His mind is as the shit in which he lives!

"You committed blasphemy when you wrote of me in your Inferno as being in Hell while I was still living! Even God does not put sinners in Hell before they die!"

"You were and are evil!" Dante cried. "Would a godly man make dogs out of men, no matter what their offense?"

Boniface screamed, "Down on your knees, Guelf pig, and confess that you have wronged me and be truly contrite! Then you may continue your journey to find your beloved Beatrice! Though you should be seeking the Truth and God, not a slut such as she!"

"A fig upon you!" Dante screamed. And he bit his thumb and stabbed it at Boniface.

"Dante empits himself; he confesses his guilt and sin. Continue to suffer your rightful punishment!"

Then the pope, slaves, henchmen, and dog pack left. Four guards stayed behind to make sure that he did not find some means of killing himself.

Tonight, as every night, it would rain so hard that he could lie down in the water and drown himself. To do that would be to commit an unforgivable sin, one that automatically damned a soul. Would that be a sin in this world? Here, when a man died, he rose to life twenty-four hours later, though far away from where he had died. Was it then a sin to kill himself? Logic said that it was not. Yet he could not be sure. What God forbade on Earth should also be forbidden in this world. Or had the commandments been changed somewhat here to fit the situation?

Unheeding the soft squishy stuff under his feet, he paced back and forth. His mind went from the unanswerable question of suicide here to the conflicts raging during his lifetime. When he was calm and logical, which was not often, he told himself that the bloody quarrels between Ghibellines and Guelfs and between Black Guelfs and White Guelfs over politico-religious issues no longer mattered.

The huge majority of resurrectees had never heard of these conflicts and would yawn if they did. Only in this area, where Italians of his era lived, did the hatred burn fiercely. Yet it should be forgotten. Far more important things stalked the Rivervalley and should be dealt with. If they were not, salvation would be beyond their reach.

But he could neither forget nor forgive.

At high noon, the grailstones thundered. The echoes from the mountains had just ceased when he heard the dogs coming toward him. Presently, the barking and the howling, mixed with the crack of the dog-tenders' whips, were above and around him. Dante looked upward, shielding his eyes against the sun. He cried out and sank to his knees. He said then, "Beatrice!"

Boniface, standing naked by the edge of the pit, a leash in his hand, said, "Your long quest is over, sinner! Your beloved whore was brought in this morning by slave dealers! Here she is, a lovely bitch who must surely be in heat!"

Dante had averted his eyes, but he forced himself to look again. Once more, he cried out with horror.

She was naked and down on her hands and knees. She was weeping, her face so twisted that he should not have been able to recognize her.

Something, some divine element, a sort of lightning flash between heaven and earth, had flashed from her to him. He had known instantly that she was Beatrice.

Boniface, grinning like a fox about to eat a chicken, pulled on her leash and kicked her, though not hard, in the ribs. She obeyed his orders to place herself parallel with the edge of the pit and very close to it. Then he gave the leash to a guard and got down on his hands and knees behind her.

"A bitch must be mounted from behind!" he shouted.

She cried out, "Dante!"

A whip wielded by another guard cut her across her shoulders. She cried out again.

"Do not speak!" Boniface said. "You are a soulless dog, and dogs do not speak!"

He eased himself forward over her. She screamed when he penetrated her.

Dante was leaping upward again and again and yelping like a dog. But he could not jump high enough to grab the edge.

"Look, look, sinner!" Boniface cried. "I am no dog, yet I am humping dog-like the bitch you love so much!"

Dante wanted to close his eyes but could not.

And then Beatrice heaved upward and lifted Boniface with her. Though the guard jerked savagely on her leash, he could not stop her. She was at this moment as strong as if an avenging angel had poured his holy fierceness into her. She turned around and grabbed Boniface. Both screaming, they fell into the pit, the leash jerking loose from the guard's hand. She landed on top of the pope and knocked the wind out of him. Immediately, she began tearing at his nose with her teeth. She ceased biting when a spear cast by a guard from above plunged deep into her back.

She gasped, "Mother of...wish...die forever," and died.

The guards shouted at Dante to stay away from the pope. He had pushed the woman's corpse aside and was scrambling to his feet. Dante, crying out with grief and rage, jerked the spear from the beloved flesh and drove its point into the pope's belly. Then he yanked it out and started to turn.

A guard who had just dropped into the pit ran toward Dante, his spear held level. But his feet slipped in the filth, and he fell hard on his face.

Dante raised the spear to stab the guard. He hesitated. If he spared the guard, he, too, might be spared. But the pope's men would only do that to torture him and then, probably, cast him again into the pit.

As the guard, slipping in the filth, tried to get up, Dante cried out, "Beatrice! Wait for me!"

He rammed the spear butt against the log wall and pushed the blade into the pit of his stomach. Despite the agony, he kept on pushing until the blade was buried in him.

He was committing the sin of suicide. But it was the only way of escape. Someday, he would find out if it was unforgivable. If he eventually went to Hell because of his evil deed—if it was evil—he was willing to pay the full price.

Beatrice had been little more than an arm's length from him. Then, within two minutes, she was gone.

But she could be found again.

Though he might have to search for a hundred years, he would find her.

Surely, God understood his great love for her. He would not be jealous because his creature, Dante Alighieri, loved Beatrice more than he loved his Creator.

Dante's last thought dwindled into darkness. Forgive...didn't mean tha...

The Last Rise of Nick Adams

Original version published as
"The Impotency of Bad Karma"
under the byline of Cordwainer Bird

"The Last Rise of Nick Adams" originally appeared in a slightly altered form in the first and only issue of the magazine *Popular Culture*, edited by Brad Lang. In that incarnation, the story was entitled "The Impotency of Bad Karma" and the author bore the strange sounding name of Cordwainer Bird. Bird, of course, is Harlan Ellison's own personal "Alan Smithee" moniker; that is, a substitute name intended to distance oneself from those projects one has been a part of but have been otherwise irreparably ruined by the shoddy work of others. Although Cordwainer Bird was not a fictional author, Farmer remedied this by placing him in the Wold Newton genealogy found in the addendums to his *Doc Savage: His Apocalyptic Life*. Accordingly, Bird is nephew to both The Shadow and G-8 and the great grandson of James Joyce's Leopold Bloom. Later, Bird appeared as a character in "The Doge Whose Barque Was Worse Than His Bight" by Jonathan Swift Somers III (*The Magazine of Science Fiction and Fantasy*, November 1976; reprinted in Pearls from Peoria, Subterranean Press, 2006). And Ellison himself wrote of Bird in his own story, "A New York Review of Bird" (*Weird Heroes, Volume Two*, ed. Byron Preiss, Pyramid, 1975).

The story in its form below debuted in Roy Torgeson's science fiction anthology *Chrysalis, Volume Two* (Zebra, 1978). Farmer rewrote it because Barry Malzberg, who chanced to have had an article published in that extremely scarce issue of *Popular Culture*, read "The Impotency of Bad Karma" and disapproved of its parody of himself.

Although some have speculated that the protagonist of the story is the son of Hemingway's Nick Adams, Farmer says he can neither confirm nor deny this.

Nick Adams, Jr., science-fiction author, and his wife were having the same old argument.

"If you really loved me, you wouldn't be having so much trouble with it."

"There are many words for it," Nick said. "If you didn't have a dirty mind, you'd use them. Anyway, there are plenty of times when you can't complain about it."

"Yeah! About once every other month I can't!"

Ashlar was a tall scrawny ex-blonde who had been beautiful until the age of thirty-seven-and-a-half. Now she was fifty. A hard fifty, Nick thought. And here am I, a soft fifty.

"It does have a sort of sine-wave action," he said. "I mean, if you drew a graph…"So now it's dependent on weather conditions. What're we supposed to do, consult the barometer when we make love? Why don't you make a graph of its rises and falls? Of course, you'd have to have some rises first…"

"I got to go to work," he said, "I'm months behind…"

"I'll say you are, though I don't mean in your writing! All right, hide behind the typewriter! Bang your keys; don't bang me!"

He rose from the chair and dutifully kissed her on her forehead. It was as cold and hard as a tombstone, incised with wrinkles that read Here Lies Love, RIP. She snarled silently. Shrugging, he walked up the steps toward his office. By the time he reached the third floor, he was sweating as if he were a rape suspect in a police lineup. His panting filled the house.

Fifty, out of breath, and low on virility. Still, it wasn't really his fault. She was such a cold bitch. Take last night, for instance. Ashlar's eyes had started rolling, and her face was falling apart underneath the makeup. He had said, "Did you feel something move, little rabbit?" (He was crazy about Hemingway.) And she had said, "Something's *going* to move. Get off. I got to go to the toilet."

Once it had all been good and true, and he had felt the universe move all the way to the Pole Star. Now he felt as if the hair had fallen off his chest.

He sat down before the typewriter and stroked the keys, the smooth and cool keys, and he pressed a few to tune up his fingers and warm up the writing spirit. He could feel the inspiration deep down within, shadow-boxing, rope-skipping, jogging, sweating, pores open, heart beating hard and true, ready to climb into the ring.

The only trouble was, the bell rang, and he couldn't even get out of his corner. He was stuck on the first word. *The. The*…what?

If only he could see some pattern in his sexual behavior. Maybe the silly bitch's sarcastic remark about making a graph wasn't so stupid. Maybe…

A bell rang, and he sprang up, shuffling, his left shoulder up, arm extended…what was he doing? That was the front doorbell, and it was probably announcing the delivery of the mail. Nick gave the mailman ten dollars a month to ring the doorbell. This was illegal, but who was going to know? Nick could not endure the idea that a hot check was cooling off in the mailbox.

He hurried downstairs, passing Ashlar, who wasn't going to get off her ass and bring the mail to him. Not her.

Since this was the first of the month, there were ten bills. But there was also a pile of fan mail and a letter from his agent.

Ah! His agent had sent a check, the initial advance on a new contract. Two thousand dollars. Minus his agent's ten percent commission. Minus fifty dollars for overseas market mailings. Minus twenty-five for the long-distance call his agent had made to him last month. Minus a thousand for the loan from his agent. Minus fifty for the interest on the loan. Minus ten dollars accounting charge.

Only six hundred and sixty-five dollars remained, but it was a feast after last month's famine. By the time he'd finished reading the fan letters, all raving about the goodness and truth of his works, he felt as if he was connected to a gas station air pump.

Suddenly, he knew that there was a pattern to the decline and fail of the Roman Empire he carried between his legs. In no way, however, was he going to take the edge off his horniness by explaining the revelation to Ashlar just now. He dropped his mail and his pants, and he hurried to the kitchen. Ashlar was bent over, putting dishes in the washer.

He flipped up her skirt, yanked down her panties, and said, "The dishes can wait, but it can't."

It would all have been good and true and the earth might have moved if Ashlar hadn't gotten her head caught between the wire racks of the washer.

"You're getting fat again, aren't you?" Ashlar said. "That's some spare tire you got. And you missed a patch on your cheek when you shaved. Listen. I know this isn't time to talk about it, but my mother…what's the matter? Why are you stopping?"

Nick snarled and he said, "If you need an explanation, you're an imbecile. I'm pulling out like a train that stopped at the wrong station. I'm going back to my typewriter. A woman will always screw you up, but a typewriter's a typewriter, true and trustworthy, and it doesn't talk to you when you're making love to it."

Two minutes later, while Ashlar beat on the door with her fists and yelled at him, the typewriter keys jammed and he couldn't get them unstuck.

You couldn't even put faith in a simple machine. You could not trust anything. Everything that was supposed to be clean and good and true went to hell in this universe. Still, you had to stick with it, be a man with *conejos*. Or was it *cojones*? Never mind. Just tell yourself, "Tough shit," and "My head is bloody but unbowed. You have to die but you don't have to say Uncle."

That was fine, but the keys were still stuck, and Ashlar wouldn't quit beating on the door and screaming.

He got up, cursing and yanked the door open. Ashlar fell sobbing into his arms.

"I'm sorry, sorry, sorry! What a bitch I am! Here's the whole earth about ready to move all the way down to its core, and I pick on you!"

"Yes, you're truly a bitch," he said. "But I forgive you because I love you and you love me and no matter what happens we have something that is good. However..."

He wasn't going to say anything about his discovery of the pattern. Not now. He'd test his theory later.

An hour afterward, he said, panting, "Listen, Ashlar, let's take a vacation. We'll go to the World Science-Fiction Convention in Las Vegas. We'll have fun, and in between parties and shooting craps, we'll make love. The good true feeling will come back while we're there"

Or should he have said the true good feeling? What the hell was the correct order of adjectives in a phrase like that'?

It didn't matter. What did was that Ashlar decided to go to the convention and didn't even complain that she had nothing to wear. Moreover, his theory had worked out. Up to a point, anyway, and that wasn't really his fault. The fans crowded around him, begging for his autograph, and he heard never an unkind word. As if this wasn't heady enough, not to mention the stimulation of his male hormones, three of the greatest science-fiction authors in the world invited him to dinner and paid him many compliments over the bourbons and steaks.

The first, Zeke Vermouth, Ph.D., the wealthiest writer in the field, didn't mention that they were going Dutch until after meal was eaten. Even this didn't lessen Nick's pleasures. And then, glory of glories, Robin Hindbind, the dean of science-fiction authors, had him in for a private supper. Nick was happy as a man with a free lifetime pass to a massage parlor. It was fabulous to sit in the suite, which was as spacious as Nick's house, and eat with the creator of such classics as *Water Brother Among the Bathless, I Will Boll No Weevil* and the autobiographical *Time Enough For F***ing*, subtitled *Why Everybody Worships Me*.

Then, wonder of wonders, the grand old man, Preston de Tove himself, asked Nick to a very select party. De Tove as probably Nick's greatest hero, the man who had rocked the science-fiction world in the 40s with his smashing *Spam!* and *The World of Zilch A.*

De Tove, however, hadn't done much writing for thirty years. He'd been too busy practicing a science of mental health originated by another classic author, old B .M. Kachall himself. This was M.P. (Mnemonic Peristalsis) Therapy, a psychic discipline which claimed to enable a person to attain through its techniques an I.Q. of 500, perfect recall, Superman's or Wonder Woman's body, and immortality.

In essence, these techniques consisted in keeping your bowels one hundred percent open. To do this, though, you had to work back along your memory track until you encountered in all details, visual, tactile, auditory, olfactory, especially olfactory, your first bowel movement. This was called the P U. or Primal Urge.

Kachall had promised his disciples that all goals could be reached within a year through M.P. Therapy. However, de Tove, like the majority of Kachall's followers, was, three decades later, still taking laxatives as a physical aid to the mental techniques. He had not lost faith, even if he did spend most of his time during the party in the bathroom.

De Tove had refused to go along with Kachall's S.P.L. Religion, a metaphysical extension of M.P. Therapy. Perhaps this was because de Tove had to wear a diaper at all times, and attendees at the S P.L services were forbidden to wear anything. In any event, the religion required that the worshipper send his C.E. (Colonic Ego) back to the first movement of the universe, the Big Bang. If the worshipper survived that, he was certified to be an E.E. (End End), one who'd attained the Supreme Purgative Level. This meant that the E.E. radiated such a powerful aura that nobody would dare to mess around with him. Or even get near him for that matter.

Aside from having had to sit by an open window throughout the party, Nick was ecstatic. Nothing better could happen now. But he was wrong. The next day, two Englishmen, G.C. Alldrab and William Rubboys, invited him to a party for avant-garde writers. This twain had been lucky enough to be highly esteemed by some important mainstream critics and so now refused to be classified as mere s-f authors. Nevertheless, when the convention committee offered to pay their airfare, hotel expenses, and booze if they'd be guests, they consented to associate, for three days at least, with the debased category.

Alldrab was chiefly famous for stories in which depressed, impotent, passive, and incompetent antiheroes passed through catastrophic landscapes over which floated various parts, usually sexual, of famous people. He was also hung up on traffic accidents, a symbol to him of the rottenness of Western civilization, especially the United States. He sneered at plots and storylines.

And so did his colleague. Rubboys was famous for both the unique content and technique of his fiction. It drew mostly on his experiences as a drug addict and peregrinating homosexual. Otherwise, he was a nice guy and not nearly as snobbish as Alldrab, though some were unkind enough to say that his camaraderie with young male fans wasn't entirely due to his democratic leanings.

Lately, he'd been getting a lot of flak from feminist critics, who loathed his vicious attitude towards all women, though he claimed it was purely literary. They couldn't be blamed. Try though they might to ignore his bias because of his high reputation as a writer, they'd gotten fed up with his numerous references to females as cunts, gashes, twats, slits, and hairy holes.

Rubboys' technique consisted of putting a manuscript through a shredder, then pasting the strips at random for the finished product.

Nick didn't care for either man's works, though he did admit that Alldrab's fiction made more sense than Rubboys'. But then whose didn't? However, to be their guest was an honor in some circles, and these were the critics with clout. Maybe they'd take some notice of him now—glory through association.

Nick was told that, even though he was middle-aged and wrote mostly square commercial stuff, he had been invited because of his experimental time-travel story, *The Man Who Buggered Himself.* This was great stuff, obscure and unintelligible and quasipoetic enough to satisfy the artiest of the arty.

Nick just grinned. Why should he tell them he had written the story while drinking muscatel and smoking opium?

The party was a success until midnight. Alldrab, pissy-assed drunk by then, tried to get his mistress to take Rubboys' rented car out and drive it at 100 mph into a lamppost. Thus he could witness a real crash and transpose it into sanguinary poetry in his next novel, *Smash!,* get to the root of the evilness in Occidental culture.

His mistress didn't care for this. In fact, she became hysterical. Rubboys wasn't too keen about it either.

Result: a stampede of pale tight-faced guests out of the door, Nick in the lead, while the girl-friend was dialing the police.

Ashlar was curious about why Nick had been so horny during the convention and for some weeks after that, then had quickly reverted to steerhood.

'What's the matter with you?" Ashlar said after one particularly distressing attempt. "Again?"

She dropped her cigarette ashes on his pubic hairs, causing him to delay his reply until he put out the fire.

"I'll tell you!" he roared. "You're always putting me down, literally and figuratively. Criticising me. You deflate my ego and hence my potency.

"The same thing happens when I get bad reviews or fan mail that knocks me or a rejection slip. But when fans and critics and authors praise me, which doesn't happen often, I'm inflated. There's no doubt about it. I've determined scientifically that my virility waxes and wanes in direct proportion to the quantity-cum (no pun intended) -quality of the praise or bumraps I receive."

"You can't be serious?"

"I drew a graph. It isn't exactly a bell-shaped curve. More like a limp cactus."

"You mean I got to say only nice things about you, keep my mouth shut when you bug me? Treat you like an idol of gold? You're not, you know. You have feet of clay—all the way up to your big bald spot."

"See, that's what I mean."

They quarreled violently for three hours. In the end, Ashlar wept and promised she'd quit pointing out his faults. Not only that, she'd praise him a lot.

But that wasn't honest, and so it didn't work out. He knew she was lying when she told him how handsome he was and what a great writer he was and how he was the most fantastic stud in the world.

To make things worse, his latest book was panned by one hundred percent of the reviewers.

"Thumbs down; everything's down," Nick said.

A week later, things got good again. Better than good. He was as happy as Aladdin when he first rubbed the bride given him by the magic lamp.

Dubbeldeel Publications came through with some unexpected royalties on a three-year-old book. The publisher offered to buy another on the basis of a two-page outline. Nick got word that a Ph.D. candidate at UCLA was writing a thesis on his works. The fan mail that week was unusually heavy and not one of its writers suggested that he wrote on toilet paper.

It did not matter now that he doubted Ashlar's sincerity. People with no ulterior motives were comparing him with the great Kilgore Trout.

He was so happy that he suggested to Ashlar that they take another vacation, attend a convention in Pekin, Illinois, which was only ten miles from their hometown. Peoria. Ashlar said that she'd go, even if she didn't like the creeps that crowded around him at the cons. She'd spend her time in the bar with the wives of the writers. She could relax with them, get away from shoptalk that wearied her so when the writers got together. The wives didn't care for science-fiction and seldom read even their husband's stuff. Especially their husband's stuff.

Nick wasn't superstitious. Even so he regarded it as a favorable omen when he saw the program book of the convention. In big bold letters on the cover was the name of the convention. It should have been Pekcon, fan slang for Pek(in) Con(vention). But it had come out Pekcor.

Later, Nick admitted that he'd interpreted the signs and portents wrongly. Had he ever!

At first, things went as well as anyone could ask for. The fans practically kissed his feet, and the regard of his peers was very evident. Some even paid for the drinks, instead of leaving him, as usual, to sweat while he settled a staggering bill.

Ashlar should have been happy. Instead, she complained that she couldn't spend the rest of her life attending conventions just to have a good sex life.

Nick got to talking with an eighteen-year-old fan with long blonde hair, a pixie face, huge adoring eyes, boobs that floated ahead of her like hot-air balloons, and legs like Marlene Dierich's. Her last name was Barkis, she was willing, and he was overcome by temptation. They went to her room, and the sexual-Richter scale hit 8.6 and was on its way to record 9.6 when Ashlar began beating at the door and screaming at him to open it.

Later, he found out that a writer's wife had seen him and Barkis entering her room. She had raced around the hotel until she found Ashlar, who hadn't wasted any time getting the hotel dick and three wives as witnesses.

All the way to Peoria, Ashlar didn't stop yelling or crying. Once there, she swiftly packed and took a taxi to her mother's house. She didn't stay there long, since she had been so angry that she'd forgotten her mother had recently gone to a nursing home. Unfazed, she moved into an expensive hotel and sent her bills through her lawyer to Nick,

Each day he got a long letter from her—each deflating. Throwing them unread into the wastepaper basket didn't work. He was too curious, he had to open them and see what new invectives and unsavory descriptions she had come up with. So, after long thought, he sold the house and moved from Illinois to New Jersey. Only his agent had his forwarding address, and Nick told him to return all letters from his wife to her.

"Mark them: *Uninterested*."

But he knew that she would find him some day.

Three months passed without a letter from her. Things went as well as could he expected in this world where hardly anybody really gave a damn how you were doing. He did find a young fan, "Moomah" Smith, who was eager to spend a night with him when he got good mail, good notices, and good royalties.

And then, one morning as he was drinking coffee just before tackling the typewriter, the phone rang. His agent's new secretary, one he didn't know, was calling. Her employer was in Europe (cavorting around on his ten percent, Nick thought), but she had good news for him. Sharper & Rake, really big hardcover publishers, had just bought an outline for a novel, *A Sanitary Brightly Illuminated Planet*, and they were going to give him a huge advance. Furthermore, Sharper & Rake intended to go all out in an advertising and publicity campaign.

The first letter was from a member of the committee which handled the Pulsar Award. This was given once a year by SWOT, the Science-Fiction Writers of Terra. Nick belonged to this, although its chief benefit was that he could deduct the membership dues from his income tax. However, one of his stories, *Hot Nights on Venus*, had been nominated for the Pulsar. And now, and now—the monster felt as if it were the *Queen Mary* heading for port with a stiff wind behind it—he had won it!

"Under no circumstances must you tell anyone about this," the committee member had written, "The awards won't be given until two months from now. We're informing you of this to make sure that you'll be at the annual SWOT banquet in New York."

Nick read the second letter. It was from Lex Fiddler, the foremost American mainstream critic. Fiddler informed him that he had nominated Nick's Novel, *A Farewell to Mars*, for the highest honor for writing in the country. This was the MOOLA, the Michael Oberst Literary Award, established fifty years before by a St. Louis brewer. If Nick won it, he would get $50,000, he would be famous, his book would be a best seller, and an offer from Hollywood was a sure thing even if it didn't get the award.

Nick opened the third letter.

Whooping with joy, he whirled around and around, the end of his mighty walloper knocking over vases and flipping ash trays from tables. He stopped dancing then because he was so dizzy. Leaning on a table for support, gazing at the ever-expanding thing, he groaned, "I've got to get Moomah here. Only… I hope she doesn't faint when she sees it."

It was Nick who fainted, not Moomah. The blood spurted from his head, driving downward as his heart constricted in a final massive endeavor to supply what the ego demanded. His blood abandoned the upper part of his body as if the gargantuan paw of King Kong had squeezed it.

Had Nick been conscious, his terror would have halted the process, reversed it, and put the brobdingnagian in its normal state, limp as an unbaked pizza. But his brain was emptied of blood, and he was aware of nothing as he toppled forward, was held for a moment from going over by the giant member, the end of which was rammed into the carpet, and then he pole-vaulted forward, his grayish slack face striking the floor.

He lay on his side while the pythonish member, driven by the unconscious, expanded. It swelled as a balloon swells while ascending into the ever-thinner atmosphere. But balloons have a pressure height, a point at which the force within the envelope is greater than its strength and the envelope ruptures violently.

The mailwoman was just climbing into her Jeep when she heard the blast. She whirled, and she screamed as she saw the flying glass and the smoke pouring out from the shattered windows.

The police found it easy to pinpoint the source of the explosion. The cause was beyond them. They shook their heads and said that this was just one of those mysteries of life.

The police did find out that the third letter, the one from the Swedish Embassy in Washington, D.C., was a fake. Whoever had sent it was unknown and likely to remain so. Why would anybody write Nick Adams, Jr., a science-fiction author, to inform him that he had won the Nobel Prize for Literature?

More investigation disclosed that the letters from the Pulsar Award committee and Lex Fiddler were also fakes. So was the call from his agent's secretary telling him that Sharper & Rake was giving him a huge advance. This was eventually traced to Mrs. Adams, but by then she was in Europe and there to stay. Besides, the police could not charge her with anything except a practical joke.

Ashlar is living in Spain today. Sometimes, for no reason that her friends can determine, she smiles in a strange way. Is it a smile of regret or triumph?

Did she write those letters and make that phone call because she knew what they'd do to her husband? Of course, she couldn't have known how much they would do to him; she underestimated the power of ego and the limits of flesh.

Or did she try to bolster his pride, make him feel good, because she still loved him and so was doing her best to make him inflated with happiness for at least a day?

It would be nice to think so.

The Adventure of the Peerless Peer

by John H. Watson, M.D.

Edited by Philip José Farmer

*American Agent for the Estates of Dr. Watson,
Lord Greystoke, David Copperfield,
Martin Eden, and Don Quixote*

*Dedicated to Samuel Rosenberg,
who has embroidered for the world
the greatest Doylie ever.*

The Adventure of the Peerless Peer: for many years out-of-print and long considered one of Farmer's funniest, most clever works. Or should I say Watson's, for here Farmer merely serves as editor.

The novella—solicited and published in 1974 by Tom Schantz of The Aspen Press—is tightly packed with references to the Wold Newton genealogy; and in a way *The Adventure of the Peerless Peer* acts as a springboard in resolving questions left hanging in Farmer's biographies, *Tarzan Alive: A Definitive Biography of Lord Greystoke* (Doubleday, 1972; reprinted by Bison Books, 2006) and *Doc Savage: His Apocalyptic Life* (Doubleday, 1973). But knowledge of Farmer's Wold Newton family is not a prerequisite for enjoying the story's often pawky wit and humor, or the intricacies of its plot. And it is a tale which contains three of Farmerian favorites—The Great Detective, The Lord of the Jungle, and Zeppelins—so it remains easy to see why Farmer decided to edit the good doctor's work. The double pun of the "Peerless Peer" may be a bit harder to discern, but I'm certain you'll have fun trying.

FOREWORD

As everybody knows, Dr. Watson stored in a battered tin dispatch-box his manuscripts concerning the unpublished cases of Sherlock Holmes. This box was placed in the vaults of the bank of Cox and Co. at Charing Cross. Whatever hopes the world had that these papers would some day become public were destroyed when the bank was blasted into fragments during the bombings of World War II. It is said that Winston Churchill himself directed that the ruins be searched for the box but that no trace of it was found.

I am happy to report that this lack of success is no cause for regret. At a time and for reasons unknown, the box had been transferred to a little villa on the south slope of the Sussex downs near the village of Fulworth. It was kept in a trunk in the attic of the villa. This, as everybody should know, was the residence of Holmes after he had retired. It is not known what eventually happened to the Greatest Detective. There is no record of his death. Even if there were, it would be disbelieved by the many who still think of him as a living person. This almost religious belief thrives though he would, if still alive, be one hundred and twenty years old at the date of writing this foreword.

Whatever happened to Holmes, his villa was sold in the late 1950's to the seventeenth Duke of Denver. The box, with some other objects, was removed to the ducal estate in Norfolk. His Grace had intended to wait until after his death before the papers would be allowed to be published. However, His Grace, though eighty-four years old now, feels that he may live to be a hundred. The world has waited far too long, and it is certainly ready for anything, no matter how shocking, that may be in Watson's narratives. The duke has given his consent to the publication of all but a few papers, and even these may see print if the descendants of certain people mentioned in them give their permission. Gratitude is due His Grace for this generous decision.

On hearing the good news, your editor communicated with the British agents handling the Watson papers and was fortunate enough to acquire the American Agency for them. The adventure at hand is the first to be released; others will follow from time to time.

Watson's holograph is obviously a first draft. A number of passages recording words actually uttered by the participants during this adventure are either crossed out or replaced with asterisks. The "peerless peer" of this tale is called "Greystoke," but on one occasion old habit broke through and Watson inadvertently wrote "Holdernesse." Watson left no note explaining why he had substituted one pseudotitle for another. He used "Holdernesse" in "The Adventure of the Priory School" to conceal the identity of Holmes' noble client. Holmes himself, in his reference to the nobleman in his "The Adventure of the Blanched Soldier," used the pseudotitle of "Greyminster."

It is your editor's guess that Watson decided on "Greystoke" in this narrative because the pseudotitle had been made world-famous by the novels based on the African exploits of the nephew of the man Watson had called "Holdernesse."

The adventure at hand is singular for many reasons. It reveals that Holmes was not allowed to stay in retirement after the events of "His Last Bow." We are made aware that Holmes made a second visit to Africa, going far beyond Khartoum (though not willingly), and so saved Great Britain from the greatest danger which has ever threatened it. We are given some illumination on the careers of the two greatest American aviators and spies in the early years of World War I. We learn that Watson was married for the fourth time, and the destruction of a civilization rivalling ancient Egypt is recorded for the first time. Holmes' contribution to apiology and how he used it to save himself and others is related herein. This narrative also describes how Holmes' genius at deduction enabled him to clear up a certain discrepancy that has puzzled the more discerning readers of the works of Greystoke's American biographer.

Some aspects of this discrepancy are revealed by Lord Greystoke himself in "Extracts from the Memoirs of Lord Greystoke," *Mother Was a Lovely Beast,* Philip José Farmer, editor, Chilton, October, 1974. However, this revelation is only a minor part of Watson's chronicle, one among many mysteries solved, and this account presents the mystery from a somewhat different viewpoint.

Your editor decided for these reasons to leave this explanation in this work. Besides, your editor would not dream of tampering with any part of the Sacred Writings.

—Philip José Farmer

1

It is with a light heart that I take up my pen to write these the last words in which I shall ever record the singular genius which distinguished my friend Sherlock Holmes. I realise that I once wrote something to that effect, though at that time my heart was as heavy as it could possibly be. This time I am certain that Holmes has retired for the last time. At least, he has sworn that he will no more go a-detecting. The case of the peerless peer has made him financially secure, and he foresees no more grave perils menacing our country now that out great enemy has been laid low. Moreover, he has sworn that never again will he set foot on any soil but that of his native land. Nor will he ever again get near an aircraft. The mere sight or sound of one freezes his blood.

The peculiar adventure which occupies these pages began on the second day of February, 1916. At this time I was, despite my age, serving on the staff of a military hospital in London. Zeppelins had made bombing raids over England for two nights previously, mainly in the Midlands. Though these were comparatively ineffective, seventy people had been killed, one hundred and thirteen injured, and a monetary damage of fifty-three thousand eight hundred and thirty-two pounds had been inflicted. These raids were the latest in a series starting the nineteenth of January. There was no panic, of course, but even stout British hearts were experiencing some uneasiness. There were rumours, no doubt originated by German agents, that the Kaiser intended to send across the channel a fleet of a thousand airships. I was discussing this rumour with my young friend, Dr. Fell, over a brandy in my quarters when a knock sounded on the door. I opened it to admit a messenger. He handed me a telegram which I wasted no time in reading.

"Great Scott!" I cried.

"What is it, my dear fellow?" Fell said, heaving himself from the chair. Even then, on war rations, he was putting on overly much weight.

"A summons to the F.O.," I said. "From Holmes. And I am on special leave."

"Sherlock?" said Fell.

"No, Mycroft," I replied. Minutes later, having packed my few belongings, I was being driven in a limousine toward the Foreign Office. An hour later, I entered the small austere room in which the massive Mycroft Holmes sat like a great spider spinning the web that ran throughout the British Empire and many alien lands. There were two others present, both of whom I knew. One was young Merrivale, a baronet's son, the brilliant aide to the head of the British Military Intelligence Department and soon to assume the chieftainship. He was also a qualified physician and had been one of my students when I was lecturing at Bart's. Mycroft claimed that Merrivale was capable of rivalling Holmes himself in the art of detection and would not be far behind Mycroft himself. Holmes' reply to this "needling" was that only practise revealed true promise.

I wondered what Merrivale was doing away from the War Office but had no opportunity to voice my question. The sight of the second person there startled me at the same time it delighted me. It had been over a year since I had seen that tall, gaunt figure with the greying hair and the unforgettable hawklike profile.

"My dear Holmes," I said. "I had thought that after the Von Bork affair…"

"The east wind has become appallingly cold, Watson," he said. "Duty recognises no age limits, and so I am called from my bees to serve our nation once more."

Looking even more grim, he added, "The Von Bork business is not over. I fear that we underestimated the fellow because we so easily captured him. He is not always taken with such facility. Our government erred grievously in permitting him to return to Germany with Von Herling. He should have faced a firing squad. A motor-car crash in Germany after his return almost did for us what we had failed to do, according to reports that have recently reached me. But, except for a permanent injury to his left eye, he has recovered.

"Mycroft tells me that Von Bork has done, and is doing, us inestimable damage. Our intelligence tells us that he is operating in Cairo, Egypt. But just where in Cairo and what disguise he has assumed is not known."

"The man is indeed dangerous," Mycroft said, reaching with a hand as ponderous as a grizzly's paw for his snuff-box. "It is no exaggeration to say that he is the most dangerous man in the world, as far as the Allies are concerned, anyway."

"Greater than Moriarty was?" Holmes said, his eyes lighting up.

"Much greater," replied Mycroft. He breathed in the snuff, sneezed, and wiped his jacket with a large red handkerchief. His watery grey eyes had lost their inward-turning look and burned as if they were searchlights probing the murkiness around a distant target.

"Von Bork has stolen the formula of a Hungarian refugee scientist employed by our government in Cairo. The scientist recently reported to his superiors the results of certain experiments he had been making on a certain type of bacillus peculiar to the land of the Pharaohs. He had discovered that this bacillus could be modified by chemical means to eat only sauerkraut. When a single bacillus was placed upon sauerkraut, it multiplied at a fantastic rate. It would become within sixty minutes a colony which would consume a pound of sauerkraut to its last molecule.

"You see the implications. The bacillus is what the scientists call a mutated type. After treatment with a certain chemical both its form and function are changed. Should we drop vials containing this mutation in Germany, or our agents directly introduce the germs, the entire nation would shortly become sauerkrautless. Both their food supply and their morale would be devastated.

"But Von Bork somehow got wind of this, stole the formula, destroyed the records and the chemicals with fire, and murdered the only man who knew how to mutate the bacillus.

"However, his foul deed was no sooner committed than detected. A tight cordon was thrown around Cairo, and we have reason to believe that Von Bork is hiding in the native quarter somewhere. We can't keep that net tight for long, my dear Sherlock, and that is why you must be gotten there quickly so you can track him down. England expects much from you, brother, and much, I am sure, will be given."

I turned to Holmes, who looked as shaken as I felt. "Surely, my dear fellow, we are not going to Cairo?"

"Surely indeed, Watson," he replied. "Who else could sniff out the Teutonic fox, who else could trap him? We are not so old that we cannot settle Von Bork's hash once and for all."

Holmes, I observed, was still in the habit of using Americanisms, I suppose because he had thrown himself so thoroughly into the role of an Irish-American while tracking down Von Bork in that adventure which I have titled "His Last Bow."

"Unless," he said, sneering, "you really feel that the old warhorse should not leave his comfortable pasture?"

"I am as good a man as I was a year and a half ago," I protested. "Have you ever known me to call it quits?"

He chuckled and patted my shoulder, a gesture so rare that my heart warmed. "Good old Watson."

Mycroft called for cigars, and while we were lighting up, he said, "You two will leave tonight from a Royal Naval Air Service strip outside London. You will be flown by two stages to Cairo, by two different pilots, I should say. The fliers have been carefully selected because their cargo will be precious. The Huns may already know your destination. If they do, they will make desperate efforts to intercept you, but our fliers are the pick of the lot. They are fighter pilots, but they will be flying bombers. The first pilot, the man who'll take you under his wing tonight, is a young fellow. Actually, he is only seventeen, he lied to get into the service, but officially he is eighteen. He has downed seven enemy planes in two weeks and done yeoman service in landing our agents behind enemy lines. You may know of him, at least you knew his great-uncle."

He paused and said, "You remember, of course, the late Duke of Greystoke?"*

"I will never forget the size of the fee I collected from him," Holmes said, and he chuckled.

---

*This is the line in which Watson inadvertently wrote "Holdernesse" but corrected it. Editor.

"Your pilot, Leftenant John Drummond, is the adopted son of the present Lord Greystoke," Mycroft continued.

"But wait!" I said. "Haven't I heard some rather strange things about Lord Greystoke? Doesn't he live in Africa?"

"Oh, yes, in darkest Africa," Mycroft said. "In a tree house, I believe."

"Lord Greystoke lives in a tree house?" I said.

"Ah, yes," Mycroft said. "Greystoke is living in a tree house with an ape. At least, that's one of the rumours I've heard."

"Lord Greystoke is living with an ape?" I said. "A female ape, I trust."

"Oh, yes," Mycroft said. "There's nothing queer about Lord Greystoke, you know."*

"But surely," I said, "this Lord Greystoke can't be the son of the old duke? Not the Lord Saltire, the duke's son, whom we rescued from kidnappers in the adventure of the Priory School?"

Holmes was suddenly as keen as an eagle that detects a lamb. He stooped toward his brother, saying, "Hasn't some connexion been made between His Grace and the hero of that fantastic novel by that American writer—what's-his-name?—Bayrows? Borrows? Isn't the Yank's protagonist modelled somewhat after Lord Greystoke? The book only came out in the States in June of 1914, I believe, and so very few copies have gotten here because of the blockade. But I've heard rumours of it. I believe that His Grace could sue for libel, slander, defamation of character and much else if he chose to notice the novel."

"I really don't know," Mycroft said. "I never read fiction."

"By the Lord Harry!" Merrivale said. "I do! I've read the book, a rattling good yarn but wild, wild. This heir to an English peerage is adopted by a female ape and raised with a tribe of wild and woolly..."

Mycroft slammed his palm against the top of the table, startling all of us and making me wonder what had caused this unheard-of violence from the usually phlegmatic Mycroft.

"Enough of this time-wasting chitchat about an unbalanced peer and an excessively imaginative Yankee writer!" he said. "The Empire is crumbling around our ears and we're talking as if we're in a pub and all's well with the world!"

He was right, of course, and all of us, including Holmes, I'm sure, felt abashed. But that conversation was not as irrelevant as we thought at the time.

---

*Under normal circumstances your editor would delete this old joke. Doubtless the reader has heard it in one form or another. But it is Watson's narrative, and it is of historical importance Now we know when and where the story originated.

An hour later, after receiving verbal instructions from Mycroft and Merrivale, we left in the limousine for the secret airstrip outside London.

2

Our chauffeur drove off the highway onto a narrow dirt road which wound through a dense woods of oaks. After a half a mile, during which we passed many signs warning trespassers that this was military property, we were halted by a barbed wire gate across the road. Armed R.N.A.S. guards checked our documents and then waved us on. Ten minutes later, we emerged from the woods onto a very large meadow. At its northern end was a tall hill, the lower part of which gaped as if it had a mouth which was open with surprise. The surprise was that the opening was not to a cavern at all but to a hangar which had been hollowed out of the living rock of the hill. As we got out of the car men pushed from the hangar a huge aeroplane, the wings of which were folded against the fuselage.

After that, events proceeded swiftly—too swiftly for me, I admit, and perhaps a trifle too swiftly for Holmes. After all, we had been born about a half century before the first aeroplane had flown. We were not sure that the motor-car, a recent invention from our viewpoint, was altogether a beneficial device. And here we were being conducted by a commodore toward the monstrously large aircraft. Within a few minutes, according to him, we would be within its fuselage and leaving the good earth behind and beneath us.

Even as we walked toward it, its biplanes were unfolded and locked into place. By the time we reached it, its propellors had been spun by mechanics and the two motors had caught fire. Thunder rolled from its rotaries, and flame spat from its exhausts.

Whatever Holmes' true feelings, and his skin was rather grey, he could not suppress his driving curiosity, his need to know all that was relevant, However, he had to shout at the commodore to be heard above the roar of the warming-up motors.

"The Admiralty ordered it to be outfitted for your use," the commodore said. His expression told us that he thought that we must be very special people indeed if this aeroplane was equipped just for us.

"It's the prototype model of the Handley Page 0/100," he shouted. "The first of the 'bloody paralyser of an aeroplane' the Admiralty ordered for the bombing of Germany, It has two 250-horsepower Rolls-Royce Eagle II motors, as you see. It has an enclosed crew cabin. The engine nacelles and the front part of the fuselage were armour-plated, but the armour has been removed to give the craft more speed."

"What?" Holmes yelled. "Removed?"

"Yes," the commodore said. "It shouldn't make any difference to you. You'll be in the cabin, and it was never armour-plated."

Holmes and I exchanged glances. The commodore continued, "Extra petrol tanks have been installed to give the craft extended range. These will be just forward of the cabin…"

"And if we crash?" Holmes said.

"Poof!" the commodore said, smiling. "No pain, my dear sir. If the smash doesn't kill you, the flaming petrol sears the lungs and causes instantaneous death. The only difficulty is in identifying the corpse. Charred, you know."

We climbed up a short flight of wooden mobile steps and stepped into the cabin. The commodore closed the door, thus somewhat muting the roar. He pointed out the bunks that had been installed for our convenience and the W.C. This contained a small washbowl with a gravity-feed water tank and several thunder-mugs bolted to the deck.*

"The prototype can carry a four-man crew," the commodore said. "There is, as you have observed, a cockpit for the nose gunner, with the pilot in a cockpit directly behind him. There is a cockpit near the rear for another machine gunner, and there is a trap-door through which a machine gun may be pointed to cover the rear area under the plane. You are standing on the trap-door."

Holmes and I moved away, though not, I trust, with unseemly haste.

"We estimate that with its present load the craft can fly at approximately 85 miles per hour. Under ideal conditions, of course. We have decided to eliminate the normal armament of machine guns in order to lighten the load. In fact, to this end, all of the crew except the pilot and co-pilot are eliminated. The pilot, I believe, is bringing his personal arms: a dagger, several pistols, a carbine, and his specially mounted Spandau machine gun, a trophy, by the way, taken from a Fokker E-1, which Captain Wentworth downed when he dropped an ashtray on the pilot's head. Wentworth has also brought in several cases of hand grenades and a case of Scotch whisky."

The door, or port, or whatever they call a door in the Royal Naval Air Service, opened, and a young man of medium height, but with very broad shoulders

---

*The good doctor probably intended to delete the references to sanitation in the final version of this adventure. At least, he always had been reticent to a Victorian degree in such references in all his previous chronicles. However, this was written in 1932, and Watson may have thought that the spirit of the times gave him more latitude in expression. *Editor.*

and a narrow waist, entered. He wore the uniform of the R.N.A.S. He was a handsome young man with eyes as steely grey and as magnetic as Holmes'. There was also something strange about them. If I had known *how* strange, I would have stepped off that plane at that very second. Holmes would have preceded me.

He shook hands with us and spoke a few words. I was astonished to hear a flat midwestern American accent. When Wentworth had disappeared on some errand toward the stern, Holmes asked the commodore, "Why wasn't a British pilot assigned to us? No doubt this Yank volunteer is quite capable, but really..."

"There is only one pilot who can match Wentworth's aerial genius. He is an American in the service of the Tsar. The Russians know him as Kentov, though that is not his real name. They refer to him with the honorific of *Chorniy Oryol,* the French call him *l'Aigle Noir* and the Germans are offering a hundred thousand marks for *Der Schwarz Adler,* dead or alive."

"Is he a Negro?" I said.

"No, the adjective refers to his sinister reputation," replied the commodore. "Kentov will take you on from Marseilles. Your mission is so important that we borrowed him from the Russians. Wentworth is being used only for the comparatively short haul since he is scheduled to carry out another mission soon. If you should crash, and survive, he would be able to guide you through enemy territory better than anyone we know of, excluding Kentov. Wentworth is an unparalleled master of disguise..."

"Really?" Holmes said, drawing himself up and frostily regarding the officer.

Aware that he had made a gaffe, the commodore changed the subject. He showed us how to don the bulky parachutes, which were to be kept stored under a bunk.

"What happened to young Drummond?" I asked him. "Lord Greystoke's adopted son? Wasn't he supposed to be our pilot?"

"Oh, he's in hospital," he said, smiling. "Nothing serious. Several broken ribs and clavicle, a liver that may be ruptured, a concussion and possible fracture of the skull. The landing gear of his craft collapsed as he was making a deadstick landing, and he slid into a brick wall. He sends his regards."

Captain Wentworth suddenly reappeared. Muttering to himself, he looked under our blankets and sheets and then under the bunks. Holmes said, "What is it, captain?"

Wentworth straightened up and looked at us with those strange grey eyes. "Thought I heard bats," he said. "Wings fluttering. Giant bats. But no sign of them."

He left the cabin then, heading down a narrow tunnel which had been specially installed so that the pilot could get into the cockpit without having to go outside the craft. His co-pilot, a Lieutenant Nelson, had been warming the motors. The commodore left a minute later after wishing us luck. He looked as if he thought we'd need it.

Presently, Wentworth phoned in to us and told us to lie down in the bunks or grab hold of something solid. We were getting ready to take off. We got into the bunks, and I stared at the ceiling while the plane slowly taxied to the starting point, the motors were "revved" up, and then it began to bump along the meadow. Within a short time its tail had lifted and we were suddenly aloft. Neither Holmes nor I could endure just lying there any more. We had to get up and look through the window in the door. The sight of the earth dropping away in the dusk, of houses, cows, horses and waggons, and brooks and then the Thames itself dwindling, dwindling caused us to be both uneasy and exhilarated.

Holmes was still grey, but I am certain that it was not fear of altitude that affected him. It was being completely dependent upon someone else, being *not* in control of the situation. On the ground Holmes was his own master. Here his life and limb were in the hands of two strangers, one of whom had already impressed us as being very strange. It also became obvious only too soon that Holmes, no matter how steely his nerves and how calm his digestion on earth, was subject to airsickness.

The plane flew on and on, crossing the channel in the dark, crossing the westerly and then the southwestern part of France. We landed on a strip lighted with flames. Holmes wanted to get out and stretch his legs but Wentworth forbade that.

"Who knows what's prowling around here, waiting to identify you and then to crouch and leap, destroying utterly?" he said.

After he had gone back to the cockpit, I said, "Holmes, don't you think he puts the possibility of spies in somewhat strange language? And didn't you smell Scotch on his breath? Should a pilot drink while flying?"

"Frankly," Holmes said, "I'm too sick to care," and he lay down outside the door to the W.C.

Midnight came with the great plane boring through the dark moonless atmosphere. Lt. Nelson crawled into his bunk with the cheery comment that we would be landing at a drome outside Marseilles by dawn. Holmes groaned. I bade the fellow, who seemed quite a decent sort, good-night. Presently I fell asleep, but I awoke some time later with a start. As an old veteran of Holmes' campaigns, however, I knew better than to reveal my awakened state. While I rolled over to one side as if I were doing it in my sleep, I watched through narrowed eyes.

A sound, or a vibration, or perhaps it was an old veteran's sixth sense, had awakened me. Across the aisle, illuminated by the single bulb overhead, stood Lt.

Nelson. His handsome youthful face bore an expression which the circumstances certainly did not seem to call for. He looked so malignant that my heart began thumping and perspiration poured out from me despite the cold outside the blankets. In his hand was a revolver, and when he lifted it my heart almost stopped. But he did not turn toward us. Instead he started toward the front end, toward the narrow tunnel leading to the pilot's cockpit.

Since his back was to me, I leaned over the edge of the bunk and reached down to get hold of Holmes. I had no need to warn him, Whatever his physical condition, he was still the same alert fox—an old fox, it is true, but still a fox. His hand reached up and touched mine, and within a few seconds he was out of the bunk and on his feet. In his one hand he held his trusty Webley, which he raised to point at Nelson's back, crying out to halt at the same time.

I do not know if he heard Holmes above the roar of the motors. If he did, he did not have time to consider it. There was a report, almost inaudible in the din, and Nelson fell back and slid a few feet along the floor backward. Blood gushed from his forehead.

The dim light fell on the face of Captain Wentworth, whose eyes seemed to blaze, though I am certain that was an optical illusion. The face was momentarily twisted, and then it smoothed out, and he stepped out into the light. I got down from the bunk and with Holmes approached him. Close to him, I could smell the heavy, though fragrant, odour of excellent Scotch on his breath.

Wentworth looked at the revolver in Holmes' hand, smiled, and said, "So— you are not overrated, Mr. Holmes! But I was waiting for him, I expected him to sneak in upon me while I should be concentrating on the instrument board. He thought he'd blow my a*s off!"

"He is, of course, a German spy," Holmes said. "But how did you determine that he was?"

"I suspect everybody," Wentworth replied. "I kept my eye on him, and when I saw him talking over the wireless, I listened in. It was too noisy to hear clearly, but he was talking in German. I caught several words, *schwanz* and *schweinhund.* Undoubtedly, he was informing the Imperial German Military Aviation Service of our location. If he didn't kill me, then we would be shot down. The Huns must be on their way to intercept us now."

This was alarming enough, but both Holmes and I were struck at the same time with a far more disturbing thought. Holmes as usual, was more quick in his reactions. He screamed, "Who's flying the plane?"

Wentworth smiled lazily and said, "Nobody. Don't worry. The controls are connected to a little device I invented last month. As long as the air is smooth, the plane will fly on an even keel all by itself."

He stiffened suddenly, cocked his head to one side, and said, "Do you hear it?"

"Great Scott, man!" I cried. "How could we hear anything above the infernal racket of those motors?"

"Cockroaches!" Wentworth bellowed. "Giant flying cockroaches! That evil scientist has released another horror upon the world!"

He whirled, and he was gone into the blackness of the tunnel.

Holmes and I stared at each other, Then Holmes said, "We are at the mercy of a madman, Watson. And there is nothing we can do until we have landed."

"We could parachute out," I said.

"I would prefer not to," Holmes said stiffly. "Besides, it somehow doesn't seem cricket. The pilots have no parachutes, you know. These two were provided only because we are civilians."

"I wasn't planning on asking Wentworth to ride down with me," I mumbled, somewhat ashamed of myself for saying this.

Holmes didn't hear me; once again his stomach was trying to reject contents that did not exist.

3

Shortly after dawn, the German planes struck. These, as I was told later, were Fokker E-III's, single-seater monoplanes equipped with two Spandau machine guns. These were synchronized with the propellors to shoot bullets through the empty spaces between the whirling of the propellor blades.

Holmes was sitting on the floor, holding his head and groaning, and I was commiserating with him, though getting weary of his complaints, when the telephone bell rang. I removed the receiver from the box attached to the wall, or bulkhead, or whatever they call it. Wentworth's voice bellowed, "Put on the parachutes and hang on to something tight! Twelve ****ing Fokkers, a whole *staffel,* coming in at eleven o'clock!"

I misunderstood him. I said, "Yes, but what type of plane are they?"

"Fokkers!" he cried, adding, "No, no! My eyes played tricks on me. They're giant flying cockroaches! Each one is being ridden by a Prussian officer, helmeted and goggled and armed with a boarding cutlass!"

"What did you say?" I screamed into the phone, but it had been disconnected.

I told Holmes what Wentworth had said, and he forgot about being airsick, though he looked no better than before. We staggered out to the door and looked through its window.

The night was now brighter than day, the result of flares thrown out from the attacking aeroplanes. Their pilots intended to use the light to line up the sights of their machine guns on our helpless craft. Then, as if that were not bad enough, shells began exploding, some so near that our aeroplane shuddered and rocked under the impact of the blasts. Giant searchlights began playing about, some of them illuminating monoplanes with black crosses on their fuselages.

"Archy!" I exclaimed. "The French anti-aircraft guns are firing at the Huns! The fools! They could hit us just as well!"

Something flashed by. We lost sight of it, but a moment later we saw a fighter diving down toward us through the glare of the flares and the search-lights, ignoring the bursting shells around it. Two tiny red eyes flickered behind the propellor, but it was not until holes were suddenly punched in the fabric only a few feet from us that we realised that those were the muzzles of the machine guns. We dropped to the floor while the great plane rolled and dipped and rose and dropped and we were shot this way and that across the floor and against the bulkheads.

"We're doomed!" I cried to Holmes. "Get the parachutes on! He can't shoot back at the planes, and our plane is too slow and clumsy to get away!"

How wrong I was. And what a demon that madman was. He did things with that big lumbering aeroplane that I wouldn't have believed possible. Several times we were upside down and we only kept from being smashed, like mice shaken in a tin, by hanging on desperately to the bunkposts.

Once, Holmes, whose sense of hearing was somewhat keener than mine, said, "Watson, isn't that a*****e shooting a machine gun? How can he fly this plane, put it through such manoeuvres, and still operate a weapon which he must hold in both hands to use effectively?"

"I don't know," I confessed. At that moment both of us were dangling from the post, failing to fall only because of our tight grip. The plane was on its left side. Through the window beneath my feet I saw a German plane, smoke trailing from it, fall away. And then another followed it, becoming a ball of flame about a thousand feet or so from the ground.

The Handley Page righted itself, and I heard faint thumping noises overhead, followed by the chatter of a machine gun. Something exploded very near us and wreckage drifted by the window.

This shocked me, but even more shocking was the rapping on the window. This, to my astonishment, originated from a fist hammering on the door. I crawled over to it and stood up and looked through it. Upside down, staring at me through the isinglass, was Wentworth's face. His lips formed the words, "Open the door! Let me in!"

Numbly, I obeyed. A moment later, with an acrobatic skill that I still find incredible, he swung through the door. In one hand he held a Spandau with a rifle stock. A moment later, while I held on to his waist, he had closed the door and shut out the cold shrilling blast of wind.

"There they are!" he yelled, and he pointed the machine gun at a point just past Holmes, lying on the floor, and sent three short bursts past Holmes' ear.

Holmes said, "Really, old fellow…" Wentworth, raving, ran past him and a moment later we heard the chatter of the Spandau again.

"At least, he's back in the cockpit," Holmes said weakly. However, this was one of the times when Holmes was wrong. A moment later the captain was back. He opened the trap-door, poked the barrel of his weapon through, let loose a single burst, said, "Got you, you ****ing son of a *****!" closed the trap-door, and ran back toward the front.

Forty minutes later, the plane landed on a French military aerodrorne outside of Marseilles. Its fuselage and wings were perforated with bullet holes in a hundred places, though fortunately no missiles had struck the petrol tanks. The French commander who inspected the plane pointed out that more of the holes were made by a gun firing from the inside than from guns firing from the outside.

"Damn right!" Wentworth said. "The cockroaches and their allies, the flying leopards, were crawling all over inside the plane! They almost got these two old men!"

A few minutes later a British medical officer arrived. Wentworth, after fiercely fighting six men, was subdued and put into a straitjacket and carried off in an ambulance.

Wentworth was not the only one raving. Holmes, his pale face twisted, his fists clenched, was cursing his brother Mycroft, young Merrivale, and everyone else who could possibly be responsible, excepting, of course, His Majesty.

We were taken to an office occupied by several French and British officers of very high rank. The highest, General Chatson-Dawes-Overleigh, said, "Yes, my dear Mr. Holmes, we realise that he sometimes has these hallucinatory fits. Becomes quite mad, to be frank. But he is the best pilot and also the best espionage agent we have, even if he is a Colonial, and he has done heroic work for us. He never hallucinates negatively, that is, he never harms his fellows—though he did shoot an Italian once, but the fellow *was* only a private and he *was* an Italian and it *was* an accident—and so we feel that we must permit him to work for us. We can't permit a word of his condition to get back to the civilian populace, of course, so I must require you to swear silence about the whole affair. Which you would have to do as a matter of course, and, of course, of patriotism. He'll be given a little rest cure, a drying-out, too, and then returned to duty. Britain sorely needs him."*

Holmes raved some more, but he always was one to face realities and to govern himself accordingly. Even so, he could not resist making some sarcastic remarks about his life, which was also extremely valuable, being put into the care of a homicidal maniac. At last, cooling down, he said, "And the pilot who will fly us to Egypt? Is he also an irresponsible madman? Will we be in more danger from him than from the enemy?"

"He is said to be every bit as good a pilot as Wentworth," the general said. "He is an American…"

"Great Scott!" Holmes said. He groaned, and he added, "Why can't we have a pilot of good British stock, tried and true?"

"Both Wentworth and Kentov are of the best British stock," Overleigh said stiffly. "They're descended from some of the oldest and noblest stock of England. They have royal blood in them, as a matter of fact. But they happen to be Colonials. The man who will fly you from here has been working for His Majesty's cousin, the Tsar of all the Russias, as an espionage agent. The Tsar was kind enough to loan both him and one of the great Sikorski *Ilya Mourometz* Type V aeroplanes to us. Kentov flew here in it with a full crew, and it is ready to take off."

Holmes' face became even paler, and I felt every minute of my sixty-four years of age. We were not to get a moment's rest, and yet we had gone through an experience which would have sent many a youth to bed for several days.

4

General Overleigh himself conducted us to the colossal Russian aeroplane. As we approached it, he described certain features in answer to Holmes' questions.

"So far, the only four-engined heavier-than-air craft in the world has been built by the Russians," he said. "Much to the shame of the British. The first one was built, and flown, in 1913. This, as you can see, is a biplane, fitted with wheels and a ski undercarriage. It has four 150-horsepower Sunbeam water-cooled Vee-type engines. The Sunbeam, unfortunately, leaves much to be desired."

---

*This mad, but usually functioning, American must surely be the great aviator and espionage agent who, after transferring to the U.S. forces in 1917, was known under the code name of G–8. While in the British service, he apparently went under the name of Wentworth, his half-brother's surname. For the true names of G–8, the Spider, and the Shadow, see my *Doc Savage: His Apocalyptic Life*, Bantam, 1975. *Editor.*

"I would rather not have known that," I murmured. The sudden ashen hue of Holmes' face indicated that his reactions were similar to mine.

"Its wing span is 97 feet 9½ inches; the craft's length is 56 feet 1 inch; its height is 15 feet 5 and seven-eighths inches. Its maximum speed is 75 miles per hour; its operational ceiling is 9,843 feet. And its endurance is five hours—under ideal conditions. It carries a crew of five, though it can carry more. The rear fuselage is fitted with compartments for sleeping and eating."

Overleigh shook hands with us after he had handed us over to a Lieutenant Obrenov. The young officer led us up the steps into the fuselage and to the rear, where he showed us our compartment. Holmes chatted away with him in Russian, of which he had gained a certain mastery during his experience in Odessa with the Trepoff case. Holmes' insistence on speaking Russian seemed to annoy the officer somewhat, since, like all upper-class people of his country, he preferred to use French. But he was courteous, and after making sure we were comfortable, he bowed himself out. Certainly, we had little to complain about except possibly the size of the cabin. It had been prepared especially for us, had two swing-down beds, a thick rug which Holmes said was a genuine Persian, oil paintings on the walls which Holmes said were genuine Maleviches (I thought they were artistic nonsense), two comfortable chairs bolted to the deck, and a sideboard also bolted to the deck and holding alcoholic beverages. In one corner was a tiny cubicle containing all the furniture and necessities that one finds in a W.C.

Holmes and I lit up the fine Cuban cigars we found in a humidor and poured out some Scotch whisky, Duggan's Dew of Kirkintilloch, I believe. Suddenly, both of us leaped into the air, spilling our drinks over our cuffs. Seemingly from nowhere, a tall figure had silently appeared. How he had done it, I do not know, since the door had been closed and under observation at all times by one or both of us.

Holmes groaned and said, under his breath, "Not another madman?"

The fellow certainly looked eccentric. He wore the uniform of a colonel of the Imperial Russian Air Service, but he also wore a long black opera cloak and a big black slouch hat. From under its floppy brim burned two of the most magnetic and fear-inspiring eyes I have ever seen. My attention, however, was somewhat diverted from these by the size and the aquilinity of the nose beneath them. It could have belonged to Cyrano de Bergerac.*

---

*The description of this man certainly fits that of a notable crime fighter operating out of Manhattan in the '30's through the '40's. If he is who I think he is, then one of his many aliases was Lamont Cranston. *Editor.*

I found that I had to sit down to catch my breath. The fellow introduced himself, in an Oxford accent, as Colonel Kentov. He had a surprisingly pleasant voice, deep, rich, and shot with authority. It was also heavily laced with bourbon.

"Are you all right?" he said.

"I think so," I said. "You gave me quite a start. A cloud seemed to pass over my mind. But I'm fine now, thank you."

"I must go forward now," he said, "but I've assigned a crew member, a tail gunner now but once a butler, to serve you. Just ring that bell beside you if you need him."

And he was gone, though this time he opened the door. At least, I think he did.

"I fear, my dear fellow, that we are in for another trying time," Holmes said.

Actually, the voyage seemed quite pleasant once one got used to the roar of the four motors and the nerve-shaking jack-out-of-the-box appearances of Kentov. The trip was to take approximately twenty-eight hours if all went well. The only time we landed was to refuel. About every four and a half hours, we put down at a hastily constructed landing strip to which petrol and supplies had been rushed by ship, air, or camel some days before. With the Mediterranean Sea on our left and the shores of North Africa below us, we sped toward Cairo at an amazing average speed of 70.3 miles per hour, according to our commander. While we sipped various liquors or liqueurs and smoked Havanas, we read to pass the time. Holmes commented several times that he could use a little cocaine to relieve the tedium, but I believe that he said that just to needle me. Holmes had brought along a work of his own authorship, the privately printed *Practical Handbook of Bee Culture, with Some Observations Upon the Segregation of the Queen.* He had often urged me to read the results of his experience with his Sussex bees and so I now acceded to his urgings, mainly because all the other books available were in Russian.

I found it more interesting than I had expected, and I told Holmes so. This seemed to please him, though he had affected an air of indifference to my reaction before then.

"The techniques and tricks of apiculture are intriguing and complex enough," he said. "But I was called away from a project which goes far beyond anything any apiculturist—scientist or not—has attempted. It is my theory that bees have a language and that they communicate such important information as the location of new clover, the approach of enemies, and so forth, by means of symbolic dancing. I was investigating this with a view to turning theory into fact when I got Mycroft's wire."

I sat up so suddenly that the ash dropped off my cigar onto my lap, and I was busy for a moment brushing off the coals before they burned a hole in my trousers. "Really, Holmes," I said, "you are surely pulling my leg! Bees have a language? Next you'll be telling me they compose sonnets in honour of their queen's inauguration! Or perhaps epitases when she gets married!"

"Epitases?" he said, regarding me scornfully. "You mean epithalamiums, you blockhead! I suggest you use moderation while drinking the national beverage of Russia. Yes, Watson, bees do communicate, though not in the manner which *Homo sapiens* uses."*

"Perhaps you'd care to explain just what," I said, but I was interrupted by that sudden vagueness of mind which signalled the appearance of our commander. I always jumped and my heart beat hard when the cloud dissolved and I realized that Kentov was standing before me. My only consolation was that Holmes was just as startled.

"Confound it, man!" Holmes said, his face red. "Couldn't you behave like a civilised being for once and knock before entering? Or don't Americans have such customs?"

This, of course, was sheer sarcasm, since Holmes had been to the States several times.

"We are only two hours from Cairo," Kentov said, ignoring Holmes' remarks. "But I have just learned from the wireless station in Cairo that a storm of severe proportions is approaching us from the north. We may be blown somewhat off our course. Also, our spies at Cos, in Turkey, report that a Zeppelin left there yesterday. They believe that it intends to pick up Von Bork. Somehow, he's slipped out past the cordon and is waiting in the desert for the airship."

Holmes, gasping and sputtering, said, "If this execrable voyage turns out to be for nothing...if I was forced to endure that madman's dangerous antics only to have...!"

Suddenly, the colonel was gone. Holmes regained his normal colour and composure, and he said, "Do you know, Watson, I believe I know that man! Or, at least, his parents. I've been studying him at every opportunity, and though he is doubtless a master at dissimulation, that nose is false, he has a certain bone structure and a certain trait of walking, of turning his head, which leads me to believe..."

---

*For the first time we learn that Holmes anticipated the discovery of the Austrian scientist, von Frisch, by many decades. *Editor.*

At that moment the telephone rang. Since I was closest to the instrument, I answered it. Our commander's voice said, "Batten down all loose objects and tie yourself in to your beds. We are in for a hell of a storm, the worst of this century, if the weather reports are accurate."

For once, the meteorologists had not exaggerated. The next three hours were terrible. The giant aeroplane was tossed about as if it were a sheet of writing paper. The electric lamps on the walls flickered again and again and finally went out, leaving us in darkness. Holmes groaned and moaned and finally tried to crawl to the W.C. Unfortunately, the craft was bucking up and down like a wild horse and rolling and yawing like a rowboat caught in a rapids. Holmes managed to get back to his bed without breaking any bones but, I regret to say, proceeded to get rid of all the vodka and brandy (a combination itself not conducive to good digestion, I believe), beef stroganoff, cabbage soup, and black bread on which we had dined earlier. Even more regrettably, he leaned over the edge of the bed to perform this undeniable function, and though I did not get all of it, I did get too much. I did not have the heart to reprimand him. Besides, he would have killed me, or at least attempted to do so, if I had made any reproaches. His mood was not of the best.

Finally, I heard his voice, weak though it was, saying, "Watson, promise me one thing."

"What is that, Holmes?"

"Swear to me that once we've set foot on land you'll shoot me through the head if ever I show the slightest inclination to board a flying vehicle again. I don't think there's much danger of that, but even if His Majesty himself should plead with me to get into an aeroplane, or anything that flies, dirigible, balloon, anything, you will mercifully tender euthanasia of some sort. Promise me."

I thought I was safe in promising. For one thing, I felt almost as strongly as he did about it.

At that moment, the door to our cabin opened, and our attendant, Ivan, appeared with a small electric lamp in his hand. He exchanged some excited words in Russian with Holmes and then left, leaving the lamp behind. Holmes crawled down from the bunk, saying, "We've orders to abandon ship, Watson. We've been blown far south of Cairo and will be out of petrol in half an hour. We'll have to jump then, like it or not. Ivan says that the colonel has looked for a safe landing place, but he can't even see the ground. The air's filled with sand; visibility is nil; the sand is getting into the bearings of the engines and pitting the windshield. So, my dear old friend, we must don the parachutes."

My heart warmed at being addressed so fondly, though my emotion was somewhat ternpered in the next few minutes while we were assisting each other in strapping on the equipment. Holmes said, "You have an abominable effluvia about you, Watson," and I replied, testily, I must admit, "You stink like the W.C. in an East End pub yourself, my dear Holmes. Besides, any odour emanating from me has originated from, or in, you. Surely you are aware of that."

Holmes muttered something about the direction upwards, and I was about to ask him to clarify his comment when Ivan appeared again. This time he carried weapons which he distributed among the three of us. I was handed a cavalry sabre, a stiletto, a knout (which I discarded), and a revolver of some unknown make but of .50 calibre. Holmes was given a cutlass, a carbine, a belt full of ammunition, and a coil of rope at one end of which were grappling hooks. Ivan kept for himself another cutlass, two hand grenades dangling by their pins from his belt, and a dagger in his teeth.

We walked (rolled, rather) to the door, where three others stood, also fully, perhaps even over-, armed. There was a window further forward, and so Holmes and I went to it after a while to observe the storm. We could see little except clouds of dust for a few minutes and then the dust was suddenly gone. A heavy rain succeeded it, though the wind buffeted us as strongly as before. There was also much lightning, some of it exploding loudly close by.

A moment later Ivan joined us, pulling at Holmes' arm and shouting something in Russian.

Holmes answered him and turning to me said, "Kentov has sighted a Zeppelin!"

"Great Scott!" I cried. "Surely it must be the one sent to pick up Von Bork! It, too, has been caught by the storm!"

"An elementary deduction," Holmes said. But he seemed pleased about something. I surmised that he was happy because Von Bork had either missed the airship or, if he was in it, was in as perilous a plight as we, I failed to see any humour in the situation.

Holmes lost his grin several minutes later when we were informed that we were going to attack the Zeppelin.

"In this storm?" I said. "Why, the colonel can't even keep us at the same altitude or attitude from one second to the next."

"The man's a maniac!" Holmes shouted.

Just how mad, we were shortly to discover. Presently the great airship hove into view, painted silver above and black below to conceal it from search lights, the large designation L9* on its side, the control car in front, its pusher propellor spinning, the propellors on the front and rear of the two midships and one aft engine-gondolas spinning, the whole looking quite monstrous and sinister and yet beautiful.

The airship was bobbing and rolling and yawing like a toy boat afloat on a Scottish salmon stream. Its crew had to be airsick and they had to have their hands full just to keep from being pitched out of their vessel. This was heartening to some degree, since none of us on the aeroplane, except possibly Kentov, were in any state remotely resembling good health or aggression.

Ivan mumbled something, and Holmes said, "He says that if the storm keeps up the airship will soon break up. Let us hope it does and so spares us aerial combat."

But the Zeppelin, though it did seem to be somewhat out of line, its frame slightly twisted, held together. Meanwhile, our four-engined colossus, so small compared to the airship, swept around to the vessel's stern. It was a ragged approach what with the constantly buffeting blasts, but the wonder was that it was accomplished at all.

"What's the fool doing?" Holmes said, and he spoke again to Ivan. Lightning rolled up the heavens then, and I saw that his face was a ghastly blue-grey.

"This Yank is madder than the other!" he said. "He's going to try to land on top of the Zeppelin!"

"How could he do that?" I gasped.

"How would I know what techniques he'll use, you dunce!" he shouted. "Who cares? Whatever he does, the plane will fall off the ship, probably break its wings, and we'll fall to our deaths!"

"We can jump now!" I shouted.

"What? Desert?" he cried. "Watson, we are British!"

"It was only a suggestion," I said, "Forgive me. Of course, we will stick it out. No Slav is going to say that we English lack courage."

Ivan spoke again, and Holmes relayed his intelligence. "He says that the colonel, who is probably the greatest flier in the world, even if he is a Yank, will come up over the stern of the Zeppelin and stall it just above the top machine-gun platform. As soon as the plane stops, we are to open the door and leap out. If we miss our footing or fall down, we can always use the parachutes. Kentov

*According to German official records the L9 was burned on September 16, 1916, in the Fuhls-büttel shed because of a fire in the L6. Either Watson was in error or the Germans deliberately falsified the records in order to conceal the secret attempt to rescue Von Bork. At the time this adventure occurred, the L9 was supposed to be in action in Europe and its commander was Kapitänleutnant d. R. Prölss, *Editor*.

insisted on bringing them along over the protests of the Imperial Russian General Staff—they should live so long. We will go down the ladder from the platform and board the ship. Kentov's final words, his last orders before we leave the plane are..."

He hesitated, and I said, "Yes, Holmes?"

"Kill! Kill! Kill!"

"Good heavens!" I said. "How barbaric!"

"Yes," he answered. "But one has to excuse him. He is obviously not sane."

5

Following orders communicated through Obrenov, we lay down on the deck and grabbed whatever was solid and anchored in a world soon to become all too fluid and foundationless. The plane dived and we slid forward and then it rose sharply upward and we slid backward and then its nose suddenly lifted up, the roaring of the four engines becoming much more highly pitched, and suddenly we were pressed against the floor. And then the pressure was gone.

Slowly, but far too swiftly for me, the deck tilted to the left. This was in accordance with Kentov's plans. He had stalled it with its longitudinal axis, or centre-line, a little to the left of the airship's centre-line. Its weight would thus cause the airship on whose back it rode to roll to the left.

For a second, I did not realize what was happening. To be quite frank, I was scared out of my wits, numb with terror. I would never allow Holmes to see this, and so I overcame my frozen state, though not the stiffness and slowness due to my age and recent hardships. I got up and stumbled out through the door, the parachute banging the upper parts of the back of my thighs and feeling as if it were made of lead, and sprawled out onto the small part of the platform left to me. I grabbed for the lowest end of an upright pipe forming the enclosure about the platform. The hatch had already been opened and Kentov was inside the airship. I could hear the booming of several guns. It was comparatively silent now, since Kentov had cut the engines just before the stalling. Nevertheless, the wind was howling and under it one could hear the creaking of the girders of the ship's structure as it bent under the varying pressures. My ears hurt abominably because the airship was dropping swiftly under the weight of the giant aeroplane. The aeroplane was also making its own unmistakable noises, groaning, as its structure bent, tearing the cotton fabric of the ship's covering as it slipped more and more to the left, then there as a loud ripping, and the ship beneath me railed swiftly back, relieved of the enormous eight of the aeroplane. At the same time the Zepelin soared aloft, and the two motions, the rolling and the levitation, almost tore me loose from my hold.

When the dirigible had ceased its major oscillations, the Russians rose and one by one disappeared into the well. Holmes and I worked our way across, passed the pedestals of two quilt-swathed eight-millimetre Maxim machine guns, and descended the ladder. Just before I was all the way into the hatch, I looked across the back of the great beast that we were invading. I would have been shocked if I had not been so numb. The wheels and the ski undercarriage of the plane had ripped open a great wound along the thin skin of the vessel. Encountering the duralumin girders and rings of the framework, it had torn some apart and then its landing gear had itself been ripped off. The propellors, though no longer turning, had also done extensive damage. I wondered if the framework of the ship, the skeleton of the beast, as it were, might not have suffered so great a blow it would collapse and carry all of us down to our death.

I also had a second's admiration for the skill, no, the genius, of the pilot who had landed us.

And then I descended into the vast complex spider-web of the ship's hull with its rings and girders and bulging hydrogen-filled gas cells and ballast sacks of water. I emerged at the keel of the ship, on the foot-wide catwalk that ran the length of the ship between triangular girders. It had been a nightmare before then; after that it became a nightmare having a nightmare. I remember dodging along, clinging to girders, swinging out and climbing around to avoid the fire of the German sailors in the bow. I remember Lt. Obrenov falling with fatal bullet wounds after sticking two Germans with his sabre (there was no room to swing it and so use the edge as regulations required).

I remember others falling, some managing to retain their grip and so avoiding the fall through the fabric of the cover and into the abyss below. I remember Holmes hiding behind a gas cell and firing away at the Germans who were afraid of firing back and perhaps setting the hydrogen aflame.*

Most of all I remember the slouch-hatted cloaked form of Kentov leaping about, swinging from girders and brace wires, bouncing from a beam onto a great gas cell and back again, flitting like a phantom of the opera through the maze, firing two huge .45 automatic pistols (not at the same time, of course, otherwise he would have lost his grip). German after German cried out or fled while the maniac cackled with a blood-chilling laugh between the booming of

---

*There was actually no danger of fire since phosphorus-coated bullets were not being used. Apparently, the grenades, which might have set off the hydrogen, were not used. *Editor.*

the huge guns. But though he was worth a squadron in himself, men died one by one. And so the inevitable happened.

Perhaps it was a ricocheting bullet or perhaps he slipped. I do not know. All of a sudden he was falling off a girder, through a web of wires, miraculously missing them, falling backward, now in each hand a thundering, flamespitting .45, killing two sailors as he fell, laughing loudly even as he broke through the cotton fabric and disappeared into the dark rain over Africa,

Since he was wearing a parachute, he may have survived. I never heard of him again, though.

Presently the Germans approached cautiously, having heard Holmes and me call out that we surrendered. (We were out of ammunition and too nerveless even to lift a sabre.) We stood on the catwalk with our hands up, two tired beaten old men. Yet it was our finest hour. Nothing could ever rob us of the pleasure of seeing Von Bork's face when he recognised us. If the shock had been slightly more intense, he would have dropped dead from a heart attack.

6

A few minutes later, we had climbed down the ladder from the hull to the control gondola under the fore part of the airship. Behind us, raving, restrained by a petty officer and the executive officer, *Oberleutnant zur See* Heinrich Tring, came Von Bork. He had ordered us thrown overboard then and there, but Tring, a decent fellow, had refused to obey his orders. We were introduced to the commander, *Kapitänleutnant* Victor Reich.* He was also a decent fellow, openly admiring our feat of landing and boarding his ship even though it and his crew had suffered terribly. He rejected Von Bork's suggestion that we should be shot as spies since we were in civilian clothes and on a Russian warcraft. He knew of us, of course, and he would have nothing to do with a summary execution of the great Holmes and his colleague. After hearing our story, he made sure of our comfort. However, he refused to let Holmes smoke, cast his tobacco overboard then and there, in fact, and this made Holmes suffer. He had gone through so much that he desperately needed a pipeful of shag.

---

*The records of the Imperial German Navy have been combed without success in a search for identification of the L9 and the crew members mentioned by Watson. Could it be that the ship and crew were secret agents also, that the L9 was a "phantom" ship, that it carried out certain missions which the German concealed from all but the highest? Or were there records, but these are still in closed files or were destroyed for one reason or another? *Editor.*

"It is fortunate that the storm is breaking up," Reich said in excellent English. "Otherwise, the ship would soon break up. Three of our motors are not operating. The clutch to the port motor has overheated, the water in the radiator of a motor in the starboard mid-car has boiled out, and something struck the propellor of the control car and shattered it. We are so far south that even if we could operate at one hundred percent efficiency, we would be out of petrol somewhere over Egypt on the return trip. Moreover, the controls to the elevators have been damaged. All we can do at present is drift with the wind and hope for the best."

The days and nights that followed were full of suffering and anxiety. Seven of the crew had been killed during the fight, leaving only six to man the vessel. This alone was enough to make a voyage back to Turkey or Palestine impossible. Reich told us that he had received a radio message ordering him to get to the German forces in East Africa under Von Lettow-Vorbeck. There he was to burn the Zeppelin and join the forces. This, of course, was not all the message. Surely something must have been said about getting Von Bork back to Germany, since he had the formula for mutating and culturing the "sauerkraut bacilli."

When we were alone in the port mid-gondola, where we were kept during part of the voyage, Holmes commented on what he called the "SB."

"We must get possession of the formula, Watson," he said. "I did not tell you, but before you arrived at Mycroft's office I was informed that the SB is a two-edged weapon. It can be mutated to eat other foods. Imagine what would happen to our food supply, not to mention the blow to our morale, if the SB were changed to eat boiled meat? Or cabbage? Or potatoes?"

"Great Scott!" I said, and then, in a whisper, "It could be worse, Holmes, far worse. What if the Germans dropped an SB over England which devoured stout and ale? Or think of how the spirits of our valiant Scots would sink if their whisky supply vanished before their eyes?"

Von Bork had been impressed into service but, being as untrained as we, was not of much use. Also, his injured left eye handicapped him as much as our age did us. It was very bloodshoot and failed to coordinate with its partner. My professional opinion was that it was totally without sight. The other eye was healthy enough. It glared every time it lighted upon us. Its fires reflected the raging hatred in his heart, the lust to murder us.

However, the airship was in such straits that no one had much time or inclination to think about anything except survival. Some of the motors were still operating, thus enabling some kind of control. As long as we went south, with the wind behind us, we made headway. But due to the jammed elevators, the nose of the ship was downward and the tail was up. The L9 flew at roughly five degrees to the horizontal for some time. Reich put everybody to work, including us, since we had volunteered, at carrying indispensable equipment to the rear to help weigh it down. Anything that was dispensable, and there was not much, went overboard. In addition, much water ballast in the front was discharged.

Below us the sands of Sudan reeled by while the sun flamed in a cloudless blue. Its fiery breath heated the hydrogen in the cells, and great amounts hissed out from the automatic valves. The hot wind blew into the hull through the great hole made by the aeroplane when it had stalled into a landing on its top. The heat, of course, made the hydrogen expand, thus causing the ship to rise despite the loss of gas from the valves. At night, the air cooled very swiftly, and the ship dropped swiftly, too swiftly for the peace of mind of its passengers. During the day the updrafts of heat from the sands made the vessel buck and kick. All of us aboard got sick during these times.

By working like Herculeses despite all handicaps, the crew managed to get all the motors going again. On the fifth day, the elevator controls were fixed. Her hull was still twisted, and this, with the huge gap in the surface covering, made her aerodynamically unstable. At least, that was how Reich explained it to us. He, by the way, was not at all reticent in telling us about the vessel itself though he would not tell us our exact location. Perhaps this was because he wanted to make sure that we would not somehow get to the radio and send a message to the British in East Africa.

The flat desert gave way to rugged mountains. More ballast was dropped, and the L9 just barely avoided scraping some of the peaks. Night came with its cooling effects, and the ship dropped. The mountains were lower at this point, fortunately for us.

Two days later, as we lay sweltering on the catwalk that ran along the keel, Holmes said, "I estimate that we are now somewhere over British East Africa, somewhere in the vicinity of Lake Victoria. It is evident that we will never get to Mahenge or indeed anywhere in German East Africa. The ship has lost too much hydrogen. I have overheard some guarded comments to this effect by Reich and Tring. They think we'll crash sometime tonight. Instead of seeking out the nearest British authorities and surrendering, as anyone with good sense would, they are determined to cross our territory to German territory. Do you know how many miles of veldt and jungle and swamp swarming with lions, rhinoceri, vipers, savages, malaria, dengue, and God knows what else we will have to walk? Attempt to walk, rather?"

"Perhaps we can slip away some night?"

"And then what will we do?" he said bitterly. "Watson, you and I know the jungles of London well and are quite fitted to conduct our safaris through them. But here…no, Watson, any black child of eight is more competent, far more so, to survive in these wilds."

"You don't paint a very good picture," I said grimly.

"Though I am descended from the Vernets, the great French artists," he said, "I myself have little ability at painting pretty pictures."

He chuckled then, and I was heartened by this example of pawky humour, feeble though it was. Holmes would never quit; his indomitable English spirit might be defeated, but it would go down fighting. And I would be at his side. And was it not after all better to die with one's boots on while one still had some vigour than when one was old and crippled and sick and perhaps an idiot drooling and doing all sorts of pitiful, sickening things?

That evening preparations were made to abandon the ship. Ballast water was put in every portable container, the food supply was stored in sacks made from the cotton fabric ripped off the hull, and we waited. Sometime after midnight, the end came. It was fortunately a cloudless night with a moon bright enough for us to see, if not too sharply, the terrain beneath. This was a jungle up in the mountains, which were not at a great elevation. The ship was steered down a winding valley through which a stream ran silvery. Then, abruptly, we had to rise, and we could not do it,

We were in the control car when the hillside loomed before us. Reich gave the order and we threw our supplies out, thus lightening the load and giving us a few more seconds of grace. We two prisoners were courteously allowed to drop out first. Reich did this because the ship would rise as the crew members left, and he wanted us to be closest to the ground. We were old and not so agile, and he thought that we needed all the advantages we could get.

He was right. Even though Holmes and I fell into some bushes which eased our descent, we were still bruised and shaken up. We scrambled out, however, and made our way through the growth toward the supplies. The ship passed over us, sliding its great shadow like a cloak, and then it struck something. The whirring propellors were snapped off, the cars crumpled and came loose with a nerve-scraping sound, the ship lifted again with the weight of the cars gone, and it drifted out of sight. But its career was about over. A few minutes later, it exploded. Reich had left several time-bombs next to some gas cells.

The flames were very bright and very hot, outlining the dark skeleton of its framework. Birds flew up and around it. No doubt they and the beasts of the jungle were making a loud racket, but the roar of the flames drowned them out.

By their light we could see back down the hill, though not very far. We struggled through the heavy vegetation, hoping to get to the supplies before the others. We had agreed to take as much food and water as we could carry and set off by ourselves, if we got the chance. Surely, we reasoned, there must be some native village nearby, and once there we would ask for guidance to the nearest British post.

By pure luck, we came across a pile of food and some bottles of water. Holmes said, "Dame Fortune is with us, Watson!" but his chuckle died the next moment when Von Bork stepped out of the bushes. In his hand was a Luger automatic and in his one eye was the determination to use that before the others arrived. He could claim, of course, that we were fleeing or had attacked him and that he was forced to shoot us.

"Die, you pig-dogs!" he snarled, and he raised the gun. "Before you do, though, know that I have the formula on me and that I will get it to the Fatherland and it will doom you English swine and the French swine and the Italian swine. The bacilli can be adapted to eat Yorkshire pudding and snails and spaghetti, anything that is edible! The beauty of it is that it's specific, and unless it's mutated to eat sauerkraut, it will starve rather than do so!"

We drew ourselves up, prepared to die as British men should. Holmes muttered out of the corner of his mouth, "Jump to one side, Watson, and then we'll rush him! You take his blind side! Perhaps one of us can get to him!"

This was a noble plan, though I didn't know what I could do even if I got hold of Von Bork. After all, he was a young man and had a splendid physique.

At that moment there was a crashing in the bushes, Reich's loud voice commanding Von Bork not to shoot, and the commander, tears streaming from his face, stumbled into the little clearing. Behind him came others. Von Bork said, "I was merely holding them until you got here."

Reich, I must add, was not weeping because of any danger to us. The fate of his airship had dealt him a terrible blow; he loved his vessel and to see it die was to him comparable to seeing his wife die. Perhaps it had even more impact, since, as I later found out, he was on the verge of a divorce.

Though he had saved us, he knew that we were ready to skip out at the first chance. He kept a close eye on us, though it was not as close as Von Bork's. Nevertheless, he allowed us to retreat behind bushes to attend to our comforts. And so, three days later, we strolled on away.

"Well, Watson," Holmes said, as we sat panting under a tree several hours later, "we have given them the slip. But we have no water and no food except these pieces of mouldy biscuit in our pockets. At this moment I would trade them for a handful of shag."

We went to sleep finally and slept like the two old and exhausted men we were. I awoke several times, I think because of insects crawling over my face, but I always went back to sleep quickly. About eight in the morning, the light and the uproar of jungle life awoke us. I was the first to see the cobra slipping through the tall growths toward us. I got quickly, though unsteadily and painfully, to my feet. Holmes saw the reptile then and started to get up. The snake raised its upper part, its hood swelled, and it swayed as it turned its head this way and that.

"Steady, Watson," Holmes said, though the advice would better have been given to himself. He was much closer to the cobra, within striking range, in fact, and he was shaking more violently than I. He could not be blamed for this, of course. He was in a more shakeable situation.

"I knew we should have brought along that flask of brandy," I said. "We have absolutely nothing for snakebite."

"No time for reproaches, you imbecile!" Holmes said. "Besides, what kind of medical man are you? It's sheer superstitious nonsense that alcohol helps prevent the effects of venom."

"Really, Holmes," I said. He had been getting so irascible lately, so insulting. Part of this could be excused, since he became very nervous without the solace of tobacco. Even so, I thought...

The thought was never finished. The cobra struck, and Holmes and I both jumped, yelling at the same time.

Something hissed through the air. The cobra was knocked aside by the impact of a missile, and it writhed dying on the ground. An arrow transfixed it just back of the head.

"Steady, Watson!" Holmes said. "We are saved, but the savage who shot that may have preserved us only so he'll have fresher meat for his pot!"

Suddenly, we leaped into the air again, uttering a frightened scream.

Seemingly out of the air, a man had appeared before us.

My heart was beating too hard and my breath was coming too swiftly for me to say anything for a moment.

Holmes recovered first.

He said, "Lord Greystoke, I presume?"

7

He seemed to be a giant, though actually he was only about three inches taller than Holmes. His bones were large, extraordinarily so, and though he was muscular, the muscles were not the knots of the professional strong man. Where a wrestler or weight lifter recalls a gorilla, he resembled a leopard. The face was handsome and striking. His hair was chopped off at the base of the neck, apparently by use of the huge hunting knife in the scabbard suspended by an antelope-skin belt just above the leopard-skin loincloth. The hair was as black as an Arab's, as was the bronzed skin which was criss-crossed with scars. His eyes were large and dark grey and had about them something both feral and remote. His nose was straight, his upper lip was short, and his chin was square and clefted.

He held in one hand a short thick bow of some wood and carried on his back a quiver with a dozen more arrows.

So this is Lord Greystoke, I thought. Yes, his features are enough like those of the ten- year-old Lord Saltire we rescued in the adventure of the Priory School for him to be a twin. But this man radiates a frightening ferality, a savagery more savage than any possessed by the most primitive of men. This could not possibly be the scion of an ancient British stock, not by any stretch of the fancy the English gentleman that Saltire had been even at the age of ten. This man had been raised in a school that made the hazing of the Priory, Rugby, and Oxford seem like the child's play that it was.

Of course, I thought, he may be mad. How otherwise account for the strange tales that floated about the clubs and the salons of our nobility and gentry?

However, I thought, he could be a product which the British occasionally turn out. Every once in a while, a son of our island, affected in some mystical way by the Orient or Africa, goes more native than the native. There was Sir Richard Francis Burton, more Arab than the Arab, and Lord John Roxton, who was said to be wilder than the Amazon Indians with whom he consorted.

During the next few minutes I decided that the first guess, that he had gone mad, was the correct one.

He said, in a deep rich baritone, "I am known as Lord Greystoke, among other things." Without offering to shake our hands or determine our identity, as any true gentleman would, he put upon the snake one naked foot, calloused an inch thick on its sole, and he pulled the arrow out. He wiped it on the grass, replaced the arrow in the quiver, and cut off the head of the reptile. While we stared in fascination and disgust, he skinned the cobra and then began biting off chunks of its meat and chewing it. The blood dripped down his chin while he stared with those beautiful but wild eyes at us.

"Would you care for some?" he said, and he grinned at us most bloodily.

"Not unless it's cooked," Holmes replied coolly.

"Cooked or raw, I'd rather starve," I said, ungrammatically but sincerely.

"Starve then," Greystoke said.

"I say," I protested. "We are fellow Englishmen, aren't we? Would you let us die of hunger while those Germans are…"

He stopped chewing, and his face became quite fierce.

"Germans!" he said. "Here? Nearby? Where are they?"

Holmes outlined our story, leaving certain parts out for security purposes. Greystoke listened him out, though impatiently, and he said, "I will kill them."

"Without giving them a chance to surrender?" I said horrifiedly.

"I don't take prisoners," he said, glaring at me. "Not any soldier, black or white, who fights for Germany. It was a band of black soldiers, under white officers, who murdered my wife and my warriors who were guarding her and burned down my house around her. I have sworn to kill every German I come across until this war ends."

He added, "And perhaps after it ends!"

"But these men are not soldiers!" I said weakly. "They are sailors, members of the Imperial German Navy!"

"They will die no less."

"Their commander dealt with us as an officer and a gentleman should," Holmes said. "In fact, we owe our lives to him."

"For that he shall have a quick and painless death."

Holmes said, "Could we at least make a fire and cook that reptile first and perhaps hear your story?"

Greystoke threw the skeleton, which was stripped of most of its meat, to one side. "I'll hunt something more suitable to your civilised palates," he said. "After all, they won't get away."

He said this so grimly and assuredly that shivers ran up my spine. "And you two stay here," he said. He was gone, taken in swiftly and silently by the vegetation.

"Good God, Holmes!" I cried. "The man is a beast, a savage engine geared for vengeance! And, Holmes, whoever he is, he was certainly never the child whom we brought back safely to the duke at Pemberley House!* Why, surely he would have recognised his saviours even though we are older! Fifteen years have not made that much difference in us!"

"But they have in him, heh?" Holmes said. "Watson, there are muddy waters in this stream. I have kept a watch on that family over the years, an infrequent watch, it is true. For some reason, we keep bumping into members of

---

*The true name of the ducal mansion Watson called Holdernesse Hall in "The Adventure of the Priory School." A description of the estate is found in Jane Austen's *Pride and Prejudice. Editor.*

the duke's family or into people who've been involved with them. It was the duchess who shot Milverton, it was Black Peter Carey who, I strongly suspect, murdered our present Lord Greystoke's uncle, you know, the Socialist duke who drove a cab for a while..."

"In the affair of the hound of the Baskervilles?" I broke in.

"You know I don't like being interrupted, Watson," he said testily. "As I was saying, Carey probably murdered the fifth duke before he came to a bad, but deserved, end at Forest Row. I have reason to believe that Carey, under another name, was aboard the ship carrying the fifth duke's son and his wife to Africa when it was lost with all hands aboard—for all the public knew, that is. Then I was called in again by the sixth duke to find his illegitimate son, who, it turned out, settled in the States instead of in Australia. It is a weird web which has tangled our fortunes with those of the Greystokes."*

"I just can't believe that this man is the sixth duke's son!" I said.

"The jungle can change a man," Holmes said. "However, I agree with you, even though his features and his voice are remarkably similar. Our Lord Greystoke is an impostor. But how in the world did he succeed in passing himself off as the real Lord Greystoke? And when? And what happened to the sixth duke's son, the child we knew as Lord Saltire?"**

"Good Lord!" I said. "Do you suspect murder?"

"Anybody is capable of murder, my dear Watson," he said. "Even you and I, given the proper circumstances and the proper, or improper, state of emotion. But I have a feeling, a hunch, that this man would not be capable of cold-blooded murder. He may be emotionally unstable, though."

"Fingerprints!" I cried, elated because I had anticipated Holmes.

He smiled and said, "Yes, that would establish whether or not he is an impostor. But I doubt that there is any record of Saltire's fingerprints."

"His handwriting?" I said, somewhat crushed.

"He would search out and destroy all papers bearing Saltire's handwriting, all he could get his hands on. There must be many that he could not obtain, however, and if these could be found, we could compare Saltire's holographs with Greystoke's. I imagine that Greystoke has trained himself to write like Saltire, but an expert, myself, for instance, could easily distinguish

---

*For a fuller description of this involvement, see my definitive biography of Lord Greystroke. *Editor.*

**It is the English custom to address the sons of noblemen with an honorary title, though legally the sons are commoners. The duke had several secondary titles, the highest of which was Marquess of Saltire. Thus, the duke's son was known as Lord Saltire. *Editor.*

the forgery. However, we are now in no position to do such a thing, and from the looks of things we may never be in such a position. Also, before I went to the authorities, I would make sure that the revelation would be useful. After all, we don't know *why* Greystoke has done this. He may be innocent of murder."

"Surely," I said, "You aren't thinking of asking Greystoke to confess?"

"What? With a high certainty that we might be killed on the spot? And perhaps eaten? I don't think Greystoke would put us on his menu if other meat were available. If he were starving, he might not be so discriminating."

I hesitated and then I said, "I am going to confess something to you, Holmes. You remember when we were discussing Greystoke in Mycroft's office? You said that you had heard about the novel, the highly fictionalised and romanticised account of Greystoke's adventures in Africa? You also mentioned that very few copies of the novel had reached England because of the declaration of hostilities shortly before the book was published?"

"Yes?" Holmes said, looking at me strangely.

"Knowing your attitude toward my reading of what you consider trash, I did not tell you that a friend of mine in San Francisco—he was my best man when I married my first wife—sent me a copy not only of the first book but of its sequel. I have read them..."

"Good Lord!" Holmes said. "I can understand your shame, Watson, but withholding evidence..."

"What evidence?" I replied more hotly than was my wont, no doubt due to fatigue, hunger, and anxiety. "There was no crime then of which we were aware!"

"Touché!" Holmes said. "Pray accept my apologies. And continue."

"The American author, and what a wild imagination he has, pretends that the real Lord Greystoke was born in a cabin off the shore of western Africa. In his novel Greystoke's parents are marooned by mutineers. Unable to make their way back to civilisation, they build a hut and young Greystoke is born in it. When his parents die the baby is adopted by a female of a band of intelligent anthropoid apes. These apes are a product of the inflamed imagination of the author, who, by the way, has never been to Africa or apparently read much about it. To make a long story short, the boy grows up, learns to read and write English without ever having heard a word of English..."

"Preposterous!"

"Perhaps, but the author makes it seem possible. Then a white girl, American, of course, and her family and associates, among whom is the youth who inherited the title of Greystoke..."

"Please speak in shorter sentences, Watson. And back up in your story a little."

"The girl's father had spent his life savings and borrowed heavily to purchase an old map showing where treasure was buried on an island off the African coast. His daughter went with him. They also happened to run into the true Greystoke's cousin in England, and he went along with them because he was in love with the girl."

"Quite a coincidence," said Holmes.

"And then the crew of their ship mutinied and set them down at the exact spot at which the real Greystoke's parents had been landed…"

"This Yank seems to rely heavily on coincidences," Holmes said, chuckling. "I could never understand, Watson, why you wasted your time on penny-dreadfuls."

"It's better than taking cocaine," I said.

"I fail to see why," he said. "But please get on with it."

"The real Greystoke, the jungle-born man, fell in love with the girl and rescued her a number of times."

"Naturally. And she, of course, fell in love with this inarticulate youth smelling of ape excrement…"

"It wasn't that way at all!" I cried. "Will you allow me to tell this, or should I just drop the subject?"

"My apology, Watson. I will restrain myself from making observations which are irrelevant."

"The real Greystoke's father had written a diary, in French, which the young Greystoke could not read, of course. It seemed that before the parents died, the baby had accidentally placed his ink-smeared fingers on a page of the diary. Years later, when the real Greystoke was in France, taken there by the young Frenchman who had become his friend, the diary was turned over to a fingerprint expert. Meanwhile, Greystoke followed the girl to America, only to learn that his cousin had proposed marriage and she had accepted. A short time later he received notice that his fingerprints proved that he was the real Lord Greystoke. But knowing that if the truth were revealed, his cousin would be stripped of titles and fortune, and the girl would be destitute, he nobly kept silence."

"In the finest tradition of housemaids' literature," Holmes said.

"Sneer if you like, Holmes," I said. "I thought it was very moving."

"What has all this claptrap fiction to do with our peer?"

"Why, it's as obvious as the nose on your face!"

"What's the matter with it?" Holmes said.

"It's a handsome nose," I said. "Perhaps the most famous in England since the first Duke of Wellington died. What I am saying is that the Yank must have heard something from somebody and that perhaps there is more truth in his fiction than anybody knows. He may have talked to someone who knew the true story of the Greystokes and based his novel on his inside information."

"Nonsense," Holmes said. "What happened is that the American read some newspaper or magazine accounts of how Lord Greystoke, a prime example of English eccentricity, or of madness, had abandoned his heritage, for all practical purposes, and settled down in Africa. To make matters worse, he'd gone native. No, worse than native, since no native would be caught dead living as he does, alone in the jungle, killing lions with a knife, eating meat raw, consorting with chimpanzees and gorillas. So, this Yank sees a highly sensational novel in all this and formulates a plot and characters which are bound to appeal to the public."

"Perhaps," I said. "Allow me to tell you what transpired in the sequel which the Yankee wrote."

I proceeded to do so, after which I waited for Holmes to comment. He sat leaning against a tree trunk, his brows knit, much as I have seen him sit for an entire night while he considered a case. After several minutes he burst out, "God! How I miss my pipe, Watson! Nicotine is more than an aid to thought, it is a necessity! It's a wonder that anything was done in the sciences or the arts before the discovery of America!"

Absently, he reached out and picked up a stick off the ground. He put it in his mouth, no doubt intending to suck on it as a substitute, however unsatisfactory, for the desiderated pipe. The next moment he leaped up with a yell that startled me. I cried, "What have you found, Holmes? What is it?"

"That, curse it!" he shouted and pointed at the stick. It was travelling at a fast rate on a number of thin legs toward a refuge under a log.

"Great Scott!" I said. "It's an insect, a mimetic!"

"How observant of you," he said, snarling. But the next moment he was down on his knees and groping after the creature.

"What on earth are you doing?" I said.

"It does taste like tobacco," he said. "Expediency is the mark of a…"

I never heard the rest. An uproar broke out in the jungle nearby, the shouts of men mortally wounded.

"What is it?" I said. "Could Greystoke have found the Germans?"

Then I fell silent and clutched him, as he clutched me, while a yell pierced the forest, a yell that ululated and froze our blood and hushed the wild things.

8

Holmes unfroze and started in the direction of the sound. I said, "Wait, Holmes! Greystoke ordered us not to leave this place! He must have his reasons for that!"

"Duke or not, he isn't going to order me around!" Holmes said. Nevertheless, he halted. It was not a change of mind about the command; it was the crashing of men thrusting through the jungle toward us. We turned and plunged into the bush in the opposite direction while a cry behind us told us that we had been seen. A moment later, heavy hands fell upon us and dragged us down. Someone gave an order in a language unknown to me, and we were jerked roughly to our feet.

Our captors were four tall men of a dark Caucasian race with features somewhat like those of the ancient Persians. They wore thick quilted helmets of some cloth, thin sleeveless shirts, short kilts, and knee-high leather boots. They were armed with small round steel shields, short heavy two-edged swords, heavy two-headed steel axes with long wooden shafts, and bows and arrows.

They said something to us. We looked blank. Then they turned as a weak cry came from the other side of the clearing. One of their own staggered out from the bush only to fall flat on his face and lie there unmoving. An arrow, which I recognized as Greystoke's, projected from his back.

Seeing this, the men became alarmed, though I suppose they had been alarmed all along. One ran out, examined the man, shook his head, and raced back. We were half-lifted, half-dragged along with them in a mad dash through vegetation that tore and ripped our clothes and us. Evidently they had run up against Greystoke, which was not a thing to be recommended at any time. I didn't know why they burdened themselves with two exhausted old men, but I surmised that it was for no beneficent purpose.

I will not recount in detail that terrible journey. Suffice it to say that we were four days and nights in the jungle, walking all day, trying to sleep at night. We were scratched, bitten, and torn, tormented with itches that wouldn't stop and sometimes sick from insect bites. We went through almost impenetrable jungle and waded waist-deep in swamps which held hordes of blood-sucking leeches. Half of the time, however, we progressed fairly swiftly along paths whose ease of access convinced me that they must be kept open by regular work parties.

The third day we started up a small mountain. The fourth day we went down it by being let down in a bamboo cage suspended by ropes from a bamboo boom. Below us lay the end of a lake that wound out of sight among the precipices that surrounded it. We were moved along at a fast pace toward a canyon into which the arm of the lake ran. Our captors pulled two dugouts out of concealment and we were paddled into the fjord. After rounding a corner, we saw before us a shore that sloped gently upward to a precipice several miles beyond it. A village of bamboo huts with thatched roofs spread along the shore and some distance inland.

The villagers came running when they saw us. A drum began beating some place, and to its beat we were marched up a narrow street and to a hut near the biggest hut. We were thrust into this, a gate of bamboo bars was lashed to the entrance, and we sat against its back wall while the villagers took turns looking in at us. As a whole, they were a good-looking people, the average of beauty being much higher than that seen in the East End of London, for instance. The women wore only long cloth skirts, though necklaces of shells hung around their necks and their long hair was decorated with flowers. The prepubescent children were stark naked.

Presently, food was brought to us. This consisted of delicious baked fish, roasted pygmy antelope, unleavened bread, and a brew that would under other circumstances have been too sweet for my taste. I am not ashamed to admit that Holmes and I gorged ourselves, devouring everything set before us.

I went to sleep shortly afterward, waking after dusk with a start. A torch flared in a stanchion just outside the entrance, at which two guards stood. Holmes was sitting near it, reading his *Practical Handbook of Bee Culture, with Some Observations Upon the Segregation of the Queen.* "Holmes," I began, but he held up his hand for silence. His keen ears had detected a sound a few seconds before mine did. This swelled to a hubbub with the villagers swarming out while the drum beat again. A moment later we saw the cause of the uproar. Six warriors, with Reich and Von Bork among them, were marching toward us. And while we watched curiously the two Germans were shoved into our hut.

Though both were much younger than Holmes and I, they were in equally bad condition—probably, I suppose, because they had not practiced the good old British custom of walking whenever possible. Von Bork refused to talk to us, but Reich, always a gentleman, told us what had happened to his party.

"We too heard the noises and that horrible cry," he said. "We made our way cautiously toward it, until we saw the carnage in a clearing. There were five dead men sprawled there, and six running in one direction and four in another. Standing with his foot on the chest of the largest corpse was a white man clad only in a leopard-skin. He was the one uttering that awful cry, which I would swear no human throat could make."

"*Der englisch Affenmensch,*" Von Bork muttered, his only contribution to the conversation that evening.

"Three of the men had arrows in them; the other two obviously had had their necks broken," Reich continued. "Von Bork whispered to me the wild man's identity, and so I whispered to my men to fire at him. Before we could do so, he had leaped up and pulled himself by a branch into a tree, and he was gone. We searched for him for some time without success. Then we started out to the east, but at dusk one of my men fell with an arrow through his neck. The angle of the arrow showed that it had come from above. We looked upward but could see nothing. Then a voice, speaking in excellent German, with a Brandenburger accent yet, ordered us to turn back. We were to march to the southwest. If we did not, one of us would die at dusk each day until no one was left. I asked him why we should do this, but there was no reply. Obviously, he had us entirely at his mercy—which, I suspected, from the looks of him, he utterly lacked."

"He claims that German officers murdered his wife," Holmes said.

"That's a lie!" Reich said indignantly. "More British propaganda! We are not the baby-bayoneting Huns your propaganda office portrays us as being!"

"There are some bad apples in every barrel," Holmes replied coolly.

Reich looked as if something had suddenly disturbed him. I thought it was a gas pain, but he said, "So, then, you *met* Greystoke! *He* told you this! But why did he desert you, leave you to fall into the hands of these savages?"

"I don't know," Holmes said. "Please carry on with your story."

"My first concern was the safety and wellbeing of my men. To have ignored Greystoke would have been to be brave but stupid. So I ordered the march to the southwest. After two days if became evident that Greystoke intended for us to starve to death. All our food was stolen that night, and we dared not leave the line of march to hunt, even though I doubt that we would have been able to shoot anything. The evening of the second day, I called out, begging that he let us at least hunt for food. He must have had some pangs of conscience, some mercy in him after all. That morning we woke to find a freshly killed wild pig, one of those orange-bristled swine, in the center of the camp. From somewhere in the branches overhead his voice came mockingly. 'Pigs should eat pigs!'

"And so we struggled southwestward until today. We were attacked by these people. Greystoke had not ordered us to lay down our arms, so we gave a good account of ourselves. But only Von Bork and I survived, and we were knocked unconscious by the flats of their axes. And marched here, the Lord only knows for what end."

"I suspect that the Lord of the Jungle, one of Greystoke's unofficial titles, knows," Holmes said glumly.

9

If Greystoke did know, he did not appear to tell us what to expect. Several days passed while we slept and ate and talked to Reich. Von Bork continued to ignore us, even though Holmes several times addressed him. Holmes asked him about his health, which I thought a strange concern for a man who had not killed us only because he lacked the opportunity.

Holmes seemed especially interested in his left eye, once coming up to within a few inches of it and staring at it. Von Bork became enraged at this close scrutiny.

"Get away from me, British swine!" he yelled. "Or I will ruin both of your eyes!"

"Permit Dr. Watson to examine it," Holmes said. "He might be able to save it."

"I want no incompetent English physician poking around it," Von Bork said.

I became so indignant that I lectured him on the very high standards of British medicine, but he only turned his back on me. Holmes chuckled at this and winked at me.

At the end of the week, we were allowed to leave the hut during the day, unaccompanied by guards. Holmes and I were not restrained in any way, though the Germans were hobbled with shackles so that they could not walk very fast. Apparently, our captors decided that Holmes and I were too old to give them much of a run for their money.

We took advantage of our comparative freedom to stroll around the village, inspecting everything and also attempting to learn the language.

"I don't know what family it belongs to," Holmes said. "But it is related neither to Cornish nor Chaldean, of that I'm sure."

Holmes was also interested in the white china of these people, which represented their highest art form. The black figures and designs they painted upon it reminded me somewhat of early Greek vase paintings. The vases and dishes were formed from kaolin deposits which existed to the north near the precipices. I mention this only because the white clay was to play an important part in our salvation in the near future.

At the end of the second week, Holmes, a superb linguist, had attained some fluency in the speech of our captors. "It belongs to a completely unknown language family," he said. "But there are certain words which, degenerated though they are, obviously come from ancient Persian. I would say that at one time these people had contact with a wandering party of descendants of Darius. The party settled down here, and these people borrowed some words from their idiom."

The village consisted of a hundred huts arranged in concentric circles. Each held a family ranging from two to eight members. Their fields lay north of the village on the slopes leading up to the precipices. The stock consisted of goats, pigs, and dwarf antelopes. Their alcoholic drink was a sort of mead made from the honey of wild bees. A few specimens of these ventured near the village, and Holmes secured some for study. They were about an inch long, striped black and white, and were armed with a long venom-ejecting barb. Holmes declared that they were of a new species, and he saw no reason not to classify them as *Apis holmesi*.

Once a week a party set out to the hills to collect honey. Its members were always clad in leather clothing and gloves and wore veils over their hats. Holmes asked permission to accompany them, explaining that he was wise in the ways of bees. To his disappointment, they refused him. A further inquiry by him resulted in the information that there was a negotiable, though difficult, pass through the precipices. It was used only for emergency purposes because of the vast number of bees that filled the narrow pass. Holmes obtained his data by questioning a child. Apparently, the adults had not thought to tell their young to keep silent about this means of exit.

"The bee-warding equipment is kept locked up in their temple," Holmes said. "And that makes it impossible to obtain it for an escape attempt."

The temple was the great hut in the village's centre. We were not allowed to enter it or even to approach it within fifty feet. Through some discreet inquiries, and unashamed eavesdropping, Holmes discovered that the high priestess-and-queen lived within the temple. We had never seen her nor were we likely to do so. She had been born in the temple and was to reside there until she died. Just why she was so restricted Holmes could not determine. His theory was that she was a sort of hostage to the gods.

"Perhaps, Watson, she is confined because of a superstition that arose after the catastrophe which their myths say deluged this land and the great civilisation it harboured. The fishermen tell me that they often see on the bottom of this lake the sunken ruins of the stone houses in which their ancestors lived. A curse was laid upon the land, they say, and they hint that only by keeping the high priestess-cum-queen inviolate, unseen by profane eyes, untouched by anyone after pubescence, can the wrath of the gods be averted. They are cagey in what they say, so I have had to surmise certain aspects of their religion."

"That's terrible!" I said.

"The deluge?"

"No, that a woman should be denied freedom and love."

"She has a name, but I have never overheard it. They refer to her as The Beautiful One."

"Is there nothing we can do for her?" I said.

"I do not know that she wants to be helped. You must not allow your well-known gallantry to endanger us. But to satisfy a legitimate scientific interest, if anthropology is a science, we could perhaps attempt a look inside the temple. Its roof has a large circular hole in its center. If we could get near the top of the high tree about twenty yards from it, we could look down into the building."

"With the whole village watching us?" I said. "No, Holmes, it is impossible to get up the tree unobserved during the day. And if we did so during the night, we could see nothing because of the darkness. In any event, it would probably mean instantaneous death even to make the attempt."

"There are torches lit in the building at night," he said. "Come, Watson, if you have no taste for this arboreal adventure, I shall go it alone."

And that was why, despite my deep misgivings, we climbed that towering tree on a cloudy night. After Von Bork and Reich had fallen asleep and our guards had dozed off and the village was silent except for a chanting in the temple, we crept out of our hut. Holmes had hidden a rope the day before, but even with this it was no easy task. We were not youths of twenty, agile as monkeys and as fearless aloft. Holmes threw the weighted end of the rope over the lowest branch, which was twenty feet up, and tied the two ends together. Then, grasping the rope with both hands, and bracing his feet against the trunk, he half-walked almost perpendicular to the trunk, up the tree. On reaching the branch, he rested for a long time while he gasped for breath so loudly that I feared he would wake up the nearest villagers. When he was quite recovered, he called down to me to make the ascent. Since I was heavier and several years older, and lacked his feline muscles, having more the physique of a bear, I experienced great difficulty in getting up. I wrapped my legs around the rope— no walking at a ninety-degree angle to the tree for me—and painfully and gaspingly hauled myself up. But I persisted—after all, I am British—and Holmes pulled me up at the final stage of what I was beginning to fear was my final journey.

After resting, we made a somewhat easier ascent via the branches to a position about ten feet below the top of the tree. From there we could look almost directly down through the hole in the middle of the roof. The torches within enabled us to see its interior quite clearly.

Both of us gasped when we saw the woman standing in the centre of the building by a stone altar. She was a beautiful woman, surely one of the daintiest things that ever graced this planet. She had long golden hair and eyes that looked dark from where we sat but which, we later found out, were a deep grey. She was wearing nothing except a necklace of some stones that sparkled as she moved. Though I was fascinated, I also felt something of shame, as if I were a peeping tom. I had to remind myself that the women wore nothing above the waist in their everyday attire and that when they swam in the lake they wore nothing at all. So we were doing nothing immoral by this spying. Despite this reasoning, my face (and other things) felt inflamed.*

She stood there, doing nothing for a long time, which I expected would make Holmes impatient. He did not stir or make any comment, so I suppose that this time he did not mind a lack of action. The priestesses chanted and the priests walked around in a circle making signs with their hands and their fingers. Then a bound he-goat was brought in and placed on the altar, and, after some more mumbo-jumbo, the woman cut its throat. The blood was caught in a golden bowl and passed around in a sort of communion, the woman drinking first.

"A most unsanitary arrangement," I murmured to Holmes.

"These people are, nevertheless, somewhat cleaner than your average Londoner," Holmes replied. "And much more cleanly than your Scots peasant."

I was about to take umbrage at this, since I am of Scots descent on my mother's side. Holmes knew both this and my sensitivity about it. He had been making too many remarks of this nature recently, and though I attributed them to irritability arising from nicotine withdrawal, I was, to use an American phrase, getting fed up with them. I was about to remonstrate when my heart leaped into my throat and choked me.

A hand had come from above and clamped down upon my shoulder. I knew that it wasn't Holmes' because I could see both of his hands.

10

Holmes almost fell off the branch but was saved by another hand, which grasped him by the collar of his shirt. A familiar voice said, "Silence!"

"Greystoke!" I gasped. And then, remembering that, after all, he was a duke, I said, "Your pardon. I mean, Your Grace."

"What are you doing up here, you baboon!" Holmes said.

I was shocked at this, though I knew that Holmes spoke thus only because he must have been thoroughly frightened. To address a high British nobleman in this manner was not his custom.

"Tut, tut, Holmes," I said.

"Tut, tut yourself," he replied. "He's not paying me a fee! He's no client of mine. Besides, I doubt that he is entitled to his title!"

---

*The parentheses are the editor's. Watson had crossed out this phrase, though not enough to make it illegible. *Editor.*

306 PHILIP JOSÉ FARMER

A growl that lifted the hairs on the back of my neck came from above. It was followed by the descent of the duke's heavy body upon our branch, which bent alarmingly. But Greystoke squatted upon it, his hands free, with all the ease of the baboon he had been accused of being.

"What does that last remark mean?" he said. At that moment the moon broke through the clouds. A ray fell upon Holmes' face, which was as pale as when he had been playing the dying detective. He said, "This is neither the time nor the place for an investigation of your credentials. We are in a desperate plight, and..."

"You don't realise how desperate," Greystoke said. "I usually abide by human laws when I am in civilisation or among the black blood-brothers of my ranch in East Africa. But when I am in my larger estate, that of Central Africa, when I am in the jungle, where I have a higher rank even than duke, where, to put it simply, I am the king, where I revert to my primal and happiest state, that of a great ape..."

Good Lord! I thought. And this is the man Holmes referred to as inarticulate!

"...then I obey only my own laws, not those of humanity, for which I have the greatest contempt, barring a few specimens of such..."

There was much more in this single statement, the length of which would have made any German philosopher proud. The gist of it was that if Holmes did not explain his remark now, he would have no chance to do so later. Nor was the duke backward in stating that I would not be taking any news of Holmes' fate to the outside world.

"He means it, Holmes!" I said.

"I am well aware of that, Watson," he answered. "His Grace is covered only with a thin veneer of civilisation."

This phrase, I remembered, was one used often by the American novelist to describe his protagonist's assumption of human culture.

"Very well, Your Highness," Holmes said. "It is not my custom to set forth a theory until I have enough evidence to make it a fact. But under the circumstances..."

I looked for Greystoke to show some resentment at Holmes' sarcastic use of a title appropriate only to a monarch. He, however, only smiled. This, I believe, was a reaction of pleasure, of ignorance of Holmes' intent to cut him. He was sure that he deserved the title, and now that I have had time to reflect on it, I agree with him. Though a duke in England, in Africa he ruled a kingdom many times larger than our tight little isle. And he paid no taxes on it.

"Watson and I were acquainted with the ten-year-old son of the sixth duke, your reputed father," Holmes said. "That boy, the then Lord Saltire, is *not* you. Yet you have the title that should be his. You notice that I do not say the title should *rightly* be his. You are the legitimate inheritor of the late duke's titles and estates. Titles and estates, by the way, that should never have been his or his son's."

"Good Lord, Holmes!" I said. "What are you saying?"

"If you will refrain from interrupting, you will hear what I'm saying," he responded sharply. "Your Grace, that American novelist who has written a highly fictionalised novel based on your rather…ahem…nonconventional behaviour in Africa, came closer to the truth than anybody but yourself, and a few of your friends, I presume, realise. Watson tells me that in the novel your father, who should have been the seventh duke, was marooned on the shores of western Africa with his wife. There you were born, and when your parents died, you were adopted by a tribe of large intelligent apes hitherto unknown to science. They were strictly a product of a romantic imagination, of course, and the apes must have been either chimpanzees or gorillas, both of which du Chaillu has reported seeing in West Africa. Neither, however, exists at ten degrees south latitude, which is where the novelist said you were born and raised. I would place your birth further north, say somewhere near or in the very country, Gabon, which du Chaillu visited."

"Elementary, my dear Holmes," Greystoke said, smiling slightly again. I warmed to him somewhat, since it was evident by his remark that he was acquainted with my narratives of the adventures of Holmes and myself. A man who read these, and with evident pleasure, couldn't be all bad.

"If it is elementary," Holmes said with some asperity, "I am still the only man complex enough to have grasped the truth."

"Not all of it," Greystoke replied. "That Yank writer was quite correct in his guess that the tribe that raised me was unknown to science. However, they were not great apes but a sort of apemen, beings halfway on the evolutionary ladder between *Homo sapiens* and the ape. They had speech, which, though simple, was still speech. And that is why I did not become incapable of using language, as all other feral humans so far discovered have been incapable. Once a child passes a certain age without encountering human speech, he is mentally retarded."

"Really?" Holmes said.

"It does not matter whether or not you believe that," the duke said.

"But the Yank had your uncle inheriting the title after his brother died and your parents were declared dead. Then your uncle, the sixth duke, died, and your cousin, the lad Watson and I knew as Lord Saitire, became the seventh duke. So far, the Yank's account was in agreement with the reality. It is the next event which, in his romance, departed completely from reality."

"And that was?" Greystoke said softly.

"Consider first what the Yank said happened. In his novel the jungle man found out that he was the rightful heir to the title. But he kept silent about it because he loved the heroine and she had promised to marry his cousin and considered herself bound by her promise. If he revealed the truth, he would strip her of her title of duchess and, worse, of the fortune which the cousin possessed. She would be penniless again. So he nobly said nothing.

"But according to Watson, a great reader of fiction, the Yank wrote a sequel to the first romance. In this the cousin gets sick and before dying confesses that he saw the telegram about the fingerprints, destroyed it, and ignobly kept silent. Fortunately, the girl had put off the marriage, so there is no question of her being a virgin, which is an important issue to the housemaids and some doctors who read this type of literature. Our hero becomes Lord Greystoke and everybody lives happily forever after—until the next adventure.

"I believe that in reality you did marry the girl on whom the novelist based his character. But that is pure nonsense about the jungle man's assumption of the title. If that had happened in reality, do you think for a moment that the resultant publicity would not have been world-wide? What a story—the heir to an English title appearing out of the African forest, an heir not even known to exist, an heir who has been raised by a band of missing links. Can you imagine the commotion, the curiosity, inflaming the world? Can you imagine what a hell the heir's life would be, no privacy, reporters trailing him at every step, an utter lack of privacy for not only him but his wife and his family?

"But we know that no such thing happened. We do know that an English peer who had led an uneventful life, except for being kidnapped when ten, at maturity goes to Africa and settles down upon a ranch. And after a while strange tales seep back to London, tales of this peer reverting to a jungle life, wandering through central Africa clad only in a loincloth, eating raw meat, killing lions with only a knife, breaking the necks of gorillas with full nelsons, and consorting with apes and elephants. The man has suddenly become a combination of Hercules, Ulysses, and Mowgli. And Croesus, I might add, since he seems to have a source of great wealth hidden some place in deepest Africa. It is distributed through illegal channels, but word of it reaches Threadneedle Street and New Scotland Yard, of course.

"I wonder," he added after a pause, "if this valley could be where the gold comes from?"

"No," Greystoke said. "That is a long way off. This valley is mostly lake, rich only with fish life. Once it was a wealthy, even grand, land with a civilisation to rival Egypt's. But it was flooded when a natural dam caved in after an earthquake, and all its works and most of its people were drowned. When the water is clear you can see at noon the roof-tops and toppled pillars here and there. Today, the degenerate descendants of the survivors huddle in this miserable village and talk of the great days, of the glory of Zu-Vendis."

"Zu-Vendis!" I exclaimed. "But…"

The duke made an impatient sound and said, "Carry on, Holmes."

"First, allow me to ask you a question. Did that Yank somehow hear an account of your life that was not available to the public? A distorted account, perhaps, but still largely valid?"

Greystoke nodded and said, "A friend of mine with a drinking problem, while on a binge, told a fellow some things which seem to have been relayed to the Yank. The Yank included parts of this account in his novel."

"I surmised such. He thought he had the true story of your life, but he didn't dare present it as anything but fiction. For one thing, he could be sued. For another, your passion for vengeance is rather well known.

"In any event, his story of how you came into your title, though fictional, still contains the clue needed to determine the true story.

"Here, as I reconstruct it, is what happened. You knew that you were the true heir. You wanted the title and the girl and everything, though I suspect that without the girl you would not have cared for the other."

Greystoke nodded.

"Very well. Your cousin's yacht had been temporarily put out of commission, not wrecked and sunk, as was depicted in the novel. You had met the party from the yacht; they were stranded on the shore near your natal cabin. All that nonsense in the second novel about your girl being abducted by little hairy men from the hidden city of treasure deep in the heart of Africa was just that, nonsense."

"If it had been true," Greystoke said, "the abductors would have been forced to travel a thousand miles through the worst part of Africa, abduct my wife, and travel back to their ruins. And then, when I rescued her, she and I would have had to travel another thousand miles back to the yacht. Under the circumstances, this would have taken several years, and the time for that allowed in the novel just would not suffice. Besides, it was all imagination. Except for the city itself and the degenerates who inhabit it."

"That high priestess who fell in love with you…?" I said.

"Carry on, Holmes," he said.

"After your cousin died, your girl and your friends told you what a lack of privacy you and your family would have from then on. So you all decided to carry out a fraud. Yet, it was not really a fraud, since you *were* the legitimate heir. You looked much like your cousin, and so you decided to pass yourself off as him. When the yacht returned to England, for all anyone knew, it had made a routine voyage from England and around Africa and back again. Your friends coached you in all you needed to know about the friends and acquaintances you would meet. The servants at your ancestral estate may have detected something a little strange about you, but you probably had an excuse trumped up. A temporary fit of amnesia, perhaps."

"Correct," Greystoke said. "I used that excuse often. I was always running into somebody about whom I'd not been instructed. And occasionally I'd do something very unBritish."*

"Lord, the mystery of the century!" cried Holmes. "And I can't say a word about it!"

"How do I know I can trust you?" Greystoke said.

At these words my mounting anxiety reached its peak. I had wondered why Greystoke was so frank, and then the sickening certainty came that he did not care what we had learned because dead men cannot talk. The only hope I had was that Greystoke had not murdered his cousin after all. Perhaps he was a decent fellow under all that savagery. This hope collapsed when I considered the possibility that he might *not* have been altogether frank. What if he *had* murdered his cousin?

Though I felt that it was dangerous to pursue this subject, I could not restrain my curiosity. "Your Grace," I said, "I hope that you won't think I'm too inquisitive. But...just what *did* happen to your cousin? Did he die as described in the second novel, die of a jungle fever after making a deathbed confession that he had cheated you out of your birthright and your lover? Or...?"

"Or did I slit his throat?" Greystoke said. "No, Dr. Watson, I did not kill him, though I must admit that the thought of doing so did cross my mind. And I was glad that he died, but, unlike so many of you civilised creatures, I felt no guilt about being glad. Nor would I feel any regret, shame, or guilt in putting anyone out of the way who was a grave threat to me or mine. Does that answer your question?"

"More than sufficiently, Your Grace," I said, gulping. He may have been lying, but my hopes rose again when I reflected that he did not have to lie if he intended to kill us.

---

*This disclosure definitely invalidates some of my speculations and reconstructions in my biography of Greystoke. These will be corrected in a future issue. Lord Greystoke himself had admitted that Holmes' theory is correct. See "Extracts from the Memoirs of Lord Greystoke," *Mother Was A Lovely Beast*, Philip José Farmer, editor, Chilton, October 1974.

"You have implied that you have read Watson's narratives," Holmes said. "Admittedly, they are somewhat exaggerated and romanticised. But his portrayal of our moral character is quite accurate. Our word is our bond."

Greystoke said, "Hmmm!" and he frowned. He fondled the hilt of the huge knife in his scabbard, and I felt as cold as the moon looked. As dead, too.

Holmes seemed to be more meditative than frightened. He said, slowly, "We are professional men, Your Grace. If we were to take you as our client, we could not disclose a word of the case. Not even the police could force it from us."

"Ah!" Greystoke said, smiling grimly. "I am always forgetting the immense value civilised people put upon money. Of course! I pay you a fee and your lips are shut forever."

"Or until such time as Your Grace releases us from the sacred bonds of confidentiality."

"What would you consider a reasonable fee?"

"The highest I ever earned was in the case of the Priory School," said Holmes. "It was your uncle who paid it. Twelve thousand pounds."

He repeated, savouring the words, "Twelve thousand pounds."

Quickly, he added, "Of course, that sum was *my* fee. Watson, as my partner, received the same amount."

"Really, Holmes," I murmured.

"Twenty-four thousand pounds," the duke said, still frowning.

"That was in 1901," Holmes said. "Inflation has sent prices sky-high since then, and the income tax rate is ascending as if it were a rocket."

"For Heaven's sake, Holmes!" I cried. "I do not see the necessity for this fishmarket bargaining! Surely.. ."

Holmes coldly interrupted. "You will please leave the financial arrangements to me, the senior partner and the true professional in this matter."

"You'll antagonise His Grace, and…"

"Would sixty thousand pounds be adequate?" Greystoke said.

"Well," Holmes said, hesitating, "God knows how wartime conditions will continue to cheapen the price of money in the next few years."

Suddenly, the knife was in the duke's hands. He made no threatening moves with it. He merely looked at it as if he were considering cleaning it.

"Your Grace is most generous," Holmes said quickly.

Greystoke put the knife back into the scabbard.

"I don't happen to have a cheque on me," he said. "You will trust me until we get to Nairobi?"

"Certainly, Your Grace," Holmes murmured. "Your family was always the most openhanded in my experience. Now, the king of Holland…"

"What is this you said about Zu-Vendis?" I broke in, knowing that Holmes would take a long time to describe a case some of whose aspects still rankled him.

"Who cares?" Holmes said, but I ignored him. "As I remember it, an Englishman, a great hunter and explorer, wrote a book describing his adventures in that country. His name was Allan Quatermain."

Greystoke nodded and said, "I've read some of his biographical accounts."

"I thought they were novels," Holmes said. "Must we discuss cheap fiction…" His voice trailed as he realized that Greystoke had said that Zu-Vendis was a reality.

Greystoke said, "Either Quatermain or his agent and editor, H. R. Haggard, exaggerated the size of Zu-Vendis. It was supposed to be about the size of France but actually covered an area equal to that of Liechtenstein. In the main, however, except for the size and location of Zu-Vendis, Quatermain's account is true. He was accompanied on his expedition by two Englishmen, a baronet, Sir Henry Curtis, and a naval captain, John Good. And that great Zulu warrior, Umslopogaas, a man whom I would have liked to have known. After the Zulu and Quatermain died, Curtis sent Quatermain's manuscript of the adventure to Haggard. Haggard apparently added some things of his own to give more verisimilitude to the chronicle. For one thing, he said that several British commissions were investigating Zu-Vendis with the intent of finding a more accessible means of travel to it. This was not so. Zu-Vendis was never found, and that is why most people concluded that the account was pure fiction. Shortly after the manuscript was sent out by one of the natives who had accompanied the Quatermain party, the entire valley except for this high end was flooded."

"Then poor Curtis and Good and their lovely Zu-Vendis wives were drowned?" I said.

"No," Greystoke said. "They were among the dozen or so who reached safety. Apparently, they either could not get out of the valley then or decided to stay here. After all, Nylepthah, Curtis' wife, was the queen, and she would not want to abandon her people, few though they were. The two Englishmen settled down, taught the people the use of the bow, among other things, and died here. They were buried up in the hills."

"What a sad story!" I said.

"All people must die," Greystoke replied, as if that told the whole story of the world. And perhaps it did.

Greystoke looked out at the temple, saying, "That woman at whom you two have been staring with a not-quite-scientific detachment…"

"Yes?" I said.

"Her name is also Nylepthah. She is the granddaughter of both Good and Curtis."

11

"Great Scott!" I said. "A British woman parading around naked before those savages!"

Greystoke shrugged and said, "It's their custom."

"We must rescue her and get her back to the home of her ancestors!" I cried.

"Be quiet, Watson, or you'll have the whole pack howling for our blood," Holmes growled. "She seems quite contented with her lot. Or could it be," he added, looking hard at me, "that you have once again fallen into love?" He made it sound as if the grand passion were an open privy. Blushing, I said, "I must admit that there is a certain feeling…"

"Well, the fair sex is your department," he said. "But really, Watson, at your age!"

("The Americans have a proverb," I said. "The older the buck, the stiffer the horn.")*

"Be quiet, both of you," the duke said. "I permitted the Zu-Vendis to capture you because I knew you'd be safe for a while. I had to get on up-country to check out a rumour that a white woman was being held captive by a tribe of blacks. Though I am positive that my wife is dead, still there is always hope. Mr. Holmes suggested that the Germans might have played a trick on me by substituting the charred body of a native girl. That had occurred to me previously. That I wear only a loincloth doesn't mean that I am naked of intelligence.**

"I found the white girl, an Englishwoman, but she was not my wife…"

"Good heavens!" I said. "Where is she? Have you hidden her out there?"

"She's still with the sultan of the tribe," he said sourly. "I went to much trouble to rescue her, had to kill a dozen or so tribesmen getting to her and a dozen on the way out. And then the woman told me she was perfectly happy with the sultan and would I please return her. I told her to find her own way back. I detest violence which can be avoided. If only she had told me beforehand.… Well, that's all over."

---

*The parentheses are the editor's, indicating another passage crossed out by Watson.

**Apparently, Watson forgot to describe Holmes' comment. Undoubtedly, he would have inserted it at the proper place in the final draft.

I did not comment. I thought it indiscreet to point out that the woman could not have told him how she felt until *after* he had fought his way in. And I doubted that she had an opportunity to voice her opposition on the way out.

"I drove the Germans this way because I expected that they would, like you, be picked up by the Zu-Vendis. Tomorrow night, all four of you prisoners are scheduled to be sacrificed on the temple altar. I got back an hour ago to get you two out."

"That was cutting it close, wasn't it?" Holmes said.

"You mean to leave Von Bork and Reich here?" I said. "To be slaughtered like sheep? And what about the woman, Nylepthah? What kind of life is that, being confined from birth to death in that house, being denied the love and companionship of a husband, forced to murder poor devils of captives?"

"Yes," said Holmes. "Reich is a very decent fellow and should be treated like a prisoner of war. I wouldn't mind at all if Von Bork were to die, but only he knows the location of the SB papers. The fate of Britain, of her allies, hangs on those papers. As for the woman, well, she is of good British stock and it seems a shame to leave her here in this squalidness."

"So she can go to London and perhaps live in squalour there?" Greystoke said.

"I'll see to it that that does not happen," I said. "Your Grace, you can have back my fee if you take that woman along."

Greystoke laughed softly and said. "I couldn't refuse a man who loves love more than he loves money. And you can keep the fee."

12

At some time before dawn, Greystoke entered our hut. The Germans were also waiting for him, since we had told them what to expect if they did not leave with us. The duke gestured for silence, unnecessarily, I thought, and we followed him outside. The two guards, gagged and trussed-up, lay by the door. Near them stood Nylepthah, also gagged, her hands bound before her and a rope hobbling her. Her glorious body was concealed in a cloak. The duke removed the hobble, gestured at us, took the woman by the arm, and we walked silently through the village. Our immediate goal was the beach, where we intended to steal two boats. We would paddle to the foot of the cliff on top of which was the bamboo boom and ascend the ropes. Then we would cut the ropes so that we could not be followed. Greystoke had come down on the rope after disposing of the guards at the boom. He would climb back up the rope and then pull us up.

Our plans died in the bud. As we approached the beach, we saw torches flaring on the water. Presently, as we watched from behind a hut, we saw fishermen paddling in with their catch of night-caught fish. Someone stirred in the hut beside which we crouched, and before we could get away, a woman, yawning and stretching, came out. She must have been waiting for her fisherman husband. Whatever the case, she surprised us.

The duke moved swiftly, but too late, toward her. She screamed loudly, and though she quit almost immediately, she had aroused the village.

There is no need to go into detail about the long and exhausting run we made through the village, while the people poured out, and up the slopes toward the faraway pass in the precipices. Greystoke smote right and left and before him, and men and women went down like the Philistines before Samson. We were armed with the short swords he had stolen from the armory and so were of some aid to him. But by the time we had left the village and reached the fields, Holmes and I were breathing very hard.

"You two help the woman along between you," the duke commanded the Germans. Before we could protest, though what good it would have done if we had I don't know, we were picked up, one under each arm, and carried off. Burdened though he was, Greystoke ran faster than the three behind him. The ground, only about a foot away from my face since I was dangling like a rag doll in his arm, reeled by. After about a mile, the duke stopped and released us. He did this by simply dropping us. My face hit the dirt at the same time my knees did. I was somewhat pained, but I thought it indiscreet to complain. Holmes, however, displayed a knowledge of swear words which would have delighted a dock worker. Greystoke ignored him, urging us to push on. Far behind us we could see the torches of our pursuers and hear their clamour.

By dawn the Zu-Vendis had gotten closer. All of us, except for the indefatigable duke, were tiring swiftly. The pass was only half a mile away, and once we were through that, the duke said, we would be safe. The savages behind us, though, were beginning to shoot their arrows at us.

"We can't get through the pass anyway!" I said between gasps to Holmes. "We have no equipment to keep the bees off us! If the arrows don't kill us, the bee-stings will!"

Ahead of us, where the hills suddenly moved in and formed the entrance to the path, a vast buzzing filled the air. Fifty thousand tiny, but deadly, insects swirled in a thick cloud as they prepared to voyage to the sea of flowers which held the precious nectar.

We stopped to catch our breath and consider the situation.

"We can't go back and we can't go ahead!" I said. "What shall we do?"

"I still live!" the duke cried. This, I thought, was an admirable motto, but it was of no help at all to us. Greystoke, however, was a practical man. He pointed at the nearby hill, at the base of which was the white clay used by the Zu-Vendis to make their fine pots and dishes.

"Coat yourselves with that!" he said. "It should be somewhat of a shield!" And he hastened to take his own advice.

I hesitated. The duke had stripped off his loincloth and had jumped into the stream which ran nearby. Then he had scooped out with his hands a quantity of clay, had mixed it with water, and was smearing it over him everywhere. Holmes was removing his clothing before going into the stream. The Germans were getting ready to do likewise, while the beautiful Nylepthah stood abandoned. I did the only thing a gentleman could do. I went to her and removed her cloak, under which she wore nothing. I told her in my halting Zu-Vendis that I was ready to sacrifice myself for her. Though the bees, alarmed, were now moving in a great cloud toward us, I would make sure that I smeared the clay all over her before I took care of myself.

Nylepthah said, "I know an easier way to escape the bees. Let me run back to the village."

"Poor deluded girl!" I said. "You do not know what is best for you! Trust me, and I will see you safely to England, the home of your ancestors. And then..."

I did not get a chance to promise to marry her. Holmes and the Germans cried out, causing me to look up just in time to see Greystoke falling unconscious to the ground. An arrow had hit him in the head, and though it had struck a glancing blow, it had knocked him out and made a large nasty wound.

I thought we were indeed lost. Behind us was the howling horde of savages, their arrows and spears and axes flying through the air at us. Ahead was a swarm of giant bees, a cloud so dense that I could barely see the hills behind them. The buzzing was deafening. The one man who was strong enough and jungle-wise enough to pull us through was out of action for the time being. And if the bees attacked soon, which they would do, he would be in that state permanently. So would all of us.

Holmes shouted at me, "Never mind taking advantage of that woman, Watson! Come here, quickly, and help me!"

"This is no time to indulge in jealousy, Holmes," I muttered, but nevertheless I obeyed him. "No, Watson," Holmes said, "I'll put on the clay! You daub on me that excellent black dirt there along the banks of the stream! Put it on in stripes, thus, white and black alternating!"

"Have you gone mad, Holmes?" I said.

"There's no time to talk," said Holmes. "The bees are almost upon us! Oh, they are deadly, deadly, Watson! Quick, the mud!"

Within a minute, striped like a zebra, Holmes stood before me. He ran to the pile of clothes and took from the pocket of his jacket the large magnifying glass that had been his faithful companion all these years. And then he did something that caused me to cry out in utter despair. He ran directly toward the deadly buzzing cloud.

I shouted after him as I ran to drag him away from his futile and senseless act. It was too late to get him away from the swiftly advancing insects. I knew that, just as I knew that I would die horribly with him. Nevertheless, I would be with him. We had been comrades too many years for me to even contemplate for a second abandoning him.

He turned when he heard my voice and shouted, "Go back, Watson! Go back! Get the others to one side! Drag Greystoke out of their path! I know what I'm doing! Get away! I command you, Watson!"

The conditioning of our many years of association turned me and sent me back to the group. I'd obeyed his orders too long to refuse them now. But I was weeping, convinced that he was out of his mind, or, if he did have a plan, it would fail. I got Reich to help me drag the senseless and heavily bleeding Greystoke half into the stream, and I ordered Von Bork and Nylepthah to lie down in the stream. The clay coating, I was convinced, was not an adequate protection. We could submerge ourselves when the bees passed over us. The stream was only inches deep, but perhaps the water flowing over our bodies would discourage the insects.

Lying in the stream, holding Greystoke's head up to keep him from drowning, I watched Holmes.

He had indeed gone crazy. He was dancing around and around, stopping now and then to bend over and wiggle his buttocks in a most undignified manner. Then he would hold up the magnifying glass so that the sunlight flashed through it at the Zu-Vendis. These, by the way, had halted to stare openmouthed at Holmes.

"Whatever are you doing?" I shouted.

He shook his head angrily at me to indicate that I should keep quiet. At that moment I became aware that he was himself making a loud buzzing sound. It was almost submerged in the louder noise of the swarm, but I was near enough to hear it faintly.

Again and again Holmes whirled, danced, stopped, pointing his wriggling buttocks at the Zu-Vendis savages and letting the sun pass through the magnifying glass at a certain angle. His actions seemed to puzzle not only the humans but the bees. The swarm had stopped its forward movement and it was hanging in the air, seemingly pointed at Holmes.

Suddenly, as Holmes completed his obscene dance for the seventh time, the swarm flew forward. I cried out, expecting to see him covered with the huge black-and-white-striped horrors. But the mass split in two, leaving him an island in their midst. And then they were all gone, and the Zu-Vendis were running away screaming, their bodies black and fuzzy with a covering of bees. Some of them dropped in their flight, rolling back and forth, screaming, batting at the insects, and then becoming still and silent.

I ran to Holmes, crying, "How did you do it?"

"Do you remember your scepticism when I told you that I had made an astounding discovery? One that will enshrine my name among the greats in the hail of science?"

"You don't mean…?"

He nodded. "Yes, bees do have a language, even African bees. It is actually a system of signals, not a true language. Bees who have discovered a new source of honey return to the hive and there perform a dance which indicates clearly the direction of and the distance at which the honey lies. I have also discovered that the bee communicates the advent of an enemy to the swarm. It was this dance which I performed, and the swarm attacked the indicated enemy, the Zu-Vendis. The dance movements are intricate, and certain polarisations of light play a necessary part in the message. These I simulated with my magnifying glass. But come, Watson, let us get our clothes on and be off before the swarm returns! I do not think I can pull that trick again. We do not want to be the game afoot."

We got the duke to his feet and half-carried him to the pass. Though he recovered consciousness, he seemed to have reverted to a totally savage state. He did not attack us but he regarded us suspiciously and made threatening growls if we got too close. We were at a loss to explain this frightening change in him. The frightening part came not so much from any danger he represented as from the dangers he was supposed to save us from. We had depended upon him to guide us and to feed and protect us on the way back. Without him even the incomparable Holmes was lost.

Fortunately, the duke recovered the next day and provided the explanation himself.

"For some reason I seem to be prone to receiving blows on the head," he said. "I have a thick skull, but every once in a while I get such a blow that even its walls cannot withstand the force. Sometimes, say about one out of three times, a complete amnesia results. I then revert to the state in which I was before I encountered white people. I am once again the uncivilised apeman; I have no memory of anything that occurred before I was twenty years old. This state may last for only a day, as you have seen, or it may persist for months."

"I would venture to say," Holmes said, "that this readiness to forget your contact with civilised peoples indicates an unconscious desire to avoid them. You are happiest when in the jungle and with no obligations. Hence your unconscious seizes upon every opportunity, such as a blow on the head, to go back to the happy primal time."

"Perhaps you are right," the duke said. "Now that my wife is dead, I would like to forget civilisation even exists. But I must see my country through this war first."

It took less than a month for us to get to Nairobi. Greystoke took excellent care of us, even though he was impatient to get back into action against the Germans. During the journey I had ample time to teach Nylepthah English and to get well acquainted with her. Before we reached the Lake Victoria railhead, I had proposed to her and been accepted. I will never forget that night. The moon was bright, and a hyena was laughing nearby.

The day before we reached the railhead, Greystoke went up a tree to check out the territory. A branch broke under his feet, and he landed on his head. When he regained consciousness, he was again the apeman. We could not come near him without his baring his teeth and growling menacingly. And that night he disappeared.

Holmes was very downcast by this. "What if he never gets over his amnesia, Watson? Then we will be cheated out of our fees."

"My dear Holmes," I said, somewhat coolly, "we never earned the fee in the first place. Actually, we were allowing ourselves to be bribed by the duke to keep silent."

"You never did understand the subtle interplay of economics and ethics," Holmes replied.

"There goes Von Bork," I said, glad to change the subject. I pointed to the fellow, who was sprinting across the veldt as if a lion were after him.

"He is mad if he thinks he can make his way alone to German East Africa," Holmes said. "But we must go after him! He has on him the formula for the SB."

"Where?" I asked for the hundredth time. "We have stripped him a dozen times and gone over every inch of his clothes and his skin. We have looked into his mouth and up..."

At that moment I observed Von Bork turn his head to the right to look at a rhinoceros which had come around a tall termite hill. The next moment, he had run the left side of his head and body into an acacia tree with such force that he bounced back several feet. He did not get up, which was just as well. The rhinoceros was looking for him and would have detected any movement by Von Bork. After prancing around and sniffing the air in several directions, the weak-eyed beast trotted off. Holmes and I hastened to Von Bork before he got his senses back and ran off once more.

"I believe I now know where the formula is," Holmes said.

"And how could you know that?" I said, for the thousandth time since I had first met him.

"I will bet my fee against yours that I can show you the formula within the next two minutes," he said, but I did not reply.

He kneeled down beside the German, who was lying on his back, his mouth and his eyes open. His pulse, however, beat strongly.

Holmes placed the tips of his thumbs under Von Bork's left eye. I stared aghast as the eye popped out.

"It's glass, Watson," Holmes said. "I had suspected that for some time, but I saw no reason to verify my suspicions until he was in a British prison. I was certain that his vision was limited to his right side when I saw him run into that tree. Even with his head turned away he would have seen it if his left eye had been effective."

He rotated the glass eye between thumb and finger while examining it through the magnifying glass. "Aha!" he exclaimed and then, handing the eye and glass to me, said, "See for yourself, Watson,"

"Why," I said, "what I had thought were massive haemorrhages due to eye injury are tiny red lines of chemical formulae on the surface of the glass—if it *is* glass, and not some special material prepared to receive inscriptions."

"Very good, Watson," Holmes said. "Undoubtedly, Von Bork did not merely receive an injury to the eye in that motor-car crash of which I heard rumours. He lost it, but the wily fellow had it replaced with an artificial eye which had more uses than—ahem—met the eye.

"After stealing the SB formula, he inscribed the surface of this false organ with the symbols. These, except through a magnifier, look like the results of dissipation or of an accident. He must have been laughing at us when we examined him so thoroughly, but he will laugh no more."

He took the eye back and pocketed it. "Well, Watson, let us rouse him from whatever dreams he is indulging in and get him into the proper hands. This time he shall pay the penalty for espionage."

Two months later we were back in England. We travelled by water, despite the danger of U-boats, since Holmes had sworn never again to get into an aircraft of any type. He was in a bad humour throughout the voyage. He was certain that Greystoke, even if he recovered his memory, would not send the promised cheques.

He turned the glass eye over to Mycroft, who sent it on to his superiors. That was the last we ever heard of it, and since the SB was never used, I surmise that the War Office decided that it would be too horrible a weapon. I was happy about this, since it just did not seem British to wage germ warfare. I have often wondered, though, what would have happened if Von Bork's mission had been successful. Would the Kaiser have countenanced SB as a weapon against his English cousins?

There were still three years of war to get through. I found lodgings for my wife and myself, and, despite the terrible conditions, the air raids, the food and material shortages, the dismaying reports from the front, we managed to be happy. In 1917 Nylepthah did what none of my previous wives had ever done. She presented me with a son. I was delirious with joy, even though I had to endure much joshing from my colleagues about fatherhood at my age. I did not inform Holmes of the baby. I dreaded his sarcastic remarks.

On November 11, 1919, however, a year after the news that turned the entire Allied world into a carnival of happiness, though a brief one, I received a wire.

"Bringing a bottle and cigars to celebrate the good tidings. Holmes."

I naturally assumed that he referred to the anniversary of the Armistice. My surprise was indeed great when he showed up not only with the bottle of Scotch and a box of Havanas but a bundle of new clothes and toys for the baby and a box of chocolates for Nylepthah. The latter was a rarity at this time and must have cost Holmes some time and money to obtain.

"Tut, tut, my dear fellow," he said when I tried to express my thanks, "I've known for some time that you were the proud father. I have always intended to show up and tender my respects to the aged, but still energetic, father and to the beautiful Mrs. Watson. Never mind waking the infant up to show him to me, Watson. All babies look alike, and I will take your word for it that he is beautiful."

"You are certainly jovial," I said. "I do not ever remember seeing you more so."

"With good reason, Watson, with good reason!"

He dipped his hand into his pocket and brought out a cheque.

I looked at it and almost staggered. It was made out to me for the sum of thirty thousand pounds.

"I had given up on Greystoke," he said. "I heard that he was missing, lost somewhere in deepest Africa, probably dead. It seems, however, that he had found his wife was alive after all, and he was tracking her into the jungles of the Belgian Congo. He found her but was taken prisoner by some rather peculiar tribe. Eventually, his adopted son, you know, the Lt. Drummond who was to fly us to Marseilles, went after him and rescued his parents. And so, my dear fellow, one of the first things the duke did was to send the cheques! Both in my care, of course!"

"I can certainly use it," I said. "This will enable me to retire instead of working until I am eighty."

I poured two drinks for us and we toasted our good fortune. Holmes sat back in the chair, puffing upon the excellent Havana and watching Mrs. Watson bustle about her housework.

"She won't allow me to hire a maid," I said. "She insists on doing all the work, including the cooking, herself. Except for the baby and myself, she does not like to touch anyone or be touched by anyone. Sometimes I think..."

"Then she has shut herself off from all but you and the baby," he said.

"You might say that," I replied. "She is happy, though, and that is what matters."

Holmes took out a small notebook and began making notes in it. He would look up at Nylepthah, watch her for a minute, and record something.

"What are you doing, Holmes?" I said.

His answer showed me that he, too, could indulge in a pawky humour when his spirits were high.

"I am making some observations upon the segregation of the queen."

THE END

EDITOR'S COMMENTS:

The reference on page 270 to the speed of the Handley Page was really in knots, not miles per hour. The editor has converted this to make it more intelligible to the reader.

The use of the word "queer" by Mycroft on page 269 has been criticized as not being realistic. Some Sherlockians have maintained that an Englishman in 1916 would not have known the word in its referent of "homosexual." However, that is the word Watson uses when he quotes Mycroft. So we must believe that some Englishmen, at least, were aware of this American term. Or, possibly, Watson's memory of the conversation was faulty. Since Watson had spent some time in the States, and had, like Holmes, picked up some Americanisms, he may have used this word because it was part of his everyday vocabulary.

The vulgarism, a*****e, on page 276, needs one more asterisk. That is, it does if Watson was quoting the English term, which Holmes probably did utter. If Holmes was using the American word because he was speaking about an American, then the number of asterisks is accurate. We'll never know.

Philip José Farmer as Fictional Author:
A Chronological Bibliography

The Adventure of the Peerless Peer by John H. Watson, M.D. (Aspen Press, November 1974; reprinted, Dell, September 1976)

Venus on the Half-Shell by Kilgore Trout (*The Magazine of Fantasy & Science Fiction*, ed. Ed Ferman, December 1974–January 1975; reprinted in book form, Dell, February 1975)

"A Scarletin Study" by Jonathan Swift Somers III (*The Magazine of Fantasy & Science Fiction*, ed. Ed Ferman, March 1975; reprinted in *Pearls from Peoria*, ed. Paul Spiteri, Subterranean Press, 2006)

"The Problem of the Sore Bridge—Among Others" by Harry Manders (*The Magazine of Fantasy & Science Fiction*, ed. Ed Ferman, September 1975)

"The Volcano" by Paul Chapin (*The Magazine of Fantasy & Science Fiction*, ed. Ed Ferman, February 1976)

"Osiris on Crutches" by Leo Queequeg Tincrowdor (*New Dimensions 6*, ed. Robert Silverberg, May 1976)

"The Doge Whose Barque Was Worse Than His Bight" by Jonathan Swift Somers III (*The Magazine of Fantasy & Science Fiction*, ed. Ed Ferman, November 1976; reprinted in *Pearls from Peoria*, ed. Paul Spiteri, Subterranean Press, 2006)

"The Impotency of Bad Karma" by Cordwainer Bird (Popular Culture, First Preview Edition, ed. Brad Lang, June 1977; revised in *Chrysalis, Volume Two*, August 1978 as "The Last Rise of Nick Adams")

"The Savage Shadow" by Maxwell Grant (*Weird Heroes, Volume Eight*, ed. Byron Preiss, November 1977; reprinted in *Pearls from Peoria*, ed. Paul Spiteri, Subterranean Press, 2006)

"It's the Queen of Darkness, Pal" by Rod Keen (*The Magazine of Fantasy & Science Fiction*, ed. Ed Ferman, August 1978, revised in *Riverworld and Other Stories*, November 1979 as "The Phantom of the Sewers")

"Who Stole Stonehenge?" by Jonathan Swift Somers III (one page fragment of an unfinished Ralph von Wau Wau story, *Farmerphile, The Magazine of Philip José Farmer*, no. 2, ed. Christopher Paul Carey and Paul Spiteri, October 2005; although published under Farmer's name, the original manuscript is attributed to Jonathan Swift Somers III)